Why readers love *Save Me from Dangerous Men*

'**Action packed** and **razor sharp** – Jack Reacher
would love Nikki Griffin'
Lee Child

'A suspenseful page-turner . . . **Original** and **inspired**'
USA Today

'If you're a fan of **Jack Reacher** or **Lisbeth Salander**, you are going
to love Nikki Griffin . . . **Highly, highly recommended**'
Douglas Preston, bestselling co-author of
the acclaimed Pendergast series

'Smart, darkly funny, and **totally addictive**'
Lisa Unger, bestselling author of *Under My Skin*

'Nikki is a dangerous woman, sort of a Lisbeth Salander,
but with **a lot more heart** . . . **Outstanding**'
Booklist, starred review

'Lelchuk winks at Nikki's similarities to a certain well-known
literary vigilante. A timely and **totally badass debut**'
Kirkus, starred review

'**Terrific** . . . the book's real appeal stems from its
powerful, **distinctive** protagonist'
Publishers Weekly, starred review

Meet Nikki Griffin . . .

Nikki Griffin owns a bookshop in California that has a resident cat, Bartleby. She drinks neat Jameson and rides an Aprilia motorcycle. She's a Private Investigator who spends her days talking about books and her nights fighting for women – and she could beat you in a fight, blindfolded.

Nikki is the hero you've been waiting for.

Meet S. A. Lelchuk . . .

Lelchuk holds a B.A. in English from Amherst College and a master's degree from Dartmouth College. The Nikki Griffin series has been optioned for film and television and the foreign rights have sold in multiple countries. *Save Me from Dangerous Men* is the first novel in the series.

To find out more, visit www.salelchuk.com

SAVE ME FROM DANGEROUS MEN

S. A. LELCHUK

SIMON &
SCHUSTER

London · New York · Sydney · Toronto · New Delhi

A CBS COMPANY

First published in the United States by Flatiron Books, 2019
First published in Great Britain by Simon & Schuster UK Ltd, 2019
A CBS COMPANY

This paperback edition published 2019

1 3 5 7 9 10 8 6 4 2

Simon & Schuster UK Ltd
1st Floor
222 Gray's Inn Road
London WC1X 8HB

Simon & Schuster Australia, Sydney
Simon & Schuster India, New Delhi

www.simonandschuster.co.uk
www.simonandschuster.com.au
www.simonandschuster.co.in

A CIP catalogue record for this book is available from the British Library

Paperback ISBN: 978-1-4711-8316-4
eBook ISBN: 978-1-4711-8315-7
Audio ISBN: 978-1-4711-8498-7

This book is a work of fiction. Names, characters, places and
incidents are either a product of the author's imagination or are
used fictitiously. Any resemblance to actual people living or
dead, events or locales is entirely coincidental.

Printed and bound by CPI Group (UK) Ltd, Croydon, CR0 4YY

MIX
Paper from
responsible sources
FSC
www.fsc.org   FSC® C020471

To my parents, Alan and Barbara, for everything

WEEK ONE

1

The bar was over in West Oakland. Just a squat block of concrete sitting in a parking lot. Neon Bud Light signs threw blue light over a dozen beat-up cars and trucks parked in front. I'd never been. Probably never go again. I pulled up at the edge of the lot, on the outskirts of the lights. Cut the engine of the red Aprilia motorcycle I was on. I walked in. Early side of a Friday night, just past nine. A half-dozen rough-looking men sat at the bar, another few at tables, and two shooting pool. Only one other girl. She was half of a couple wedged into a dark corner booth, a pitcher of beer in between them. She had a nose ring. I'd always wondered if nose rings were as painful as they looked.

I stood at the bar. "Heineken."

"That's five dollars." The bartender was a big, paunchy guy, better side of fifty, graying hair. He eyed me without bothering to hide it. So did the rest of the bar. So what.

I took the beer, took a swig, headed into the ladies'. The smell of Lysol and floor polisher. Stared into the chipped mirror and took a careful look at myself. I was tall, five foot eight. Taller with the heavy motorcycle boots I wore. I smoothed out my auburn hair from the helmet. I'd never be called skinny, but I kept my body toned. I looked over my tight stonewashed jeans, and a black, scoop-necked tank top under an unzipped black leather bomber jacket. A touch of shadow around my green eyes. A touch of red lipstick I'd never ordinarily wear. I looked okay.

I could start.

I headed over to the pool table. Threw a quarter on the table. "Next up," I said.

The two men playing were about my age, thirty-three. They gave me that hungry look that men give women. Predatory, almost. As though they wanted to snap me up in a quick bite. As though by talking to them I'd walked up and nibbled on an earlobe, whispered something dirty. The taller one held his cue casually in one hand. Turned back to the table. He wore a backward black-and-silver Raiders hat. Aimed carefully and sank the final stripe ball. Hitting harder than he needed to. Men did, usually. Only the really good players were able to resist the temptation of shooting hard, showing off. He aimed again. Shot a bit slower, the white ball glancing off the eight and sending it softly into a pocket. Game.

He turned back to me. "You're up, then." Started to bend to put quarters in.

"I'm challenging. My dime."

He stopped and shrugged. "Suit yourself."

I took my quarter off the table and three more from my pocket. Set my purse next to my beer and bent to put the coins in. Could feel the whole bar staring at my ass in the tight jeans. I racked.

"You know how to hold a stick?" his friend asked me. Leering as he said it, emphasis on stick. Shorter, a beer gut hanging over a stained T-shirt. Like his question would make me want to take him into the bathroom for a quick hand job. I didn't bother to answer. Just went over to the rack, pulled the straightest-looking cue, rolled it on the table. Seen better days, but it would do.

"You play for kisses, honey?" This from my soon-to-be opponent. Raiders Hat. The same shit, every bar in the country, probably. Every bar in the world.

I looked up at him. "I want to make out with someone, I'll go to prom."

"Playing tough," he said, like I was flirting. "But you all warm up eventually."

I kept my eyes on him. "I don't play tough. I play for money. Unless you just want to play for drinks. Your table. Your call."

When I said that, he didn't have a choice. "I don't usually take money from girls."

I reached into my back pocket. Threw a fifty-dollar bill on the table. "Smallest I got."

He exchanged a look with his friend. Wondering.

The bar was watching us.

Good.

"Fine." He fumbled in his wallet. Put down two twenties and a ten. "I break."

When money was down people always woke up a bit. He hit a good break. Sunk two solids and got lucky on the roll. Made another two before missing a midrange bank shot. Which put him about at par for the kind of pool players found in any bar that had a table. Not really bad, not really good. Average. That was fine. The first game wasn't really about winning. More about finding out what kind of things the other person wanted to do and how likely it was he could pull them off. Winning was secondary.

I took a big swallow of beer and ran half the table without saying a word.

Gentle, unhurried. Letting each shot position itself for the next one. Sequential. One move setting up the next. Thinking not about what I was doing but about what I wanted to do next. The balls making polite little clicks across the scuffed green felt. They said the only thing that separated amateur chess players from the grandmasters was how many moves ahead they could see. Pool was like that, a little, I'd always figured.

When I missed he took his cue up with a resolved look in his eyes. Focused. Seeing he had more than a pretty ass on his hands and not wanting to lose his fifty bucks. I didn't blame him. I'd never met anyone who liked losing money.

He shot and missed. Nerves, maybe. More people were watching now.

I was feeling good. Easy. Relaxed. Ran the other half of the stripes. Tapped the far corner pocket with my cue, aimed at the eight, not saying a word.

Sank it softly. Game.

I took his money off the table and pocketed it. Left my fifty on the table. "You want to try to get your money back, Jack?"

He was pissed now. "Hell yeah I do. And this time I'm gonna try."

"Money down, then. You lost. Rack 'em."

I left my fifty-dollar bill sitting there like I didn't have a care in the world. Went over to the bar. "Shot of Jameson and another beer."

An older guy leered over. He wore a Warriors T-shirt and had potato chip crumbs across his chin. "That's nice of you, sweetheart. You didn't have to buy me anything."

I didn't bother to even look at him, just skewered him with my silence. His face reddened and he turned his eyes back to the counter. I knocked the whiskey back. Threw one of Raiders Hat's twenties on the bar and walked away with the beer, not bothering to ask for change.

He had racked the balls but left a centimeter of space between the lead ball and the rest of the triangle. Trying to be sneaky. Which meant he didn't think he could beat me fair. I went over and took the triangle and reracked without a word.

"Must've rolled," he said, embarrassed. Caught.

"Must have," I said. "Money down."

He fumbled with his wallet again. This time the bills were smaller, a few dollar bills making up the last of the fifty. I took a swallow of cold beer and broke. By this time most of the men in the bar had drifted around the table.

"Little firecracker has a shot."

"Wonder if she's this good at other things."

"I could watch her bend over all night long, tell you that much."

I ignored them. Beat Raiders Hat again. Took his money. He was done. He eased his way toward a wall and slouched against it.

His beer-bellied friend wanted to take me on next. Maybe vengeance, maybe to stare down my cleavage some more. What did I care. I took twenty dollars off him because that was all he had.

Then I saw him.

He must have walked in while I was wrapping up the last game, because I hadn't seen him at the door. He leaned on the bar with a beer in front of him. I checked my watch. 10:40.

I went over to the jukebox. Men watching me. Took more quarters out of my pocket. Dialed in a Rolling Stones song. Walked back to the table. Moving my hips a bit this time. Took a long, slow sip of my beer. "Who's up?"

I beat someone else. One of them. I didn't care who it was. The man who had come in had settled in at the bar but was watching the little crowd at the pool table with curiosity. Watching me. Wondering. I had his attention.

I took my money off the table. "I'm thirsty. Table's open. I'm done."

Back to the bar. Took my jacket off for the first time. Sat down near him, one empty stool between us. It was him, all right. A couple of years older than me. A thickset guy with a black goatee and dull eyes. Broad shoulders, blue-green tattoos running down both forearms.

I caught the bartender's eye. "Another Heineken. And another shot."

This time I didn't take the shot right away. Left it on the bar, sipped my beer, and stared into the chipped wood. Someone had carved initials into the surface. RS & CJ 4EVER. I wondered if RS and CJ were still together. My money was on no.

"They say it's bad manners to drink alone."

I looked over. Directly, for the first time since he'd walked in. "Who says?"

He laughed. "They. The fuck who. I have no idea."

"So have a drink."

"Think I will." He nodded at the bartender. "A shot of whatever she's having, Teddy. Both on me."

"No," I corrected. "I pay for my drinks."

He looked at me, surprised. "Never known a woman to turn down a free drink."

"First time for everything."

"Guess you can afford it with that pool action you got going on."

"I could afford it when I walked in. Still can."

He laughed again. "You're a little sparkplug, ain't you?"

"You don't know me," I said.

"But I could."

"Could?"

"Know you. Better, anyway."

"If?"

His turn to shrug. "If we keep talking, I guess."

I held up my shot. "Cheers."

We clinked shot glasses. Drank.

"Haven't seen you in here before," he commented.

"That's because I've never been in here before."

"Why tonight?"

I traced a red-painted nail through the wood scarring in front of me, wondering again about RS and CJ. "Do you really care?"

"Not really."

"Exactly. I'm here. You're here. Why search for origin?"

"Fair enough." He looked up at the bartender. "Two more. She pays for hers." Turned to me. "Who says you can't teach an old dog new tricks?"

"You an old dog?"

He threw a wink my way. "Not too old."

"Then maybe we'll try and teach you a few tricks."

Two more Jamesons. We drank.

"I'm bored," I said. Slid off my barstool without looking back. Back to the jukebox. Put on a slower song. "Love Me Two Times," by the Doors. Started moving slowly by myself near the machine. Eyes on me, the whole bar. I felt him behind me. Sensed it. Like I was watching him through the back of my head. Felt a big hand tentatively cradle my hip. Moving with me. I didn't stop him. Felt him press against me from behind. My tongue was sharp against my teeth but I didn't stop him. We danced out the song together.

"You should come over," he said when the music stopped.

I smiled a little. "Is that right?"

"You've been drinking. You shouldn't be driving."

My smile grew. "You're looking out for me."

He grinned. "I'm lookin' out for both of us. Come on, I'm a mile down the street. Got a great bottle of whiskey we can get into." He paused significantly. "And I got some eggs and coffee. For breakfast."

I stared frankly at him. "I want to tell you something. The two of us won't ever have breakfast together. Not in the cards."

His eyes flickered with anger. "Could've told me that an hour ago. Waste of time."

He turned on his heels and headed toward the bar.

I let him get three steps away before I spoke.

"I never said I wouldn't come over."

He turned back around in a hurry.

2

I followed him. Loving the night air on me, the feel of leather-clad fingers on the handlebars, the solid force of wind streaming into my chest. I hated riding with windscreens. I needed to feel the wind holding me, steadying. Sometimes I thought my motorcycle was the only place I could feel at peace. I couldn't tell if it was a scary thought. Or a true one.

He lived in a little Craftsman house in West Oakland. Close to the docks. Close enough that I could hear the freeway traffic, see the Port lights. Massive cranes and stacked shipping containers curtaining the dark, flat water. The orange glow rising vaporously into pale night. The glinting city across the Bay.

I saw his car turn into a driveway but I continued another block before I parked. Locked my helmet to the bike and put my gloves in my purse. Headed back toward the house. He was waiting for me at the front door. "Why didn't you park in the driveway?"

"I never park in a stranger's driveway."

"We won't be strangers for long."

"Maybe not."

His living room was plain. A couple of old armchairs and a black leather couch in front of a television playing ESPN. An Xbox controller on the coffee table along with several unwashed plates. He muted the show, disappeared into the kitchen, came back with a bottle of whiskey and two glasses. Good whiskey. It was The Famous Grouse. God. What did he think was bad whiskey?

He turned on some rock band that sounded like a cheap knockoff of

Metallica, all of the volume but none of the talent. Poured into the glasses and gestured. "Pull up a chair. Don't be shy."

I took a sip. "I should slow down before I get drunk."

"Is getting drunk a bad thing?"

"Depends what happens, I guess."

"What do you want to happen?"

"You'll see."

"My God!" he exclaimed. Somewhere between amused and annoyed. "Talking to you is like cracking code."

I ignored him. Looking around. Feeling things building together. It was past midnight.

Almost time.

I nodded at a couple of lavender curtains over the window. "Didn't figure you for a decorator." There was a picture hanging on the wall above the couch. The man in front of me, his arm around a woman, each smiling and holding a drink. She wore a black dress and he wore a scarlet tie over a maroon shirt. People milled behind them. Holiday office party, maybe, or wedding reception. Something social. The woman in the picture wasn't especially pretty. She was on the heavy side, with plain features. But she looked happy. Her smile was real.

He followed my eyes to the curtains, embarrassed. "Not me."

"Roommate? Girlfriend?"

"Call her a roommate, sure."

"Is she here?"

"No."

"Coming back tonight?"

"No, but who cares?" He poured more whiskey into his glass. "What does it matter?"

"Guess it doesn't."

"Look, I'm not trying to be a dick, but it's been a long week. I'm talked out. You want another drink, or just head in there?" He nodded toward a half-open door. The bedroom.

"I told you. You'll know what I want."

"What's with the goddamn riddles?" he exclaimed. "I picked you up at a bar. We're not high-school sweethearts. We know what we want. Why beat around the bush?"

"You have a temper," I observed.

"I have a hard-on."

"I'll have that drink."

"Sure." He poured.

I took the glass. Drank. Got up. Took off my jacket. Set it on the chair. Stood there in my black tank and jeans and boots, glass in one hand. "Is that better?"

"Shit," he said. "You're a serious ten. And I'm a seriously lucky bastard."

"Your turn."

"Now we're talking." He drained his drink and rose. He was a big guy. Maybe six foot one, over two hundred pounds, solidly built. He took his T-shirt off, revealing a thatch of black hair across his chest.

"More," I said.

"Suit yourself. I ain't never been shy." He unbuckled his belt. Kicked his shoes off. Pulled his jeans off. Stood there in boxers and socks. He hadn't been kidding about the hard-on. He sat back down in his chair. Comfortably. "Get over here, girl. We gotta get those boots off you."

I looked at him.

Put my drink down.

Took my motorcycle gloves out of my purse. Slid the first one on. Adjusting the leather so that the armored ridge fit perfectly over my knuckles.

He stared at me. "You got a leather fetish?"

I said nothing. Pulled the other glove on.

"Look," he said. "I don't know what you're into but I don't do kinky shit. Not getting spanked or whipped or bending over."

I looked down at him. "You know something?"

"What?"

"I don't think I'm in the mood."

His eyes narrowed in anger. "Are you kidding?"

"Nope."

"You can't pull that shit."

"Why not?"

"You came over here, drank my booze, had me take my goddamn clothes off. You think I had you over 'cause I needed the conversation?"

"Where's your girlfriend?" I asked.

"What are you talking about?"

"Right. Roommate," I said, my voice dripping with contempt as I nodded at the picture.

"We broke up."

"I'm not going to screw you, all the same."

"You're serious?"

"Serious."

"All right," he said. "Then get the hell outta my house, you crazy bitch. Go on, now."

"And if I don't?"

His features shifted into a different look. A dangerous look.

A look that said *Run for the hills if you know what's good for you.*

I stayed right where I was.

His hands were clenched into fists and his jaw was tight. "I've had it with your cock teasing. I don't know who you are or what you want, and I don't care."

"You should," I said. "That's the thing. You should care about those things."

He ignored me. "All I know is that you're on my property and if you don't get out in five seconds I'm gonna dump you headfirst on the damn curb with yesterday's garbage."

I looked evenly at him. Said nothing.

"I mean it."

I was quiet.

"Five."

I didn't say a word.

"Four. Three. I'm serious."

Kept looking down at him. Silent.

"Two. Last chance. I mean it."

I took an even breath in. Blew it out slow. Feeling my pulse starting to hammer in that familiar way. We were almost there.

Almost.

"One."

I drew in another breath.

Let it out slow.

"Okay, you asked for it." He started to get up, hands still clenched.

I waited until he was halfway out of the chair. Off-balance, legs bent, weight shifting forward awkwardly.

Then I stepped forward and hit him.

I was a southpaw. Delivered a hard crack with my left hand. A short, twisting punch that had the full weight of my body behind it. Felt my fist explode into his nose with a crunch, the yielding, squishy feeling of cartilage. Different feeling than hitting a jaw or cheekbone or temple. A long time ago I'd gotten sick of busting my knuckles up. The armored motorcycle gloves were designed to hit asphalt at eighty miles an hour. They did wonders. Now I barely even bruised.

He fell back into the chair, clutching his nose with both hands. "Shit," he said. His voice was muffled. "You broke my nose."

I stayed where I was. Drew in another breath, let it out. Controlling my breathing, my pulse. Scrapingly aware of every tiny detail like I was on some kind of drug. The world coming in sharp and clear, every movement, every sound. I chose my words carefully. "You ready for another taste? Or do you need a minute?"

That got him back up. This time he rose cautiously. Nose dripping blood steadily out of both nostrils. He ignored the blood, never taking his eyes off me. He didn't lunge forward this time. Gained his feet, faked a rushing tackle, then stepped forward and threw a massive right hook at my head. The kind of punch that would knock someone into next week and have them wake up wondering what bus they'd stepped in front of.

I slipped it easily.

Came under his arm while he was off-balance, our faces three inches apart. I hit him four times in two seconds. A hard uppercut to the jaw and a short right hook to the side of the head. Just above the ear to destroy his equilibrium. A left to the broken nose and finishing with a nasty hook into his drink-sodden kidneys.

He went down face-first into the coffee table.

I didn't talk this time. I didn't wait. I lifted his left arm away from his body and carefully positioned myself. Then I brought up my boot about six inches under his left armpit and drove the heel down as hard as I possibly could. There was a cracking sound. He screamed loudly. I looked at him lying there. No more fight in him. Done.

"You have a landline?" I asked.

He didn't answer. Just lay there moaning and holding his side.

"Do you have a landline?" I repeated.

His breath came in gasps. "You broke my damn rib. Oh, God, it hurts."

This wasn't getting anywhere. "If you don't have a landline, can I borrow your cell phone, please?"

"Why?"

"To call you an ambulance."

"No, why'd you hit me?"

"Because you had it coming. Can I get that phone now?"

He raised himself slowly off the shattered coffee table. "My jeans."

I went over to his pants and found the phone. I didn't need the passcode for the number I was dialing.

"Nine-one-one, what is your emergency?"

"This guy I'm with," I said. "I think he was in a fight. I think he lost."

3

I was hungry. I rode around until I found a twenty-four-hour diner a few miles away. Three black guys were walking out, laughing as they got into a Jeep. One of the newer models, headlights narrowed to squinted strips. They saw me as I took my helmet off and one called out, "Damn, girl, you got *style!*"

I grinned at him and gave them a wave as they pulled away. Inside, a sign by the front said SEAT YOURSELF so I did, at a booth in the back. The place was mostly empty. It was past one in the morning. A slow period for diners, after the graveyard shift had been in to eat, and before the drunk crowd headed in after the downtown Oakland bars closed at 2:00 A.M. The waitress came over almost immediately and I ordered coffee and one of the big Lumberjack breakfasts, eggs over easy and sausage and bacon and hash browns, a short stack of pancakes, and buttered sourdough toast. I read until the food arrived and then tore into it, still reading. Ordered more coffee and got three refills on my ice water, feeling the last effects of the whiskey slowly trickling away.

There was a table of four men nearby. White guys in their late twenties or early thirties. They were throwing a few looks my way. I didn't care. Kept eating. The food tasted good. I was hungry.

The four guys were whispering and laughing to each other. I seemed to be the subject. One of them finally walked over. He was handsome, with a slender build and three or four days of tobacco-colored stubble. Curly brown hair cut short, wire glasses. He wore a corduroy jacket and with bemusement I saw a little golden cardboard crown atop his head, like what Burger King gave away to birthday kids. "Permission to approach the bench," he said.

I finished chewing and put my book aside. "And why would you want to do that?"

He came a step closer. "My friends said you wouldn't talk to me."

"Sounds like they think very highly of you."

He giggled. "I mean—you're really pretty and you seem really focused. I've learned that's a bad combination if I'm trying to talk to a girl. For me, I mean, not the girl. The pretty, focused ones usually ignore me. Actually, even one out of two and it doesn't work out so well."

I sighed. "Look. You're talking to me. And I'm talking to you. You win the bet. You can go back to your friends now and tell them that the really pretty focused girl talked to you."

I picked up my book and my fork. Went back to the eggs.

"Look, I wasn't trying to bother you."

"It's okay," I told him. "You didn't bother me."

Then he surprised me. "'Infinite resignation is that shirt we read about in the old fable. The thread is spun under tears, the cloth bleached with tears, the shirt sewn with tears; but then too it is a better protection than iron and steel.'"

I put my book back down. The cover visible again. *Fear and Trembling*.

"Okay, hotshot," I said. "You're a Berkeley grad student and you can quote Kierkegaard. I'm guessing philosophy?"

Now he was surprised. "English, actually. I just have a soft spot for long-dead Danish existentialists. How'd you know the rest?"

"Because you're up too late to be a professor and you're too polite for an undergrad. And if you were at Stanford you'd be going out in San Francisco, not Oakland. So that leaves Berkeley."

"Those are a lot of assumptions."

"Everyone makes assumptions. The only question is if they're right or not."

He frowned. "So I'm of little to no mystery to you? That's depressing."

"I do have one question."

"Yeah?"

"The crown," I said. "Can't figure that one out. Very mysterious."

He rubbed his head self-consciously. "I finished my dissertation today. We've been celebrating."

"Congratulations."

"Well, it still has to pass. But this is a step, anyway."

"Who did you write on?"

"William Hazlitt."

"*The Fight*. A favorite."

"Wow," he said. "Nobody knows Hazlitt anymore, except maybe his Shakespeare stuff. But *nobody* knows *The Fight*. Are you in school, too?"

"Nope. Just a working girl."

"Working where?"

"I work in a bookstore."

"Around here? I know them all."

"Then maybe you'd know this one."

He glanced around the nearly empty restaurant. "So why are you here tonight?"

"You mean I don't look like I just finished a dissertation?"

He grinned, showing white teeth. "You're way too sober to have done that."

I liked his smile, I realized with mild surprise. "Okay. Fine. You can sit."

"I was waiting for you to say that," he said, sitting down. "I'm Ethan. And you are . . . ?"

"Nikki."

"You like Kierkegaard?"

"Sometimes," I said, "I feel he's the only thing holding me together."

"Look," Ethan said. "I don't usually give out my number to strange women."

I had to laugh. "Was I asking?"

"Your eyes betray you."

"I see."

He winked at me. "I'll make an exception. Just this once."

"You will."

"But we don't sleep together on the first date," he said sternly. "That I'm sticking to. Not up for debate. I don't care what you say."

I sipped my coffee and tried not to smile. "Setting terms, are you?"

"Well, someone had to. Now, if you would be so good as to lend me your phone, I'll put in my number, and then you can pretty much go ahead and call me, like, whenever."

"I don't have a cell phone."

He was surprised. "Everyone has a cell phone. My grandmother has a cell phone and she doesn't know how to turn it on. Literally, I'm not exaggerating, she would not know where the Power button is. But she *has* one."

"Well, I don't."

"Why?"

"For the same reason that I don't have a pet hamster. Because I don't like them."

He took a hash brown off my plate and chewed it thoughtfully. "Be careful. Now I'm starting to really like you."

"Is that so?"

"Come on," he said. "We're going to go out together, and it's gonna be fun." He took a napkin, pulled a pen from his jacket pocket. "That's my number. How do I reach you, No-Cell-Phone Girl?"

He had blue eyes. Soft ones. And he did have a good smile.

"Fine." I took the napkin, tore off half, wrote down a phone number and address, and handed it back to him.

He took the napkin, surprised. "Your address? You barely know me."

"Monday," I said. "You can come over for dinner this Monday, seven o'clock. If you want."

"You're inviting me to dinner? I feel like I should be inviting you to dinner."

"Well, you didn't. Besides, I promise you that I'm a better cook than you are."

"How do you know that?"

"Call it another assumption."

"I'm kind of a shitty cook," he confessed. "But I love to eat."

I checked my watch again. Almost two thirty. It was time.

I threw a twenty on the table and got up. "I have to go now. And by the way," I added. My fingers brushed his jeans pocket, where his Cal ID peeked out. "Sometimes it's only a matter of looking close."

Then, because I couldn't resist, I took his crown, put it on my head, and walked out of the restaurant.

4

Ten minutes later I was back at the Craftsman house.

Again, I left my bike down the block. The homes on either side of the street were darkened. Cars littered the curbs and the Port's sodium glow spread spookily through the sky. The street was quiet.

I'd noticed a funny thing about people who left home in an ambulance. They never remembered to lock their door on the way out. Just wasn't something they thought about. They had bigger concerns. The paramedics never locked the doors, either. It wasn't their job.

So I wasn't surprised to find the front door unlocked.

I let myself in.

He wasn't back yet. Friday night in Oakland, the emergency rooms were running at full capacity. Even with a broken nose and rib he'd have to wait a bit. Oakland was a city, and kind of a violent one. Not as bad as it used to be, but people still got shot, run over, stabbed. All kinds of bad things happened every day, and Friday nights seemed to bring out the worst in people. The ER wasn't going to drop everything for a guy with a broken rib and busted nose. No one was going to die from a broken rib. But they wouldn't leave him sitting there forever. He hadn't come in with a sprained ankle. I figured I'd have to wait one hour, maybe two at the most. Depending on how busy the night had been. Depending on how many bad things had happened to people I'd probably never meet.

He'd mentioned coffee.

I rummaged through the kitchen and found a bag of Peet's, pre-ground. Could be a lot worse.

I brewed a big pot in the coffee machine and settled in to wait.

I heard the door just before three thirty. I didn't bother to get up. Stayed in the armchair as he walked in. I wasn't worried about police being with him. He wasn't going to tell anyone that he'd had his ass kicked by some girl he'd invited over. And the last thing on his mind was the possibility of me still being there.

Of me having come back.

I waited until he had closed the door. "Robert," I said, and clicked on a light.

"What the hell!" He literally jumped backward. His nose was partly obscured by a white bandage and both his eyes were blackened from the break. A few stitches on his forehead from where his head had hit the coffee table. Probably ACE bandages under his shirt. There wasn't much to be done about broken ribs except to let them heal without doing anything to stop that from happening. Not a fun injury. He winced in pain as the words left his mouth. With broken ribs even breathing hurts pretty badly at first. He was backing away from me. "Why are you here?"

"Relax," I said. "I'm not going to hurt you. We're going to talk."

"You want to talk? After what you did to me?"

"Yes, I do. Sit down. Please."

His face showed fright and anger. "You're in *my* house, telling me to sit down?"

"I'm asking you to sit. I've never yet told you to do anything."

"You're not going to hurt me? You promise?"

I got up, went into the kitchen, and came back with a mug. I handed it to him. "I made coffee. I hope that's okay."

"You made coffee," he repeated. Now he just looked confused.

"Figured we could both use a cup."

He took the cup skeptically, as though I'd dropped in a cyanide pill. We sat in the living room. Except for the broken coffee table, everything looked the same as when we had first arrived. "What do you want?" he asked.

I opened my purse, took out a narrow sheaf of pages, and handed them to him.

He saw the first page and looked up, startled. "What is this?"

"Your girlfriend's name is Angela Matterson. Your name is Robert Harris. She works as a special education teacher in San Leandro and you're a mechanic at Sharkey's Motors. You've been with Angela for two years and seven months."

"How do you know that?"

I ignored the question. "Six weeks ago, you two got in a bad argument. Tempers flared. And then you hit her. You hurt her pretty badly."

He stared at me. "Who are you?"

"I don't pretend to know who was in the right. I don't give a damn who said what. But as shown in those hospital intake records you're holding, you put your girlfriend in the ER with a broken nose. The broken rib she got when she fell down the front steps trying to run. She told the police that she had tripped, and stuck to it. She wouldn't admit you had touched her."

"I lost my temper," Robert said in a more subdued voice. "I felt bad about it. I'd never laid a hand on her before."

Maybe it was true. Maybe it wasn't. "After the hospital, she checked into a women's shelter," I continued. "She received counseling and then she came back here to get her things. She had decided to move out, and start a new life. She made those decisions for herself."

He looked at me but said nothing.

"When she came back here, though, you were waiting."

"To apologize! To ask for another chance."

"You did apologize. That's undisputed. But she didn't change her mind. She packed a suitcase." I set aside my coffee. "That was when you showed her the gun. Said you'd find her and make what you'd done look like nothing."

I was quiet. Challenging him to contradict me.

He wouldn't meet my eyes. "I never would have done that. I wasn't serious, I was upset. I just really wanted her back."

Again, maybe true, maybe not. Didn't matter. "Sure. Maybe you were bluffing. Maybe you did really love her. Maybe you still do. I don't know. I don't pretend to know. But what you said was enough to terrify her. And that's where I come in."

He bit his lip. "I was angry, but I'd never hurt her. I have that gun for self-defense. I work in a bad part of town, been carjacked twice."

"How many Percocet did they give you at the hospital?"

"What?"

"How many pills? And what milligrams were they? Did you happen to notice?"

"Only one. They wouldn't give me more until the booze was out of my system."

"So you're feeling clear-headed? Cognizant?"

He looked at me in confusion. "Yeah, I guess."

"Good." I reached into my purse a second time. This time I took out a small black pistol.

People reacted differently to guns being pointed at them. Some screamed, some froze, some ran. All kinds of reactions. Robert started jerking his head this way and that. Back and forth like some grotesque jack-in-the-box.

"This is a Beretta subcompact chambered in forty-caliber hollow points," I told him. "The subcompacts aren't worth jack for target practice because the barrel's too short. But from five feet away that doesn't matter so much."

"You said you weren't going to hurt me!"

I pulled the slide back and the gun cocked loudly.

The only safety I ever used was an empty chamber.

He started jerking around even more frantically. "Please!"

I left the gun on him for a long moment. Then in one smooth motion I pulled the slide back, popped the live cartridge out of the chamber, and put the gun down. "I need you to understand your situation. How it's escalated."

"Please," he said again.

I walked over to him. Put a hand lightly on his shoulder. Put something in his hand. The cartridge. A small brass cylinder, pointed at one end, still warm from my hand. "I want you to keep that, Robert," I said, sitting down again. "Think of it as your restraining order. If you ever get mad or lonely and start thinking about maybe finding Angela, I want you to hold this bullet and look at it and remember this conversation. Because if you ever try to talk to her or see her again, I'll use a bullet identical to this one and shoot you in the head."

He stared at the oblong cylinder in his palm, saying nothing. I let him think.

He looked up. "I understand," he finally said.

"Good." I put the gun away.

"So in the bar tonight, all those lies about wanting me, flirting . . . You were planning this the whole time, weren't you?"

"I didn't lie. I don't lie. I didn't tell you a single word that was untrue."

"You hit on me."

"No. I let you hit on me. And I let you make assumptions about what I wanted."

"Why'd you have to hurt me, then?"

"You put your girlfriend in the hospital. What happened to you is fair. Your injuries."

"So why come back here?"

"The two parts are a system, Robert. If I just hurt you, that might make you angrier. If I just pulled a gun, you might not take me seriously. This way, you do."

"How did Angela find you?"

"That's not the point. The point is that *I* found *you*. It's not about her anymore. It's about us—me and you. That's what matters now."

"So you've done stuff like this before."

I didn't answer him.

"You must think I'm a real scumbag."

"I'm sure I've met better and I'm positive I've met worse."

"I did love her. Maybe I still do."

"Okay."

"What if you hadn't been able to take me? If I'd gotten to the kitchen, grabbed a knife?"

A door opens. A step forward onto the sunlit floor. A sticky iron smell. Dusty sunlight along the wall. Another step.

"I don't like knives. A knife would not have helped resolve things."

He took that in.

"Any other questions?" I asked.

"No."

"Then this concludes our business." I stood. "There's more coffee, if you want. I left the pot on just in case. Get some rest. And then go meet a new girl. Be nice to her. Or enjoy the single life. Not my business. Sound okay?"

He spoke the single word somberly. "Okay."

"You won't see me again. Not unless you try to find her. Then you'll see me once more."

I left him there, looking blankly at the broken coffee table, and walked outside into the night.

5

On the freeway heading north, I slowed at my Berkeley exit, then changed my mind and accelerated past it. I wasn't tired. The drive from Oakland to Bolinas was normally about an hour and a half. On the Aprilia, late at night, no traffic, I could do it in under an hour. I worked my way onto the 580 and headed north, taking the Richmond Bridge over the Bay. Loving the night, the speed, the wind. Across the water, I passed the bulk of San Quentin looming over the Marin coast.

Trying not to think about what I always thought about when passing the pale stone walls.

Who I always thought about.

I twisted up and then down around Mount Tamalpais, leaning into hairpin curves, headlight lancing the night. At Stinson Beach I picked up my speed for the last few miles as the road straightened. Bolinas had changed a lot since my childhood. Mainly, the homes had all gotten about tenfold more expensive, the hippies and artists joined by millionaire tech boys wanting to play surf bum for the weekend. A crowd that didn't think much of slapping down a couple of million bucks for a little place by the ocean that would have sold for thirty or forty grand only a few decades before. But the town was still tiny, and proudly held on to its original character despite the unrequested changes.

I turned off the main street onto a narrow, curving road that led up to the high bluffs above the ocean. Halfway up the road I got off the bike. Cut the engine. Walked quietly up to a blue house that was just visible in the dim predawn light. A small, single-story house. A neat brick walkway bisecting the clipped grass of the lawn. I noticed a child's tricycle had been left in the yard. I bit my lip as I imagined a kid pedaling frenetically around the path. I could hear the crunching sound the plastic wheels would make, rolling over the pavement. Could hear the happy laughter.

A cheerful blue house.

I stood there looking at the house. No lights on. No one awake. The night quiet. I could hear the waves below. Felt that same choking feeling I always got.

"I'm sorry," I whispered to the house. "I'm so, so sorry."

"Nikki, yes? Nikki Griffin? Why don't you tell me a little about yourself?"

"Myself. Like anything in particular?"

"Wherever you'd like to start."

"That sounds like a trick question. Like a job interview."

"There's no trick. Why don't you start at the beginning?"

"Okay. My brother and I grew up in Bolinas. My parents were the Bohemian California type, drove down to the Fillmore for shows on the weekends, weed and wine and bonfires on the beach."

"Are you close with your brother?"

"I try to look out for him."

"And you are close to your parents?"

"Can we talk about something else?"

"Of course. May I ask you something, Nikki?"

"Sure."

"How's the violence?"

"The violence."

"Yes."

"Well, I wanted to slug my waiter the other night."

"Your waiter? Why?"

"Ordered a martini and he brought it over with vodka."

"Vodka? That was a problem?"

"Gin. Someone orders a martini, you bring them gin. That's the default. Not vodka. Gin."

"But you didn't."

"Didn't hit him? No. Just asked for gin. I was mostly kidding, anyway. About hitting him."

"I'm very glad to hear that."

"But I wanted to. Kind of. A little. Vodka. God."

"Are you drinking a lot, Nikki?"

"Why would you ask me that?"

"Just a question—you know, drinking can be a trigger for other things."

"Other things?"

"For impulsive behavior of any kind."

"Look. Ninety-nine percent of the time I don't consider myself impulsive."

"Maybe we should talk about the one percent."

"I don't mean to be rude, but can I go now?"

"We can end early, I don't see why not. I'll see you next week, same time?"

"Sure. Next week. Same time."

"And Nikki?"

"Yeah?"

"Try to be good."

I walked out into bright afternoon sunlight. Squinting, putting on black Ray-Ban aviators. Reached into my purse for lip gloss, tasted vague citrus. The therapist worked out of her home in North Berkeley. She had been dressed casually in blue jeans and a faded sweater. We'd sat in her living room, me on a couch, her in an armchair. A desk adorned with crayon pictures, probably the work of grandchildren. A worn Persian carpet over the hardwood floor, a high bookcase filled with many of psychology's prominent names, as well as others I didn't recognize. I liked the setup. A home was better than tile floors and clipboard questionnaires. For this kind of thing. The therapy thing. Outside, speed bumps in the road rose in gentle asphalt waves. Colorful homes lined the quiet streets. A gardener's clippers buzzed. A comfortable neighborhood. A safe neighborhood. The late September air pleasant.

I pulled a hair tie off my wrist and worked my hair into a bun, put my helmet on. The big engine thrummed, the sound filling my ears even through the padded helmet. I left my leather jacket unzipped to feel the wind. Clicked my foot down into First, eased my hand off the clutch, rolled onto the street, headed south toward Oakland.

I had a job to do.

7

The man's bare behind was the same shade as an uncooked parsnip.

I aimed the black crosshairs, centering them directly over his back.

Click.

I took several shots, the powerful zoom lens of the camera making it seem as though he was only a few feet away, instead of across the street in a second-floor apartment. The woman walked into view, wearing only a bra and underwear. The apartment was rented under her name. She looked about forty, maybe two decades younger than the man. She had the body of a woman who spent her fair share of time in the gym. I idly wondered if he paid for the apartment, some kind of sugar daddy relationship. I didn't care. It didn't matter to me one way or the other. What mattered was that the two of them were here, in front of me, together. The woman looked awfully pretty for him, though.

They embraced. His hand caressed the back of her neck, under her blond hair.

Click. Click-click-click.

I watched through the zoom as his fingers worked her bra open.

Click. Click.

As they moved from window to bed they disappeared from my line of sight. That was fine. I put the big camera into my backpack and walked down the block to wait. I found a deli and bought a coffee and a copy of the *Chronicle*. There were the usual headlines, seemingly all of them bad. Skyrocketing housing prices, North Korea shooting off missiles, human rights abuses in the

Middle East. In the U.S. & World section there was a blurry picture of a curly-haired man with a missing front tooth, inset next to another picture: an overhead shot of yellow police tape surrounding a body bag. The caption identified him as the late Sherif Essam, a prominent blogger who had decided to leap from a thirtieth-floor rooftop in Cairo while breaking a story about government human rights violations. The police were treating it as an open-and-shut suicide. I pushed the paper away. The world was a depressing place. Not really the most groundbreaking thought, but one that I had frequently. Maybe due to my work.

Given what I did, I didn't generally see the best side of people.

Best side, indeed. I stood. Even the most passionate couples only shacked up for so long.

When the man and woman emerged from the apartment, the zoom lens brought them again into perfect focus. He wore a pinstriped navy suit and red tie, looking like the successful lawyer that he was. She wore jeans and a T-shirt, hair still damp from a shower. Their faces flushed. Happy with their secret. He leaned in to kiss her.

Click-click-click.

It always amazed me how easy it was to catch people having affairs. Trysts in apartments, cars, hotels. Thinking they were being clever. I'd never had an affair, but maybe that was part of the thrill. The illicitness. Spy games. Getting to sneak around, check into an anonymous motel. Some people were more cautious than these two, the pictures harder to get. But they were always gettable. I didn't mind the endless waiting, learning routines and preferences, but I didn't like the intrusion. The weird voyeurism of seeing and photographing men and women, women and women, men and men, often in explicit sexual contact. People chose to have affairs. Had nothing to do with me. Some probably deserved to be forgiven. Some probably didn't.

But a job was a job and I'd do the work if I had the time. It was amazing how set most people's habits were. A week or two would show most everything. Where people ate, worked, shopped. Sometimes the person who hired me already had e-mails or texts or proof. Others, just vague suspicion, coalescing into an itch that could no longer be ignored. Sometimes it would be nothing. Sometimes it would be. I always billed for the affair jobs. Not like the women from the shelters. Infidelity was one problem. Being trapped, threatened, hurt—that was different.

Those people deserved protection.

I watched as the man got into a silver Mercedes S550. The paint gleamed, freshly washed. A vanity plate read LAW1981. I didn't care much about cars, but it was easy to tell that this was a nice one, the roof curved and taut, as though the whole car was eager to spring forward. The Mercedes pulled away as the woman went back inside.

I had seen a pay phone down the block by the deli. I put coins in and dialed. A woman's voice answered. "Hello?"

"Brenda, it's Nikki."

There was a pause. The woman on the other end bracing herself. Like getting lab results from the doctor. "Hi, Nikki. Any updates?"

"Why don't we meet for coffee?"

8

She was coming into East Bay from San Francisco, so I suggested a tiny coffee shop just off the Bay Bridge in West Oakland, not far from where I had paid the visit to Robert Harris. A sign said BAY COFFEE. The sign made sense. They had coffee, and there was the Bay. It was an industrial neighborhood, the road's battered pavement waving a white flag high after years of the big trucks that jolted along on their way to the Oakland Port. Some parts of Oakland had gotten nice fast. Some were taking their time.

Brenda Johnson was a stylish, pretty woman of about fifty. Her hair was honey-colored and professionally styled, her hands manicured. She wore suede boots and a three-quarter-length black Burberry jacket with the belt knotted fashionably. She eyed the small café anxiously, as though they'd hand her bad news printed right across the menu. I thought again of the lab results.

"Coffee's on me," I said. "What are you having?"

She blinked and looked at me. "Just a cappuccino if they have it. Otherwise coffee with cream and sugar. Thanks, Nikki."

"I'll be out in a minute," I said. "We can sit outside."

At the counter I ordered from a pretty black-haired girl in her mid-twenties. "Can you do cappuccino?" I asked.

She nodded. "Sure." She had a slim body, brown eyes, and small white teeth. A brown-yellow discoloration, like a large birthmark, spread across her right cheekbone. I smelled cigarettes and Tommy Girl perfume. I'd worn the same stuff myself all through high school.

"One of those, and a large black, no sugar."

She handed the full cups over unlidded, and a few drops of coffee splashed over the rim onto my jacket as I reached to take it. "I'm so sorry," she said. She looked more than sorry. She looked like instead of a little coffee she'd spilled two million barrels of crude into a harbor full of otters. I saw the tattoo of a rose on her thin forearm, the long stem twisting along skin. Thorns protruded at intervals as though pinning the stem into her arm.

"It's okay," I said. "Don't worry about it."

"Here, let me." She grabbed a handful of paper towels and dabbed awkwardly at my arm. "I'm so sorry," she said again. "I'm such an idiot."

"Hey," I said, nonplussed. "It's no big deal. Seriously."

"It's just—I'm having the worst day. I know that's not your problem."

"Anything I can do?"

She shook her head as though at the silliness of the question. "I'll be fine. Thanks for not yelling at me. You wouldn't believe what some people are like."

"I believe it." The yellowish mark on her face. It didn't look quite like a birthmark after all. It had that unhealthy, overripe look of injured skin. She caught my gaze and seemed to shrink into herself. She tore little corners off the napkin she was holding and white flecks drifted to the counter with the determined instability of snow.

"I'll be fine," she said again.

"I'm Nikki," I said. "What's your name?"

"Zoe," she answered hesitantly. She had a faint accent. South American. I couldn't place the country. The smattering of Spanish left over from high school didn't take me that far.

"We can talk," I said. "If you'd like. Sometimes it's nice to have someone to talk to."

She blushed and shook her head without a word.

I picked up the two cups. "I work at a bookstore over on Telegraph." I handed her a business card. "A few of us do a kind of book club thing. We're meeting next Friday afternoon. Maybe you'd like to come."

She blushed again and looked away. "I can't remember the last time I've even read a real book. I didn't even finish high school. I wouldn't fit in."

"You might be surprised. You might fit in just fine."

She took the card carefully, as though it was made of the most delicate glass, and slid it into the tight pocket of her jeans. "I'll think about it." She had torn the napkin into a blizzard of tiny pieces that covered the counter.

I impulsively put my hand over hers and gave it a light squeeze. "A lot of the women there have had bad days, too. Think it over."

Down the block from the coffee shop there was a small city park. A boy in a red jacket went back and forth on a swing while two little girls played hopscotch. Motes of colorful chalk dusted up from the asphalt and swirled in the afternoon sun. Overhead traffic rumbled from freeways that looped up in gray circles. The Bay Bridge stretched toward San Francisco.

"Your husband is having an affair," I said. There wasn't really a good way to start.

She put her hands to her mouth. "Oh my God. You're sure?"

I thought about the man and woman in the window. "I'm sure."

"I can't believe it." She ran a hand through her hair. "You think you must be crazy. You *hope* you're crazy. I mean, I did all the crazy things people do. I made a secret copy of his office keys, as though I was going to break in and catch them on his desk. I checked his clothes for I don't even know what— lipstick stains or stray earrings. I hired *you*." She laughed. The kind of laugh someone might make when realizing they had just spent five hours accidentally driving north instead of south. "But then . . . you learn you're not crazy. And somehow it's worse." She set the coffee down on the ground. "He's a lawyer, always doing this top-secret work for all these stupid tech firms, treating it like national security. Always running around or shutting himself up in his office until late at night. And now I don't even know if he's been lying about all of that the whole time . . ."

"I understand." I felt badly for her. People who had affairs embarked on all the usual deceit, never really thinking that it could start to make their spouses feel like they were in Gogol's *Diary of a Madman*. "You didn't do anything unusual," I added. "You had a right to know."

"Who is she, anyway?"

I took a second to answer. It was no good blurting out everything at once. I'd learned that early on from a case. After being told that her husband was sleeping with his secretary, a client had walked into the office, by all accounts calm as could be, chatting and smiling, before hitting the unlucky secretary over the head with a three-hole punch. The police had found her at home in bed an hour later, drinking rosé and watching *Grey's Anatomy* reruns. She had been charged with aggravated battery and narrowly avoided a felony.

So now I was cautious about giving out too much information too quickly.

"A personal trainer," I finally said. "From his gym."

Her eyes flashed with anger. "That son of a *bitch*! I got that out-of-shape prick a personal training package so he wouldn't die of a heart attack at sixty-five like his father. And he goes and *screws* her?"

I put my hand over hers, reminded yet again that it was impossible to know which words would provoke which emotions. "I know. It's not nice hearing it." This was part of the job. It was impossible to only be a messenger. Not after delivering news that often changed the trajectory of a life. Therapist, friends, family—eventually my clients would reach out to people. But initially? It was just me.

Brenda stood up and tried to take off her jacket. The belt knot got stuck and she cursed and threw the jacket onto the sidewalk. Her arms were toned and firm. Her voice was neither. "I'm going to get that son of a bitch. He's not going to *believe* what hit him. You can prove it?"

There was a loud metallic grinding as a BART train passed. The tracks ran mostly underground but here they rose overhead briefly before plunging down under the Bay to connect Oakland to San Francisco. I waited until the noise faded. "I have photographs."

"I want to see them."

"I'll have them to you in the next day or two."

"I want to see them now!"

"Soon. I promise." I thought again about the hole-punch woman. I intentionally kept a gap between delivering news and pictures. Photographs could be incendiary.

She was pacing; short, pent-up steps. One of the hopscotch girls watched curiously. "We're going to find him right now, him and his *whore,* and we're going to teach them a lesson."

"Why don't you sit down?" I suggested.

"I'm not in a sitting mood," Brenda snapped. "I've heard stories about you, Nikki. My niece referred you, remember? The one who works at the Brighter Futures shelter. I need you to teach my husband a lesson. I don't care how much it costs, I'll pay. Isn't that what you do?"

"You're upset. I understand. But I can't do that."

"I *need*—"

"Brenda. Listen." She heard the difference edged in my tone and quieted. "I'm not in the lesson-teaching business," I continued more gently. "Save the drama for the soaps. It doesn't end well, talk like that. What you need right now is a stiff drink, a hot shower, and a good divorce lawyer."

"But, as one woman to another, Nikki . . . you have to help me."

"That wouldn't help you. Honest. You'd be trading a bit of short-term satisfaction for all kinds of long-term problems. It's better this way, believe me."

Brenda slowly bent down and picked up her coat. The hopscotch girls were gone and the swing was empty. Her cotton candy–colored manicure had started to flake away, leaving bits of bare nail, and there were dark circles under her eyes. "I'm sorry. I didn't mean to get angry." She rubbed her hands across her head, massaging her temple. "I haven't been sleeping well."

"Angry is normal. I get it."

"I guess." She sounded exhausted. "I should head back home."

I squeezed her hand. "You'll get through this."

Five minutes later I was headed toward Berkeley. I had a few things to wrap up at the bookstore and then was thinking about a movie and Chinese food. Saturday afternoons were supposed to be quiet.

Supposed to be.

I had yet to meet Gregg Gunn.

9

"Hi, Jess. How's business?"

"Hey, Nikki! It's been busy, all the Cal kids settling into fall term. Can't believe we're almost through September already."

The Brimstone Magpie was a used bookstore on Telegraph Avenue in Berkeley. I'd been lucky and bought the shabby two-story building just before East Bay prices really skyrocketed. Now, no way I could have afforded it. Until the next big quake, Bay Area real estate seemed to only be heading up. At the time, I'd thought the building would be a good way to collect steady money from a long-term tenant. The large street-level space was filled by a trendy bakery with a five-year lease and plans to expand. Then came the recession, and suddenly nobody was jumping to buy six-dollar lemongrass shots or gluten-free birthday cakes anymore. The bakery folded fast.

With the bakery gone and no other prospective tenants in sight, I'd started using the empty space for storing books. I acquired too many books and was constantly getting more. I couldn't help it. I loved books. Boxes and boxes from garage or library sales, the free books put up in Craigslist ads, along with walking into every bookstore I passed. So eventually I had put up a few shelves, then a few more. An armchair so I could sit with a cup of coffee and read. I paid for the damn space, I'd figured. Might as well enjoy it. And then one rainy winter day a woman holding a dripping umbrella hurried in and asked how much was the copy of *Bleak House* that she'd seen from the street. I'd never sold a book before. I told her to give me whatever she wanted. She checked her purse and asked if five dollars was okay. I said why not. She paid. My first sale. More people came in, both locals and the university crowd. I started leaving a pot of coffee on the counter. Bought a few more chairs. Put up a few more shelves. At some point, I realized I'd better get a cash register.

The timing was oddly lucky. After Borders folded along with many of the independent bookshops, people started realizing that bookstores weren't exactly guaranteed in the Bill of Rights. All over the East Bay there was a concerted effort to buy local. I started selling more books. I didn't really worry about cash flow or balance sheets. I just liked the idea that people could walk in and read. People started arriving with books to sell, more came in from estate sales, book drives, all over. I talked to local libraries and put up signs. So many books piled up that I had to rent storage space in Oakland to hold the stacks I hadn't had time to sort. I hired a couple of part-timers who came and went before eventually realizing that I needed a full-time manager. I ran an ad and Jess answered it on the second day. She was my age, a raven-haired Los Angeles native who'd walked in wearing cobalt Prada glasses, a miniskirt, and high black boots. During what passed for the job interview she had announced herself as a lesbian with a degree in architecture that she'd never used, a fondness for single malt scotch and rescue animals, and a distaste for cheap coffee, social media, and Lakers fans. She also told me that she expected equity after the first year, zero micromanaging, and permission to bring her cat to work.

I'd hired her on the spot. One of the best decisions of my life.

We got along. She knew when to let me be. Didn't come running in every two seconds with some breathless question about restocking. Pretty soon she was running the place far more efficiently than I ever had, dealing with accounting and insurance and a hundred other details I never would have thought about. Business picked up. Customers liked the coffee, the armchairs, the casual vibe. And Jess's tendency to expel anyone who answered their cell phone while in the store. Sales increased. A year passed and I made her a partner. It wasn't just the sales bump, or that we got along.

Jess understood that I sometimes did other work. She understood that sometimes a woman would come by the store needing something other than a book.

Jess was okay with that. We shared certain views.

"Any good weekend plans?" she asked, turning from a high stack of newly arrived paperbacks that she had been sorting.

"Catch a movie tonight, I think." Remembering, I laughed. "And apparently I have a date on Monday. Don't ask me how the hell that happened."

Jess grinned. "How the hell did that happen?"

I rolled my eyes. "Why do I tell you anything?"

"You on Match, Nikki? Or Tinder? Going for some casual love?"

"Ugh. Please." I went over to the espresso machine, a Lavazza. A big brass Italian model that was the pride of our shop. We officially offered an espresso to customers who made a purchase, but usually just ended up giving out a lot of free coffee without bothering to toe the line. "Want one?"

"Always."

I made two, bending down to scratch Bartleby, the bookstore's resident cat. He was a gray, yellow-eyed cat, and he meowed as I scratched between his ears, his fur warm from the morning sun. True to her word, Jess brought him into the store every day, where he prowled amongst the shelves and took naps of tremendous length, often, for obscure cat reasons, directly atop the register. Maybe he liked to keep track of things more than he let on.

We stood by the counter and sipped our espressos. Customers leisurely browsed the shelves or sat, reading quietly. Sunlight from the windows stretched a slice of brightness against the floor. Jess had a Billie Holiday album playing and the beautiful, vulnerable voice drifted through the store, backed by unhurried big band instrumentals. I took pleasure in the languid pace of the bookstore, the slow movements, the soft voices, the smells of fresh coffee and aged paper, the people who circulated comfortably between the high stacks with gentle semi-purpose, like fish in an aquarium. My bookstore was a place of calm for me—a calm all the more meaningful given how much chaos and unpredictability and pain was out there, outside the doors. Much of my childhood had been anything but calm, so much so that for years I had given up any hope of finding it for myself. Maybe the bookstore had started accidentally, but as I brought in the boxes of books and filled the shelves, I must have known, deep down, that what I was truly doing was building the refuge I had always been so desperate for, and so unsure of ever finding.

"So? Who is he?" Jess wanted to know.

I shook my head. "I knew I shouldn't have said anything."

"Too late now."

"Fine. He's a grad student."

"Got yourself a Berkeley boy! Business? Law? You gonna marry rich and retire?"

"English, sadly. I think I'll keep my day job."

"So what's the plan for the first date?"

"Have him to dinner."

Jess laughed. "You're one of a kind. A strange guy coming to dinner on the first date."

"Right," I said. "'Because he's gonna slip something in my drink or tie me up. I think I'll survive, but if you don't hear from me, tell the cops to check the English Department for clues."

"Or," she winked, "they should check the bedroom . . ."

"My God. You never stop." I saw an older, white-haired man in the fiction section, looking lost. He was dressed impeccably in polished cordovan loafers, a blazer, and a polka-dot blue tie. "Help you find something?" I asked, walking over.

He turned with a relieved look. He had a pleasant face and sharp eyes. "My grandson's birthday. I'm afraid I've fallen out of touch with whatever twelve-year-old boys read these days. But I was sternly warned by his mother that he has every Rowling and Tolkien book in existence."

"What's your grandson like?" I asked.

"Very active. Boy Scouts, loves wilderness, adventure—anything outdoors."

I thought for a second, then started moving up and down the shelves, pulling books. "Jack London, the gold standard. Lived down the street from here, too. *White Fang, Call of the Wild*. Wildness to domestication and the inevitable reverse." I moved down a few letters and grabbed another. "Gary Paulsen, *Hatchet*. Can't go wrong. Classic wilderness survival." Another title caught my eye and I pulled it. "*The White Company*. Knights and battles."

He looked at the book. "Arthur Conan Doyle . . . Sherlock Holmes?"

"This one's different. He'll like it. Trust me." I was already headed down the shelves and grabbed another. "Robert Louis Stevenson. I'm sure he's read *Treasure Island*, but try *Kidnapped*." I lingered in the Ss, scanning titles. "Ernest Thompson Seton. Helped found the Boy Scouts, actually. *Lives of the Hunted*." I handed the man the last paperback. The cover was frayed and the pages were heavily marked up. I saw him notice. "Don't worry. Your grandson is going to be happy."

"You know your books," the man commented as I rang him up.

"Goes with the territory. If I worked as a florist I bet I could tell you all about peonies."

His eyes crinkled. "Somehow I don't see you with peonies."

I put the books in a paper bag and dropped a couple of bookmarks in with the receipt. "Hope he enjoys. Tell him happy birthday from me."

I rang up a few other customers while I finished off my espresso. Across the store I heard voices raised in argument. The ZEBRAS were in, occupying their usual corner. The ZEBRAS were the Zealous East Bay Ratiocinating Amateur Sleuths, a group of East Bay residents who convened a few times a week. Their stated purpose—as their business cards happily stated—was the "Solving of Crimes, Reading of Mysteries, and Nitpicking of Everything," but they leaned decidedly toward the latter parts. As far as I knew, they'd never solved anything more than whose turn it was to pay for lunch, and they were usually a month behind on that. What the ZEBRAS were best at was having spirited literary debates over endless amounts of coffee and deli takeout.

"Don't forget, by the way," Jess said. "Book group this week."

I nodded. "I invited someone new, actually. Her name is Zoe. Who knows if she'll show up, but keep an eye out for her just in case."

Jess gave me a look.

I shrugged. "Maybe. She looked like some company would do her good, anyway." I enjoyed the book club, made up of women I met through my other work. Everyone from English professors to women who had never made it through a copy of *People* until they started coming. They were my favorite. I loved seeing them get so excited about something they'd always been told was a waste of time. When a woman realized there were situations, lessons, knowledge in books that applied to her own life more than she'd ever imagined.

"All right," I said. "Back to the joys of paperwork."

Jess's voice followed me. "Nikki?"

"Yeah?"

"It's good that you're dating again. After what happened with Bryan, I was starting to wonder if you'd end up in a nunnery."

"Yeah, well, we'll see. That's still a definite option." I started toward a door marked EMPLOYEES ONLY but was stopped by another voice. I had been spotted by the ZEBRAS.

"Nikki, we need you to settle something." The request was from Zach, a bearded Cal biology postdoc in his usual uniform of tortoiseshell glasses and army green cargo shorts. He waved his bagel at me to underline the importance of the approaching question.

"I'm busy, Zach."

"Come on, it will just take a second."

I turned toward the group, doing my best to pretend to look irritable. "Fine. What?"

"You're on a cruise ship and people are getting knocked off one by one. You suspect the killer is on board. Who do you want in the cabin next to you: Hercule Poirot or Auguste Dupin?"

I considered. "Poirot. He's got more of a track record. Besides, *Death on the Nile* proves he wouldn't get seasick."

"Not bad, but let's go double or nothing," said Laney Garber, silver bangles on her wrists clinking. She was a Berkeley native, owned an art gallery near campus, and was the only woman I'd ever met who regularly smoked a pipe. Whenever she was in the store, the fragrance of apple tobacco accompanied her. Much to her displeasure I didn't let her smoke in the shop, but the pipe sat next to her even now, a beautiful hand-carved meerschaum that seemed to eye me resentfully for its lack of freedom. "Your great-aunt left you a fortune in rare gems but your loafing, good-for-nothing brother-in-law swiped it all and headed for San Francisco. You can't go to the cops because they're all crooked as hell. What's Philip Marlowe's street address?"

This time I didn't hesitate. "Trick question. Marlowe works L.A. If that rotten, thieving bastard headed for San Francisco I'm calling Sam Spade."

There were approving nods. Abe Greenberg looked up from spreading cream cheese, fingers working the knife across his bagel with the care of a violinist. He was the founder of the ZEBRAS, and, happily adrift somewhere in his eighties, probably the oldest. He'd had a long career as a physicist at the nearby Lawrence Livermore Laboratory and people said he'd forgotten more about nuclear research than most in his profession ever knew. When it came to mysteries, he seemed even more knowledgeable. "Okay, here we go, for all the marbles. You have to beat the goddamn Commies before they take over the world. George Smiley or—"

"Just stop right there. Smiley's the only man for me. Now look, are you gonna buy some books or just sit around talking all day?"

Abe cheerfully ignored me as he cut lox into postage-stamp-size squares and applied them to his bagel as though plastering a collage. His blue eyes were bright under unkempt gray eyebrows and a corduroy beret. "Lisbeth, why so busy? Would you like to request use of our deducing abilities? We all need help sometimes."

I ran a hand through my hair and tried not to smile. If I ever allowed Abe to suspect that I found him even the least bit charming he'd never leave me alone. "I can't afford your rates, Abe. And stop calling me that."

"Anything you need, Lisbeth, we're here for you."

"Just save me one of those bagels."

"Sesame, right? Light schmear?"

"You know me so well."

"He doesn't ask what my favorite bagels are," Laney put in.

"With all that pipe smoke fogging up the air you wouldn't know a sesame bagel if it bit you on the *tuchus*," Abe shot back.

"Okay, sadly some of us have to work," I put in. The ZEBRAS moved at their own pace. When I had the time, I could easily spend an hour bantering as we tried to stump each other with esoteric mystery and detective references, but this wasn't one of those days. "Speaking of which," I added pointedly, "we're closing soon."

Abe threw me a wink and cupped an ear. "Going a bit deaf, I'm afraid. I didn't quite catch that last bit."

I shook my head in mock despair and went upstairs. The day almost at its end.

My upstairs office was plainly furnished with some chairs and a beat-up metal desk. In the corner was a steel safe, next to some struggling houseplants. I'd tried an aquarium once but the cat had gotten up there one calamitous morning. After that, we figured one pet was enough. The back window faced out to Telegraph, and a cube of four black-and-white television monitors sat stacked on a file cabinet. I liked to know what was going on. The only decorations were framed pictures and portraits of favorite authors: Thomas Hardy, Carson McCullers, Graham Greene, Flannery O'Connor, George Eliot. I liked looking at their faces. Some people prayed, went to synagogues or mosques or churches to find support. I had my writers. Wise men and women, even long dead. I liked to think they were capable of guidance nonetheless.

I slid a couple of inches of scotch into a mug. It was almost five and there was a seven o'clock showing of *Double Indemnity*. I'd finish up the time log and invoice for Brenda Johnson and then take off. My favorite Chinese restaurant was a block from the theater. I looked out the window, watching people pass on Telegraph. A couple holding hands. A homeless guy pushing a shopping cart. A group of laughing undergrads. A silver Tesla pulled up and parked across the street. The vehicles were all over San Francisco and Silicon Valley, but scarcer in Berkeley. Only so many people spending $100,000 on an electric car.

A man holding a briefcase got out. The man squinted toward the bookstore, then jaywalked across the street. I turned back to the time log. The details drove me crazy: times, mileage, locations. But divorce cases had a tendency to end up in a courtroom, and I'd been called to testify more than once. In court, documentation and precision ruled.

The intercom on my desk crackled. "Nikki? Man here to see you."

"He say what he wants?"

I heard fuzzy laughter through the intercom. "Do they ever?"

"He can come up."

On one of the monitors I watched Jess talk silently to the Tesla owner. She walked him over to the EMPLOYEES ONLY door. On another monitor I watched the man climb upstairs with brisk, energetic steps. He disappeared from the frame and the next monitor picked him up at the door. There was a knock. I got up and opened the door.

I was greeted with a broad smile and an avalanche of enthusiasm. "Nikki Griffin? How do you do? I'm Gregg Gunn. Call me Gregg." He glanced around. "Oh, Nikki. We're going to get along so well, I can feel it. This street—this charming little bookshop—it's all so wonderfully seedy."

"Seedy," I repeated. "That's the look I gave the decorators. Come on in, I suppose."

That was how Gregg Gunn entered my life.

10

"You'll have to understand," I said. "You caught me as I was heading out."

"I'll be no time at all!" my visitor said, sitting down unprompted.

The first thing I noticed about Gregg Gunn was his energy. He was constantly moving. His hands, his feet. He wore fitted selvedge jeans and black New Balance sneakers and a button-down blue shirt. Late forties, an athletic build, curly sandy hair, clean-shaven. A long time ago someone had told me that the best way to guess a man's worth was by looking at his shoes and his watch. A lot of rich people liked to dress casual. A suit, even a nice one, didn't mean much anymore. Especially in Silicon Valley. Gunn's sneakers were nothing special. Along with the jeans and button-down or polo shirt, the de facto uniform of the Valley, from CEOs to interns. The watch peeked out under the shirt cuff. Soft gold dial, leather strap.

I took another look. A Patek Philippe. Meaning it probably cost about as much as his car. Definitely not something the interns had.

"You don't talk much, do you?" He held up a finger. "Wait! Don't tell me. ISTP, right?"

"Huh?" I looked at Gunn, confused.

"ISTP," he repeated proudly. "You have to be, right? I'd bet anything."

"IS-what now?"

He gave me a funny look as though I was teasing him. "Don't tell me you don't know your type?"

"My type? You mean, like tall, dark, and handsome?"

He laughed. "I love it! You truly are a diamond in the rough. Take Myers-

Briggs sometime, Nikki. ISTP, I guarantee it." He glanced around affably. "I can't remember the last time I was in a bookstore. And people still come in? To buy books?"

"As crazy as it sounds. What can I do for you?"

His knee bounced up and down like a jackhammer. "I'm correct in my belief that you sometimes handle . . . delicate work?"

"All I know about delicate," I said, "is that it's a setting on my dryer."

"You do have a reputation for discretion."

"This line of work, you don't get too far by writing in to the *Chronicle* about what you had for breakfast."

He switched knees. Bouncing the other one now. He hadn't been still a moment since he'd walked in. "With lawyers, of course, there is attorney-client privilege."

I nodded. It was a common question. People came to me with private problems. They wanted the problems fixed. They also wanted the problems to stay private.

"But you're not an attorney."

I spread my hands in a what-can-I-do gesture. "Sorry to disappoint. But if you need a lawyer, San Francisco is right next door. I bet you could find yourself one or two."

Gunn laughed. Now the original knee was bouncing along like an off-kilter metronome. "The last thing I need is another lawyer. I have too many already. I just need to know how you handle information that is of an extremely confidential nature. Call me paranoid, but one can't be too careful."

I sat back in my chair. "You walked into my office. You need something, you tell me. Maybe I can help. Maybe not." I gestured, taking in the plain white walls, the plants and secondhand furniture. "No megaphones or microphones in this place. I get subpoenaed? Let me tell you loud and clear, I don't do perjury. Not for love or money. So if you have a body on your hands and you're looking to dump it? Save your time and go somewhere else. Anyway. I got sick of kick-the-can back in grade school. You talk to me, or not, Mr. Gunn. It's all the same."

He took this in. "Okay. I'll trust you." He paused. "But I must ask you to sign this." He opened his briefcase, removed a packet, and handed it to me. I took the papers and flipped through them. A nondisclosure. This one happened to be about ten times longer than normal. I didn't bother to read through it. Just set it aside.

"You're not going to sign it?"

"I might sign it," I said. "And I might not. Depends on a few things. Including what exactly you want me to do." I had pegged him for a blackmail job. He seemed the type. A male or female prostitute with an illicit video, maybe a rogue coke dealer—some enterprising and immoral figure realizing they'd stumbled across a gold mine in the form of Mr. Gregg Gunn.

He was on his feet. "Okay," he said. "But I should begin with some context."

I nodded. Trying to resist the urge to check my watch.

"I'm the CEO," he explained, "of a company down in Sunnyvale called Care4 that plans to revolutionize childcare. We make monitors and sensors that can live-stream a child's every sound and gesture to a parent via cloud-based wearable technology." He reached into his briefcase again, this time handing me a small white object that resembled a golf ball. There was a slight indentation on one side so it could be placed on a surface and not roll. "Motion and voice activated, longest battery life on the market, HD video, multiple microphones for stereo audio, widescreen lens with digital zoom." He sounded proud enough that he could have been talking about an actual child.

"Looks good. When I have kids, I'll come find you," I said, turning the little ball around in my hands. There was a tiny aperture in the sphere, barely visible. A lens. I tossed the thing into the air, caught it. The material felt like some kind of polymer and was very light.

I handed it back to Gunn but he shook his head. "Call it a souvenir. I have plenty more." He smiled easily. "I hand those suckers out like business cards."

I shrugged and put the thing on a nearby bookshelf. "So you sell cameras?"

"In a sense. We like to think of ourselves as being a communications company that happens to be in tech. We sell communication. That's what today's busy mothers and fathers crave—constant communication and uninterrupted access. Four million babies born each year in this country alone. The daycare and childcare services market in the U.S. is over fifty billion. Care4 stands at the crossroads of technology and the fundamental humanity of parenting—"

I felt like I was drowning. "Save the pitch. Whatever I can do, it's not going to be writing you a check."

He stopped, startled, and laughed. "You're right. What we do doesn't matter, does it? The point is, there's a huge amount of money at stake. And unfortunately, in this day and age, corporate espionage has never been a greater problem."

I glanced at my watch. Dinner was out. I could get some popcorn at the theater.

"The Chinese and the Russians are the worst," Gunn was saying. "But these days it's everywhere. All over the world, gangs discovering that cyber-crime is a lot easier than trying to move heroin over a border." His fingers tapped his knee. "It's a cesspool, Nikki. Everyone willing to steal, cheat, bribe."

I could have made some guesses by that point. I didn't. The point wasn't to convince a client you were smart. The point was to shut up and find out what they wanted.

"Recently," Gunn went on, "we have had crucial intellectual property stolen. We suspect a specific employee is taking it."

"And that's where I come in."

"That's where you come in, yes."

"A question." I didn't wait for an okay. "You run a big company down in the Valley, but you're here talking to me. Why aren't you at one of the big firms that specialize in this?"

"Good question." For the first time he sat still. "I could go to one of those firms, but they're in my world—we move in the same circles. I can't risk even being seen visiting one of them or people will suspect there's a problem. That's all it takes for word to get out that we're in trouble. There are sharks every-where, circling, looking for weakness. You see, Nikki, we've received several rounds of funding and we're on the verge of receiving our last private invest-ments before a public offering. If investors spook now it would be catastrophic."

"So what do you want me to do?"

"I need this employee followed. We have to learn what she's taking and who she's giving it to."

"Why not just fire her?"

Gunn nodded as if he had expected the question. "I wish it were that easy. But then whoever she's working with will keep probing for another weak spot until they find someone else. We need to learn who is trying to steal from us."

It had been a slow month. I had the time. I shrugged. "Sure."

Gunn smiled. "Wonderful. How do you bill?"

"Retainer up front," I said. "Hourly or daily rates after that. Depending on what I have to do, how far from home it takes me."

He turned to his briefcase a third time and handed a bulging manila envelope to me. I opened it and saw stacks of green bills. I pulled out one of the stacks, seeing "100" on the corner.

"That's twenty thousand dollars. Is that sufficient to begin?"

Usually my retainers were a few hundred dollars. So much for the movie. "Can I offer you a drink? Water? Scotch? Coffee?" I figured twenty grand bought him a drink.

Gunn shook his head. "I have." He took out a bottle filled with a murky green liquid. "Cold-pressed juice. The vegetables all come from a sustainable farm down in Gilroy. Want me to send you a case?"

"No thanks. I've never been able to drink my dinner. Anyway, tell me who I'm following."

He took a big glug of cold-pressed whatever. "Sure. But first, I really do need you to sign that document."

Was he telling me everything? Of course not. Then again, they usually didn't. With any luck I could make a decently quick job of it and leave my corporate espionage career behind.

I accepted the pen he handed me and reached for the papers.

11

Following another human being was both simple and incredibly complicated. Simple, because following was just a basic set of actions. Especially if someone didn't suspect they were being followed. In a car, drive after them. On foot, walk after them. Get on the same bus. Sit in the same restaurant. Complicated, though, because people could be unpredictable and it was a big world, one that was increasingly easy to move around in. Someone could jump in a cab, go to an Amtrak or Greyhound station. Or an airport. A person could be thousands of miles away in a matter of hours.

And with a tail you only got one chance.

I'd lived in California my whole life but still didn't really get Silicon Valley: an unplanned constellation of cities with San Jose roughly in the center. Sunnyvale, Santa Clara, Cupertino, Mountain View, Milpitas, Palo Alto, Menlo Park. Each with the same bland little downtown strip of shops and restaurants. Impossible to tell when you had left one and reached another. Endless pavement, endless freeways. Building after building, vast glassy complexes, arid hills. Often passing signs for some household name, Yahoo!, eBay, Apple. More often passing a hundred names that meant nothing. They might someday. They might not.

Care4 was in Sunnyvale, a large building at the edge of a huge office park that must have held ten other companies. The motif seemed to be black tinted glass. A parking lot full of late-model cars. Tech paid. It was hotter than in Berkeley, away from the chilly breezes and fickle weather of the Bay. I started working my way through the parking lot. I had a make and a license plate, plus the employee, Karen Li, drove a distinctive car. A red Porsche Boxster convertible. License plate 5LA7340. I cruised up and down the rows. Not a small parking lot, but not huge. I wasn't searching an airport lot with a hundred different lettered and numbered sections. I saw a red convertible but it was a Mustang. I drove down a few more rows and then I saw it. A little red roadster. Soft top, jaunty, fun to drive. At least as fun as anything else on four wheels. Cars had never been my thing. I stopped nearby and looked around. No one in sight, the employees hard at work inside. I strolled in the direction of the Boxster and dropped a pen I was holding as I walked past. It rolled near the back tire. I squatted down by the Boxster's rear bumper, one hand fumbling for the pen, the other reaching under, toward the chassis. I felt the powerful magnet grip onto the metal underside of the car.

A minute later I was gone. I'd passed a little plaza on my way in. Nail salon, Starbucks, fast-food restaurants. I ordered iced coffee from the Starbucks, bought a newspaper, and settled in to wait.

Following someone used to mean turn by turn, but these days, an average civilian could buy products that would have made a Stasi agent sick with envy. Voice recorders and hidden cameras, keystroke loggers that recorded and transmitted every letter typed on a computer. And GPS trackers. I'd never felt the need to own a lot of the modern technology being sold. Not out of any deep philosophical belief. I just didn't see how fitness trackers or toasters that connected to the Internet would make me happier. But technology had its uses. Instead of standing in eighty-degree heat with a pair of binoculars, I was sitting in an air-conditioned café working my way through my second iced coffee. The device I had used was barely bigger than a matchbox, enclosed in a weatherproof magnetic case. The batteries were good for close to a month and it transmitted to an old iPad Jess had given me. The display showed a map, and a dot on the map.

That dot meant Karen Li could no longer drive anywhere without me knowing exactly where she was.

I waited for almost three hours. We hit lunchtime and groups of people began filling the plaza. Almost all of them men between their twenties and fifties. Almost all of them white, Chinese, or Indian, in jeans and polo shirts with little laminated badges clipped to a belt or lanyard. Tens of thousands like them. Building whatever new world lay around the corner.

The lunch rush ended. The plaza quieted again. I was on my third coffee.

The iPad emitted a beep. The dot was moving.

I got up fast.

By the time the Boxster passed the plaza I was on my motorcycle, watching the road.

I pulled out behind the little red car.

She drove fast, headed north on the 101. We passed NASA's vast Ames Research Center, the enormous airplane hangars looming with otherworldly dimension like something out of an H. G. Wells novel. Reaching Palo Alto I saw signs for Stanford University, and soon after for the SFO airport as we neared San Francisco. A billboard stated WRITE CODE. SAVE LIVES in happy, bright colors. Another, marked with a cute little sky-blue logo, advertised a cloud storage service that presumably was better than other cloud storage services. I stayed a couple of cars back and one lane over from the Boxster. It was midday and even though the freeway was, as always, packed with cars they moved quickly. That made it easier. When people drove, they focused on the road. When they sat in bumper-to-bumper traffic they fidgeted, craned their necks, looked around trying to figure out the holdup. Bored people became unintentionally observant.

As we reached San Francisco, the Boxster exited by AT&T Park. We passed huge Giants pennants and then the bulk of the stadium itself. The day was loud with construction from a hundred different building sites. In the sky, more cranes than clouds. On King Street the Boxster slowed abruptly. Looking for parking. Too close to brake, I accelerated past it. There was an empty metered spot on the right. She'd take it. I continued a block up and wedged my bike between two delivery vans, then unhurriedly walked back down.

I got my first look at Karen Li as she got out of her car. She looked about my age, a pretty Chinese woman in her early thirties with glossy black hair and large sunglasses. She was dressed stylishly, tight jeans and a leather jacket, a black leather handbag slung over her shoulder. She walked purposefully into a coffee shop.

I crossed the street and waited a full five minutes, eying the sidewalk to make sure she didn't leave. If this woman was stealing company secrets she'd be highly alert. When I finally entered the coffee shop I went straight to the register. I ordered coffee and a bagel and bought a copy of the same newspaper I'd read that morning.

Karen Li was at a back table, alone, facing the door.

I sat as far away as I could, in the front corner.

There were about a dozen people around me. A middle-aged guy reading the paper, a college-age girl with an open textbook, a few couples, an old man filling out a crossword puzzle. Karen Li should have fit right in, but something about her was different. She wasn't reading or doing crosswords or eating. A coffee and blueberry muffin stood in front of her, untouched. She was noticeably tense, fingers tapping against the table. One hand rested lightly on her handbag. She checked her watch and drummed her fingers restlessly.

Twenty minutes passed and then two men walked in. One wore a leather jacket and blue jeans, the other a beige sports coat over a red polo. Both were over six feet but the guy in the leather jacket was clean-shaven, with deep set, muddy eyes and the bulk to match his height, while Polo was thin, with a bristly Vandyke beard and a sharp triangle of nose like the prow of an icebreaker. They looked around while they ordered coffee. They looked like men who would notice things. I felt their gaze pass over me and kept my head buried in the newspaper.

They paid for their coffee and sat across from Karen Li.

She was nervous. But she knew them. That was clear.

The three of them fell at once into an intent, urgent conversation. I didn't even consider pictures. The two men were very different than Karen Li. Definitely not the tech crowd. Something else. Something about them felt vaguely dangerous. Like feeling a nascent sunburn long before the skin reddened. I was thinking that whoever Karen Li was, and whatever she was trying to do, she had bitten off way too much. If offering advice I would have told her to forget all about corporate theft and find somewhere else to live. A different city. Maybe a different country.

After a half hour the two men stood. She stayed where she was. The one in the jacket leaned down, whispered a parting word, and the two of them walked past me to the door. A completely normal sight. A coffee, three friends, casual good-byes.

Except for one strange detail.

When they walked away, the man in the leather jacket was holding her handbag.

Karen Li sat for a few more minutes, then pushed her coffee away and gave the muffin a puzzled look as though wondering how it had gotten there. I got a good look at her face as she walked out. She was very pretty. Almond brown eyes, a delicate jaw, pronounced cheekbones, a small nose. She was thin but had a physical vitality as though she spent weekends paddleboarding and skiing. I waited another few minutes and then left as well. It didn't really matter where Karen Li was going. I'd know where she was. I was thinking about something else. Human faces and expressions. In my line of work, I saw more than my fair share of intense emotion. Grief, confusion, anger, shock, lust. Usually the expression matched the situation. Catch someone cheating and you got shame. Track down a thief and you got fear. Faces mirrored feelings.

So Karen Li's nervousness hadn't surprised me. That was normal for someone in her situation. Someone involved in high-stakes corporate espionage. Someone doing something wrong. She was bound to be nervous.

Her face had been different, though. Karen Li hadn't looked like someone stealing. She had looked like she was being marched to the firing squad. On her face had been nothing but naked terror.

12

I'd taught myself basic cooking in junior high, out of necessity, and got better in college while sharing an off-campus apartment with other undergrads. I had bounced around in my early twenties, lived in Marin for a while with an older guy who taught poetry at Sonoma State and couldn't grease a pan to save his life. My favorite thing about that place had been a family of peacocks who'd wandered onto his property and seen no reason to leave. I hand-fed them blueberries every morning. After we split I missed the ex-peacocks more than the ex-boyfriend.

I hadn't grown to really enjoy cooking until I had my own place and my own kitchen. My apartment was a one-bedroom in West Berkeley, close to the water and a few miles from the center of campus. The industrial part of the city, auto repair shops and warehouses and quirky artist spaces with glass-blowing studios and sculpting. Close enough to the train tracks that I could hear the blasts from the Amtrak and cargo trains that rattled through. From the roof of my building it was possible to glimpse the lights and towers of San Francisco. I had lived there close to ten years and the area was changing noticeably, sleek new developments springing up at a breakneck pace, but the neighborhood still retained much of its former identity.

I had gone by the bookstore after following Karen Li to the coffee shop, and by the time I got home it was past six. I had to hurry. I jumped in the shower, took a few extra minutes to wash my hair and shave my legs. I threw together an antipasto plate in between blow-drying my hair into an auburn sheen. Artichoke hearts, olives, salami, cheeses. I left my hair down. Put on my favorite jeans and a thin cashmere sweater that hung loosely off one shoulder, a pair of simple silver pendants in my ears. I added a little blush to offset the naturally pale skin that had always driven me crazy as a kid, when a good beach tan was the only thing I wanted. The phone rang and I felt a moment of disappointment that it would be Ethan, calling to cancel.

I picked up, blow-dryer still running in one hand. "Yeah?"

"Is this Nikki Griffin?"

I flicked the blow-dryer off. "Who is this?" Definitely not Ethan. A slurred, unfamiliar voice. Some drunk guy, maybe, accidentally hitting the wrong number.

Except he was looking for me. By name.

"You met with a man named Greggory Gunn recently."

I set the dryer down. "Who is this?"

"He talked to you about an employee. You should know there is more to the situation."

"There usually is." I was focused on the voice as much as the words. Not quite a slur. A strange, unnatural bass. A voice that didn't sound quite human. I looked at the caller ID. Nothing except the word PRIVATE. "If you have something to say, then say it," I prompted.

There was a dial tone. I put the phone down slowly. Wondering why a strange man using a voice changer was calling me about a tech company, and what it meant.

Through the kitchen window, I saw Ethan bicycle up to my building. He wore a helmet and backpack and that same corduroy jacket from the diner. A bouquet of flowers sprouted out of his backpack. When he leaned to lock his bike to the gate, the flowers fell onto the ground. I had to smile as his lips moved in a silent flurry of curses through the glass. He buzzed and I rang him in, hearing footsteps on the stairs as I opened the door. "Look who showed up."

"Hello! These are for you." He thrust the rumpled bouquet toward me. Irises, courtesy of Trader Joe's. He leaned in and I thought he was going to try to kiss me, but instead he gave me an awkward half hug and stepped back quickly as though worried I'd take offense. I couldn't remember the last time someone had brought me flowers. I couldn't find a vase. I put the flowers in a decanter instead. Close enough. "What would you like to drink?" I asked.

"What are you having?"

"Martini."

"You know something weird? I'm not sure if I've ever had a martini before. I thought people only drank them in John Cheever stories."

"Well," I said, "we can't fix all the world's problems. But we can fix this one."

I mixed us a couple of martinis. "I thought they were supposed to have vodka," he commented.

I skewered olives on a toothpick. Three, because one wasn't enough and two were bad luck. "If you want this to work, don't ever say that again." I handed him his drink. "Gin. Cheers."

He sipped cautiously, then smiled. "That's kind of awesome." He took another sip. "Usually my friends tell me to find a six-pack and a bottle opener."

"Maybe you need new friends."

He was walking around, curious. "Record player . . . no television . . . you weren't kidding about the technology thing." He stopped by a bookshelf. "Who's this guy? In the picture?"

I glanced over. "That's my brother. Brandon."

The two of us. Years ago. We stood together on Mount Tam, the California landscape spread out gloriously below. The blue of the Bay, the green of thousands of acres of trees. The two of us in sweat-stained tank tops, grinning like we'd just summited Everest. My brother's eyes clear and bright.

"And this one—your parents? It's a nice picture."

I bit my lip. Took a big swallow of my drink. "Thanks." I didn't need to turn around to see the picture he meant. The four of us. Standing on the beach in Bolinas. The ocean behind us. My brother five or six, me nine or ten. My mother blond, willowy, tall, tanned, wearing a bikini top and cut-off jean shorts. My dad's long black hair touched with gray, bearded, bare-chested, wearing a ridiculous polka-dot bathing suit. The four of us. Together.

"You look really close. You're lucky."

I joined him at the small table. "Have some food."

He placed a piece of cheese carefully on a cracker. "So you work in a bookstore?"

"Technically, I own a bookstore."

He was impressed. "You're full of surprises. Which one?"

"The Brimstone Magpie, over on Telegraph."

He nodded. "I've been there. Where's the name from?"

"The first book I ever sold, *Bleak House*. One of the characters, Grandfather

Smallweed, used the phrase as a curse word. I always liked it. Where are you from?" I shifted.

"A small town near Bozeman. I went to U of M on scholarship even though my parents weren't into higher ed. They thought it would turn me gay, Commie or, worst of all, liberal. I met a few professors who gave me a lot of encouragement, got lucky, and ended up at Cal. They give me a stipend that still seems too good to be true. Over twenty thousand a year to read and teach."

I thought about the envelope holding $20,000. A year's salary, for him. But I didn't want to think about Gregg Gunn. Didn't want to think about the strange telephone call or the job I had taken on, motives as murky as one of those cold-pressed juices. Not now. Not tonight. There was a blasting horn and the apartment shook slightly with a passing train. I could tell by the volume that it was a cargo train, not Amtrak. I was used to the trains and didn't mind.

I stood as the noise faded. "I'll start dinner."

"What are you making?"

"Trout *grenobloise*."

"Trout what?"

"You'll see." I unwrapped a pair of gleaming, silvery brook trout. Added a sizeable piece of butter to a hot pan and got some sliced lemons and capers ready while waiting for the butter to brown. I had a mushroom risotto that I had been stirring for the last hour.

Trout were quick. Ten minutes later we were eating. I opened a bottle of white wine and poured.

"This is delicious," he said. "And this wine is amazing. Even though I don't know anything about wine."

"Good wine is just wine that you like." I also liked Ethan. His enthusiasm, his obvious love of books. And his smile. I caught myself wondering what his chest was like under the corduroy jacket and shirt.

He looked up from his plate. His eyes were blue and pleasing. "Question."

"Sure."

"If we were skipping all of the, like, first date awkwardness. The BS where we try to pretend there's nothing wrong with us. What if this was, like, date number ten?"

"Ten. Wow. You're an optimist."

"I'm serious. What would it be like?"

I thought about it. "Probably," I said, "we'd be arguing about books. Then maybe you'd ask me some questions about my job that I wouldn't want to answer, so I'd change the subject. After dinner, we'd take a bottle of wine and some blankets, go sit up on the roof. That's what number ten might look like."

He took this in. "Why wouldn't you want to talk about your job? I love bookstores."

"Ask me something else."

"Mysterious."

"No. That's the thing." I wanted him to understand. "People think mystery is good, exciting. Except usually it just means that something bad is around the corner."

"Are you saying you're bad?" He wasn't being lascivious.

"I don't think I am. I hope I'm not. But the parts of me you don't know might not be the parts you'd like. They might not even be the parts I like. But they're there, just the same." I was quiet. Feeling what I wanted to say fighting through my natural reserve like someone underwater swimming up toward that spot of brightness that means light and air. I couldn't stay under forever, playing Miss Havisham. No matter how peaceful that sounded.

He was clearing the table. He'd been a waiter. I could tell. The way he cradled the wineglasses between his fingers and lined the plates along his forearm. No one who'd ever worked as a waiter stacked plates when they cleared. I pictured him in college, in Montana. Friday night, maybe working a late shift. Ignoring the frat parties and kegs. Coming home alone, exhausted. Roommates probably out having fun, hooking up, getting drunk. Doing carefree college things. And him alone, worn out, tired. But planning. Planning how to move forward. Past the bad things and toward the good ones.

I wondered which one of us I was even thinking about.

"Look," I finally said. "Don't worry about the plates. Grab those blankets from the couch. It's nice out. We can go sit on the roof for a bit."

WEEK TWO

13

"Nikki, how have you been?"

"You're gonna laugh."

"I won't laugh."

"Okay. I met this guy."

"You met a guy."

"That sounds totally high school. I know."

"And you like him?"

"Yeah. I had him over to dinner. We kinda hit it off."

"That sounds very nice."

"I—am I allowed to tell you, like, personal stuff? Or is that weird?"

"Of course you can."

"I . . . um, slept with him."

"You slept with him."

"Yeah. Which was ironic because we had joked about *not* doing that. On the first date, anyway."

"And you enjoyed it?"

"Uh . . . yeah. Actually, I did. Kind of a lot. It was a nice evening."

"I'm glad to hear that, Nikki. And you're going to see him again?"

"We're going to a concert in Oakland this weekend with another couple, friends of his. I can't remember the last time I've been on a double date. What do people even do? Maybe we'll get gelato afterwards. Or play Scrabble."

"Does this man you met know that you see me? Why you see me?"

"Why I see you?"

"Yes."

"You mean what happened."

"Yes."

"Why? I just met him. It's not like I have to tell him everything at once."

"I know it's only our second meeting, but we haven't addressed this yet. You aren't here voluntarily."

"Like I could forget."

"I'm not trying to upset you. But just to get all of the elephants out of the room."

"Sure. The elephants."

"Your last boyfriend, Bryan. That was his name, right?"

"Bryan. Yeah. Sure. What about him?"

"I feel compelled to point out that you struggle with—with certain tendencies. How you react to certain things."

"Aren't you supposed to be on my side? Bryan was an asshole. I was protecting him. *Protecting* him. Did you get that in my file?"

"Nikki, I know you're upset."

"Let me finish. Okay? Since we're herding the damn elephants or whatever. You know that he didn't even bail me out after it happened? That I got to spend a day in a cell with the DTs puking two feet from my cot and a bunch of sleazy male guards telling us all the fun things they wanted to do to us— did that go in my file, too?"

"You feel betrayed by Bryan."

"I'm not complaining. I can handle worse. I *have* handled worse. A lot worse."

"I believe you, but my point is that problems become problems when they have a negative effect on your life. Legal consequences, the end of a relationship, risks to your health and safety. This has to be addressed. Why didn't you want to talk about your parents last time? Can you tell me?"

"Can we call it a day?"

"We still have some time left."

"I know."

"We can finish early if you like. I'll see you next week, same time?"

"Like I have a choice."

"Be good, Nikki. I'll see you next week."

14

Gregg Gunn had asked to meet me at a fitness center in San Jose, a couple of miles from the Care4 building where I had begun following Karen Li. I pulled up to the big glassy building and walked into a sun-filled atrium, dodging potted ferns and finding the main desk just past a smoothie bar with lemons and oranges painted along its walls. The effect was like a corporate kindergarten. Around me everywhere were young staff in white polo shirts and khakis, all smiling and moving with the precise efficiency of robots. Gunn must have given them my name because a moment after I checked in, a good-looking Korean guy bounced around the desk and offered to show me upstairs. "He's on the racquetball courts," he explained. My guide looked to be college-age, with a wide smile and muscular arms that strained his sleeves. A name tag identified him as Kevin. We walked past the Sales offices, where a handful of attractive men and women were on the phone or leaning forward in earnest conversation.

"You're a trainer here?" I asked.

Kevin nodded with vigor. "Most definitely! Do you work out? You look it."

"When I can."

"Ask for me if you ever want to book some individual sessions. I'd love to help you achieve your goals!" We reached the racquetball courts on the second floor. "He's on court three," Kevin said. He flashed me a parting smile and offered a strong handshake. "Don't be shy about getting in touch!" As he walked away I thought again of the robots.

The back wall of the racquetball court was glass. I watched Gunn move within. He wore athletic clothes and hit with energy, leaping side to side across the polished maple, arm winding back and sweeping across his body with each shot. The glass stripped the scene of audio; I watched sneakers squeak silently off wood and the paddle bounce soundlessly off the ball. When I walked into the court he glanced at me over his shoulder but didn't stop. "Nikki. Thanks for coming. Any updates?"

I told him briefly what I'd seen of Karen Li in San Francisco, omitting only the strange phone call I'd gotten at my apartment. Gunn kept hitting while I talked. I tried to stay out of the way. "You're sure about this?" he said. "Did you record the conversation?"

"No."

He gave the ball a hard slam and repositioned himself for the bounce. "Why not? Isn't that what I'm paying you to do? No offense, Nikki, but I can't just take your word for everything that happens. I need *proof.* You of all people should know that."

I stepped out of the way of the ball as it angled toward me. Gunn's paddle came within six inches of my head and sent the blue rubber ball spinning toward a corner. "The woman is scared out of her mind," I said. "Meaning she's hyperaware. A hundred thousand years ago, that's probably why we didn't all get eaten by lions. If I had been snapping pictures, someone would have noticed. Once that happens, forget about following her anymore." I wasn't exaggerating. Being professionally followed was an experience that the majority of the population never encountered. The feeling tended to be deeply unsettling. It could keep a person looking under the bed for years to come.

He sidestepped to take the ball on his backhand and smashed it downcourt. "So you physically *saw* her leave her bag. And the two men took it? You're sure?"

"Yes," I said, trying not to sound annoyed. I reminded myself the guy had paid me twenty grand. For that money, I could play parrot.

Gunn abruptly stopped and set the paddle down, breathing hard. The ball rolled away from us. "So I was right."

"That I can't tell you. Not yet, anyway."

"Of course I was right," he snapped as though I had called him a liar. "What do you think, she's giving them her dry cleaning?"

"Would you like me to stay on her through the weekend?" I was hoping he'd say no. It was the first weekend in October and I was looking forward to seeing Ethan again. I didn't want to cancel. Not for any reason, but especially not for Gregg Gunn.

He shook his head, wiping sweat away with a gym towel. "No need. We have a company retreat down in Big Sur. She'll be there the whole time."

"Okay." For once, I wanted to say more. I wanted to ask why the woman I was following looked like she was standing three stories up in a burning house, if all she was doing was stealing documents. I wanted to ask why a man using a voice changer would have gone through the trouble of digging up my home number to warn me about unknown danger. I wanted to ask him, again, why he had hired me in the first place instead of picking one of the big, sleek corporate security firms that specialized in handling exactly this kind of case. For that matter, I wanted to know how exactly he had found me, and why he had decided to pay me a retainer far in excess of my normal rates. I wasn't buying that he'd flipped darts into the Yellow Pages until my name came up, either. I wouldn't have minded learning a bit more about Gunn or his company. There were plenty of things I wanted to know.

I kept quiet.

Gunn drank from a water bottle, still breathing hard. Under the sheen of physical exertion he looked tired, eyes reddened as though he hadn't slept well. Together we left the court, closing the glass door behind us. "Are there things about Karen Li you're not telling me?"

He gave me a sharp look. "What makes you ask that?"

"Maybe I like questions."

Gunn started to say something, stopped, and shrugged. "I suppose there's always something we don't know. I told you what is relevant."

"Is Karen Li working with anyone else at your company? Do you suspect anyone else?"

Gunn narrowed his eyes. "Not that I'm aware. But if she is, I hope you can find that out."

"And there's nothing else I should know? About who she is or what she wants?"

"I told you the salient details," he replied. "That's what you should be focused on."

He stopped by a door leading to the men's locker room. "We'll be in touch. Make sure I can reach you."

Outside in the parking lot I had just gotten on my motorcycle when there was a double honk behind me. I looked over my shoulder and saw a little white BMW, one of the boxy hybrid models. I raised my visor, irritated by the constant impatience of Silicon Valley. "You can have the spot," I said. "Just give me a second."

The driver looked at me through his open window. He was Gunn's age, in his late forties, but had the opposite manner of the charismatic CEO. His brown hair withdrew from his forehead in a pronounced widow's peak and he had prominent eyebrows set above an intelligent, uncertain face. The uncertainty was telegenic. He could have been cast in a commercial as the guy thinking about switching from one phone company to another after his best friend tells him what he's missing while they're watching a baseball game. "I don't want your parking spot," he said. "I want to talk to you." His voice was soft and careful.

"If you want to hit on a woman, I think you're supposed to do it in the gym, not the parking lot. And you're never supposed to honk. Just a tip for the future."

He didn't smile. "I'm not hitting on you, and we can't stay out here all day. *He* might see us. He'll be out any minute."

I took a closer look at the driver. I'd never seen him before. "You don't mean—"

"Follow me," he said. "Hurry."

I generally wasn't in the habit of letting strange men pull up in a parking lot and tell me where to go, but this time I nodded. I followed the white car onto the freeway, heading north. It was early afternoon, before the South Bay's hellish commuter traffic really got bad. In North San Jose, the white car exited and we drove down wide roads crammed with construction cranes and new apartment complexes. Even through my helmet, noise assailed me, clanging and hammering descending from the little troops of orange-vested men on scaffolding and catwalks. I was relieved when the BMW took another, narrow road that spun us out away from the craze of buildings, and then we were weaving between high unkempt grass and, beyond that, marshy water that must have been the southernmost tip of the Bay.

The car pulled over on the side of the road and the driver got out. I pulled up behind him and we faced each other. I wasn't worried. Nothing about the man in front of me seemed dangerous. He was a little shorter than me and wore high-waisted blue jeans and a tucked-in black T-shirt. Sock-clad feet filled leather sandals. The skin on his hands was soft, fingernails neatly clipped. He had the expression, out here in what passed for wilderness, of someone who seemed far more comfortable indoors.

"Your name is Nikki Griffin," he said. "You're a private investigator."

"I've been called worse. And you are . . . ?"

"That doesn't matter."

Something about him seemed familiar, even though I was sure we'd never met. I took a long-shot guess. "You called me the other night, didn't you? At my home."

His eyes shifted. "I don't know what you're talking about."

"Using a voice changer. You were trying to warn me about something."

"I don't know what you're talking about," he repeated weakly. He pulled an orange plastic bottle from a pocket and removed two small white pills, dry-swallowing them. I glimpsed the label. Lorazepam. Jess had a prescription for the same thing because she hated flying.

"You okay?" I asked.

"I'm fine. I'm fine," he repeated.

"You never got around to giving me your name," I added.

"No! I'm not used to this cloak-and-dagger stuff," he continued more quietly. "It's very stressful. I don't know how people like you manage it constantly."

"Don't tell me your real name if you don't want to. We're not in *The Secret Agent*."

"The what?"

"Conrad. Never mind. But I have to call you something."

He hesitated. "Call me Oliver."

"Okay. So, Oliver, why are we here?"

"You took on a job that you shouldn't have," he finally said. "There's a lot more going on than you know, and what you're up against is a lot more than you can deal with."

"You really know how to build up a girl's self-confidence."

He didn't smile. "You should walk away," he said. "Better yet, run. Away from the whole mess, before it's too late. Because after a certain point, there's no going back."

I was getting tired of the whole Nostradamus act. "I thought you had something to tell me. Something *real*." I glanced around at the grass, dead brown after the dry summer. "As much as I like the beautiful view and scintillating conversation."

"I'm getting to that."

"Well, you're not breaking any speed limits."

"First I need to know that I can trust you."

I spread my hands apologetically. "Oliver. Please. There's no way I can make that happen. And that's not a bad thing. You don't know me. You'd be stupid to take anything I say at face value. But, sure, if you insist—how can I earn your trust?"

"Well, you're doing a pretty bad job of it so far," he retorted.

"How long have you worked at Care4?"

He drew back suspiciously. "Who says I do? How do you know that?"

"Because you knew Gunn would be at the fitness center, which means that you either have access to his calendar or work at the gym." I remembered the biceps and smile of the charismatic Korean guy who had walked me up to the racquetball courts, the cluster of energetic salespeople we'd passed. "You're definitely not a trainer, and frankly—no offense—there's no way you're in sales, because if you were, the whole place would be bankrupt."

"You really know how to build up a guy's self-confidence," he returned.

I had to laugh. "Sorry. Guess we're even. So what do you do at Care4?"

The flash of humor faded as he gazed out at the weed-choked water. "I'm in security."

"I think you forgot your gun and badge."

"Not that meathead goon crap. I mean the security that matters—network security. The stuff that people should actually worry about."

"How about me? You told me I should worry. So what do I worry about?"

His lip pinched his teeth. "Why were you hired by Care4?"

I made a fast calculation of the pros and cons of disclosure, and decided that I almost definitely wouldn't be telling him anything he didn't already know. "To follow an employee. Karen Li. To find out if, and what, she's stealing from the company."

He nodded. "Have you talked to her?"

"Of course not. You think I can just walk up and ask if she had eggs or oatmeal for breakfast? That's not how it works."

He unwrapped a candy bar that he took from his pocket. "What do you know about Greggory?" he asked, biting into the dark chocolate.

"I know that he's the CEO of a tech company that's going to change the world one baby monitor at a time. Look, Oliver. I appreciate the questions, but I can't do the runaround all day. What do you want to tell me?"

"Not tell you. Show you." He reached into his car and handed me a sheaf of folded papers. I unfolded them and looked up questioningly.

Airline itineraries.

The passenger name on each was Mr. Greggory A. Gunn. "Are these real?"

He nodded. "It's easy enough to verify a couple of flights if you don't believe me."

The destinations jumped out. Grozny, Chechnya, with a stop in Moscow each way. A three-day round trip to Riyadh, Saudi Arabia, and then a third trip to Cairo, Baghdad, and Istanbul. I did my best to memorize the flight numbers and dates. Three separate trips in total, all within the last ninety days, all commercial. It was the last part that made me skeptical. "You're telling me your CEO is too cheap to fly private? Have you seen his watch?"

"On the contrary. He always flies corporate. Except on these trips."

"Why?"

"Look at the destinations."

"I did."

"A lot easier for people to know where you're going if you're in a company jet."

"So what was he doing?"

"I have no idea."

"Can you take a guess?"

Oliver gave me a sour look. "I thought that was *your* job, Detective."

"You think Karen Li is part of this? Or knows something about it?"

"No idea. And I'm not about to get involved."

"Then why talk to me now?"

Even the question seemed to make him nervous. "I'm not a hero, but I don't plan to end up in prison, either. If my company is doing something wrong I don't want to be complicit."

"Why not go to the police?"

"To report a travel itinerary?" He slid his sandaled toe around the dusty paving and watched little tracks form. "Look—just take my advice and walk away. I'm sure there are a million people out there who will pay you to fol-low someone or snap pictures or whatever you do. Don't get involved in this. It's not worth it, I mean it."

"Thanks for the advice. To be continued."

He didn't like that. "*No!* Not to be continued! This was a one-time favor. Don't think we're getting into a whole . . . arrangement."

I didn't bother to answer that. Putting my helmet on, I tried once more. "No guesses? Why your CEO would want to visit those countries? He doesn't seem the type to be into the whole extreme tourism thing, but maybe I'm wrong."

Oliver started to say something, then stopped. "No idea whatsoever."

"Nice to meet you, Oliver."

I rode away, thinking about the destinations, what they had in common.

Wondering what a tech CEO was doing visiting the world's hotbeds for extremism.

15

There might have been worse parts of Oakland than Castlemount, but I didn't know about them. I parked on the sidewalk, right by the door of the six-story apartment building I was headed into. In addition to breathtaking coastline and sweeping redwood forests, the Bay Area also had the distinction of being statistically the best place in the country to have a car stolen. Something like fifty thousand vehicles gone each year. I wanted to come back to a motorcycle that was still there. Across from me was a small white house. A rusted car sat in the front yard on tireless rims. Two young men sat on the porch, staring openly, passing a bottle in a paper bag. A dog barked somewhere down the street. I took grocery bags out of the lockable metal storage cases on either side of the motorcycle.

Inside, what passed for the lobby smelled like cigarettes and stale vomit. The stained tile floor was sticky against my shoes. I pushed the button for the elevator. Nothing. I pushed the button again, then gave up and started up the staircase. On the fourth floor, I used my key, knowing the door would be locked. "Hey," I called out. "It's me."

"Nik?"

The apartment was dark. Heavy blinds hung over the windows, no lights on. Instead of a sunny afternoon it could have been the middle of the night. The furniture would have gone on the Free section of Craigslist and then waited a couple of years for someone to pick it up. A beat-up red couch, pockmarked with cigarette burns; a couple of chairs that looked like they were biodegrading right into the floor. Pizza boxes and random clothing were strewn around, along with empty cans, crumpled cigarette packs, and liquor bottles like something out of a Bukowski story. Cigarette butts, some in ashtrays, plenty not. A cheap red plastic bong on the coffee table. I tried not to see the syringe next to it. The air stunk of smoke and sweat and bong water. I set down the shopping bags and turned on the overhead light.

Brandon was lying on the couch. A shirtless man of about my age slumped in an armchair, asleep. He had a green Mohawk and a face full of piercings. A girl sat on the floor, slouched against a wall. She smoked a cigarette and looked at me dully. Her hair was peroxide blond with darkening roots. She could have been sixteen or twenty-six. "Who're you?" she slurred. Her pupils were bright and tiny. She wore torn black jeans and a stained gray T-shirt with pink Be-Dazzling spelling out the word PRINCESS.

I looked at her. Thinking that she and Mohawk could probably go on the Free section right along with the furniture. They'd probably have to wait a lot longer to get picked up. "You should leave." I jerked my head over to Mohawk. "Both of you. Now."

"Hey, c'mon, Nik," Brandon said. "What're you doing? I invited them. They're my guests." His words dripped out of his mouth.

"Who're you?" the girl said again. Insistent. She fumbled for words. "You can't just barge . . . just barge in here. Tell us what to do. What gives you the right . . . ?"

I went over to Mohawk. He'd been smoking a cigarette and it had fallen out of his mouth or hand. It lay on the floor, steadily burning into the wood.

I stomped it out. Shook his shoulder. "Hey. Get up."

There was no response. I shook harder. Still no response. I took one of his earrings in my fingers. The upper lobe. More sensitive. I tugged the earring sharply. Once, then again. Like ringing a doorbell. His eyes slowly opened. "What the fuck?"

"You. Up. Go take a walk."

"Who the hell are you?"

"Come on, Nik," Brandon said. "These are my friends."

"You can't tell me shit," said Mohawk. He seemed to have woken up in a bad mood. He blinked his eyes, the tiny pupils glaring up at me. "We're his friends. You heard him."

"Where are we supposed to go?" argued the girl in that same dull voice. Still sitting on the floor. Her cigarette smoked down to nothing. She took another drag anyway. I wondered how the filter tasted. "You think we have anywhere to go?"

"Sit on the damn curb," I said. "Same as what you're doing now. Only there, not here."

"You can't talk to her like that," Mohawk said. He looked like he was trying to get himself out of the chair. His voice not quite aggressive, but getting somewhere in the vicinity.

I looked away. Took a breath. "Brandon," I said, ignoring Mohawk and the girl. "These two should really go. Immediately. Because I'm getting kind of sick of asking nice."

Brandon laughed. He had an endearing laugh, at odds with the grim surroundings. A high-pitched near-giggle that faded into a long smoker's cough. "That's your cue," he said to Mohawk. "I wouldn't make her mad."

"She shouldn't make *me* mad," Mohawk said. "She has no idea what I'm capable of."

Brandon laughed again. "If you make her mad you'll get a *reeeeeaaal* surprise. I'd listen to her, I really would." He laughed more.

"Come on," Mohawk said haughtily to the girl. "I can see we're not wanted."

I didn't look at him. Let him pause in front of me, light a new cigarette, blow a cloud of smoke into my face. I didn't move. The two of them left. The door slammed. Footsteps faded.

"Why'd you have to kick them out, Nik? They weren't doing any harm."

The two of us alone, now. The apartment quiet.

"No harm?" I said. I turned away from the wall. Once my kid brother had been handsome as hell. Unforgettable green eyes that danced with energy, and smooth clear skin. Given a normal childhood, he would have been juggling girlfriends right and left. There would have been girls stopping by the house for help with chemistry homework or to borrow a CD or whatever high school girls did when they liked someone. Traces of that Brandon were still there but I had to look close. He was thin, no longer in a coltish teenage way but just a parched, unhealthy look. A couple of inches taller than me and probably ten pounds lighter. He wore a black sleeveless tank top and dirty blue mesh gym shorts, and his lightly freckled face was covered with scraggly stubble. A Band-Aid on his cheek, his brown hair unwashed. I wanted to cry. I wanted to shampoo his hair, sponge hot water over the dirty skin. His green eyes didn't sparkle. The pupils were small, the eyelids puffy.

"Are you hungry? You want me to make something? An omelet? Grilled cheese?"

"Not hungry, Nik-Nik," he said. "But thanks."

I took the shopping bags into the kitchen. I couldn't have done much cooking anyway. The sink was piled high with dirty plates and moldering food, the stovetop greasy, covered in pizza boxes and empty takeout containers. A cockroach scuttled across the counter and took refuge behind the stove. I opened the refrigerator. Two six-packs of Bud Light, a bottle of Sriracha hot sauce bearing the telltale rooster, and a rotting head of lettuce. That was it.

I took cleaning supplies from where I kept them under the sink. I threw out the lettuce, scrubbed away the liquid rot that had pooled underneath. Began unloading groceries. Fresh vegetables and fruit, delicatessen cold cuts, eggs, bread, cans of soup. I scrubbed ash and dried food off the dishes, filled two large Hefty bags with trash. In the bedroom, the sheets were rank. I put them all in another trash bag to be laundered, got clean sheets from a shelf in the closet. The air was stale. I managed to get a window open and jumped as a loud jangling went off from the night table by the bed. An old analog alarm clock, a vivid Mickey Mouse imprinted on the bright yellow face. I shook the clock and turned dials until it stopped ringing.

Brandon was just as I had left him. "That alarm clock scared the crap out of me," I said. "You want a new one that actually goes off when you want it to?"

He shook his head emphatically. "Mom and Dad gave it to me for my first day of first grade. Mom said I'd actually have to start waking up on my own."

"Sorry," I said, suddenly guilty. "I knew that."

"Maybe this one doesn't work perfectly. But neither do I. We're a good fit."

I changed the subject. "You're sure you're not hungry?"

"Let's have a drink."

"A drink? Seriously?"

"We're both over twenty-one."

I looked at my brother, draped comfortably across the couch. "You're just a regular Oblomov, aren't you? Sure, we can have a drink. Why not?" I went into the kitchen and twisted the tops off two bottles of Bud Light. He was sitting up now. I handed him a beer. "Here. How much do you need?"

"Could I get a thousand?"

"I took care of rent already. You need a grand on top of that?"

He laughed. "Inflation, Nik. Basic economics. The dollar doesn't go as far anymore."

"Dammit, Brandon. It's not about the money. I give you that, it goes into your arm."

"This month will be different."

"Right."

"Please, Nik-Nik."

"Don't give me that Nik-Nik shit! Okay?" His name for me. When he was barely old enough to talk. Running around the house playing hide-and-seek, chasing me down the beach, crowing delightedly as he snatched a piece in checkers. Nik-Nik. His older sister.

"I need something," he said. "Can't not have *something*. What's the harm?"

Harm. That word again.

I bit my lip and counted out five hundred-dollar bills. "The harm? That I come in here one day and— Can't you be careful? And who knows what's in the needles?"

He laughed merrily again and drank more beer. "I already got most things you can get from a needle, Nik." Traces of his old smile. "It's the damn needles should be scared of me."

I took a vicious swig of my bottle. Feeling the cold beer hurtle down my throat. "Here. Five hundred is all you're getting. Take it." I handed him the money. "Naloxone. You have some here?"

Brandon giggled. "We did, but Eric—the guy you kicked out—he took a bad hit the other day. Here one minute, gone the next. I used the dose I had here to pull him out of it." He giggled again, gestured to his Band-Aid. "He was so mad when he woke up that he head-butted me."

"The asshole with the Mohawk did that?" My hand gripping the beer bottle. If I'd known that, I wouldn't have bothered tugging the earring. Mohawk would have been awakened by a bottle breaking over his head.

"He didn't mean it."

I took two plastic nasal spray tubes out of my purse and put them in the drawer of the coffee table. If someone overdosed on an opiate, naloxone was a literal lifesaver. No need for paramedics or hospitals, although a side effect was sending the OD into an instantaneous state of acute withdrawal. There were all kinds of stories of junkies mindlessly attacking the paramedics who'd just saved their lives. But the stuff worked almost magically. One day, one of

those little white tubes might save my brother's life. "You're sure you don't want to live somewhere nicer? I'll find you a place in my neighborhood."

"Naw," he said with a gentle smile. "The gritty underbelly is where I stay."

I got up to pee, guiltily aware that I was bringing my purse. I doubted my brother would take money from me unasked, but a small part of me never wanted to have to find out. The bathroom was in the same shape as the living room. Cigarette butts, ashtrays, empty baggies. The only thing that wasn't there was toilet paper. I used a Kleenex from my purse. Suddenly I was sobbing. Nothing gradual. Not a few tears or whimpers leading up to the main event. Just full-on choking sobs. Striking like the most explosive thundershower out of a clear sky. I got control back. Splashed tepid water on my face and went back into the living room. "Why won't you let me help you?"

He ignored my question. "You made it. Look at you. I love you. You made it."

"Why?" I asked again. Like talking on different frequencies. Yet hearing each other fine.

"You beat the odds, Nik. Neither one of us should have. But you did."

"Don't say that."

He stood. Slowly, carefully. His eyes that beautiful green. He put his arms around me. Hugged me. "You look out for me," he said. "Like you always have."

"Like I always *haven't*."

"You have. And you got through. And maybe I couldn't. But that's on me, Nik."

"I should have been there. You were there." I wasn't even pretending not to bawl. Just clutched his thin shoulders to me as tightly as I could. "I should have been there, Brandi." The name had driven him crazy when he was a kid. Brandi. A girl's name. He'd hated it. Obviously ensuring that that was the only thing I'd ever call him. "Let me help you. Please. Get you checked in somewhere. And then I'll get you a place close to me."

He hugged me back. I could feel the weakness in his thin arms. It was strange, feeling not the presence of strength but its absence. "I know you would," he said. "But that's not me. You know that. I'm on my train, you're on yours. And I'm really happy that I get to rattle along and look out the window and see you. But we're on different tracks. We can't change that."

I took a step back. Looked into his eyes. The black pupils larger now.

Wishing I could make his words somehow less true. "Is there anything you need? Anything?"

He grinned. "I could use another beer."

"My God. Anything you *actually* need?"

"Naw," he said, sitting back down on the couch. "I have everything I need right here."

"Well, I'm hungry, anyway. I'm going to order a pizza."

His voice brightened, puppyish. "Half ham and pineapple? Please?"

I shook my head. "Now he perks up."

"Whatever. I'm allowed to change my mind."

"Won't let me make you an omelet but you'll take a damn Hawaiian pizza."

His eyes danced. "Omelets are breakfast food. It's lunchtime. Get with it."

I punched his shoulder. Lightly. "Close your damn mouth and let me borrow your phone. See if we can find a place that'll deliver without freaking out when you tell them the address."

16

I left my motorcycle parked sideways between a white delivery van and a Volvo with a faded College Prep bumper sticker and headed into the bookstore, where Jess was arranging an empty circle of chairs in the back. "Shit," I said. "Book club."

"You forgot." She smiled.

"Too much going on." I thought of something. "Hey. Important. When was the last time you were on a double date?"

Jess laughed. "Umm, like last week. Why?"

"What do people do on them?" I felt something brush against my leg and looked down. Bartleby the cat looked up at me with large yellow eyes and meowed sharply. I leaned down and scratched his head. He rolled onto his back and I scratched his belly, then the soft gray fur under his chin. He purred in pleasure.

"You're hopeless. Double dates are like regular dates. Except with two extra people."

I shook my head. "I have one tonight. I'm gravely unprepared."

"Never heard you say that before."

"Excuse me, do you work here?"

I turned to see a freckled woman in a lilac blouse. She had an open, friendly face and a wide, frank mouth. "What can I help you find?"

"I'm on a mission. My daughter can't get enough of mysteries. She's a junior in high school, reads everything, wants to be a writer. I was thinking any female mystery writers would be perfect, but I don't know much more than Mary Higgins Clark or *Gone Girl*."

"Sure. Follow me. She goes to College Prep?"

The woman gave me a surprised look. "How'd you know?"

"And you drive a Volvo."

She laughed. "The bumper sticker, I see. You keep your eyes open."

In the Mysteries section I began pulling books from the shelves. "We're going for variety. Let's give her a bit of everything. *The Hours Before Dawn*, Celia Fremlin. Patricia Highsmith, *Strangers on a Train*; Joyce Maynard, *To Die For*. Margaret Millar, *Beast in View*; Ottessa Moshfegh, *Eileen*; and *Beautiful Lies* by Lisa Unger." I thought of something. "Oh—and of course something by Sara Paretsky. I think I have the first in the series . . . here we go. *Indemnity Only*." I handed her the stack. "Try these—if she likes them, send her in and I can recommend some more."

The woman looked at the titles with curiosity as I rang them up. "Thank you. These look perfect." She took the stack of books and nodded good-bye.

"Ready?" Jess asked.

"I'll be down as soon as I can. Start without me." I headed up the stairs into my office. Thinking about my client. Gregg Gunn. Trying to figure out what felt off. We had instincts for a reason. Ignoring instinct was a waste of a critical resource. Like ignoring sound just because you trusted sight. I thought about Karen Li. The fear on her face. The mysterious Oliver, trying to warn me of something. A CEO of a tech company taking secretive, unexplained trips to dangerous parts of the world. People I hadn't known even to exist, a week ago. And now I was wrapped up with them.

But wrapped up with what?

I glanced at the monitors. Downstairs the chairs Jess had arranged were filling up with women. I was going to be late. And then I had to go home, change, and race back to Oakland to meet Ethan. Instead I picked up the phone. A voice answered on the third ring. "Yeah?"

"Charles, it's Nikki. I need you to check something."

"Animal, vegetable, or mineral?" Charles Miller had a strange sense of humor.

"A man named Gregg Gunn. He runs a company called Care4 down in Sunnyvale. They make some kind of baby monitoring system. Also an employee, Karen Li, L-I."

"Okay." There was a pause. I knew he'd be writing things down. "Anything specific?"

"I just want to know a little more about them. Anything you find."

"Give me a day or two."

"You working weekends now?"

He laughed a little bitterly. "What, I'm gonna watch the kids play baseball?"

In a previous life, Charles Miller had been an investigative journalist in Houston. Then he'd written the wrong piece, targeting a notoriously press-shy billionaire who had a habit of dumping money into shady, hard-to-trace foundations. The kind of guy who had probably opened every champagne bottle in the cellar the day of the Citizens United decision. The billionaire hadn't taken kindly to being the subject of a story. Charles had been followed, his phones tapped. Undeterred, he had continued. When finally published, the article had been a success. The billionaire had filed suit that same day. Facing a nine-figure lawsuit, Charles had been fired. Hung out to dry. Because he had been named personally in the lawsuit, it didn't stop there. Without a newspaper to pay for lawyers, the outcome wasn't in doubt. After the dust settled on the bankruptcy and divorce, Charles ended up in the Bay Area. Burnt out on journalism and looking to start over. We'd done each other more than a few favors. I liked him. He was a loner. For most people, that was unnatural. In my book, it was fine.

Downstairs the small circle of chairs was full, the group in mid-conversation. There were murmurs of greeting as I sat and poured myself a cup of coffee from a pot. Besides Jess there were six other women, ranging from early twenties to late sixties. Some I knew better than others. I'd helped each of them at some point. I noticed Zoe, from the coffee shop where I had met Brenda Johnson. So she had come after all. She sat quietly in long sleeves, her chair slightly pushed back from the rest of the circle. The bruise on her face looked better.

"So does Flannery O'Connor always make her characters suffer this much?"

We were reading *The Violent Bear It Away*. The question was from Samantha. She was gorgeous, a tall black woman with an orange silk Hermès scarf wrapped high around her neck. She had a beautiful husky voice and sang jazz at the local East Bay clubs. She always wore the scarf. I was probably the only one in the room who had seen the lurid scar that the scarf concealed. Or met the person who put it there. A drunk heckler at a nightclub in Oakland. He'd gotten angry when she made some mild joke after an hour of him shouting for her to take off her top. Supposedly the heckler was a local tough guy. The house bouncer had conveniently gone deaf.

"Suffer, sure. But not only suffer," I said. O'Connor was a favorite. "Her characters struggle. With themselves, with the world, with their faith and identity. With who they are. With what they believe."

Samantha nodded. "I get the struggle part." A few of the women smiled. Knowing nods. There had been some struggle in that group. I saw Zoe smile for the first time. Her eyes were excited. I saw Jess had given her a spare copy of the book.

That night, in response to Samantha's joke, the heckler had thrown a highball glass that shattered on the brick wall behind her, spraying a burst of glass splinters. I'd held a dish towel against her neck until the ambulance arrived. The heckler had left quickly after he heard the screams. Self-preservation in the very lowest form. The security cameras had been down and Oakland kept the cops busy. Maybe they'd tried hard to track him down. Maybe they hadn't. I'd always privately felt that if there wasn't a body laid out neatly next to a smoking gun, some cops seemed to suddenly care a lot less about getting to the bottom of things. I'd seen plenty of cops seem more excited about giving a traffic ticket than solving a cold case. It didn't surprise me that eventually they had given up the search.

I hadn't.

It had taken me three weeks. Asking around up and down the city. Bars, gyms, backdoor card games, barber shops, liquor stores, the works. Finally, I got a name. With a name, everything became much easier. Pretty soon I had an address to go with the name.

Afterward I was pretty sure the heckler wouldn't throw glasses anymore. He probably wouldn't be much good at throwing anything. Maybe a few years down the line he'd be able to lob a bocce ball, although he hadn't seemed like the bocce ball type.

"Have a cookie, Nikki. Fresh-baked this morning," said Marlene, offering me a plate piled with oatmeal cookies. She was a wide-hipped, cheerful woman who was the head chef at one of Berkeley's most beloved restaurants, The Redwood Tavern, just down the block. Marlene never failed to show up to the book club meetings with something delicious.

"I can't," I said apologetically.

"Don't tell me *you're* watching your weight," she exclaimed. "Where's that leave me?"

I'd met Marlene a few years earlier. She'd been having a hard time, working at a San Francisco restaurant owned by one of the celebrity chefs, the handsome, enfant terrible type who not only got their own cookbooks but then went and posed shirtless on calendars with a cigarette and scowl. A genius in the kitchen, but not really a nice guy at all. Not to his female employees, anyway.

I'd helped her move on.

"I have a dinner right after this," I explained. "No cookies. I need my appetite."

"A *date*," clarified Jess. "A double date. And our poor Nikki is terrified." There was laughter and I theatrically threw an arm over my eyes and slid down in my chair. I liked the book club sessions. Half talking books, half just talking. I'd been in the habit of informally inviting some of the women I helped to drop by the store and stay in touch. But the actual idea, the book club idea, had been Jess's.

The door opened and a voice called out. "Anyone work here?" The speaker was a Hispanic guy of about thirty, brooding eyes and black hair frozen solid with styling gel. Stubble shadowed his face and I smelled his cologne from halfway across the store. He held a plastic-wrapped bunch of red roses in one hand.

Jess stood and hurried over. "Sorry, right here! Can I help you find a book?"

The man shot her a broad smile and gestured with the roses. "Actually, you can help me find my girlfriend."

Her tone changed. "This is a bookstore. That's what we have. Books."

Zoe was already standing. "What are you doing here, Luis?"

"Can I talk to you, baby?"

"I'm busy now, I can't talk."

His voice lowered, pleading. "I came by to say sorry, baby. That's all."

Our group had fallen quiet; one of those awkward moments when talking and trying not to listen seemed equally impossible. "Just come here for a second," he said again. "You know I love you."

Her voice was determined. "No, Luis. Leave me alone. I'm busy. I mean it."

He gestured again with the flowers. "Fine, baby. I just wanted to give these to you." His voice changed, some of the affection fading to disinterest. "I don't want to bother you. I'll get out of here."

She hesitated for a moment, her eyes showing a blatant indecision. Like a smoker, trying to quit, staring at a pack of cigarettes. As he turned away she hurried over. "Give them to me, then." She took the flowers and his hand grazed her wrist. She pulled her hand away, slowly, and his fingertips stretched to brush her skin. I watched his fingers against her hand.

"I'm sorry," he said again. "I really am. You know that, baby. You know I didn't mean it. You know how much I love you."

"I'm busy," Zoe said quietly. "Leave me alone."

"You look so damn beautiful right now, baby. Can I talk to you? Just for a minute? Then you can go back and do your thing."

She said something I didn't hear and he tugged her toward him, whispered something. She shook her head and looked down, flowers in one hand. "Come on," he said, his voice coaxing. "I made us a reservation already. You know it's your favorite place."

"I'm with people," she said softly. "My friends. You shouldn't be here."

Luis whispered something else and bent his head to kiss her. She turned her head and took the first kiss on the side of her face. The next one, following fast like a boxer's combination, caught her lips.

"Looks like Nikki's not the only one going on a date," Marlene whispered.

Zoe looked over at us. "I gotta go," she murmured. "Thanks for everything."

I didn't say anything. Just nodded good-bye. Luis shot the group of us that high-wattage smile again. It was a good smile, one that showed his white teeth and dimpled his cheeks. I would have bet that plenty of women had fallen for that smile. "Sorry, ladies, didn't mean to drag her away," he apologized, still smiling. "Guess I just can't stay away from her."

No one answered him. I watched the two of them leave, his arm around her waist. Zoe held the flowers. Luis held Zoe. Someone walking past them on the street might have thought *cute couple* and not given them a second look.

I turned back to the group. "Anyway, the title—from the biblical passage, Matthew eleven, verse twelve. 'The kingdom of Heaven suffereth violence, and the violent bear it away.' Let's talk about that. Who are the violent here? What are they trying to bear away?"

"Seems like he's bearing away that poor girl," muttered Jess.

Along with the rest of the women, I looked involuntarily toward the door. Wondering if I should have done anything more. Knowing that however much I might want to, I couldn't charge through the world trying to fix every broken thing I came across. Yet here, sitting all around me, were women who had all needed something. Different things, but the same thing. Where was the line? Broken things didn't always fix themselves.

Especially when there was someone trying hard to keep them broken.

"Nikki?"

"Sorry," I said. "Was thinking about something. One more time?" I turned my attention back to the book group, trying to focus on the discussion while in the back of my mind trying to place a foreign scent. After a moment, I realized what was distracting me.

I could still smell a trace of Luis's cologne, heavy and dangerous in the air.

17

"Sorry I'm late," I said. "Got caught in traffic."

"No trouble at all, Nikki. You missed the first round, but plenty more."

Ethan came over. He was wearing a blazer and chinos. The sleeves on the blazer spilled almost to his knuckles. He kissed me on the mouth, surprising me. To my greater surprise, I didn't mind. "Meet Lawrence and Katherine Walker," he said. "Good friends. Lawrence has taught me everything I know about tennis."

"Which isn't much, Ethan, I'm afraid. But we persevere."

Lawrence Walker was a tall, solidly built man in his late thirties, with carefully kept jet-black hair, a close-cropped beard, and wire-frame glasses that together would have left him looking perfectly at home in the October Revolution. He wore a green cashmere sweater, gray flannel pants, and brown oxfords. His accent seemed East Coast. His wife, Katherine, was a tall blonde about the same age. Maybe five years older than me. She wore a flowing tangerine skirt, with a necklace of heavy pieces of turquoise looped around her neck. Each wore a rose gold wedding ring.

I greeted them and handed Lawrence a bottle.

"A Barolo," he said, impressed. "I can see *you're* going to teach Ethan a thing or two."

"She already has," said Ethan with a smile. He was happy. Happy, and a little buzzed.

They had a spacious apartment in the trendy Lake Merritt neighborhood of Oakland. My brother's apartment was probably less than a fifteen-minute drive away, but it could have been in another world. I looked around. The place screamed intellect and whispered money. Tasteful, but able to indulge that taste, too. High oak bookcases in the living room. My eyes picked up a hodgepodge of names as I walked past—Foucault, Marcus Aurelius, Guy de Maupassant, Pushkin, Tolstoy, Jean Genet, Anthony Trollope, Harold Bloom, Thomas Mann, Goethe, of course the mandatory Sophocles and Euripides and Shakespeare and Chaucer and Joyce. They had everything covered. Literature, history, drama, philosophy, cultural studies.

One of the reasons I hated e-readers was because bookshelves showed so much about the people who owned them. Here, clearly, was an academic couple, probably able to discuss Greek tragedy, Russian literature, and French political science with equal fluency. Also, here was an apartment whose occupants were broadcasting a message a mile high: they wanted anyone who knew anything about books to know that they did, as well. I took another look at the titles. The proportions were too perfect. A little of everything, not too much of any one thing. A careful display. In the living room was a sculpture, a crouched warrior with spear raised in one hand. Paintings, a series of nude prints, Saville, a Tracey Emin, a Modigliani. The living room was comfortably appointed, a heather-gray upholstered couch, deep armchairs, a striking dining table legged with marble pillars.

"What can I offer you to drink, Nikki?" Lawrence asked. "We'll have a few cocktails here and then we can drive over to the Fox Theater."

I sat. Conscious of my motorcycle boots on the hardwood floor. I hadn't known what to wear and had settled on jeans and a conservative turtleneck sweater for the chilly October evening. I ran a hand through my hair, hoping the helmet hadn't mussed it too badly. "As long as it doesn't come out of a blender, I'm hard to disappoint."

"No blenders allowed in this house, I assure you," said Lawrence. "We've had a round of Negronis to start and were debating the prospect of a second."

"A Negroni works fine, thank you."

"Excellent. And please, help yourself." There was a large wooden board covered with cheeses and meats and expensive-looking crackers. Even a small silver bowl of black caviar with a small porcelain spoon. The Walkers knew how to entertain, and they had the means to do so. Lawrence moved off to a wet bar in the corner of the living room. He poured Campari, gin, and sweet vermouth into a glass beaker and stirred vigorously with a long bartender's spoon. A picture on the opposite wall caught my eye. Lawrence, wearing blue headgear and a pair of blue boxing gloves that looked about sixteen or eighteen ounces. Too large a size for him to have been pro, at least based on that photograph. "Where did you box?" I asked.

"You *are* observant. Just some amateur stuff back East. When I was too young to know any better."

"Lawrence is being modest," Katherine said. "At Princeton he was in the New Jersey Golden Gloves three years running."

"You must take me for a terrible barbarian, Nikki. We didn't use cestuses, I assure you."

"Cestuses?" Ethan asked. He sat next to me. Close, his leg touching mine.

"Spiked leather straps," I explained. "The Greeks and Romans wrapped them around their hands. Turned what passed for boxing back then into blood sport."

"How do you know all that?" Ethan wanted to know. "At first I thought Golden Gloves was an a cappella group."

"Someone taught me how to box. Ages ago. I guess a little stuck."

"He had something against soccer?" Ethan teased.

I smiled back. "He just didn't want me beating up the boys anymore."

Lawrence came over with two Negronis, on the rocks, the color of the drinks a deep ruby. He handed a glass to me, a twist of orange bent carefully around the rim. He gave the second drink absently to Ethan, eyes still on me. "Boxing *and* bookstores? Nikki, you continue to impress."

"I think I lucked out," Ethan agreed.

I squeezed his knee affectionately but didn't answer. I couldn't remember the last time I'd done something like that. Like squeezing someone's knee. Some casual affectionate touch. It felt good. Natural. "What do you both do?" I asked.

"I teach in the Cal history department. Katherine is in French. Still scratching our heads wondering how we ended up three thousand miles west of where we began."

"I blame the Cambridge winters," Katherine said.

Lawrence smiled. "Indeed. The chill winds of New England practically sailed us across the country."

"Harvard? Grad school? You met there?" They had just told me that, loud and clear. Humanities plus Cambridge equaled Harvard. They just hadn't *told* me. An East Coast tendency, I'd noticed.

They exchanged a glance. Nodded. "Exactly. And how about you, Nikki?"

"Nikki runs a bookstore," Ethan said proudly. "*Owns* a bookstore. The Brimstone Magpie, over on Telegraph."

"Did you ever consider the academic life?" Katherine wanted to know.

I finished my Negroni. "I think at some point I've considered everything."

"Is your family from California originally?"

I shook the ice around in my glass and nodded vaguely, wondering how to change the subject. Lawrence saw my empty glass. "Another one, coming up."

I nodded in relief. As if sensing my reluctance, Katherine sipped her drink and shifted the conversation. "So where *did* you two meet, anyway?"

"Over breakfast," I answered.

"How charming! Such a pleasure to hear a story other than 'online.' Lawrence and I were together before the whole eHarmony craze, or whatever those things are called. Thank goodness. The thought of swiping frantically through all those random faces strikes me as such a dismal way to spend one's time."

One of them had to come from money, I was thinking. Maybe both. The apartment was too expensively furnished. And they were too young to be tenured. I wondered if they owned the apartment or rented. I would have bet owned. Lawrence was speaking. "We've been trying our best to civilize Ethan here from the wilds of Montana."

"Hence the tennis," I said.

I didn't love the comment. A little patronizing. I glanced at Ethan. He seemed fine with it. Maybe—I had to smile at the thought—I was feeling protective.

"Indeed," Lawrence agreed. "Hence the tennis."

There was another round of drinks. A bottle of wine was opened, then another. At some point Lawrence, with a mischievous grin, opened a carved wooden box and took out a small joint. "Does anyone indulge? After all, it's in the spirit of musical appreciation."

A slightly blurry hour later Lawrence started herding us to the door for the concert. "We'll get a cab. We're going to miss the opening act as it is," he said. "But I'm afraid," he added, "that driving would be less than responsible."

"Let's walk, honey," Katherine said, tugging his arm. "It's barely two miles and it's nice out. I could use the fresh air."

They looked back at us. I shrugged. "Fine by me."

We made our way along the curve of Lake Merritt, heading toward downtown Oakland. The night air was cool and the street quiet. Only the occasional car. A sliver of moon. Ethan and Lawrence walked ahead, talking excitedly about the upcoming Cal-Cardinal game. As we left their neighborhood, the streets became grittier, the streetlights scarcer. Katherine was talking. "Lawrence and I think it's wonderful that Ethan met you. We really do."

"Thanks," I said. This was the heart-to-heart part of the double date, I supposed. Girl talk. The part where the two men chatted sports and the two women confided over whatever. But I was in a good mood. The drinks and pot buzzing in my head.

"We can see that you have a sense of culture. It's so good for him. We've been doing our best to move him along in that respect. To build things up."

I gave her a look. "He's not a Habitat for Humanity project."

She took my arm, squeezed it affectionately. "No, no. Of course not." Her voice lowered confidentially. "I just mean—I'm not sure if you know, but Ethan doesn't come from a background that provided him with a lot, in that respect. He's been having to learn all on his own. He's come a long way. I like to think we've helped. I mean that as a true friend of his. You understand, Nikki."

I did understand. Loud and clear. "Sure. A modern-day *Jude the Obscure*, stonemason to scholar." There were a few other things I wanted to say. But I didn't. I'd learned that usually it was talk that landed people in trouble.

A defensive look crossed Katherine's face as she started to reply, but she tripped on something, a pothole or gap in the paving. I caught her arm and steadied her. "They need to fix these streetlamps," she said, our exchange forgotten. "Someone will break their neck out here. This city is getting better, but still."

I could see the lights and buildings of downtown Oakland in the distance. Probably less than a mile away. I heard Lawrence's raised voice from up ahead. "What the hell is this?" His voice was no longer jocular. Katherine caught the change in his tone, too. "What's going on, honey?" she called, concern in her voice. Up ahead Lawrence and Ethan had stopped. I could see their still shapes. Katherine quickened her pace into an anxious half-jog. "Is everything okay, honey?" she asked again, her voice louder.

I kept pace with her. But cautiously. I'd gotten close enough to see the shapes of other people. In front of us. Blocking the way.

"What's happening?" Katherine said. "Is everything okay?"

I heard Lawrence's voice. Thin and frightened. All the confidence stripped away like bark off a tree. "We're being robbed."

We reached Ethan and Lawrence and I took another look. There were three of them, big guys. The city had gotten a lot safer since the '60s and '70s. Tech money and gentrification paid for a lot of extra law enforcement. The homicide rate had plummeted. But still far from perfect. Over three thousand robberies a year in a city of less than half a million. Almost ten a day, one every other hour. Like clockwork. Maybe we happened to be the first people these three had ever tried to rob. Maybe they were doing it on a drunken dare, some spontaneous decision. Or, maybe, they'd done a hundred of these, and people like our little group were their bread and butter.

I stood next to Ethan, watching the three men and wishing I hadn't touched the pot or the last bottle of wine. Two immediate questions. How many? And what weapons? I had my first answer. Three of them. No one hiding off to the sides. The lead guy was almost as tall as Lawrence, and heavier. He wore an Oakland A's baseball hat and work boots and held something in his hand.

A knife.

It was a hunting knife. The lower half of the blade serrated. The point wickedly sharp. A six-inch blade gleaming coldly. The kind of knife someone would use to gut and skin a deer. The kind of knife that could do all kinds of awful and permanent things to a human body in less time than it would take to lace up a pair of shoes.

When it came to violent crime, the longer it went on the likelier that something would go wrong. Robbers tended to show whatever weapons they had in the interests of immediate intimidation. The whole shock-and-awe thing. A guy with a bat would wave it. A guy with a knife would brandish it. A guy with a gun would pull it. There were plenty of normal, regular people who might fight back against an unarmed robber. Especially on a weekend night, when they'd been drinking themselves into false confidence. No one wanted to give up their possessions. But the number of people who would risk fighting back against an armed assailant, risk being stabbed or shot for a few bucks—that was a much smaller number.

So maybe no guns. Probably no guns. But no way to tell for sure. Not yet.

Ethan held my hand. He was shaking. I could feel it. "Don't worry," he whispered. "They won't hurt you, Nikki. We're going to be okay."

The guy with the knife stuck it toward Lawrence. "Your wallet and your watch. Hurry."

I watched closely, wondering what the big ex-boxer would do.

Lawrence licked his lips. "Please," he said. "Take the money and don't hurt us." His big hands fumbled in his back pocket.

Katherine was handing over her purse. She took off her necklace and wedding ring unprompted. Extended her hand out, palm up. Like a child feeding a horse an apple. "Please," she said. "Please."

"Shut up, bitch. Shut your damn mouth."

Ethan was next. He held out his wallet. Obedient as always. "Here, take it."

"Hurry up." The A's guy shoved Ethan backwards, hard.

I took in a breath. Blew it out. There hadn't been a need for that.

He turned to me. Working fast. Not wanting to be out here all night. "Purse, bitch."

I met his eyes. Breathing evenly. Deep inhales, deep exhales. My purse still slung over my shoulder. Feeling familiar adrenaline fill me. Breathing. Controlling it. Feeling my senses sharpen. "You should know something important," I told him quietly. "I don't like knives."

He stared at me. "Well, this one's about two inches from your damn face. So give me the damn purse."

I felt Ethan's whisper close to my ear. "It's going to be okay, Nikki, just do what he says. I know you're scared."

"Put the knife away," I said. "Please. And then we can work to resolve this."

I heard Lawrence's voice explode, angry, edged with panic. "Are you nuts, woman? Shut up and give him your purse! Are you trying to get us killed?"

The knife blade was in front of my face. Close enough that I saw the blade crosswise between my eyes. Blurred by proximity. Like trying to look at the tip of your nose.

"Last chance, bitch. You don't give me that purse, I'm gonna cut pieces off you."

I shrugged.

"Okay. Have it your way." I held up my purse. "I guess you'll be happy, then. I have cash. A lot." I reached inside. "Here. Let me give it to you."

I took a wad of bills. I knew they were hundreds.

Slowly removed my hand. Letting him see.

"Shit," he said. "That's what I mean. That's right. Gimme all that."

I extended my hand. Let him start to reach for the money.

He reached.

Opened my fingers.

The bills fell gently to the ground like dry fall leaves.

"Whoops."

He cursed. Kneeled, started picking money off the ground with one hand. The other hand still holding the knife. The gleaming tip still pointed up at me.

I took a look around. Everyone's eyes on the money. Hundred-dollar bills did that to people. You could have ten million bucks in your bank account and your eyes would still be riveted by a hundred-dollar bill falling to the ground.

I took a single step back. My hand back in my purse. Finding what I wanted.

When my hand emerged the second time I gripped a rubberized handle.

This particular object was illegal in multiple states. California included. It was also useful as hell in situations like these. I pressed the latch button and a powerful thirty-pound spring mechanism caused a twenty-inch black steel rod to materialize out of the handle. Like a switchblade action. Telescoping out faster than the eye could follow.

The metal tip was weighted. I was effectively holding a steel baseball bat.

He was still on the ground, still picking up the last few bills. Starting to look up toward the unfamiliar sound. Instinctual.

Not fast enough.

I took a breath in.

Blew it out.

Swung the baton in a downward arc as hard as I could. A careful, controlled motion.

The baton struck his forearm above the wrist. About where the carpus joined to the radius in a mass of small, delicate bones and nerves and tendons.

I was conscious of a few different sounds coming in quick succession.

The sound of bone shattering with an audible crack.

The metallic noise of the knife clattering to the pavement. Steel scraping tar.

The instantaneous, childlike howl of agony.

And then the shocked noises from everyone around us.

I looked down. The man was rolled into a ball. His hat had fallen off and he clutched his arm. I could see why the batons were illegal, more or less. They tended to have a nasty effect on whatever part of the body they encountered. The hand hung limp, bleeding, useless. It would be a long time before anyone got his autograph.

There was general confusion for the next second or so. Things could go many different ways. It was important to assert control.

I took a deep breath in. Blew it out.

Extended the baton outward. Pointing toward the other two men.

They watched me. Frightened, unsure. Not fully comprehending what had happened. But starting to. Starting to process why their friend was now curled up on the ground.

I saw a hand creeping toward a pocket. "Choices," I said. "We all get to make them. He did. Now it's your turn." I hovered the baton roughly between them. Arm's length away so they couldn't grab it. Daring one of them to try to pull something. I was pretty sure I could crack a head faster than they could raise an arm. Or two heads, if need be. I was willing to bet on it. Maybe we'd find out. Maybe not.

Choices. We all had them.

They exchanged a look. Glanced down at their friend. Still on the ground, bills scattered around him. Still clutching his arm. Groaning and cursing as the initial shock wore off and the full magnitude of the pain set in.

They turned on their heels and ran.

I looked down again. He was no longer a threat. Not even close. I saw the knife, gleaming against asphalt. The needle point. The razor edge. Serrations for sawing through flesh or bone. I watched the knife. But I was seeing something else.

She takes a step into the room. Seeing the dark stain, larger, now. Sticky-looking. Bright afternoon sunshine streaming through the window. A pot bubbling on the stove. A strange smell. She's never smelled this smell before. Not a pleasant smell. A sour, iron smell. Not a kitchen smell. The stain spreading outward. She squints in the sunlight. Looking at the floor.

I took a breath. Looking down at the knife. Thinking of Ethan being pushed backward. Thinking of Luis, that afternoon. Remembering all kinds of things. Seeing the knife.

The knife.

The knife.

"I *told* you I didn't like knives," I exclaimed. And swung the baton a second time.

A hard, backhanded arc directly into the man's upper lip.

There was a crunching sound and suddenly half his front teeth appeared all over his sweatshirt. I assumed the other half had gone down his throat.

He put his hands over his face and started moaning softly. Blood dripped through his hands. He lay there, making that moaning sound. The blow had knocked his hat off. The white A still visible above the brim. I was conscious of Ethan grabbing me. "Nikki, no more. Enough."

Lawrence was holding Katherine. The two of them staring at me. A strange look. The same look from both of them.

Like I was an animal.

I retracted the baton. Pulled a Clorox wipe from a travel packet in my purse and wiped blood off the tip. Knelt down and took back everything that had been taken from us, ignoring the guy on the ground. He had rolled to a seated position and leaned against a fire hydrant, holding his good hand against his head and mumbling small noises.

I handed Katherine her purse. She accepted it without a word.

Maybe two minutes had gone by. The same amount of time it took to brush one's teeth or soft-boil an egg. I looked at the three of them. "We can probably still make the show."

Lawrence had his arm around Katherine. Breathing hard. Watching me. "Are you insane? You could have killed him."

"Or he could have killed you," I said. "Or your wife."

"He only wanted money! He wasn't going to hurt us."

"It wasn't his money. And you don't know what he would have done."

"You could be going to jail for manslaughter," Lawrence said. "Why did you hit him a second time? Are you some kind of sociopath? Are you sick?"

Ethan stepped forward. "Leave her alone, Lawrence. She saved us."

Lawrence glared at him and whispered something to his wife. They turned and started walking away from us. Fast, without a backward look.

"We should go," I suggested.

Ethan nodded at the figure on the ground. "Are you going to leave him?"

"Why not," I said sullenly. "He can walk. His legs are fine."

"I'd feel better if I called nine-one-one."

I shrugged. "Suit yourself."

Ethan took out his phone and dialed. "I'd like to report an injury," he said. He gave the cross street and then said, "No, thank you!" and hung up hurriedly. "They asked for my name. Will I get in trouble if they trace it?"

"It doesn't matter. He won't say anything."

"How do you know?"

I looked at Ethan patiently. "Because he was *robbing* us."

"Oh."

We soon reached downtown. A regular Friday night. Neon, people, cars, shouting, laughter. Normal. Ethan was shaking a little. Shock.

I put my hand in his. "We should talk."

18

We sat in a little all-night donut shop. The smell of pastry was sweet and aromatic. I got us coffee and a few donuts and we sat across from each other in a bright red booth. I didn't like the fluorescent lights. I would have been happier in a dim, comfortable bar. But something was telling me that coffee was the way to go. "Take one," I said, pushing the donuts to him.

He sipped his coffee, wincing at the hot liquid. "I don't think I'm hungry, to be honest."

"Eat one if you can. The sugar will help."

He took a piece of a maple glazed donut. Took a bite. "I'm sorry," he said. "I—I've never been mugged before. I think the last time I saw someone throw a punch was in high school."

"And it bothers you? What happened?"

"It was scary."

"Sure."

He was watching me. "You run a bookstore."

"Yes."

"But—but you did that."

"Yes."

"Were you lying? About the bookstore?"

"Ethan. Let me tell you three things about myself. And then you can ask questions. Is that okay?"

He nodded.

"First of all. I don't lie. Ever. Not to you. Not to anyone. It's just a thing."

"Okay."

I wasn't done. "But I sometimes choose not to reveal the whole truth. I'll never lie to you. But I might not always tell you everything, either."

He took another nibble of donut. "That seems like a sort of imperfect arrangement."

"Let me finish. Second. There are pieces of me that I don't talk about. Not to anyone."

"You're really selling yourself."

"Ethan?"

"Yes?"

"Shut up. Please. Okay? Just listen. For a minute."

"Sorry."

"And third. I sometimes struggle."

"Struggle?"

"With certain impulses."

"Impulses? What do you mean, impulses?"

"Look. As an example. My last boyfriend."

He groaned. "Please don't tell me you're sleeping with an ex. That's happened, like, at least three times to me. And it really sucks. You'd think it gets easier with practice, but turns out it doesn't. Just continues to basically all-out suck."

"No," I said. "There's no one else. Definitely no one else."

He was watching me closely. "So what do you mean, with your ex?"

"I guess it ended with him because of how I act. Sometimes. In certain situations."

"Like tonight?"

"Yeah. Like tonight."

"So you mean . . . violently?" He thought this over. "What happened last time?"

"We were at a bar. Some dive. Having a drink, minding our own business. There were a couple of assholes who came in looking for trouble."

"What happened?"

I drank some coffee and shifted my weight. "They hassled a couple of other people, then started trying to pick a fight with Bryan, my ex. Stupid stuff. Dumped a drink on him. Said suggestive things about me. The bartender knew them. Didn't want to get in the middle of it. They wouldn't leave us alone. Kept trying to get a rise out of him."

"And?"

"Eventually they did. Only they didn't get a rise out of *him*."

"They got a rise out of you," Ethan finished.

I nodded. "Yeah."

"What'd you do to them?"

I looked down at the yellow linoleum table, seeing directly under me the white-rimmed black circle of my coffee and next to it the dark circle of my uneaten chocolate donut. "I overreacted. In hindsight."

"Overreacted?"

"Two of them had to be hospitalized. Not for anything major. But still."

"Hospitalized? You used that thing? That stick?"

I shook my head emphatically. "No. I wouldn't use a weapon unless someone threatened or attacked me with one. I believe in proportional response."

"So how did you handle them?"

I looked at my two hands. Somehow I'd chipped the maroon polish on my left thumbnail. I'd have to repaint it. "A couple of drunk assholes. I didn't need much."

"So what happened?"

"I was arrested."

"Arrested?"

"First time in my life. They plea-bargained the charges to a misdemeanor after they saw the security tapes. But I had to attend court-ordered therapy sessions. For my . . . issues."

"The violence."

"It's not that I'm some raging psycho, Ethan. I'm not running around bashing heads or out of control. And I've never picked a fight in my life. But I tend to be . . . overprotective. Of people I care about. And certain situations end up setting something off."

"Like tonight?"

"Like tonight."

"Why?"

"Ask me a different one."

"Okay. Anything else to confess?"

I had to laugh. "I think that's enough for one night."

"So you're working on your . . . issues. In therapy."

"I guess. When you put it that way."

He sipped his coffee. "What kind of person carries that—that weapon around with them? That stick you pulled."

I sighed. This was where questions led. "My job."

"I thought you owned a bookstore."

"I do. But I do some other work, too. On the side. Kind of after hours."

He laughed uncomfortably. "I'm starting to see what you mean about the not-telling-me-everything-at-once thing. What do you do?"

"Sometimes I help people find things they're looking for. Or learn things they're trying to figure out. And sometimes . . . I help women. Women who need my help."

"Help them how?"

"I help them get out of situations that aren't good for them. I help them get away from people who are bad for them."

"How do you do that?"

"I talk to those people in a language they understand."

He took this in. "Do you carry a gun?"

"Ethan," I said. "All in due time. But now I have a question for you."

"Okay."

"Can you handle it?"

"Handle it?"

"Me. If you can't, I understand. Bryan—my ex—he couldn't. But I want to know. Because if you can't, then there's no point in talking any more about it."

He toyed with donut crumbs, pushing them around the table. "Honestly, Nikki, I'm a little freaked out. An hour ago we were on a double date to a jazz concert. Now I'm sitting with a girl who I just watched take out three guys with knives. And I kind of feel like I'm dating Dirty Harry. So can I think about all of this for a bit?"

"Of course you can. And for the record, it was *one* guy with one knife. And my legs are way nicer than Dirty Harry's. If you don't agree with that, we have bigger problems."

He smiled for the first time since we had sat down. "I'll give you that."

There didn't seem to be much else to talk about. I got up. "I guess I'll go. Get in touch if you want."

I walked out of the shop. Feeling lousy. Thinking again of celibacy. Solitude. This time for real. This time for good. Maybe I wasn't cut out to be the relationship type no matter what I wanted. Maybe it would never work with anyone normal. Someone like Ethan.

Choices. Maybe we couldn't choose everything. No matter what we wanted.

I felt my mood overtaking me. I knew that after I walked back to Lake Merritt for my motorcycle I wouldn't go home. Didn't matter how late it was. Knew I'd head north, toward the ocean. To the little blue house above the beach.

WEEK THREE

19

"How have you been, Nikki?"

"This guy I met. Ethan. I think I blew it."

"What do you mean, blew it?"

"I showed him too much of myself."

"Was someone hurt? What happened?"

"We were on a double date. Some guys tried to mug us. So much for my suburban Scrabble fantasies."

"You're all okay?"

"One of them got hurt a little. But that's what he gets."

"You did something to him?"

"Look. I've lost plenty of sleep over plenty of things. But this guy? Nope. He pulled a knife. I told him I didn't like knives. What does he do? He goes and waves it in my face. That was deeply irresponsible. That's on him."

"And Ethan—it upset him when that happened?"

"Yeah. His friends, too. Actually, everyone seemed upset. Except me. But what was I supposed to do? Let him rob us? Be a normal girl and cry for two hours afterwards while her boyfriend strokes her hair and calms her down? Is that more honest?"

"Do you consider yourself self-destructive, Nikki?"

"Of course not."

"But you find yourself in these situations where you seem to . . . raise the stakes."

"I don't. That's the thing. Why does no one understand that? I *match* the stakes. That's what I've always believed in."

"Harassed by a group of men, you refuse to walk away, respond with violence. Held up by muggers, you refuse to hand over your possessions, respond with violence."

"I'm not self-destructive. I like life. I've worked hard for what I have."

"But your responses. That bar fight, costing you a relationship, legal fees, time. This mugging, perhaps costing you another relationship. Are those positive outcomes?"

"I was *protecting* them."

"This notion of protecting people. Your previous boyfriend, now Ethan— did they want the kind of protection you offer?"

"There's not really time to have them fill out a questionnaire."

"Why are you so swift to act violently to protect these people?"

"Because I *care* about them."

"Was someone's life in danger?"

"*Bad things happen in this world. They needed me.*"

"*Who needed you.*"

"Never mind."

"Tell me more about your family. Why are you holding back?"

"Because I don't talk about them."

"Why won't you let me see these parts of your life? You have a brother. During our first meeting you said you take care of him. Do you protect your brother?"

"*I told you I don't want to talk about him.*"

"This urge to protect. Where did it start?"

"Don't ask me that."

"I'm worried about you, Nikki. Your refusal to face your past—whatever's there."

"I face it every day. You have no idea."

"I've studied many types of impulsive behavior. Over time, it tends to worsen. Alcoholics drink more, addicts use more. People who engage in risky behavior don't fix themselves. And I'm worried, Nikki, that at some point you'll react to a situation in a way that has permanent consequences. That you'll do something you can't take back."

"Maybe sometimes there *should* be permanent consequences."

"Even if they destroy your life?"

"I'm not self-destructive. I'm not some psycho. There are people in this world who need help."

"And you think you need to help them."

"I think somebody does."

"We're out of time. I'll see you next week, okay?"

"Like I have a choice."

20

I met Charles Miller on the fishing pier in the Berkeley Marina. It was windy and the water of the Bay was choppy. The long pier extended toward San Francisco like an outstretched arm. He was standing near a bench watching a woman tossing handfuls of corn kernels to a group of pigeons and gulls. Smaller brown sparrows hopped efficiently between the larger birds. Charles was an unusually short man, maybe five foot two or three, in his late fifties. Clean-shaven, with sparse hair and wire glasses. He wore blue jeans and a plain white athletic sweatshirt.

"Morning, Charles."

"Morning, Nikki."

We walked out onto the pier. Men fished. Some alone, some in clusters of twos and threes, coolers on the ground to hold the catch. I wondered what they caught. What was out there in the cold water. Across the Bay I could see the San Francisco skyline. A vast bank of fog loomed over pale buildings. I could barely make out the Golden Gate Bridge, shrouded by mist. A sailboat cut through the water, leaning steeply to one side as it tacked. I nodded at it. "What happens if they tip?"

He followed my gaze. "Then they're in the water."

He lit a brown, foul-smelling cigarillo. Charles loved the things. He puffed and the end glowed to life. Gray smoke trickled away. "Everything he told you checks out. Gunn is classic Valley. Dropped out of Stanford—technically got kicked out for bad grades, but who's counting—did a hitch in finance in New York, came back to California, founded three start-ups that all went bust. Still managed to raise enough to start Care4. Just one funny thing. They're not waiting on any investments. All of that went through years ago."

"Maybe I misunderstood."

"Guess so. Here, I even got this." With evident pride, he handed me two photocopied sheets of paper bearing the distinctive tree seal of Stanford. In the upper corner of the top page was a blurry black-and-white photo of a much younger Gunn, a confident grin spread across his face. Next to the photograph was housing information: a dorm (Wilbur Hall), a room number, and two other names who must have been roommates, Martin Gilman and George Levinson. The second paper was a transcript. Bs and Cs first semester became Cs and two Fs second semester. Gunn had evidently not been the studious type by the time he reached college. Seeing the unimpressive transcript, I wondered how he had even gotten in.

My face must have showed my thoughts. "A tennis recruit," Charles added pointedly.

I folded the paper into a pocket as we walked on. "How about Karen Li?"

"I couldn't find much beyond the basics. Born in Beijing but came over to the States in 1990, when she was ten, to live with relatives. Standard B.S. in computer science, standard LinkedIn profile, nothing unusual. I got in touch with a former boss who said she was a great employee, easy to work with, friendly, and a brilliant programmer. Certainly doesn't seem the type to make waves. She's been at Care4 for about five years. That's about it."

We'd reached the end of the pier. There was a gap of water, and then maybe twenty yards out was a chunk of a different pier that I'd never figured out. An island. No one would ever walk on it. It led nowhere and nothing led to it. It was just there. San Francisco didn't seem any closer, but looking back I could see how far we were from shore. The sailboat was gone. Nearby, a man reeled in something small and wriggling.

"Thanks, Charles," I said. "I appreciate it."

He gave me a look. "I can't help wondering what they need you for."

After leaving the Berkeley Marina I headed straight to the bookstore. The first thing I did was to call Ethan. Not knowing if the urge was right or completely wrong. He didn't pick up. Half-relieved, I left a message. "Hey, it's Nikki. I just wanted to say—" I stopped, phone pressed against my cheek. There was a lot I wanted to say. "I hope you're having a good day." I hung up. Feeling the familiar empty feeling curling around me, a voice assuring a lifetime of solitude. A feeling that whispered to me I had ruined whatever good thing I'd had. Just like I always had, and always would.

A woman in her mid-forties was browsing the Staff Picks table that we had set up at the front. She had a solitary air that connected to my own mood. She didn't seem to be looking for assistance but I went over anyway. "Can I help you find something?"

She looked up, surprised. "I'm not sure." She was dressed formally for Berkeley, a slate-colored dress with a high neckline, face carefully made-up. Her hair had been done recently and pearl earrings were fastened in her ears.

"What kind of books do you like?"

"I haven't read much lately," she admitted. "Blink and a decade or two goes by, and all I have to show for it are a handful of summer beach reads." She didn't smile when she talked but her manner was not unfriendly.

"I'm sure you have a lot more to show than that."

"Would you like a glass of wine?" she asked abruptly. "I have some with me."

"It's eleven A.M.," I pointed out. I regretted the words as soon as I spoke them. I lived a life of odder hours and fewer rules than most. It wasn't my place to question when this woman wanted a drink.

She was unfazed by the question anyway. "Then I'm just in time for lunch." She drew a bottle from her handbag. The label said SAINTSBURY. I searched my mind, wondering why it was familiar. "Any relation to George Saintsbury, the writer?"

She shrugged. "I have no idea. A wine shop down the street recommended it."

"*Notes on a Cellar-Book*—it must be the same person." I looked at the bottle curiously. A Napa pinot noir. I'd have to make my way over sometime. I felt a strong alliance to businesses referencing nineteenth-century English writers. After all, I had my Brimstone Magpie. "Have a seat, why don't you?" I gestured to an armchair and found a couple of clean coffee cups and a bottle opener. I twisted the cork off and poured. "Cheers," I said. "To something or other."

"To something or other," she agreed. We drank. She put her mug down and tugged at one of the jeweled rings she wore where a wedding band would normally go.

"What brings you into the neighborhood?"

She looked at her wine in the mug and then up, showing sad, intelligent brown eyes. She spoke in measured, thoughtful sentences, and as she spoke her gaze roved around the store. "Two weeks ago my husband told me he was leaving. I thought he meant for work. He meant for another woman. Arguments, couples therapy . . . he skipped all of the local stops, you might say. He was on the express train. Stop one, a happy marriage, stop two, no marriage at all. He's a professor of mathematics and I woke up today to a house precisely fifty percent empty. One of our two dogs, gone; one of our two cars, gone; even half the bath towels. I'm surprised the mattress wasn't chopped in half. Formulaic. One marriage, divided by two, equals divorce." She interlaced the fingers of her hands, pulled them apart.

"I'm sorry to hear that."

"Everyone says you shouldn't let those things derail your life, even though by definition that's exactly what they do. So I decided to put on nice clothes, buy a good bottle of wine, take myself out to a nice restaurant for lunch. Only I forgot to make a reservation, and so now I'm on some waitlist, waiting, which is kind of how I feel the rest of my life will be. Waiting to be seated, waiting for something good. When really all you get is a very young, very beautiful hostess telling you with dreadful politeness that you can't come in."

She poured more wine for both of us.

"Which restaurant?"

"The Redwood Tavern. Right down the block."

I got up. "Be right back." At the counter, I called The Redwood Tavern and asked for Marlene, giving my name. I knew she'd be in. She wasn't one of those chefs who opened a restaurant and then made themselves as scarce as possible the moment it became popular. After a minute's hold she picked up. "Nikki?"

"Can I get a friend off the waitlist? She's had a hard day."

The answer was immediate. "Send her in. We'll have a table ready by the time she's here."

I paused by a shelf on my way back to the woman, who sat there quietly with her wine. "Go get lunch. Tell them you were over here."

She was perplexed. "Will that matter?"

"Give it a shot." I handed the woman a paperback. "Take this, too. I've always felt that you're not dining alone if you have a good book. *The Days of Abandonment*—you know it?"

She took the book curiously. "No, I'm afraid not."

"Sort of a sad book, but a good one. You might like the ending especially."

The phone was ringing again. I excused myself and picked up, thinking Marlene had forgotten to tell me something and was calling back. "Brimstone Magpie."

"Nikki? Is that you?" It was Gunn, his voice raw with tension. "Karen Li. She disappeared and we have no idea where she is." His words came hurriedly. "You have to find her, Nikki. This time she's gone too far. We think she's stolen something crucial, and we need to find out for sure." He fell silent, as though trying to organize and control his words. "You need to find her and stop her. Before it's too late."

21

Buster's World Class Bike Smog & Auto Repair was in Vallejo, over the Carquinez Bridge. Even in the Bay Area, Vallejo was just far enough and plenty ugly enough that no one was jumping to buy homes there. The kind of city that most people would only drive through on their way to somewhere else. Buster's World Class was buried between a Jack in the Box burger place and a payday lender. I'd never been to either and never planned to. But I went to Buster's from time to time. I ignored the small parking lot out front and instead rode around to the back, straight into an open garage bay. Roughly half the garage was devoted to cars, the other half motorcycles. Two cars were up on lifts, a few more on the ground. None of them looked anything close to under warranty. The motorcycles were newer. I saw a Ninja and a Ducati, a few Harleys, a massive Honda Gold Wing.

I got off the Aprilia and one of the mechanics came over. He was a skinny teenager with a bad complexion and a buzz cut. "If you're looking for the waiting area it's down that way." His eyes wandered openly around my body before settling on the area of my chest. I didn't know why. My zipped-up leather jacket wasn't exactly showing a lot of skin.

"I'm not looking for the waiting area," I told him. "I'm looking for Buster."

He stopped looking me over quite so obviously and nodded across the garage. "He's working. Might not want to bother him. Some friendly advice."

I found Buster halfway under a blue Acura coupe. He was horizontal on a wheeled creeper seat. Only his legs stuck out. I could tell it was him because he always wore the same beige Timberland work boots with a scuff in the left toe. I kicked his boot without bothering to be gentle. Buster wasn't a gentle guy and he didn't demand that quality in others.

A deep voice growled out from somewhere under the car. "Whoever did that better be here to tell me I won the fucking Powerball."

"You won the fucking Powerball, Buster."

"I know that voice. It haunts my dreams." He rolled out from under the chassis and squinted up at me, a lit Camel cigarette stuck in the corner of his mouth. "Nikki Griffin, in the flesh? What brings you into the fancy part of town? Get lost coming off the freeway?"

"Tea at the Ritz," I said. "Forgot the biscuits. Hoping you had a few to spare."

He grinned, getting to his feet. It was a process. Buster was big. A year or two north of forty, he wore his hair in a black ponytail that matched up with a long black goatee. Tattoos all over his bare forearms and probably plenty more elsewhere. He must have been six foot five, over 250. The kind of guy that would make some people cross the street at night. "What do you want?" he asked. "Need your carbs cleaned? New spark plugs?"

"Was hoping for coffee."

"Coffee we can do."

Cigarette still in his mouth, he started toward the front of the shop, moving with a slight limp. "Jimmy!" he shouted. "Goin' on break. Anyone who needs me, tell 'em to hold their breath and count to a billion backwards."

The skinny mechanic who had pointed me over nodded. "Sure, Buster."

"Oh, and Jimmy?"

"Yeah?"

"You keep checking out this girl's ass, and she'll kick your skinny worthless tail a hell of a lot worse than I will, and twice as fast."

Buster's office was a tiny, claustrophobic space off the garage. Maybe eight feet by eight feet. It was one of the messiest rooms I'd ever been in. Almost literally not a square inch of flat space. He didn't seem to believe in file cabinets, so there were stacks of papers almost to the ceiling. Fluorescent lighting, a dirty linoleum floor. A metal desk took up a chunk of the small space, a big executive-style leather chair on the far side, a metal folding chair on the other. A Mr. Coffee machine perched precariously on a slanted stack of coffee-stained papers. Cigarette butts and ash everywhere. I had to smile. The fact that the place hadn't burned down yet was astounding.

"Buster," I said. "You should fire the maid. She's slacking off."

He laughed. A big, booming laugh that filled the office even more than the papers. "Somehow I don't see a maid working out here." He went over to the coffee machine and dumped in ground coffee from a giant red forty-eight-ounce container and flicked the button. An orange light came on and, a second later, unhealthy hissing and sputtering noises issued from the machine. "See, Nikki? Only the red-carpet treatment for you." He smirked crookedly my way. "A fresh pot for a fresh gal."

I had to laugh. "Jesus, I thought people stopped buying Folgers in 1950-something."

Buster sat back, shoving a stack of papers across the desk to make room for a ponderous elbow. "Well, this is how the other half lives, out here in the sticks. Folgers and Styrofoam cups. You've been spoiled rotten by those Berkeley tree huggers, I can see. Probably gone vegan by now."

"Speaking of spoiled, when'd you get the exec chair? Now all you need is a corner office. Beautiful views out over the Vallejo skyline."

He grinned. "Fancy, eh? When I hit forty, my back started to go. Too much time on the damn floor. The folding shit wasn't doing it no more." The coffee machine gave a final, wheezing sputter, and he poured two full cups. Styrofoam, true to his word. He took his cup and lit another cigarette, filling the tiny space with smoke. "If you need any soy milk or whatever, I know a great place about thirty miles down the street." He stretched back comfortably in his chair and scratched the stubble on his neck. "They call it, what is it again? San Francisco."

I laughed and took a sip. The coffee was hot. Its only redeeming quality, but an important one. "I'm getting you a new coffee machine for Christmas. This one's gonna die before you do."

I'd met Buster through, of all people, his ex-wife. His fourth ex-wife. She was the one who had hired me, ironically. The dissolution of his first three marriages had taught Buster that lawyers had their uses. He'd also learned, the hard way, that every divorce divided his net worth by half, not to mention child support. So, by the fourth he'd decided to play hardball. His lawyer had his marching orders. Apparently, Buster had told him if he budged an inch in the negotiations, Buster would be standing in his living room that night, wanting to ask why. Buster was a big, scary guy. His lawyer wasn't backing down, come hell or high water.

I'd been hired to communicate to Buster, delicately, that lawyers were all well and good, or would have been, if his about-to-be-ex-wife hadn't found out that he ran a thriving chop shop out of his garage. I didn't want to know exactly how many of the Bay Area's missing cars passed through Buster's World Class each year, but I figured he put most auto dealerships to shame. I'd had to explain to him that it was better not to fight the divorce in court. The marriage hadn't gone well. There was a surplus of ill will. He didn't want his wife talking about his side business, which she most definitely would.

Eventually, we reached a point where we understood each other.

The divorce went through, Buster's retirement got pushed back by a few years, and doubtless he started working the chop shop harder than ever to make up for the financial hit. According to him, he'd also sworn off marriage and gotten a vasectomy, but he sometimes exaggerated. There was no way to tell for sure if Buster's pipes still worked.

He lit another cigarette and topped off our cups. "What do you need?"

"Weekend getaway package."

"We can do that."

"I'm seeing the neon letters," I said, gesturing with both arms. "Buster's World Class Travel Agency. Getting Places in Style."

"I *like* that. Wheels are spinning. You wanna invest? You can be the silent partner."

"You got something comfortable for me? Not sure how far I'll be going."

"Harley do ya?"

"Sure." I smiled affectionately. "I've always wanted to feel like a fat middle-aged man."

Buster shook his head. "Trust me, the novelty wears off after the first ten years." He pushed his chair back and lumbered to his feet. "Let's go take a look."

We headed back into the garage. There were three different Harleys. An older Softail, one of the massive Street Glides, and a Fat Boy S. The pipes blacked out, matte black paint, no chrome, big engine. I nodded to the Fat Boy. "True love, Buster. It exists after all."

He shook his head dismissively. "Say that until you get married."

"I can take it?"

He nodded. "Guy dropped it off last week for a tune-up that it didn't need. A doctor who does the weekend warrior shit. Get it back by Friday and we're good."

There were times when the Aprilia was too distinctive or I didn't want to be seen twice by the same person. Sometimes I didn't want anyone to get a license plate or describe a motorcycle that could be traced back to me. Buster's was a sort of library. He constantly had new motorcycles coming in for repairs. I'd borrow one, here and there. Untraceable. Owners didn't notice an extra few miles on the odometer.

"Here." I handed him an envelope. There were five hundred-dollar bills inside.

"Not needed. Haven't you ever heard of comps?"

"Got an expense account this time."

"Why didn't you say so?" The envelope vanished. I got onto the Harley. It had a different feel from the Aprilia. The handlebars tilted back, the front tire angled out, the seat much closer to the road.

"This work for you?" Buster asked.

I nodded. "This works. How's the leg holding up?"

"Eh, it's fine. Feel it when it rains, is all."

"Lucky you don't live in Seattle."

He laughed again. "No shit. Look what it did to Cobain. And that sonofabitch had a hell of a lot more to be happy about than I do."

When I'd come to the garage after hours to deliver the bad news that he wouldn't be able to fight his divorce in court after all, Buster hadn't been happy.

Not at all happy.

The divorce had stressed him out, he'd explained later. Lawyers stressed him out. The prospect of losing a lot of money stressed him out. His about-to-be-ex-wife stressed him out. He hadn't been sleeping well. Plus, he'd always had a temper problem. Which was why he'd pulled a big stainless steel .357 revolver, pointed it, and given me five seconds to leave his garage.

I gave him a big spiel about not wanting to shoot the messenger, but it hadn't dissuaded him.

He'd started counting.

Since then, he'd always been grateful that I'd only shot him in the leg. Considerately avoiding bones and arteries and instead putting a bullet through the fleshy part of his ample left thigh. It was true. I had done Buster a favor. He'd pulled a gun. He knew as well as I did that he'd escalated things to a point where anything could have happened. A gunshot to the leg was a fairly workable resolution. And I'd driven him to the hospital afterward. He'd cursed me out the whole way, but later admitted the gesture had been sweet.

He'd recovered nicely. Just a very slight limp.

After the divorce went through and the matter was settled, I'd felt bad. Maybe because my former client—his former wife—had driven *me* crazy. She was not an easy woman. Not at all. And I'd only been mixed up with her five weeks, not five years. One of the few cases I regretted taking. Five years with Buster's ex-wife and I probably would have behaved worse than he had. So, I showed up to his garage one afternoon with a case of Red Label. By way of apology. Turned out that however Buster felt about me, he liked scotch more than a little.

We spent the afternoon sitting in a giant red-finned Cadillac convertible parked in the back of the garage. Something that would have been right at home in about 1965. The car was comfortable. Big, spacious bucket seats, the radio going. Top down, so Buster could do his chain-smoking without driving me nuts. We sat there working our way through the first bottle and into a pretty decent chunk of the second, Buster putting down two or three to each of mine.

By the time I rose rather unsteadily out of the Cadillac, we'd become friends, of sorts. Scotch would do that to people. He was a good guy, Buster. At least in my book. He was honest. That counted. We stayed in touch. Doing each other the occasional favor. A few more bottles of scotch here and there. The people I trusted—people like Buster, Charles, and Jess—helped me in different ways. And I counted them as friends. I didn't have that many friends. It was good to have a few.

The Harley came to life with a visceral rumble. I rode out the open bay door. I had everything I needed in a backpack. Outside, I checked the iPad. Assuming she was in her car, the GPS tracker would tell me where to go.

It was time to find Karen Li. Time to find out what she had taken.

22

She was in San Francisco but heading north. Even as I watched, the dot edged up on the map. Toward the Golden Gate Bridge and the 101 freeway that ran all the way up to Seattle. That gave me a choice. I could loop around, follow, and try to catch up. Or gamble on where she'd end up. Not many choices immediately north of the city. If she wanted a freeway, the 101 was it.

I gambled. Worked my way around San Pablo Bay on the 37, riding fast, aiming to link up with the 101. It was a chilly, gray day. Light rain swept out of the sky and wind gusts rocked the big motorcycle. When I reached Novato I pulled over and checked the iPad. Karen Li was only a few miles north, still on the 101. I had guessed right. I moved faster, cutting through traffic until I saw the red Porsche. It was doing a steady eighty in the left-hand lane, the top up. I drifted closer until I could see Karen Li's black hair in the little rear window. It was her.

Satisfied, I eased over a lane and dropped back a few cars.

We stayed on the 101 through the rolling hills of Petaluma and Santa Rosa, passing vineyards and pastures full of sheep and black cows standing with that angular flat shape, like cardboard cutouts. We continued north.

Then something interesting happened.

Without signaling, the little red convertible cut into the right-hand lane. I followed. Still a few cars behind, I saw the Boxster's brake lights as it slowed onto an exit ramp. Then, very suddenly, it swerved back onto the freeway, cutting over the solid line and rumble strips. Cars honked. A trailer truck just missed the little roadster and its loud horn blared.

Already on the exit ramp, I didn't bother to try to follow the Porsche back across the divider. Instead, at the intersection I took the entrance ramp straight back onto the freeway. Either I had seen a confused driver nearly take the wrong exit and catch herself just in time—or I had watched the fumbling, rookie maneuver of someone trying to ditch a tail. A basic trick. Like getting onto a subway car and jumping off before the doors closed. Counting on the fact that any pursuers would have to exit, or would make such a fuss trying to cut back over that they'd be spotted.

Interesting.

I caught sight of the Boxster as it turned off the freeway a second time, this time exiting. I followed, letting more space grow between us. Fewer cars meant it was easier to be spotted. Did Karen Li suspect she was being followed? She couldn't have recognized me. Was she just generally cautious?

Or were other people following her?

We were on the 128, a narrow two-lane road that angled sharply up while curving back and forth in hairpin twists. I let the Porsche get still farther ahead, out of sight. There was nowhere for her to go except forward. It began to rain harder. Drops splattered off my helmet visor. The road descended sharply into Anderson Valley and I caught a glimpse of the red convertible on the flat road in front of me. We drove through several small towns, Yorkville, Boonville, Philo, passed meadows and vineyards and signs for wineries and farms, and then abruptly we were in a redwood forest, the high trees blocking what little light there was. The redwoods fell away as suddenly as they had appeared and we were on the coast, the choppy, gunmetal water of the Pacific stretching to the sky. The Boxster headed north on Highway 1. Out by the ocean it was windier. Sharp gusts rocked the Harley. A driving rain lashed into me.

We reached the town of Mendocino and the Boxster braked and turned in.

I continued until I was out of sight, then pulled an illegal U-turn. A minute later I was in Mendocino proper, in sight of the high bluffs looking over the Pacific. Little shops and restaurants and a two-story hotel stood along one side of the main street. The side closer to the sea was an expanse of flat, high grass, threaded with trails that led to the bluffs. On a sunny, warm day the trails were probably full of hikers and families. Today they were empty.

I could see Karen Li. She had parked by the hotel and stood in the rain. A long black raincoat over her slim figure. She unfurled a black umbrella and took a black handbag from her car. Oddly, she didn't walk toward the town. She seemed oblivious to the cozy little cafés and pubs that any normal traveler would have hurried into after a long, wet drive. She set out in the opposite direction. I watched her figure diminish into a small black dot.

Moving toward the high bluffs and gray sea.

Most people tended to be better at remembering details than faces. A blue hat, a red T-shirt—these would wedge into memory far more than eye color or bone structure. The hotel on Main Street was furnished in a Victorian style— plush armchairs, rugs, a crackling fireplace. I found a restroom and changed hurriedly, pulling clothes from my backpack. When I emerged I had traded my boots for white sneakers and was dressed in blue running tights and a black athletic halter top. My hair now swept up in a ponytail under a cherry red 49ers cap, and a pair of white Apple earbuds in my ears. The unconnected cord tucked into a fanny pack on my waist.

I had pulled up on a Harley, in a leather motorcycle jacket. That was one person.

Now I was a jogger. Someone else.

I left the backpack under a couch in the lobby and headed out into the rain.

I ran slowly, feeling the wind raise pinpricks along my arms. Feet squelching into wet grass, white sneakers already muddied beyond repair. Not entirely sure if I was being watched. If Karen Li had wanted to choose the ideal place to spot someone following her, she couldn't have picked a better setting than this flat, open landscape. I found a twisting path that wound toward the edge of the bluffs. Below, maybe fifty or sixty feet, the sea churned over craggy rocks, the water forming whirlpools, white patches of foam frothing up, swirling away, reappearing. I caught a glimpse of a black umbrella, far ahead. Behind me, the little town faded. The ocean swirled and foamed. As we drew closer to the edge of the bluffs, the ground became rocky and uneven.

I stopped. I could see her. A motionless dot on the gray landscape, roughly a football field length away. Framed by the gray sea, she suddenly seemed a fragile and at-risk figure right out of literature, somewhere between *Anna Karenina* and *The Woman in White*.

She wasn't alone.

In front of her were two other people.

I pulled a pair of binoculars from the fanny pack and lay down in the wet grass, not caring about the mud. I was soaked, anyway. The binoculars were small but powerful. Faces sprang into focus. The two men from San Francisco. Also wearing black raincoats and holding umbrellas. I watched as Karen Li set down her black bag. The skinnier man picked it up, said something, walked away. The other man was saying something, too.

I took a sharp breath. Without warning he had suddenly leaned in and seized her thin shoulders. Her back was to the ocean. I could see her shaking. See him saying something. Underneath, a fifty-foot drop into the whirlpools and rocks and frigid Pacific currents.

I remembered their watchfulness, the whiff of danger that had rolled off them in the coffee shop. The expression of terror on her face as she left. That had been a very safe and public place. Now she stood literally at a cliff's edge.

Alone. No one else in sight.

No one to help her.

In the space of several seconds my role had fundamentally changed.

I no longer needed to follow Karen Li. Now I needed to save her life.

In perfect conditions the world's fastest man could cover one hundred yards in just under ten seconds; the fastest woman, about a second longer. On a track, I could run it in less than double that time, but given the wet grass and treacherous footing, there was no way I'd reach them. I didn't need to, though. I just needed the man to see me. I didn't much think about what would happen then. Maybe he'd run. Maybe a more aggressive reaction. But he wouldn't push someone off a cliff in front of a witness.

He'd want to leave either two bodies, or none at all.

I ran. All out, straight toward them. My heart banged, my breath rasped.

She took a backward step away.

He stepped forward, hands gripping her shoulders.

I ran faster.

Another step back. Now she was only a few feet from the edge.

I was close enough to see the wind whipping at her raincoat. Her mouth moved as she said something I couldn't make out.

They saw me.

The man's hands fell from her shoulders and he stepped away from her.

She edged away from the ocean.

I slowed to a fast jog, gave them a look of casual curiosity, just someone wondering what on earth two people were doing standing around in this weather. Threw a little wave as I passed by. A friendly hello. A gesture that said I'd remember seeing them.

The man turned and started hurrying in the same direction his partner had gone.

Karen Li started walking quickly toward town.

I was of no more use to Care4. But I had saved a life. It seemed a good trade.

I found her back in town, getting into her car. I crossed the street and walked over. Still in my muddied jogging gear. The rain still coming down hard.

"Karen," I said. "I think we should talk."

23

"You've been following me. Haven't you?"

We sat on the wide front porch of the hotel where I had first changed into my jogging gear, barely more than an hour before. Below us stretched the Pacific, gray water joining an equally gray sky in an invisible horizon.

Karen Li was drinking hot tea with lemon. Both her slender hands wrapped around the ceramic mug as though seeking its warmth. I was reminded again how pretty she was. The pale, delicate face, not much makeup. Dark, expressive eyes and whitened teeth that looked orthodontist perfect. We sat in a pair of rocking chairs off to one side of the porch. I had changed out of my wet running gear and back into my original clothes.

"You've been following me," she said again. "For how long?"

I sipped coffee from my own mug. I had ordered a strong French roast and was drinking it black, as always. The coffee, brewed by the hotel café, was good. Good coffee wasn't a guarantee at hotel restaurants. It was always nice to encounter it. "Longer than today."

"Are you the only one who's been following me?"

"As far as I know. I can't answer that definitively."

She raised her mug, drank. Still looking out to sea. "Who hired you?"

"Ask me a different one."

She shrugged. "It doesn't matter. I can guess."

I said nothing. Watched a couple walk out the front door of the hotel. They started down the stairs, the man's arm around the woman, whispering something. She laughed, nestled into his arm as he raised a jaunty blue umbrella. They looked happy. An anniversary, maybe, or a spontaneous getaway. I thought of Ethan and wondered if I'd hear from him.

"Why did you want to talk to me?" Karen wanted to know. "If you were hired to follow me, doesn't that defeat the point? Now that I know about you?"

It was a fair question. "I don't know much about you. But best I can tell, you're swimming in deep water. May be time to get out."

Her dark eyes flashed. "What *do* you think you know about me?"

I considered my response. An odd situation. She was right. I was working for Gregg Gunn. He had paid me. At the same time I wasn't going to let someone die on my watch. Twenty grand didn't buy that. Nothing did. Karen Li was giving something to someone. And I'd tell Gunn what I'd seen, as I'd been hired to do. She would also stay safe. I wasn't about to stand by and let the woman in front of me get pushed off a cliff. "They're concerned," I said. "About their information. Their secrets. Which is logical."

She looked at me, confused. As though trying to figure out exactly what I meant. "You think you know about their secrets? You have no idea. Whoever you are."

"So tell me."

She laughed. A brief, rueful laugh. "That would be nice, wouldn't it? Get another person dragged in. Were you telling me to get out of the water? Or had you wanted to jump in?"

"Those men. You were with them in San Francisco. You gave them something. What was it?"

She set her cup down. "You were there?"

I said nothing.

"Forget it," she said. "I don't know why I'm even talking to you. I don't know why I'm sitting here." She ran a hand through her black hair, made as if to stand.

"Sit down, Karen."

"You're telling me to sit?"

"I'm asking you to sit. You asked me a question. I'll answer it."

She sat back in her chair, slowly, defeated. As if the prospect of getting up, of walking off the porch into the chilly, wet afternoon, was suddenly too much to even contemplate. "Fine," she said. "Answer my question."

"You're talking to me because something has scared you. Badly. I don't know everything. I know it's connected to the people you work for and to the men you met today. But you're talking to me for one reason only. You're in danger. And you know it."

I gave her a hard look, challenging her to disagree.

She was silent. Biting her lip, the mug back in her hands. "It's not only me."

"What do you mean?"

Her face openly weighed how much she wanted to say. "It's not only me," she said again. "What I'm trying to stop—people will die. A lot of people. Innocent people. And if I can't stop them, it's going to happen soon."

"Stop who?"

"Care4, of course. My *company*." She said the last word with special emphasis. Like she was describing the type of cancer she had.

"If you're not trying to sell their secrets, how'd you get caught up in this?"

"Selling secrets? *That's* what they told you? You think I'm doing this for *money*? My God. You know how much easier it would be for me to just walk away?"

"Why don't you, then? Why take these risks?"

Her voice was coiled with anger. "If you really knew me, you'd know why. If you knew anything about me, you'd get it. Some things are worth taking risks for. My parents taught me that in a way you won't ever understand."

"I think I might," I said. "Give me a chance. Tell me. How'd you get caught up in this?"

"You actually care?" she asked, still upset. "You really want to know?"

"I'm asking because I do."

Some of the tautness left her voice, and her eyes softened. "It started with an e-mail. That's all. Just an e-mail with a weird subject line."

"An e-mail?"

"Someone accidentally CC'd me on a chain I wasn't supposed to see."

"All this from an e-mail? That seems extreme."

"It wasn't so much the e-mail. If it was just the e-mail, I probably would have forgotten about it. We get hundreds and hundreds each day. It's impossible to even read all of them."

"What was it, then?"

"Their reaction. It was like they panicked. They shut down my account, reset the password, told me it was routine maintenance even though that was obviously BS. Then when I was finally able to log back in, the e-mail had been deleted. Only that one. That was weird enough, but it didn't get scary until a few days later, when some of their lawyers called me in and read me the riot act. It didn't matter how many times I explained I hadn't done anything wrong—they didn't seem to believe me. It got worse. After that meeting I started to feel like I was being watched. Finally, I decided that if they were so suspicious, I should learn more about what was worrying everyone so much." She finished simply. "Sometimes I wish I could take that back. Because the more I learned, the more I understood about what Care4 is actually doing."

"You mentioned a weird subject line. What was it?"

She gave me a quick, guarded look and then stared back at her mug. "Is this a trap?"

"No trap. I'm just asking."

"'In Retentis.' That was the subject line."

I took that in. "You said people would die. Who is going to die?"

Her face changed, becoming almost hostile. "What do you care? You were hired by people who hate me. And you think you might know some things. But I promise you—whoever you are. You don't know the half of it. You don't know a *tenth* of it. About what you're doing, or who you're working for, or what you're getting into."

"We both work for the same people," I observed.

She laughed again, that short, humorless laugh. "I know them a lot better than you do. And they're a lot more dangerous than you realize."

"Yeah? Tell me about them."

"Why?"

"So I can help you."

"Why do you want to help me?"

"Because you need help."

"You're actually going to help me? That's what you're saying?" Her voice was a mixture of defiance and its opposite quality. "You're going to save me from these dangerous men?"

I finished off the last of my coffee. "If you want me to try to help you, Karen, you tell me what you're wrapped up in. And if you don't want my help, I'm out of town in the next five minutes. Either way, I'm done following you. You want me to leave you alone, say the word."

She was quiet. I had nothing else to do so I counted to myself. Almost a full minute went by before she spoke. "I'm staying at the Narwhal Cottages." She pulled a wallet out of her purse and opened it. I saw her California driver's license in a translucent plastic sleeve next to tiers of colorful plastic cards. She pulled aside a red Bank of America card and a yellow Hertz card and a blue Visa and then found what she was looking for, handing me a business card bearing the silhouette of a whale. A little horn extended from its forehead.

"Meet me there at ten o'clock tonight."

"Who's going to die?" I asked again. "What did you mean when you said that?"

She seemed to ignore the question. "The whole company is focused on one thing right now. If you want to know what's going on, you have to understand that."

"What one thing?"

She raised her mug and then put it down again. It was empty except for a pale wedge of tea-stained lemon at the bottom. "Care4 has almost arrived at a milestone they've spent years trying to reach. They've staked the company's whole future on this—and they're almost there. They're doing final internal troubleshooting as we speak. It's set to go live on November first."

"November first? That's barely over two weeks away."

"Exactly." Her eyes turned from the empty mug to me. "Once that happens, all of this will be too late to stop."

"Stop? What do you mean, stop? Who will it be too late for?"

Momentarily quiet, she appeared to make a decision, and then her words came in a rush. "It will be too late for the people who are—"

There was a sudden shattering sound.

Our heads jerked around to the noise and Karen half sprung out of her chair. A waiter had dropped a plate that had broken against the porch. The loud noise seemed to have jarred Karen away from her thoughts, away from what she had been about to say. Her face closed off, regained its wariness. "No more now," she said. "I'll explain everything tonight."

"Why not now?"

She had been so close. On the verge of telling me. And if what she said was true, that left almost no time to act. The sooner I learned what Karen Li knew, the better.

She looked cautiously around as the waiter used a dustpan to sweep up the ceramic fragments. "I don't even like being outside like this, talking to you. We shouldn't even be here. It's too risky, too easy to be heard. They had *you* follow me—how do I know there aren't others, too?"

I looked at her with sympathy. There were small lines of worry and tension in her face and her hands were unsteady. I wondered how much she'd been sleeping. Her attitude wasn't uncommon. People who learned they were being followed tended to flash into paranoia that was hard to pull away from. To a woman as frightened as Karen Li, this quiet seaside town might seem rife with more menace than a battlefield.

"If not now, when? And can you prove what you're saying?"

She nodded. "I have something hidden. Not here," she added. "It's not safe with me. My house isn't safe. The people I know aren't safe. But if you show me I can really trust you, I'll tell you everything I know."

"Narwhal. Ten o'clock. I'll be there." Seeing the anxiety in her eyes, I added, "And if I can, I'll help you." I squeezed her hand.

I got up, headed down off the porch toward town. In spite of the urgency, if she was telling the truth, I didn't want to push too hard for what she knew. I *had* been following her, after all. I had accepted money from the people she was most frightened of. The woman was in a scary situation and it had taken a visible toll. If she was going to trust me, part of that meant respecting her terms rather than pressing hard for everything at once. I'd show up at ten, as she wanted, and if she really was in danger I'd get her out of town and somewhere safe.

Her voice called after me. "One more thing."

I paused on the stairs. "Yeah?"

"Whatever you think. Whatever you've guessed. It's much worse."

24

The Narwhal Cottages were reached by a long, curving driveway that slanted up from Highway 1. I left the Harley at the bottom of the driveway. The big engine was too loud. Especially grinding up a winding incline, people would hear it and remember it. With some effort I eased the heavy motorcycle off the paving into the trees. Glad I had chosen the blacked-out model. No chrome made it harder for headlights to pick up. Not invisible, but hard to notice and easy to miss. It was a cold night, but the exertion of walking fast up the steep driveway warmed me. The rain had let off and misted into a heavy fog. Swaths of cloud swirled over a dim moon.

When I reached the top of the driveway I was far above sea level. On clear days, the view of the Pacific was surely stunning. Now, not even the stars were visible. There was a house off to one side, probably where guests could check in, maybe containing a restaurant as well. Farther on, cabins of varying sizes were set between the trees. Each had a chimney. To allow for the romance of a fireplace. Behind a few of the cottages I could see redwood hot tubs. A couple could open a bottle of wine, sit in the warm bubbling water under the stars. I thought again of Ethan. Imagined us, someplace like this, doing something like that. It sounded good. It sounded like a fantasy and not much more.

Post–Labor Day meant the off-season. Rates lowered, fewer check-ins. Each cabin had an adjoining parking spot and almost all the spots were empty. Mid-week, bad weather. Not many guests. I found Karen's convertible parked at the last cabin, farthest from the driveway. It was surrounded on three sides by tall trees. A tradeoff. No ocean view, but the most privacy.

Whatever you've guessed, it's much worse.

I wondered if that was true. A lot of people who found me were badly scared of something. Sometimes they were right to be scared. Sometimes their fears were exaggerated. I liked to form my own impressions. The small cabin looked uninhabited. Blinds down, no light visible, no smoke from the chimney.

I knocked softly. No response.

Knocked again. Still nothing.

The night was quiet. Far below I heard an engine, a car passing on Highway 1. The noise grew, then faded without slowing. I turned the knob slightly. It was unlocked. I opened the door. The cabin was dark. I walked in and shut the door behind me. Felt around for a light switch and flicked it up. A rustic, homey décor came into view. Wood-paneled walls, a closed door leading to the bedroom, a kitchenette off to one side next to a bathroom. Music was coming from a radio. Some '40s pop song, a fuzzy big-band sound, a man crooning about love and heartbreak. On a desk, there was an open bottle of red wine next to a black corkscrew bearing the same little Narwhal logo that was on the card she'd given me.

All normal.

Except no Karen Li.

I walked around the living room. Looked around. No sign of her. I checked the bathroom, saw an electric toothbrush, a few containers of makeup and facial lotion, contact lens solution, a hairbrush. Someone was staying here. Drops of water beaded the sink. The faucet had been used in the last hour or two. Maybe she was eating a late dinner at the restaurant. So close to the cabin she wouldn't have bothered to lock the front door.

I took another look at the bedroom door. My neck prickled. The door was closed but not latched shut. It couldn't latch. Not anymore. Someone had forced it. A heavy blow, probably a kick. I saw scrapes where the brass lock had dug into the soft wood of the doorjamb.

The song continued. Romantic verses of moonlight and love-struck couples.

I opened the door. The small room was empty. A big queen bed in the middle of the room. No one had slept in it. The sheets were still perfectly arranged. A closet set into one wall was empty except for a black raincoat, hanging like a silhouette.

No Karen Li.

I shivered, feeling a gust of cold air. Coming from a window set at head height on the opposite side of the room, across the bed. The window was closed. I took another look and saw that one of the panes had been broken. That was where the cold air was coming from.

I walked around the bed and then I saw her.

She lay slumped against the wall under the window. Whoever had hit her had used something blunt and hard. The left side of her face was fine. The thin eyebrow, the snub nose and eye, although now bloodshot and unfocused. The right side of her face was different. Ruined. Blood matted into her black hair. I swallowed hard as I saw the white of bone through what would have been her cheek. Blood had pooled over the wood floor. I bent to check her pulse. Knowing there was no point.

She'd removed her makeup and was wearing flannel pajama pants and a cotton sleeveless top, no bra. Comfort clothing. The kind of clothes you put on when you were in for the night. In bed, maybe, watching a movie with a glass of wine before going to sleep. The kind of clothing you put on when the only guest you were expecting was another woman coming over to talk. I saw a pair of wire-framed glasses on the floor nearby, smashed. She'd taken her contact lenses out. Gotten comfortable. Waiting for me.

Because I had said I'd help her.

There was a vivid red-yellow bruise on her left shoulder. I bent close. The bruising was worse on the back deltoid. Her left forearm was bent at an unnatural crook. Probably broken.

Imagining what had happened was easy.

I could already tell that not imagining it was going to be much harder, for a long time.

Whoever had come to the cabin hadn't wasted time talking. Hadn't bothered to pretend everything would be okay. She must have come to the door, maybe hearing a knock. Expecting me. Maybe wondering why I was early. Maybe relieved.

And then seen whoever was at the door and known, more or less, what was about to happen.

She'd gotten away from the front door without having the chance to lock it. Maybe a foot had been pushed in the frame or a shoulder set against the door so she couldn't get it shut. Fled into the bedroom because there was nowhere else to go. Locked that door and then frantically tried to get through the window.

Knowing it was her only chance.

I looked at her hands. Her right hand was badly cut around the knuckles. A shard of glass embedded in the palm. I closed my eyes for a moment. Pictured her expression as she'd punched through the windowpane, too rushed, too panicked to bother trying to open it. Probably barely aware of the glass that had splintered into her hand. There was something on the floor by her left hand. A small glossy square, maybe two by three inches, creased and crumpled as though it had been squeezed. It was a grainy photograph of a young Chinese couple, posing formally for the camera. The woman bore an unmistakable resemblance to Karen Li and held a little girl of about six or seven. A family photograph. Whoever had been inside the cabin couldn't have missed it, had clearly deemed it unimportant. I looked around the cabin again. Envisioning Karen fleeing to the bedroom. Maybe she'd been holding the picture, looking at it, when she'd answered the door.

Not fast enough.

Meanwhile, the bedroom door kicked in. A flimsy door. Light wood, basic brass knob. It had probably lasted one good kick, two at most.

The window was a small one but Karen Li hadn't been a big person. She probably could have hauled herself up through it. Gotten outside to safety or at least the chance of escape. She could have gained the two most precious commodities in that situation: space, and time.

The first blow must have caught her on the shoulder as she was trying to get through the window. The impact had probably knocked her down. Off her feet. Pain would have disoriented her. Maybe she'd tried to regain her feet. Maybe, by that point, she was begging.

The rest was clear enough.

I opened my eyes, then closed them again. Seeing, and not wanting to see. Her attacker had swung again. This time, she'd been facing him. She'd seen it coming. Had raised her arms instinctively. That second blow had broken her arm. And then the third, the one she hadn't been able to stop. Maybe she had closed her eyes and waited for it. The impact had knocked her over, pulped her face, splattered blood. A vicious blow. Delivered by a person—almost definitely a man—of unusual physical strength.

I was picturing the burly guy who had grabbed her by the ocean that afternoon.

I opened my eyes again. Not wanting to see any more.

A pretty, defenseless woman, crying in pain, pleading for mercy. Not an easy psychological target. A lot of people could throw a punch or swing a bat in fear, or self-defense, or anger. If provoked, people could do all kinds of things they'd never imagine. But to murder with physical force in cold blood? That took a different type. A type that was either pretty far gone mentally, or had done plenty of similar things already.

Maybe both.

A bad way to go. The final seconds full of pain and terror and suffering. Knowing what was happening. What was about to happen. With any luck, she hadn't felt the final, killing blow. Had slipped into unconsciousness or shock. I hoped so. I doubted I would ever know.

I spent five careful minutes going around the cabin, wiping prints off anything I'd touched. There wasn't anything worth taking. Her purse was gone. Only a small open overnight bag with some clothes and shoes, her toiletries in the bathroom. I saw her black umbrella, placed neatly by the door to dry.

Whatever you've guessed, it's much worse.

She had been right. As for me?

I hadn't protected her. I hadn't saved her.

I had let her die.

I took a last look at the dark-haired woman slumped against the wall. Silently apologizing for leaving her like this. And making her a promise. Then I was outside. Down the fog-choked driveway, on the motorcycle. I didn't know much about the two men from the afternoon, but I knew their faces and was pretty sure I knew who they worked for. That would have to be enough.

I had failed Karen Li. I had let her go to a very bad death when she needed me most. I couldn't change that. But when I found the people who had done this, I intended to do everything I could to minimize their remaining time in this world. I'd make sure they knew why. The road unwound. The cold wind rushed against me. The big motorcycle roared as I hurtled along, headlight slashing through the heavy mist.

I was half an hour south of Mendocino before I realized what I'd forgotten.

The GPS tracker still on her car. Directly linking me to a murder. It was too late to go back. Couldn't take the chance that police might find me there.

Would they find the tracker? Maybe not. It was easy to miss. An unpleasant thought settled into my mind just the same. If they did find the little device, it had my fingerprints on it and, worse, electronic records that would lead directly to me. Which meant that if the tracker was discovered I would almost definitely find myself a murder suspect. One with no alibi, at that. Surely people had seen me with Karen Li in town. As we ordered our coffee and tea inside. As we sat talking on the hotel porch. Then, later, I'd been at the scene of the murder, near the time of her death. I had come into town for no apparent reason. Alone.

Which all added up to one thing.

If I didn't find the men who had killed her, it was entirely possible that I could be charged with the crime myself.

25

I reached the Care4 headquarters the next morning after dropping the Harley back at Buster's. I hadn't slept much. That was okay. A couple of shots of scotch in the first of three morning coffees had left me more or less where I wanted to be. A little reckless, a little hot, and all about getting things done.

In the lobby, huge screens on the walls played silent looping videos, endless smiling parents and gurgling babies, all happily connected by technology. More screens showing impoverished villages, dirt streets and huts, panning images of hospitals and grateful patients. Images and captions touting the nonprofit money the company was generous enough to contribute to the world. Two glowing, backlit words were engraved into the wall. WE CARE. A security guard in a black suit jacket sat behind the desk. I didn't slow down as I walked past him toward the elevators, my boots clicking on polished marble.

"Miss, hold on! You need to check in." The guard saw I wasn't stopping. He got up fast and headed to intercept me. A tall, goateed man with sloping shoulders and a bald, shiny head.

"I have an appointment with your CEO." I pushed the elevator button but nothing happened. It was equipped with an electronic security reader, I realized.

"Did you hear me? I said you need to check in."

"Call your boss if you want. But I'm in a hurry. I'm going up."

His hand was on my arm. Squeezing. "You're not hearing me. You need to check in."

I'd never much liked having my arm squeezed. "You're not hearing *me*. I'm going up. And you should take your hand off me."

His grip tightened to the point of pain. "You're not going anywhere."

Maybe the scotch was making me impatient. Maybe it was the squeezing. Maybe I was getting sick of being nice. "Fine. Have it your way." I took a step away from the elevator and felt his hand relax. Then I brought my boot down hard onto his right ankle and gave him a rough shove sideways. He yelped in pain as he fell. I leaned down and snatched the security badge off his belt. Waved it at the electronic reader. There was a beep and I was in the elevator. I pushed the button for the top floor.

When the doors opened again I was on the executive level. I walked through a set of frosted glass doors into a reception area that felt different from the public lobby. No screens showing babies or hospitals up here. No warmth. The furnishings were expensive and minimalist, monochrome colors. Water ran down a wall of black marble.

I walked right up to the surprised receptionist. "I'm here for Gregg Gunn. Urgent."

She looked at me suspiciously. "Mr. Gunn is in an executive meeting. Whoever you are, you're not on his calendar for this morning."

"Where is he?"

"I can't tell you that."

"Then I go knocking on every door in this place until I find him."

She reached for a phone. "I'll call security."

I waved the badge. "Who do you think I am?"

She bit her lip. "He's in the Meadows Conference Room."

I walked past her down the hallway. Some of the doors were marked by surnames, some by words. The conference rooms. I passed a Forest, Grove, and Copse.

Meadows was the fourth.

I let myself in.

Inside, three people were seated around a long table. Sun feebly scratched at tinted windows. Gregg Gunn sat at the far side. Down a little to his left was a tall, red-haired woman, and across from her a big, beefy guy in a royal blue polo shirt who looked like he'd played as a D3 tackle in college. The three of them stared at me. The faces of the two strangers expressed curiosity and hostility. Gunn's face was just confused.

"Nikki?" he sputtered. "What are you doing here?"

"We need to talk."

"Can it wait?" He turned several papers over, absently rearranging them into a new pile.

"If it could wait," I said, "I would have called your secretary and asked to be scheduled in for sometime next week."

He caught my tone. "Fine. Wait in the lobby. When I'm through here, we can talk about whatever is so pressing."

I sat down in the chair closest to me and kicked a muddy boot up on the varnished table. "I don't usually ask for much from people," I said. "Never been the needy type. I don't even want flowers on my damn birthday. But right now we need to talk, and until we do, I'm not going anywhere."

"How the hell did she get past security?" This was from the beefy guy. His face was red and angry, big biceps flexed under tight sleeves. He looked like he was about ready to throw me out himself. I wondered if he'd try.

Gunn's eyes hadn't left me. "Talk about what?"

Before I could answer, the conference room door burst open. The security guard. Limping, his face red. And holding a gun.

This made things more interesting.

"She snuck past me," he said.

I tossed his badge to him. "You dropped this."

He gave me a look of hatred and pointed the gun at me using two hands, arms braced in a classic triangle stance. Maybe he was an ex-cop or ex-military. Maybe just a guy who spent nights alone on the couch watching too many YouTube videos, hoping his big hero moment would one day come along. I gave the gun a closer look. A Glock 17. People who didn't know guns bought the Glock 17 the way people who didn't know vodka bought Grey Goose. The whole brand-name thing. A good brand, without a doubt, even if not the single best. Nothing was the single best. But people wanted to think there was, and so they bought Glocks, and so here we were. The only thing that made the Glocks different from most other nine-millimeter semiautomatics was that they didn't have a push-button safety. Instead the safety was built into the trigger. Which basically made it easier to shoot someone, whether you intended to or not.

"Get up," he told me. "Slowly."

I looked back at him. Boot still up on the table. "No."

"You're coming with me."

"You're mistaken if you think that."

"You're trespassing."

"So go find a judge."

I saw his hands tighten on the black pistol. "If you don't get up right now, I'll shoot you. You're trespassing on private property."

That made me laugh. "If you want to shoot an unarmed woman in your CEO's executive boardroom you go right ahead. That's a great headline."

"David," said Gunn. His fingers drumming on the table. "You're being melodramatic. Put the gun away."

The guard half lowered the pistol. "You're sure, sir?"

"Well, it doesn't seem to be doing you or anyone else much good, now, does it?" Gunn exclaimed. He looked around the room. "This meeting is adjourned."

The other two got up to leave. The big guy looked like he still wanted to tackle me. I hoped he wouldn't. Things were settling down a bit. The security guard stood in the doorway. "Do you need me?"

Gunn looked at him. "I think, David, that if I had needed you, it was about five minutes ago, when she was in the lobby. I don't need you anymore."

The guard didn't look happy. There were a few ways to take that last bit. He walked out of the room and the two of us were left alone together.

"Nikki," Gunn said. His voice was cold. A different man than the bubbly, energetic guy who had walked into my bookstore like he was delivering a million-dollar pitch. "Do you always burst in on your employers like this? I can't say it's an endearing habit."

I shrugged as I took my boot off the table and sat up. The boot left a muddy streak against the smooth wood. "You've been to my office. Figured it was about time I stopped by yours."

"Except that I hired you. You work for me."

"That's the thing." I poured myself a glass of ice water from a pitcher and took a swallow. "I *did* work for you. But not anymore. I came by to submit my resignation."

That surprised him. "What? I paid you a considerable sum of money, in case you forgot."

"That's true. You did." I took the same manila envelope from my purse and slid it across to him. "Twenty thousand dollars. Fully refunded. Every penny. Not even billing you for expenses."

He looked at the envelope but didn't touch it. "You came here to quit. Why?"

"You hired me to follow a woman. Karen Li."

"Yes. So?"

"Karen Li is dead."

He reared back in his seat. "Dead? What are you talking about?"

I was watching Gunn closely. If he had known, he was doing a good job of hiding it. There was a pretty healthy mix of shock and disbelief on his face.

"Last night. She had her head knocked in."

"Someone killed her? What are you talking about?"

"You hired me to tail a woman. That woman was murdered. I don't much like the idea of blood money, and I sure won't be following her anymore. I quit."

"She's dead?" He looked distressed. "You're sure? How do you know?"

"I know," I said, standing. "And now you do. That's what I came here to tell you."

His gaze wandered around the room and then found its way back to me. "Next time, an e-mail will do."

I paused at the door. "One last thing, Mr. Gunn."

"Yes?"

"Karen Li. I didn't know her well, but she didn't deserve what she got. She got a pretty lousy ending, you know. Not really the storybook type."

Gunn sat completely still for the first time since I'd met him. "What's your point?"

"She didn't deserve what she got. But the people who gave it to her— they deserve what they'll get. Do you follow?"

"No." His voice was soft. "I don't follow you, I'm afraid."

"I'm not accusing you of anything. Not yet, anyway. But a woman is dead."

"I agree," Gunn said. "Whatever problems she was causing, you're crazy if you think I wanted something like this to happen to her."

"I don't know much about you, your company, or what you want. But if you know something about how Karen died, you should tell me now."

"Nikki," he said. His brown eyes were flat and hard. "You look exhausted. Like you haven't slept. Maybe you should head home, take a nap. Take a vacation, even. Hawaii's nice this time of the year. No tourists clogging the beaches. I'll pay, even—spend a couple of weeks snorkeling and kicking sand, send me the bill. I'm happy to pick it up; you did good work." He leaned forward. "But you should think about these crazy accusations you're making. Think about that nondisclosure you signed and what you're insinuating, before you go running around acting out some misguided revenge fantasy."

"Hawaii," I said. "One day. In the meantime, though, I think I'll stick to California. Plenty of sand to kick here, without getting on a damn plane."

Gunn pushed his chair back and shrugged. "You take care, Nikki."

"I'll let myself out."

I walked out, thinking about the paper I had glimpsed in the conference room before Gunn turned it. Bullet points, the date "NOVEMBER 1" just visible at the top, like they had been going through a checklist item by item. I would have given a lot for a few more seconds with that piece of paper. I didn't see anyone else as I took the elevator back down to the lobby. As though everyone in the building was so busy they were nailed to their desks. Or had been told to keep away from me. For the hundredth time that day, I felt a rush of stomach-turning self-hatred for allowing Karen Li out of my sight in Mendocino.

I hadn't protected her. I hadn't saved her. I had shrugged off her fear as mere paranoia. Now she was dead and, worse, I hadn't learned whatever it was she had intended to tell me.

People will die.

The whole company is focused on one thing right now.

Innocent people.

I had betrayed her trust. I had ignored the danger she was in. I hated myself for it. The worst mistake I could have made, with the worst consequences. I was worthless—every time in my life when it most mattered, worthless to the people who needed me.

Pulling out of the parking lot, I had to brake hard to avoid a silver Mercedes that passed as though the driver hadn't even noticed me. I looked around in annoyance as the big sedan turned into a handicapped parking spot right in front of the Care4 entrance. One of those drivers who seemed to operate on the principle that the most expensive vehicle should be given unquestioned right-of-way. The driver was already getting out. He didn't seem handicapped as he pulled a black briefcase from the trunk and headed toward the lobby. He wore a navy pinstriped suit and bold red tie that was out of place in the excessive casualness of the Valley. Something about the man's self-satisfied stride was familiar. I'd seen it before. Photographed it, in fact. As he walked from an apartment building to that same car with a woman who was not his wife.

I took a last look and then pulled away, wondering what Brenda Johnson's husband could possibly be doing at Care4.

26

I had been up for almost two days, running on not much more than adrenaline and caffeine. I still didn't want to sleep, but I was becoming too tired to think, let alone do anything else. I reminded myself that in my current state I wasn't much good to anyone, went home, and got into bed. Twelve hours later, I woke up feeling more or less normal. I went for a run, had breakfast, and got to the bookstore by mid-morning.

"What do you think of this poster?" Jess wanted to know. "It's rough, I know." In the last year she had been expanding the number of local author readings, and these had proved popular. Lately she'd been working overtime setting up for Thrillers in the Fog, a new event we were putting on featuring local mystery writers. I looked over the glossy twelve-by-fourteen paper she was holding up, gray and black tones, a rusty slice of Golden Gate Bridge daggering out from swirls of fog, the lettering done in that same brick-rust color as the bridge.

"I love it." It felt good to think even for a moment about anything besides Care4. "Who do we have lined up so far?"

She smiled, proud. "It's going to be awesome. Martin Cruz Smith and Laurie King for sure are confirmed, and I'm working on a few others. Possible shot at Joyce Carol Oates if she's out here teaching at Cal again."

"Does she count as thriller?"

Jess gave me a look. "Have you read DIS MEM BER? The Barrens?"

"Good point."

"Excuse me?" I turned, seeing a red-haired girl in a flannel skirt and black stockings and boots. "I'm looking for a book for my boyfriend," she said. "He's really into jazz, plays trumpet, but doesn't read that much. I'm trying to get him into more fiction."

I thought again, relieved for the mental change of pace. "Hang on. I think I have something perfect, if it's in stock." I was back a minute later and handed her a book.

"*1929*? I've never heard of it."

"Historical fiction, Bix Beiderbecke. If he likes jazz, I bet he'd like it."

As the girl paid, Jess handed me an envelope. "Almost forgot. Either they hired a cute new postman or grad students are starting to deliver their own mail."

"Thanks." I tore the envelope open. A few lines of neatly slanting handwriting.

> Dear Mysterious No-Cellphone-Girl,
> Having been duly warned about your million and one shortcomings, I would like to proceed full steam ahead. I was thinking we could check out this Vietnamese place I like. This week, if you aren't out cracking heads.
> *PS: the last part was a joke (I hope).*

The note gave me a good feeling. I wanted to have dinner with Ethan. I wanted to forget about Gregg Gunn and Care4 for a few hours, forget about trying to understand what Karen Li had meant when she talked about hiding something, forget that there were people walking around in the world—in this very city—who would bash in a woman's head for a couple of missing files.

Jess wasn't done. "Someone else stopped by, a little guy, stank of cigars. He said you should get in touch as soon as you can."

Charles Miller. I wondered what he wanted to tell me.

"And one more thing. That girl Zoe, from the book club. She was outside when I opened up this morning. She wouldn't tell me what it was about, just asked when you'd be in."

"She's here? Now?"

Jess nodded. "She doesn't look like she's had the best day, either. Must be going around."

We sat on a pair of red beanbags in a corner of the bookstore. The shabby, understuffed bags were more comfortable than most of the thousand-dollar leather armchairs I'd encountered. Above us the reassuring solidity of book-shelves rose up to the ceiling. Like the walls of a confessional: comfortable, secure. The air itself smelled good. Pressed paper and the leather of the spines. The outside world seemed distant in the best possible way. I remembered Gunn's initial skepticism, whether people still needed bookstores. To me, sit-ting here, the answer was all around us. Like asking a fly fisherman, knee-deep in a clear stream, why he didn't just go to the supermarket for farmed tilapia.

"I'm sorry," Zoe said. She'd been crying. Her long black hair hadn't been straightened and it was springy with curls. "I don't have anyone else to talk to. I shouldn't have left like that the other week. I was having a good time."

Since she had brought it up, I was curious. "How did he know you were here?"

Zoe looked surprised. "My phone, of course. He has me keep the location-sharing turned on so he knows where I am."

Her answer made me dislike cell phones even more than I already did. "He doesn't seem to trust you much."

"He's had girlfriends go behind his back, cheat on him. He likes to know where I am."

"You're okay with that?"

"I live at his house, he takes care of me. My kids, too. Luis is good to them. You know how hard it is to find a man like that?" She ran a hand through her hair, pulling distractedly at a curl. "If he ever got sick of me, I don't know what I'd do."

"Can I ask you a question? Has he touched you before?"

"Touched me?"

I looked at her. "You know what I mean."

She looked away. "He takes care of me."

"There are other people out there, you know. Who take care of you. Without the other stuff. And along the way you get better at taking care of yourself."

She laughed. "For you, maybe, sure. You talk good, you're beautiful, read all these books, probably went to college. Me? I'm a high school dropout with two kids. Luis gets mad sometimes, sure, but all men do. It's not his fault."

"Are you safe around him? Has he threatened you?"

"I'll be okay."

"What did he come in to apologize for the other day? With the flowers."

She looked at the rows of books. "Nothing. He just overreacted about something and felt bad. It was my fault, really. I should know what gets him mad."

"I could talk to him," I suggested quietly.

She was surprised. "You? Talk to Luis?"

"I could explain that it might be better if he gave you some space."

"Where would I go?"

"I could help you with that."

She ran a hand through her hair again, like the very idea made her anxious. I saw her fingers untwist another curl, saw it bounce back into shape. "He wouldn't listen."

"If I talk to him he'll listen."

"He doesn't listen to anyone. Why you?"

I put a light hand against her knee to emphasize. "Luis would listen to me because I'd make him feel."

"Feel?"

I wanted her to understand. "I'd explain things so that he would feel the same things he's made you feel. And then he'd get it."

Zoe laughed. "Feelings . . . I don't think so. He doesn't go for the sentimental stuff."

I didn't laugh. "Neither do I."

"You don't know him," she said again. "You've already been too good to me. I don't want to get you in trouble." She looked around uneasily. "I should get back. Thanks for listening. Sometimes I just want someone to talk to so badly."

"You don't have to leave," I told her. "You can stay a bit."

"I don't want to get in trouble," she said.

I watched Zoe hurry out, knowing she was right. It was all well and good for me to tell her to stay. I didn't have to worry about what she'd come home to. Her form seemed to blur, to become Karen Li, to become Samantha, Marlene, all the women I had known over the years, everyone I had tried to help. I watched her walk out of the bookstore. Hating myself for wondering if she'd ever walk back in.

I rode up through the Berkeley campus, passing the empty football stadium, the wide flagstone plaza and enormous whale sculpture that marked the

Lawrence Hall of Science. The road steepened as I worked my way into the hills, and I throttled up to match the grade. I rode through brown hills and viridian scrub spilling thousands of feet down, an immense terrain of hiking trails and untouched land, until I spotted Charles's Honda Civic parked in a small dirt turnoff. One of the many scenic viewpoints that jutted off from the narrow road. Charles sat on a bench at the overlook. A little puff of smoke rose from his cigarillo and dispersed into harsh blue sky. I sat down next to him. "Never figured you for a hiker."

He nodded at me. "Who said anything about hiking? I just enjoy a good bench."

We sat quietly. For mid-October it was a hot day. A hawk wheeled around on the thermals. We both watched it. Charles finished his cigarillo, stubbed it out against the ground. "You said this fellow Gunn originally came to you because he didn't trust the big security firms?"

"Right."

Charles shook his head. "That doesn't add up. Those places wouldn't be in business two weeks if they weren't totally discreet."

I gave him a look. "You brought me all the way up here to tell me that? Come on, Charles. Clients bullshit. Horses eat apples. What else is new? I took the job."

Charles took a brass cigarette case and a gold Zippo lighter from his pocket. He lit another cigarillo and puffed the tip into an orange glow. "It was the money that stuck in my mind—the funding. Why lie about that? The logical lie is to say they had money if they *didn't*—project stability. But why lie about *not* having the funding if it had already gone through? Where's the benefit in that?"

"What does that change?"

Charles seemed to ignore the question. "I looked closer at Gunn. He worked on Wall Street for a couple of years, like I said, until they got him on insider trading. He took a plea bargain and traded names, got off with a fine. Gotta love nineties New York, right? As long as you weren't dealing crack or jumping turnstiles it was hard to get into trouble."

"So the guy who hired me is a white-collar crook? Sorry to shatter your illusions, Charles, but I've worked with worse."

Charles puffed smoke out of his mouth. "It's one thing to lead a private company. The Valley tends to be forgiving when money's at stake. But a publicly traded company is different. If you're talking about getting money from state pension funds, university endowments, mom-and-pop investors? All kinds of regulation and scrutiny kicks in."

"Meaning?"

"If you're the CEO of a publicly traded firm, they look at you funny if you get too many speeding tickets. There's no way Care4 would issue an IPO with Gregg Gunn at the helm." Charles stubbed out cigarillo number two and placed the stub next to the first one. "So then I looked much closer at the company itself."

"The baby monitors."

"But really, what's a baby monitor?"

Charles wasn't prone to redundancy. I thought and answered. "Something to watch with. Make sure the kid is sleeping. Make sure the babysitter doesn't have the boyfriend over when you're at the movies."

"Something to watch with. In other words . . . surveillance."

"Surveillance?"

"They make cute little baby cameras and it sounds warm and fuzzy. A website filled with smiling families and a bunch of feel-good stories about how they're devoted to improving childcare. They even have a nonprofit arm, healthcare, global poverty, all that. That's all sugarcoating."

"But he even showed me one of their cameras." I thought of the sleek white sphere, the pinpoint lens. "I still have the damn thing sitting in my office somewhere until I can find someone to give it to. That's real enough, right?"

"They make hardware, sure, but that's unimportant. Anyone can find some cheap Chinese factory to outsource manufacturing to. Cameras are easy. Surveillance *software* systems are Care4's real business."

For one of the first times in my life I found myself wishing I had paid more attention to the omnipresent tech world that I usually tried so hard to ignore. "Isn't surveillance basically just cameras?" I thought of my own work, aiming the zoom lens at Brenda Johnson's husband through the apartment window. "It sure is when I do it."

"You're old-fashioned, Nikki. Times have changed. Have you heard the term 'CNNs'? Not the news channel," he added. "Technology."

I gave him a look. "Please, Charles. I don't even date guys who work for Google."

"CNN stands for convolutional deep neural networks, used in computer vision. Essentially, deep learning models the biological brain's way of learning new information based on what it already knows. Show a computer a picture of a dog, tell it that it's looking at a dog, and then the next time the computer sees a dog it can remember and identify it without being told. Just the way a person would."

I was starting to see where he was going. "So show a computer a picture of a face . . ."

He nodded. "Exactly. It can be taught to recognize the next face. The technology is filtering down everywhere, from tagging photos on Facebook to autonomous vehicles. But Care4 has developed proprietary algorithms aimed directly at large-scale surveillance, offering its customers massive crowd-scanning capability. Let's say you're an NFL team and you want to know if anyone coming to your games isn't supposed to be there. Anyone from people on no-fly lists to the drunk guy who picks fights in the parking lot. Hook up a Care4 camera system, scan everyone walking in, and input photographs of the people you want to know about. The system flags them instantly and security grabs them. Easy as pie."

"How'd you learn this?" I wanted to know.

Charles smiled and scratched one of his thick eyebrows. He took pride in his work. "Not all that thrilling. If you want to learn what a company is up to, the first step is to look at who they want working for them. Investigative Journalism 101. I examined hiring ads across a half-dozen of the major job search engines, going back years through cached pages, called some headhunters for good measure." He was working his way through yet another cigarillo and I wrinkled my nose as the acrid smoke hit me. "A little over three years ago Care4 started aggressively hiring graduate-level computer scientists, Ph.D.s who specialize in AI and neural networks. Which is no different than plenty of the companies around here, except it made less sense for Care4 to want those types, given what they ostensibly do. I found that significant and looked closer."

"So besides sports teams, who buys that stuff? Airports? Police departments?"

"Sure. Or governments."

"For what, antiterrorism or something?"

"That was my first thought," he agreed.

"Okay. I understand why Gunn would lie about that if they're selling to foreign countries. Public image. But why lie about the IPO?"

Charles leaned forward. "Exactly. What's significant is not that he lied, but the nature of the lie. Gunn isn't worried about an employee ruining him by going public, because he has to know that will never happen."

"So what do they want?"

"As far as I can tell? Nothing. They seem happy to be churning out money and keeping a low profile. The last thing they want is to go public and have to hold quarterly earning calls and divulge who they do business with."

I was adding things up. "They probably never even wanted to go public."

"Which means three things. You're not dealing with some little start-up. Care4 is a global, well-established company that deals with rough, shadowy clients. And unlike every other company I've heard of, they're not peacocking, acting bigger and more successful than they actually are—they're pretending to be much smaller."

"Okay, that's one."

"Next. This woman you were tailing, Karen Li. If they weren't worried about her ruining an IPO, what were they actually scared of? What was she taking?"

"Charles, she—"

He wasn't finished. "Third. Maybe most important. A company that literally *makes* surveillance equipment. With contacts all over the world. Why would they come to you?" He looked intently at me, eyes serious. "You have to approach this woman you're following, Nikki, and find out why Care4 is so scared of her, and what she is trying to take."

"That's the problem."

"What do you mean, problem?"

"This woman. Karen Li. They got to her. She's dead."

27

I spent the night sleeping fitfully, wondering what Karen Li had hidden and how I could possibly figure out where it was in the next two weeks. It was starting to seem impossible. By early morning I had given up sleeping. I got dressed and headed for a taqueria down the block. If I was going to be awake thinking, coffee and breakfast might as well be involved. It wasn't quite a plan, but having made even this small decision felt better. Outside the air was warm, the sky clear.

They grabbed me on the sidewalk.

Two of them. One on each arm. Hard. Squeezing up close to me so I couldn't kick. Manhandling me toward a waiting black sedan. Someone inside the car shoved the rear passenger door open. They'd done this before. The whole thing took about five seconds.

Statistically speaking, the chances of surviving a kidnapping decreased dramatically as soon as you left public space. For instance, as soon as you were shoved into the backseat of a car. I waited until I was almost at the car door before I jerked my head sideways into the right-hand guy's chin. He swore loudly and spit blood. His teeth must have caught lip or tongue. That encouraged me. I gave his instep a hard kick and jerked my arm away, pivoting to my left and aiming a right hook at the man on my left. That didn't work as well. He rolled his shoulder up and caught the punch without releasing my arm. Then he got the other arm around my neck and pressed in with his full weight. He must have had at least fifty pounds on me. I poked for an eye but missed. By that time the first guy had stopped cursing and grabbed me again.

He crammed in on top of me, crushing me into the car, the one on the left already inside, pulling me by the neck. The choreography wouldn't have got them hired by the Bolshoi Theatre, but it was effective enough. They got me in the car.

The man to my right slammed the door shut.

The car accelerated.

I forced my body to relax. No point in wasting more energy. Not yet.

"You almost made me bite my tongue off!" The right-hand guy spit blood savagely onto the floor mat and added a few extra words that wouldn't have made it onto network television.

"You're talking just fine," I pointed out.

He swore again but I wasn't paying attention. Because I'd been able to take a look at my captors. I'd thought I was in a bad situation. It was actually worse. I was sitting in between the two men from Mendocino. The one on the left was heavily built, wearing the same leather jacket as he'd had in the San Francisco café. He had a ruddy face, short neck, and sandy hair. His mud-colored eyes watched me closely. The one on my right was thinner, with a Vandyke beard and sports coat. Both his hair and skin were the color of pumice. Both men had obvious holsters under their jackets.

I was seated in between the two men who had killed Karen Li.

They didn't seem concerned that I'd seen their faces.

When it came to kidnapping, that was another not-so-good sign.

The man in the leather jacket was rooting around in my purse. He found the Beretta first, then the collapsible baton, and my keychain with a little container of pepper spray clipped onto it. He tossed the purse onto the front passenger seat and said, "We gotta pat her."

The one on the right glared at me. "Don't try to stop us."

"Or?"

He shook his head impatiently. "So tough, aren't you?"

The man in the leather jacket ran his hands down my body. I forced myself to allow it. Not that I had much of a choice. He was thorough. Also, to his credit, not lecherous. He didn't shy away from feeling between my breasts, against my hips, and between my thighs, but he did it without pausing or groping or any of the million dirty tricks men did when patting a woman down. He found everything. The brass knuckles in my jacket pocket. The flat black leather sap I kept in my back pocket. The tiny .32 Derringer pistol in the ankle holster in my right boot.

The man in the leather jacket gave me a look. "Who are you looking to hurt, Nikki?"

I ignored the question. "You know my name. What do I call you?"

"You can call me Mr. Ruby."

The guy on my right chimed in. "You can call me Mr. Jade."

"How's your tongue, Mr. Jade?" I asked him.

He swore. I laughed. "Mr. Ruby. Mr. Jade. Sure, whatever. Where are we going?"

I could see we were headed south along the freeway, skirting the east side of the Bay. Still unable to let go of the thought that they hadn't bothered to blindfold me or wear masks or do any of the things people did to avoid being identified later on. Kidnappers essentially fell into one of two categories. Those who intended to release their victim. And those who didn't.

Mr. Ruby spoke. "Nikki, we're going to ask you some questions."

"What kind of questions?"

"The easy kind." He paused. "If you want to make them easy, of course."

"And if I don't?"

"Then they get harder."

I watched the landscape blur by. We were doing a safe, unspectacular seventy. In a boring black Buick driving in a middle lane. Not slow, not too fast. Impossible that we'd attract the attention of some idling Highway Patrol cruiser. "Maybe I like the hard way," I suggested.

Mr. Ruby gave me a slow, semi-interested look. "No, Nikki, you don't."

"And you know that how?" I was making conversation. Seeing what they'd say. It didn't really matter what we talked about.

"There are two types of people," he answered. "The people who know they don't like the hard way, and the people who think they do, but then realize they don't."

"How about Karen Li? She didn't seem like she liked the hard way. But she still got it."

Mr. Jade spoke, his words slightly slurred from his wounded tongue. "We're going to talk about Karen Li, I promise you."

I didn't reply. I could hurt one of them. Everything after that was up for grabs. The car was moving far too fast for me to jump out. Best-case scenario, I stunned the two of them long enough to get behind the driver. I could maybe get an arm around his throat, hit the wheel, or pull the emergency brake, and hope we didn't bang into anything too permanent. Worst-case scenario, one of them shot me. Or the car ran into a concrete divider or over a guardrail.

I decided to wait.

We took an Oakland exit and got onto the Webster Street Tube, a stretch of underwater tunnel connecting Oakland to Alameda Island. We emerged and drove down quiet paved streets, heading west. Alameda lay in between Oakland and San Francisco. It had been used by Pan Am and then later the navy; more recently, a handful of distilleries had sprung up on its western side, taking advantage of huge, deserted hangars that seemed as ideal for gin as they were for airplanes. The streets were empty. Row after row of drab, uniform government-built buildings. The military didn't have much interest in memorable architecture. The emptiness was striking, like we were driving through some abandoned movie set or plague-hit city.

The car stopped in front of a building that looked like all the others. Fading blue paint over concrete, like a police barracks in a state that had sharply cut its budget a few years back. Mr. Ruby said, "We're going to get out of the car and go inside, Nikki. I know you're calculating odds. There are three of us. Don't try anything."

I didn't reply. There was no point. Mr. Jade got out quickly, and Mr. Ruby started edging me over to the open door, pushing his bulk against me, forcing me sideways. I considered trying to get to the driver's seat, but the driver was turned watchfully toward me. Outside, Mr. Jade again took my right arm and Mr. Ruby my left. The driver walked ahead of us to unlock a plain metal door. Inside a pitch-black hallway he hit a switch and fluorescent lights came on. He unlocked another door, hit another light switch as we walked in. More fluorescents.

We were in a room that looked identical to an elementary school classroom. Sky blue paint, tile floor, even a blackboard and a big metal desk up front. Facing the desk were several rows of desk-chair units, the chairs molded from cheap orange plastic and welded to little pine desks that came around from the right-hand side. Being a lefty, I used to hate them even more for this. I turned to Mr. Ruby. "You're not going to make me take the SAT, are you?"

He didn't smile. "Sit down."

I looked around. Shrugged. Sat. Unlike in most classrooms, these desks were bolted to the floor. The chair was too small and my knees pressed uncomfortably against the underside. "If this is the hard way," I said, "you convinced me. How do third graders handle this torture?"

Mr. Ruby sat on the big metal desk. Mr. Jade stood off to one side. The driver leaned against the door. The three of them watching me.

I shifted in the chair, trying to get comfortable. "Which one of you killed Karen Li?"

They exchanged a look. Turned back to me, smiling.

"Are you crazy?" asked Mr. Ruby. "*We* didn't kill Karen Li."

He sounded like he meant it. "Then who did?" I challenged.

Mr. Jade laughed harshly and stepped closer, looming over the desk. His lip had started to swell up and he dabbed at it with a red-stained handkerchief. "Save the bullshit, Nikki. We didn't kill Karen Li. *You* did."

28

I stared at them. "What are you talking about?"

Mr. Ruby was walking toward me. Hand reaching under his leather jacket. I tensed. He took an object out of his pocket and put it on the desk in front of me.

The GPS tracker.

"We know this is yours," he said.

"And we know you were following her," added Mr. Jade. "We saw you in San Francisco."

"So you went back that night," I said, understanding. "To the cabin. You killed her and then you went back there—looking for me? Because of what I had seen?"

They exchanged another look. "Not exactly," Mr. Ruby said. He took something else from inside his jacket and placed it next to the tracker.

Suddenly, everything was very different.

I was looking at a gold badge topped with a gold eagle. Three letters across the front.

FBI.

"Bullshit," I said.

Mr. Ruby gave a humorless smile. "Who did you think we were?"

I tried to think what this changed, if I actually had two federal agents in front of me. I couldn't decide whether it made things better or worse than if they had been a couple of run-of-the-mill hit men. "Am I under arrest?"

"You should be," Mr. Jade said, rubbing his swollen lip. "Assaulting a federal agent."

I laughed. "You call that assault?"

"Easy, tiger," said Mr. Ruby. I thought again of the moment by the ocean in Mendocino. His hands on her shoulders as I sprinted toward them, trying to save her life.

"I saw what you were about to do to Karen," I said.

He was confused. "Do to her?"

"You were about to push her off a cliff."

Their reaction wasn't what I was expecting. They both broke into loud laughter. Even the driver started chuckling. Like some private joke everyone except me was sharing. "What?" I asked, annoyed. I didn't like feeling dumb.

"Push her into the ocean?" Mr. Ruby was still smiling. "You read too much pulp fiction, Nikki. I was comforting her. The woman was on the verge of a breakdown. She almost fainted."

"Bullshit," I said. "And don't talk to me about pulp fiction when the woman had her head knocked in that same day. What was she to you, anyway?"

The smiles left their faces. Mr. Jade sat on a desk in front of me, his long legs crossed. "Karen Li was going to be our star witness."

"What?"

"Forget that," said Mr. Ruby. "We brought you here to ask *you* questions." He waved the GPS tracker at me. "We have you in the same town as the deceased, on the same day. We know you were following her. We know you talked to her that afternoon. And we can put you at the scene of her death that night. Tell us, Nikki—why did you kill her?"

I thought about everything they'd said so far. Smart money said to pronounce one word, "lawyer," and then shut up. But they didn't seem like they were going after me with a full-court press. They were probing, not attacking. Wanting to see what I'd give away. Saying they could put me at the scene was different from telling me directly that I had been seen. Which probably meant I hadn't been.

I made up my mind. "I didn't kill Karen Li. But you know that already."

"Don't tell me what I know," Mr. Jade said, fingers twisting his goatee.

"I found her. We were supposed to meet at her cabin. I showed up at the time we agreed on. She was already dead. I took off."

Mr. Jade squinted skeptically. "You left her there? Didn't call an ambulance?"

I shook my head disdainfully. "Don't try to guilt-trip me. The woman was dead. As far as I knew, the people who did it were still in town."

"I don't buy it," Mr. Ruby said. "Why were you even there in the first place?"

I shifted my legs again under the desk. Cops were cops. Half clever, and half not. They'd set a nice hidden trap and then get so proud of it they'd build a monument a mile high to mark the spot. "You already know that. I was hired to follow her by the company she worked for, Care4."

Mr. Jade looked at me. "Why should we believe that?"

"Because you know it's true."

"Prove it."

"The last time I sat at a desk like this, I was in elementary school. I didn't like it then and I don't like it now. If you want to show some cards, I'll match. If not, book me or call me a cab."

They exchanged a look. "You want to play show-and-tell? Fine, you first," Mr. Ruby said.

I stood. "I'm getting a cramp. How'd you end up here, anyway, they slash your budget? Can't afford San Francisco?"

Mr. Ruby grunted. "Believe it or not, even the government tries to save money every now and then."

It was a relief to leave the cramped room and walk outside onto the street. We strolled along the potholed pavement, past rows of dilapidated buildings clad in the same faded blue paint. Across the water to the west was the San Francisco skyline. From the east spread the Oakland Port, high cranes silhouetted, shipping containers stacked into high walls.

"You got your walk," said Mr. Ruby. "So talk."

I told them most of it. Omitting only the parts involving Charles, Oliver, and Buster. When I finished I said, "Your turn. What was she taking, and what was she scared of?"

Mr. Ruby's face was drawn. "I'm not entirely sure we should share that."

"Cops," I said. "Always holding up their end of a bargain."

"It's an ongoing investigation."

"Fine," I said. "Don't go banging on my door if you think of any questions you forgot to ask. And I won't go banging on your door if I happen to think of anything I forgot to tell you."

Mr. Jade glared at me. "Withholding information from federal agents is a felony."

I glared back. "Go sit on your damn felony." I started heading off in the general direction of Oakland.

"Nikki!"

I kept walking. Not looking back.

"Come on, Nikki. Wait."

I stopped and turned to Mr. Ruby. "What?"

"You have to understand about Care4. You walked into quite the wasp nest."

"I didn't walk into anything," I answered. "The wasp nest walked into me."

"Karen Li wasn't selling tech secrets on the open market or whatever crap Gregg Gunn told you. She didn't care about that. Besides, she had enough money. The woman was very good at what she did and worked in an industry that throws more money at talent than the NBA."

"So what did she want?"

Mr. Jade joined in. "She found out about something."

"Don't be too specific."

"That's the problem—there's plenty to choose from. We believe Care4 has done all kinds of things wrong, everything from embargo violations to bribery. We've been building a case against them for some time."

"So Karen was helping you?"

"Not at first," said Mr. Ruby frankly. He scratched the side of his thick neck. "At first she refused, said she'd done nothing wrong, and that we should go find someone else and leave her out of it. Then, much more recently, she came back to us on her own. She had found out something new. Something worse—something bad enough that it changed her mind."

"What was it?"

"We're not sure, but it was urgent. Something extremely time sensitive. She had managed to hide some kind of evidence, but we have no idea what—could be anything from a warehouse full of gold bars to a single flash drive. We were supposed to meet her later in the week so she could give it to us."

"She didn't tell you anything else about what it was?"

People will die. Innocent people.

"Just a name. 'In Retentis.' Some kind of internal project. All we know is that it was enough to scare her, badly."

It was the second time that week I had heard the strange phrase. In Retentis. The subject line of the e-mail that, according to Karen, had set every-thing in motion. "Can't you find out what it means?"

Mr. Jade answered, absently braiding the hairs of his goatee. "It's not so easy. According to Karen, whatever is happening is being planned abroad. We don't have jurisdiction. We're trying to get subpoenas and search warrants, but we don't have enough solid evidence to take to the courts and start the process. Which is a disaster, given that she told us that whatever is going to happen will—"

He caught a glance from Mr. Ruby and stopped mid-sentence.

"Happen on November first," I finished. "So if we don't figure it out by then, it's too late."

They looked at me uncomfortably but said nothing. "Right?" I asked.

Their eyes met and Mr. Ruby gave a barely perceptible shrug.

"Right," agreed Mr. Jade. "She told you, too?"

"Yeah. So any guesses what it is?"

Mr. Ruby answered. "We know that the CEO, Gunn, has been traveling recently to all kinds of rough places."

"The kinds of places where bad guys sit around drinking strong coffee and planning how to get the next truck bomb into the next building," added Mr. Jade.

"Terrorism?" I had thought about it and was skeptical. "What benefit could it possibly be for an American tech company to help terrorists attack Westerners? What's the upside? Wouldn't that just instantly make them our government's public enemy number one?"

Mr. Jade nodded in agreement. "It's anyone's guess, but Silicon Valley is dead set on protecting client privacy at all costs. They're notorious for it. These companies are like the Swiss banks of the twenty-first century."

"We have to go through the courts just to open a goddamn iPhone," Mr. Ruby put in bitterly. "As though some AR-wielding nutjob who just mowed down an office full of innocents needs to be protected from the big bad FBI."

Mr. Jade wasn't done. "Our best guess is that Care4 had gotten hold of information about some kind of cell or strike, quite possibly unintentionally. Only they can't say anything or they lose the trust—and more importantly, the revenue—of their most lucrative clients. The Eastern Bloc pack, the oligarchs and Middle East petro-states, that crowd. No way those guys let Care4 do business in their countries if they think the company is passing any kind of info back to the States."

I was still unconvinced. "So someone at Care4 essentially decided that letting a handful of Westerners possibly die was preferable to taking a devastating financial hit?"

"That would be the thought process, yes. Factoring in the calculus that they'd never get caught for said decision and were not doing anything to actively aid and abet."

"And this bad thing, whatever it is, this attack, is going to happen on November first?"

"Everything we've learned so far is pointing strongly to that."

"Have you talked to other intelligence? CIA, NSA?"

Mr. Ruby nodded. "We've been in touch with our counterparts, sure. But there's always so much online chatter about pending attacks that it's almost impossible to say what's real and what isn't. If you're not exposed to the kind of information that we look at, it's hard to describe the flood that hits our desks daily. There's extremely credible evidence for a dozen different attacks to happen on any given day, every day, somewhere in the world. Most the public never hear about. Some fall apart on their own, some are stopped—and some happen."

"So where do you go from here?"

Mr. Jade looked glum. "Try to find someone else willing to talk. But Karen Li had unique access. Even under the best of circumstances she'd be hard to replace. By November first, impossible. That's less than two weeks from now. We don't know what kind of evidence she had. Whatever it was, there's no trace. We've checked everywhere."

I nodded absently. Thinking that "checked" could mean one of three things. Maybe Karen had been lying. Maybe Care4 had found and destroyed whatever it was.

Or maybe these two hadn't checked the right places.

The two men in front of me seemed competent. But they didn't seem wildly creative.

Mr. Ruby asked, "Can we count on you, Nikki? To help us if you learn more?"

I rolled my eyes. "Sure, I'll be your man in Havana. Graham Greene would love this."

"It's not funny." This from Mr. Jade again. "We got to you today. Which means other people can, too."

29

"I need your help," I told Jess.

"Sure, gimme a sec." She was finishing with one of our regular customers, Lennis. He was an old man in a blue flannel shirt, jaw roughened with white stubble like moss over bark. He came in about every other week to clean out our science-fiction section and swipe pours of bourbon. He saw me and winked, mug in one hand and a stack of worn paperbacks cradled under his arm. "Great coffee you serve here."

"Aren't you supposed to wait until after lunch?"

He grinned. "After lunch it might not be free."

Jess rang him up while I hung a CLOSED sign on the door. "What's up?" Jess asked when we were alone in the store.

"Remember that man who came to the bookstore when we were closing the other week? The one with the briefcase who you sent upstairs?"

She thought for a second and nodded. "Yeah, vaguely. Something happened to him?"

"Not exactly. He hired me to follow an employee of his, a woman named Karen Li. So I did. Now she's dead."

"Oh my God, dead? Like, murdered? What happened? Who did it?"

"I don't know." Saying it made me see it. The cabin. That broken window. That broken body. The cracked pane of glass somehow suggesting all of the futility and desperation about the whole thing. I forced the memories out of my mind. "She hid something that she wanted me to know about. I need to figure out what it was."

"And you're going to find out how . . . ?"

I placed a stack of paper on the desk between us. Jess looked from me to the papers and back. "Don't tell me Ethan's making you edit his dissertation?"

"Printouts of locations. From the GPS tracker I put on her car. Everywhere she went recently. That's how we're going to find whatever she hid."

"What if it happened before you started following her?"

I thought about the look on Karen's face. The fear. "I don't think so. It was close to the end. After she was scared by whatever it was she found. If she hid something it won't be too obvious. She suspected people were watching her. But also somewhere she could get to it again."

"And you know this how?"

"I don't *know*. Not for sure. But it's all we have."

"Okay." Jess shrugged. "Tell me where to start."

Each paper was a printout showing a time-stamped location. I started going through the stack one by one, reading out the addresses. Jess had her laptop open to Google Maps. She looked up each address as I read it off, skipping the repeats. As we worked, Karen Li's life began to coalesce with haunting accuracy. Most people stuck to routines. Karen was no different. We put all the repeats in one pile. The Care4 office, her home. I'd been by there already. A bland townhouse in San Jose, surrounded by rows of identical homes. A new development, probably built within the last few years. I hadn't even bothered to try to get in. By this point the police would have been inside. Probably other people, too. Now it would just be her family. The long, sad task of retrieving possessions that were no longer needed. Going through books and silverware, jeans and underwear and shoes, paintings and souvenirs, making those hopeless and meaningless decisions. What to give to charity, what to throw away, what to keep.

I shut my eyes, again seeing the cabin.

"Her poor parents," Jess said, as if reading my mind. "Can you imagine?"

"I don't think they're alive," I said, remembering the family photo clenched in her hand.

"The poor woman."

"Let's keep going," I said. "We have a lot to get through."

Other addresses came up frequently enough that we put them in a second pile. Several restaurants, a Starbucks and a wine bar, both near where she lived. I pictured her at the bar. Sitting alone, a glass in front of her, maybe with a laptop open. Probably having a second glass but not a third. We kept at it. Moment by moment, her life rewound. A fitness club. A yoga studio. Normal places for an energetic, successful woman in her midthirties. All the things people did and places they went when they were alive.

In the third category went the addresses that came up less frequently but didn't seem out of step with routine. Restaurants and bars, a spa at a fancy hotel, a few different apartment buildings that I assumed were addresses of friends. A location a dozen miles south of San Francisco, just off the Bay, that turned out to be a rental car facility serving the San Francisco Airport. A Kaiser hospital, an AMC movie theater, a nail salon. A nonprofit in San Francisco called Tiananmen Lives, various stores and parking garages, and a handful of random addresses that looked to be street parking.

The stack of papers in front of us steadily diminished.

There was a fourth category: addresses that actually meant something. Potential hiding places. Except we got through the printouts without putting anything there. "Now what?" Jess sounded exhausted.

I pushed my chair back from the counter and rubbed my eyes. "Lunch."

We ate at a little Mediterranean place up the block from the bookstore, taking gyro wraps and fries and salads on plastic trays to a table. "Here I was thinking you were running around being exciting," Jess said. "If this is how you spend your spare time, I'll stick with the bookstore. I have more fun reading Gogol than Google." She took a bite of her gyro, holding it carefully so that the juice leaked downward into the foil wrapper. "Also, what if she walked somewhere? She could have ditched the car entirely."

"You don't spend enough time in the South Bay," I said. "Nobody ditches their car. They can't. It's worse than LA."

"How can anything be worse than LA?"

"LA has a subway."

"Okay, fine. But how do you look for something if you don't know what it is? You said the fourth pile would be the key. So how do you find something that isn't there?"

"It's there," I said. "We just have to know how to look."

"You mean *where* to look?"

I wiped my chin with a napkin and finished chewing. "When I was a kid my family went to a Seder every year, hosted by a Russian couple, Mr. and Mrs. Berkovich. They managed to get out of the USSR in the seventies and wound up in Bolinas. They always said they wanted the exact opposite of Moscow, and Bolinas was the closest they could find."

"Soviets—so did they teach you spycraft or something?"

I laughed. "God, no. They would have made terrible spies. He was a painter and she taught piano. But the Seder. Everything is ritual, the whole meal. Early on, Mr. Berkovich would break a piece of matzah in half. He'd wrap half in a napkin and then sneak away from the table to hide it. The afikoman, it's called. Then later on, us kids would try to find it, and we'd get a reward if we did."

Jess interjected. "I grew up in SoCal. I've probably been to more Seders than Moses. But this applies how . . . ?"

"The rule was that it always had to be hidden in plain sight. Just a matter of *looking.*"

"Let me guess who found it each year."

I smiled. "Not trying to boast. But if Karen Li hid something, it's there for us to see."

"Talk about a needle in a haystack."

I thought about Mr. Berkovich. "It's not, though. What we're looking for was hidden by a person. A needle in a haystack is a random occurrence. But finding something hidden is the opposite of random. Because *people* hide things. And people can't hide things randomly no matter how hard they try. There's always a decision process. Choosing, eliminating, choosing. It's like coming up with an e-mail password. The security experts always say make it totally random, just a jumble of letters and numbers. But no one actually listens. We're people. Coming up with something truly random is unnatural. Finding something is just about figuring out how the person doing the hiding thinks."

"So what do we do?"

"We narrow it down. One: it has to be a place where she could physically hide something. In Mendocino she told me it wasn't with her."

"Okay, what else?"

"Two: she was scared. She had to assume they would check the obvious places. Three: she had to be able to get to it again. So, accessible on relatively short notice. Not halfway across the world or in a time-locked bank vault. And four: she had to make sure that someone else wouldn't accidentally find it in the meantime."

Jess thought. "Maybe that Starbucks or the wine bar she liked?"

"Possible, but I don't think so. Food service is tricky. Too many staff members constantly doing inventory, cleaning, moving around. I don't see how a customer could hide something and be confident a busboy or barista wouldn't run into it."

"The movie theater, maybe? Under a seat or something?"

"That's how we should be thinking, but not a movie theater. She wouldn't chance it. Again, too easy for a janitor or employee to accidentally come across it."

"What if she got on a plane and stashed it thousands of miles away? She went to the airport, remember?"

"She needed it to be accessible."

"How about a friend's house? Someone she trusted."

"She was too scared. She wouldn't have risked getting someone she cared about wrapped up with Care4."

"But how do you hide—" Jess pushed her tray away in excitement. "The hotel and spa that she went to. A spa is perfect. Lockers, cubbyholes, privacy, all kinds of hiding places. And single gender. Harder for the Care4 goons to go in looking."

I thought about the idea. "Where was it again?"

"The Ritz-Carlton, in Half Moon Bay. We went once for our anniversary. I think I'm still paying off that credit card."

I thought about Buster. He'd laugh. I was going to the Ritz after all.

30

Like many coastal towns, at some point Half Moon Bay had traded fishing for tourism as its major source of revenue. The hotel was a massive stone and beige palace on manicured green grounds and golf courses, set high above the ocean. It looked like a place where Henry James would have happily placed one of his European scenes. We were in Jess's old black BMW convertible. It was a stick shift and she drove aggressively, top down, the heater running to compensate for the foggy coastal air.

After parking, we followed signs to the spa. "Do you have an appointment?" asked one of the receptionists, a pretty college-age girl with a perfect smile and a perfect manicure.

I shook my head. "Referred by a friend. We were hoping to talk to her masseuse."

"We love our referrals!" said the receptionist. "Do you know the name?"

"No. But my friend was Karen Li. L-I."

She typed into her system. "She had Kaitlyn." She clicked around more. "Kaitlyn is totally booked today, but can I schedule you with someone else? Everyone's amazing."

"Is it okay if we just meet her quickly?"

"I think she's in between appointments right now. Let me check."

We waited. I flipped through a home decoration magazine showing perfect outdoor firepits and pools lined with geometric rows of beach chairs, wishing that waiting rooms like this one could be bothered to stock a few paperbacks along with the magazines. Then again, with smart-phones everywhere, even finding a *Reader's Digest* wasn't guaranteed any-more.

The receptionist came out with a tall blond woman who smiled, reveal-ing whitened teeth. "Hey guys! I'm Kaitlyn."

We introduced ourselves. "Our friend loved you," Jess said. "Karen Li."

"Pretty Asian woman, late thirties, looked younger," I added.

Kaitlyn laughed. "You totally described about half my clients."

I gave a more detailed description and her face pinched in thought. "I thiiiink I remember her." She paused, trying to be helpful. "I think she did the Pearlescence Facial. Maybe? Anyway, I gotta run!"

She vanished into the door she'd come out of. "Now what?" Jess asked.

"We're here. Might as well look around. They must sell day passes."

In the locker room, we changed into comfortable bathrobes and slippers at one of the lockers. It was a weekday afternoon and the locker room was almost empty. Soft music played and the lighting was dim and generous. The lockers were stacks of empty cubes set against the walls. Multiple signs warned that they were emptied nightly. No way something was hidden in one of them long term. The rest of the room would have been equally difficult to hide something in. The counters were sterile, the only objects hair dryers and jars of Q-tips and facial lotion. Even as I watched, a cleaner came through to empty the used towel bin. I thought briefly of the laundry room but wrote it off. The laundry room probably handled the hotel as well as the spa. Cheaper than running two separate facilities. Meaning it would be going twenty-four hours a day, staffed constantly, maids in and out. Whatever we were looking for wouldn't be there.

We found our way through an opaque glass door to a smaller room with an emerald hot tub set into the floor. Candles glowed from crannies in the walls and Eastern instrumental music played. I hit a button on the wall and the jets came to life. The water frothed appealingly. "Might as well," I said. "We paid for the damn day passes."

We left our bathrobes on a teak bench and got in. The bubbling water felt good. I leaned back into a jet, feeling it pulse against the center of my back. "Maybe she put it somewhere in the hotel," Jess suggested. "But I don't know where we'd start."

I shook my head, thinking of the laundry room. "Too many employees everywhere, cleaning. It's impossible to hide anything because the whole point is to make each person feel like they're the first ones to ever arrive."

Jess sank lower in the water until the bottom of her chin brushed the surface. "How are we supposed to find this thing if we literally don't have a clue?"

I thought again about those childhood afikoman searches through the Berkoviches' house. "We're looking, but we're not *seeing*. Spas, movie theaters, restaurants—those are just places she went. They don't mean anything. We could spend a year looking that way. Like digging random holes in the ground to see if we strike oil."

Jess blew an exasperated mouthful of water. "Sorry, I don't get it. We thought about everywhere she went—everywhere she drove, at least. This is why I run a bookstore and don't solve cold cases, Nikki. I thought my spa idea was genius. After that I got nothing."

"It wasn't a bad idea," I said. Jess had been right about the Seder. I had always been the one to find the carefully folded napkin every year. It drove the older boys crazy. They couldn't figure out why a little girl always beat them to it. It wasn't coincidence. While they ran around straining adolescent muscles to lift up the couch or checking the sleeves of the record collection, I'd stood thinking. Not looking for hiding places that I'd choose, but places that Mr. Berkovich would pick. That was the difference. Adding up both the physical and nonphysical characteristics I had observed in him over the years: a mischievous, playful side; fairly short; deliberate by nature; a bad knee that made him less likely to bend low; very proud of his creativity. Adding up those things told me a lot about where he might hide something. Everything there to see, so long as I *looked*. Each year the hiding places got tougher as Mr. Berkovich became more determined to stump me.

I always figured them out. Because I knew how to look.

Like now. The answer lay somewhere in the papers we'd gone through, somewhere in Karen Li's life. And her life had been here. She hadn't gotten on a plane and deposited it thousands of miles away. I was certain. Yet Jess was right. *We thought about everywhere she went. Everywhere she drove, at least.* We had considered everything.

Where she drove.

Drove.

And then I knew.

"The airport," I said.

Jess was surprised. "The airport? I thought you said she didn't take it on a plane."

I was thinking about the pages of timestamped locations we had pored through. "Not the airport, exactly."

"Then where?"

"She went to the rental car center next to the airport."

"Nikki. Not sure how long it's been since you got on a plane? That's kind of how things work. Take a flight, rent a car—what's weird about that?"

"Exactly," I agreed. "Take a flight, rent a car. Normal. But Karen Li didn't get off a plane in some other city and rent a car. She rented a car *here*."

"So?"

"She had a car. Why rent one?"

"Maybe her car broke down?"

"The woman drove a brand-new Porsche. The dealership would've given her a loaner. And besides, if the car *had* broken down I bet anything it was still under warranty, so the last address the tracker would show would be the dealership service center, or at least a mechanic. But she never brought it anywhere for service."

"So what does that mean? If she didn't want her car for some reason, why *not* just bring it into the dealership for some made-up reason and get a loaner? Or rent one in San Jose, where she lived? Why bother going through the inconvenience of renting from the airport?"

I nodded. "Exactly. The airport is the last place you rent a car if you have a choice, because it's not only out of the way, it's always the most expensive. Have you ever looked at one of those mile-long receipts, a dozen different fees and surcharges? Travelers don't have the luxury of choosing. They're rushed, they don't know the area, so they pick the nearest option. Meaning the airport. Maximum convenience. But anyone needing to rent a car in their home city would go anywhere *except* an airport. Why would Karen Li rent a car *here*?"

"I don't get it, then. Why?"

"For the same reason we missed it. We overlooked it just the way she planned. Maybe she thought she was being followed. Maybe she even suspected her car was on someone's radar. She was scared. Rent a car out of the blue and it draws suspicion. People wonder why. But park at an airport, visit a rental car center? No one thinks twice. Those two actions fit together. Like getting popcorn at a movie theater. We don't notice things that seem to add up. We notice things that don't."

I was already getting out of the water, reaching for my robe. "Her car was at SFO for a day. But nothing says she even got on a plane. Karen Li didn't go to the airport to fly somewhere. She went for cover."

31

At San Francisco Airport we followed signs to the rental car facility. Different car companies were arrayed in a line of desks: Avis, Enterprise, National, Hertz, Budget, Dollar. It was busy. Lines in front of every desk. Travelers, most looking frazzled or sleepy. People wanted very different things out of life, but they united around certain commonalities. For instance, no one wanted to be standing in line at a rental car center. Didn't matter who you were.

"How do we know which one?" Jess asked.

I had thought about this. I remembered Karen pulling the Narwhal's card out of her wallet. The colored edges of the credit and membership cards. The strip of yellow. "Hertz," I said. "That's the one." We skipped the front desks and lines, instead heading for the elevator. I pushed the button for the Hertz floor and we rose smoothly.

"What are we going to do?"

"Now we try plan A," I said.

"What's plan A?"

"I am."

"And what if plan A doesn't work?"

"Then it gets more complicated."

I walked into the garage alone, weaving through rows of spotlessly washed cars until I found a Hertz employee near a little booth that was set up like a makeshift office with a desk and computer and phone. The main rental desk would be downstairs, but up here was this outpost to ensure that frequent travelers and rewards members could get their cars with a minimum of hassle. The Hertz kid looked like he was just out of college. He wore a white button-down and a red tie that had the paradoxical effect of making him look younger rather than older. The knot on the tie was off a little. It was cute. I wanted to adjust it for him. Instead I silently apologized for how much of a bitch I was about to be. "My friend recently rented a car here and forgot something important in it. I need to pick it up for her."

He looked uncertain. "Is she with you?"

"No. I have her name."

"I'm not sure if I'm allowed to do that."

I smiled at him. "Where I come from, not sure usually rounds to yes."

He rubbed his nose uncomfortably. "We really can't confirm or deny customer information. They tell us that pretty much the first day we start training."

"It's important," I insisted.

"I'm not sure," he said again. His voice was hesitant.

Feeling guiltier, I added pressure. "I don't have time to come back."

The pressure had been a mistake, I saw at once. He bit his lip and tugged on his name tag uneasily as he edged away. "I should get a manager."

I had nothing else to do, so I stood there watching the cars. A tall Indian man was trying to decide between a red Ford Fusion and a black Hyundai. A family dragged suitcases toward a beige minivan. An annoyed-looking businessman in a rumpled suit and scuffed wingtips headed toward a Chrysler sedan. Meanwhile other cars were lining up behind traffic cones for the return. People getting out, attendants moving down the line swiping handheld electronic readers over the vehicles. I wondered how many cars this place rented each day. Hundreds, at least. Seven days a week.

The kid was back, accompanied by an older woman. She wasn't so cute. She had fraying, bleached hair and a set line of mouth framed with pink lipstick. She smelled like her last cigarette break had been about five minutes ago and looked like she'd been ready for the next one since getting out of bed. Her feet were squashed into stubby black pumps and her legs were stockinged. She didn't even bother to play nice. "I understand your friend thinks she forgot something in one of our vehicles?"

I nodded. "Karin Li, L-I. She rented a car here between one and two weeks ago, I can get the exact date if you need it. She's out of town so she asked me to check for her."

"Your friend's not with you?"

"No."

"We don't give out customer information, ever. Tell your friend to call us or come in and we're happy to help."

Nice clearly wasn't going to cut it. I tried to look like the type of woman who billed six hundred dollars hourly. "I didn't come here to waste my time. This is urgent."

"So what are you looking for? Describe it and we'll check." She was tough. She could have pulled off the pumps and hit the beach at Normandy. The kid's head was going back and forth, watching our exchange like a tennis match.

The question was the one I'd been hoping she wouldn't ask. I had no idea what I was looking for. "It's private," I insisted, adding, "I wouldn't want you to get into trouble."

She didn't even blink. "Lady, I haven't been in trouble since the early eighties. Let's not worry about me. No dice, good luck, and if you don't plan to rent a car, the door's right over there." She was walking away before she finished the sentence.

I took the elevator back down. There was a bus stop with a bench down the street from the rental car facility. I sat on the bench and watched planes slide up and down from the sky.

Parking shuttles seemed to stop at the bus stop every eight minutes. I counted three of them, with a fourth in sight, when a silver Range Rover pulled up to the curb. The other two people waiting at the bus stop watched me jealously as I got off the bench and climbed in. I relaxed into the comfortable seat. Whoever had built the thing had ordered extra scoops of leather with generous sides of sleek aluminum trim and wood accents. It rode smoothly, the engine quiet. Beyond that I didn't have much of an opinion. I'd always liked to hear my engines.

"Plan B," I said.

"Plan B," Jess agreed from the driver's seat.

"How did it go?"

Not taking her eyes off the road, she smiled proudly. "Just like you said. After you left, the first thing she did was go over to a computer and then to this car. She tore through it with that kid for at least ten minutes."

"They didn't find anything?"

"Nope. Then I waited a bit, walked up, and did my best Valley girl voice. *'Oh my god, I love that Range Rover! My boyfriend has an orange one just like it!'*"

I winced. "I'm okay with missing that part."

She took a ramp onto the freeway. "So this is what Karen Li rented?"

"I'd bet anything," I said. "After my little scene, there was no way the manager wasn't going to at least check and make sure no one had dropped a diamond ring behind the seat."

"It was in this special Prestige row, over three hundred dollars daily."

"That was smart of Karen," I said. "I was watching the pace of the rentals while I waited. The regular cars are going in and out constantly, but nobody went near the Mercedes or Range Rovers in that row. Way more car than most people need for a family vacation or business rental. The more expensive the car, the less likely someone rents it."

Jess nodded, understanding. "So the better the chance it's sitting right there when Karen was ready to go back for it."

"Exactly."

"Now what?"

"Now we look."

A few exits down, we got off the freeway and followed signs to a Home Depot. We drove to the back of the big parking lot. A few Hispanic men leaned against a wall, watching us hopefully. I wasn't worried about drawing attention. They were day laborers. Almost definitely undocumented. Groups like this congregated at Home Depots all over California. Work was their only concern. Work, and not attracting the attention of law enforcement. We could have set our SUV on fire and they wouldn't have called the cops.

We went through the Range Rover from end to end. I barely bothered to check the obvious places. We ignored the glove compartment and center console after a cursory look. Whatever Karen Li had wanted to hide, it wasn't going to be anywhere a cleaning crew or customer would accidentally find it. We spent about a half hour going through every part of the vehicle, inside and out.

Nothing.

Jess stepped back in frustration. "Remind me again how we know there's even something here?"

"It's here," I said, trying to sound confident. Maybe there was a perfectly good reason to rent a car for a day. Or maybe this wasn't the car. Or maybe Care4 had found whatever Karen had hidden and they were letting me chase my tail. So many possibilities. I was thinking again of Mr. Berkovich. Not what was hidden but who had hidden it. Karen Li. I added up what I knew. She wasn't a drug smuggler. She wasn't going to chainsaw a fake compartment into the trunk or solder hollow metal tubing onto the chassis. And it was a rental. She couldn't go cutting the seats up or drilling into the door panels. But, more importantly, she was a computer scientist. A software engineer, not hardware. An electrical or mechanical engineer might pride himself on his mastery of the physical world. He might take great pains to create a hiding place that would put a smuggler's best idea to shame. As much out of intellectual pride as a desire to conceal. Taken to an extreme, a mechanical engineer might end up caring less about what he was hiding and more about how well he was hiding it. Like greyhounds chasing a rail-mounted wind sock around a track.

But not Karen. She wouldn't try to switch out one of the tires or build a compartment between the interior ceiling and the roof. That wasn't how she thought. Not how she'd hide something. Her greatest creativity had been exercised outside of the physical world. Besides, code was complicated enough. I'd been around software engineers enough to know that they didn't seek out needless complexity. To them, that was inefficiency. Nothing drove them crazy like having to untangle extra lines of code that didn't need to be there. From that first Java course, they were trained to look for the simplest solution that worked.

Karen was smart. Resourceful. And she had gone through the trouble to rent a car she didn't need at an airport she hadn't flown into. She would have been aware that a rental car wasn't exactly private property. A driver might run over a nail. Maybe a kid would drop a soda onto the backseat. Something could happen necessitating a mechanic or detailing. She needed a hiding place accessible but not accidentally accessible. Invisible but basically in plain sight.

I borrowed Jess's phone, turned the light on, and got down on the ground to check every square inch of the chassis. I rechecked the tires and doors and trunk and the backsides of the accelerator and brake pedals and between the sunroof glass. I popped the hood to check the windshield wiper fluid.

Nothing.

"That's it, then," Jess said. "Unless she dropped it in the gas tank."

I shook my head. "It would corrode, or be discovered."

"So what do we do?"

"I'm not sure."

One of the day laborers approached. He wore a workman's belt with a hammer and wrench hanging off. "Do you need any help, miss? Is your car broken?"

"No, thanks," Jess said. "We're okay."

"Sure," he said. "Let me know if you need help."

Jess laughed as he walked away. "If only he knew."

I watched the man walk back toward his friends, his tools swinging against his narrow hips. Jess was right. We did need help. Just not the kind of help he was thinking of. We didn't have a flat tire or overheated radiator. Nothing that needed a tool kit or auto expertise. Because Karen Li hadn't been a mechanical engineer. She wouldn't have approached the problem with a carbide-grade cutting wheel or a 5000°F oxyacetylene welding torch and a desire to create the world's best hiding spot. Chances were, she had been like 99 percent of the population, comfortable with little more than a hammer or screwdriver.

I thought of something. "Wait a second," I called out. "Do you have a screwdriver?"

The man looked back, puzzled. "A screwdriver? Sure."

I fumbled in my jeans and came out with a twenty. "Let me borrow it."

The man looked at me suspiciously. "You'll give it back?"

"Five minutes."

It was probably the easiest money he had ever made. He handed over the screwdriver and walked back to his friends. They leaned against the wall and watched us.

"What was that about?" Jess wondered.

I kneeled down in front of the Range Rover and unscrewed the license plate. I pulled the thin metal rectangle away, thinking again of Mr. Berkovich and his flat, folded napkins.

Nothing.

I screwed the plate back on. Went to the rear bumper and did the same, prying the thin metal outward.

There was a white envelope flush against the black plastic of the license plate holder.

"Holy shit," Jess said. "You were right."

I reattached the plate and gave the guy back his screwdriver before we got back into the Range Rover. The white envelope had been wrapped in tight layers of plastic wrap. Waterproofing. Clever. Rental cars were washed constantly with high-pressure jets. I unpeeled the crinkled layers of plastic wrap and opened the envelope carefully. There was a stack of papers inside. Print-outs done with a high-quality color printer. On each page was a photograph.

Faces.

The faces, both men's and women's, had been captured in everyday actions by what seemed a mix of security cameras and distance lenses. Most seemed on the younger side, somewhere between their twenties and forties. Nothing seemed to connect one face to the next. A range of ethnicities: white, black, South American, Middle Eastern. About thirty of them. A tall, bearded man wearing a backpack and sunglasses. A Slavic woman in her twenties, full lips and blue eyes, getting off a bus, face set watchfully. A man with a missing front tooth, sipping espresso at a sidewalk café. A college-age kid with a wispy mustache wearing aviators and a T-shirt. We flipped through more pictures. I could make out a few words in the background, signs for stores and streets and brands. Arabic, Cyrillic, and English, mostly.

"Who are they?"

We looked through more of the pictures. "I'm not sure."

"The pictures look like law enforcement surveillance," said Jess. "Could they be terrorists or criminals, you think? Like different cells? What do you think they're planning?"

"I don't know." I checked the envelope once more and stopped, seeing ink on the inside. I pulled it apart. Two words: IN RETENTIS. Whatever e-mail Karen had gotten, whatever the FBI men had been looking for, I was holding it.

People will die. Innocent people.

Under the words were three numbers. 11/1.

A date less than one week away.

A milestone they've spent years trying to reach . . . and they're almost there.

"Latin," Jess said. "Which I dropped sophomore year of high school. What's it mean?"

"*In retentis.* A legal term. Documents held back from a court's regular records."

Jess's voice was uneasy. "Nikki. If they're planning some kind of strike, you have to take these to the police. If a bomb goes off we'd both be complicit."

"I know."

Her voice grew still more uneasy. "If Karen Li knew about this, and if the people in these pictures found out that she knew . . ."

Again, I was silent. Again, I had been thinking the same thing.

"How do you find out for sure? Can you get to anyone else at the company?"

I thought. "There might be someone I can reach."

32

I hadn't seen Oliver since the day he'd pulled up to me at the gym to show me Gunn's flight itineraries. The strange little man's precautions while setting up our meeting were so elaborate that they might have been funny. Except Karen Li was dead. That made them not funny. I couldn't blame him for being careful. I had thought about telling Mr. Jade and Mr. Ruby about both Oliver and the photographs, but something held me back. Part of it was that I trusted them about as much as I would any pair of strange men who had thrown me into the backseat of a car by way of a handshake. The fact that they were FBI agents didn't do much to tip the scales, either. Law enforcement types were notorious for pursuing their own ends, which sometimes happened to parallel those of the people they dealt with, and sometimes did not. Our goals regarding Care4 might seem to align, but I wanted to learn more for myself before I shared. More importantly, they had let their star witness be murdered almost under their noses. Whether that was bad luck, indifference, or incompetence didn't matter all that much. If Oliver learned I was working with them, that would be the end of that relationship, and the whole company might be spooked into lockdown.

There was another part, under the logic. I'd gotten used to relying on myself in life.

I'd fill in the FBI when I was good and ready, and not before.

Following Oliver's instructions, I took a train to the San Francisco Ferry Building, getting there at one in the afternoon. The Ferry Building was a grand, rectangular building done in the Beaux Arts style, the exterior composed of a double series of arches, three large central arches supporting a clock tower rising hundreds of feet above the water. In front was a palm-filled plaza; behind, the water, the titular ferries cutting around the Bay.

I found a seat at the Hog Island Oyster Bar and, according to instructions, waited. It was a good place to wait. I ordered a dozen oysters and drank a draft pint and watched the oyster shuckers. There were two of them. One seemed to shuck at a steady three-oysters-per-minute rate. The other was faster. His technique seemed better. More fluid. He didn't waste a motion. He seemed to get about four oysters a minute. He worked the oyster knife with small, easy gestures, flipping each full shell onto the bed of display ice and the empty shells into a trash can under the bar.

An hour went by. More than four hundred oysters shucked, sold, and served.

A waitress came over and handed me a paper. "Your friend said you forgot this."

I took the paper. It was a ferry schedule. Dense rows of locations and departure and arrival times. A single line was circled in blue ballpoint pen. A 2:05 departure to Sausalito, across the Bay. I checked my watch. 1:59. I had to hurry.

I was the last one to board, hurrying onto the walkway as the engines powered up. Onboard, the ferry had three levels. The bottom, where I had boarded, was indoors, with a small bar at one end. The bar was crowded. Sea voyages seemed to inspire people to drink. A ferry across the Bay wasn't a steamship crossing the Pacific, but the water was salty enough and we were floating. The essentials were there. I bought a coffee and walked upstairs to the middle level, feeling the engines thrum through the deck as we eased out. People sat on benches and milled around. Easy to pick out the tourists from the locals. Only a question of who was taking the pictures. It was a bright, windy day and the water surged with whitecaps. Behind us the wake frothed. I walked up to the top level. It was much windier up there. Fewer people. Most of the benches empty.

I found him leaning against the railing, watching San Francisco recede. I remembered the thin face, that mix of intelligence and caution. He wore a scarlet windbreaker emblazoned with the Stanford tree logo and the usual socks and sandals combination, a blue Clipper card visible in his pocket. One of the Bay Area all-purpose transportation passes, good for busses, trains, and ferries. "Hey, Oliver," I greeted him. "You picked a nice day for a boat ride."

"Did anyone follow you?" he wanted to know.

"No."

"You're sure?"

"Reasonably."

His mouth tightened and he glanced around. "That's hardly reassuring."

"How'd you choose Oliver?" I asked. "Out of all the names. You a Dickens fan, too?"

"What?"

"You know, *Oliver Twist*."

He gave me an uncomfortable look. "I don't understand."

I put my elbows on the railing and watched the water. "I always used to think it was just a brilliant name. Oliver Twist. Then I realized it's actually a Cockney accent, asking, 'Olive 'er twist? Olive or twist?' One of the most famous names in literature, just a bartender asking about a drink. It always made me wonder. Were martinis around back then and, if so, how did Dickens take them?"

He shook his head and peeled an orange that he had taken from his pocket. "I don't read Dickens and I don't drink. So I don't see how that applies to me."

"Careful," I warned. "You're starting to sound like you have too much fun."

He angrily threw a piece of orange peel over the side. I watched the peel until it became invisible against the water. "Spare me your jokes, okay? A woman I work with—*worked* with—is dead. *Dead*. For doing pretty much what I'm doing. Talking to people I shouldn't be talking to, about things I shouldn't be talking about. Go find someone else if you want to crack jokes. I shouldn't even be here. I should be as far away from you as I can get."

He had a point. "Sorry. You're right. No more jokes." I drank some coffee. The hot liquid felt good against the breeze. "So tell me, what *shouldn't* we be talking about?"

"Everything."

"That might limit the conversation."

"I shouldn't be here," he said again. "They killed her."

"Who killed her?"

His face was pinched and fearful. "How am I supposed to know? There were rumors that the company was investigating employees, and then she turns up dead. They sent an e-mail—that's all she was worth in the end.

We are deeply sorry to inform you that a beloved colleague passed away . . ." He rubbed his eyes with the heels of his palms. "I can't believe I'm here."

"So why are you?"

"If there's a right side and a wrong side, I want to be on the right side."

"Then tell me about In Retentis."

I had thrown the words at him like a fastball. His eyes widened and his gaze shifted to my left for a split second. Then his features were back to normal. "In what?"

"You know," I said. "Or you don't know. I'm tired of guessing. If you know, tell me. If not, I don't know why we're talking, because that means I know more than you do, and don't need you to tell me anything."

His eyes were wary. "You first. What do you know about it?"

I pulled a photograph from my jacket and put it on the railing between us. I had to keep my finger pressed tightly down to prevent the picture from blowing away like the orange peel. A Middle Eastern woman with a set, determined jaw and large sunglasses. I slapped down another like I was dealing blackjack. A young, dark-skinned man, photographed walking out of a café, coffee in one hand, wearing jeans and a soccer jersey. I put down a third. A fourth, a fifth. "That's what I know."

His eyes were focused intently on the photographs. I took another look at his Clipper card, the upper edge jutting out of the small side pocket of his jeans. Easy to reach when rushing through a turnstile with people crowding from behind. No one wanted to be the person fumbling in a wallet and holding up the line. He was still staring at the pictures. I let one of my hands fall from the railing toward his pocket. There was a huge cargo ship stacked high with rust-colored containers, working its way toward us on the other side of the bridge, Chinese lettering on the side. I wondered what the cargo was.

Oliver pushed the photographs back to me. "I've only heard vague rumors."

"I'll never consider myself too good for cheap whiskey or vague rumors."

As usual, he didn't laugh. "The company became unintentionally involved with something big. Our networks were linked to so many cameras, we were collecting so much data, so much raw footage, all over the world. In hindsight, they should have realized that at some point certain parties would approach us, wanting to use what we had collected in ways we hadn't anticipated."

"Parties?"

He shook his head in distaste. "You're making me spell it out? I thought you were some kind of detective. Foreign governments, or affiliated agencies."

"Affiliated agencies . . . you mean security services? Counterterrorism?"

He nodded.

"And Karen Li was involved in this? She had been working on In Retentis, right?"

He shook his head emphatically. "She found out accidentally."

I relaxed a little. He was telling the truth, at least here.

"How did you find out about any of this?" he wanted to know.

"That doesn't matter. There was a date," I pressed. "Something major happening on November first. What is it?"

Now his head shake was definite. "I don't know anything about a date."

"Who are the people in the photographs?"

He shrugged. "Isn't it obvious?"

"Humor me."

"Are you even listening to me?" he said impatiently. "Which countries we're talking about—which parts of the world? They breed radical extremism like stagnant ponds breed mosquitos."

"So these are terrorists? Planning some kind of attack? Is that what Karen was talking about when she said people will die? Something happening on November first that the people in these pictures are planning, and Care4 won't release information it got hold of?"

That frightened him. He chewed his lip nervously. "An attack? Is there going to be one?"

I looked straight into his eyes. "We should go to the police. This is too much for us."

"Really?" He looked even more nervous. "The police? Are you sure?"

"I think we need to. I know some people I'll get in touch with this week."

He licked his lips. "When, exactly? Will the company find out I was involved?"

"Don't worry. I'll keep your name out of it."

Oliver took this in. We were nearing the shoreline. I could see the main street of Sausalito, just above sea level, a border of toothy black rocks set against the water. A charming street full of antique stores and ice-cream shops. Above the town jutted steep green hills flecked with homes. "Look," Oliver finally said. "It's not safe for me to be seen with you. I'm serious. I'm going to disembark. You stay on the ferry, take it back to San Francisco. If anyone asks, we never spoke."

The ferry was slowing as it approached the gangway. Below I could see a line of people waiting to board. Oliver headed for the staircase without another word. My coffee had gotten cold but I sipped it anyway, feeling an emotion that I wasn't used to encountering in my professional life. Self-doubt. Whatever I had gotten caught up in was starting to feel unmanageable, and each step forward seemed to lead to impossible new questions. There were too many missing parts, too many unconnected pieces, and only a handful of days between now and the first of November.

Time was running out.

Even worse, I still didn't know what would happen when it did.

33

The next morning I went for a long run in the Berkeley Hills. I often did my best thinking while running, and I was starting to feel desperate. I had exhausted every lead, every piece of information. There had to be a way to take the next step—but what?

The trail I was on ascended gradually for a few miles before looping around. I was high up and could glimpse fragments of the Bay in between the hills and trees. Like glimpses of Care4. Pieces, fragments. But I couldn't see everything. I passed a pair of plodding hikers with a leashed golden retriever. The dog jealously watched me pass. The trail steepened and I forced myself to keep my pace. I leapt over a branch, ran faster. Gregg Gunn hired me to follow Karen Li. Next. Karen Li was killed. Next. I found the photographs she hid. Pictures that she had wanted me to have.

And then?

I got another glimpse of the Bay. From this distance, the water looked still and artificial. Those faces. Where did they lead? What did they mean? If there was a pending attack, where would it be, and what was Care4's role? Pieces. All I had were unconnected pieces. How could I see the whole picture? My foot snagged a root and the next thing I knew I had sprawled onto the ground. I caught myself on the palms of my hands and rolled over to a seated position, laughing for no good reason at my clumsiness.

I had started with Care4 by following Karen Li. And ended up back there after finding her. Circular. A loop, like this trail. Offering glimpses but not the whole view. My visit to Care4, Gunn's soft tone, warning me to leave it alone. But leave what alone?

Leaving Care4, hating myself for having failed Karen, pulling away, almost being sideswiped by the Mercedes.

The man in the Mercedes.

Still sitting on the trail, rubbing dirt off my leg, I said two words. "Brenda Johnson."

Brenda's contact information was at the bookstore, where I kept all my client files. When I arrived that afternoon I was met by loud voices raised in argument. The amateur sleuths, the ZEBRAS, were in their usual corner. "You can't tell me Kay Scarpetta is more memorable than Carlotta Carlyle!"

"We're not talking about individual quirks of character, we're talking about where they stand in the pantheon! The woman's powered almost twenty-five novels over the better part of two decades!"

"Don't start with the quantity-over-quality argument, Abe, it's beneath you."

"I'm surprised you ever got past the Hardy Boys. You have the mind of an adolescent and always will." Abe, the passionate founder of the ZEBRAS, accentuated his point by crumpling up the page of *The Times* he was reading and hurling it toward Zach, his antagonist of the moment. The crumpled paper bounced off Zach's glasses and rolled to the ground.

Zach shook his head. "When words fail, resort to physical assault. Classic."

I picked up the ball of paper, smoothing it. "In Abe's defense, sometimes words do fail." I handed the paper back to him. "You dropped your newspaper."

Abe drank his coffee and shook his head sadly. "My apologies, Lisbeth. We didn't mean to expose your delicate sensibilities to such turmoil."

I pinched his ear. "If I was fifty years older I'd show you turmoil." About to walk away, I stopped. "Hey, let me see that." I took the newspaper I'd just given him and looked closer at the small photograph of a man, recognizing immediately the curly black hair and missing tooth. I read the few lines of print under the photograph.

ANTI-CORRUPTION BLOGGER'S DEATH NO SUICIDE, FAMILY CLAIMS

Sherif Essam, a Cairo blogger who had devoted his career to exposing government corruption following the Arab Spring, was found dead after leaping from a rooftop this past September—only his family insists his death was anything but willing. Reports from friends, relatives, and human rights organizations are insistent that Essam never would have jumped. "My husband had the courage to point at powerful people and accuse them of crimes. We received threats, he knew he was in danger . . . but to call it a suicide?" said his wife, Dina, 31. "He spoke too loudly, and so they murdered him."

The last time I had seen his face had been in a different newspaper. While taking the affair photographs for Brenda Johnson. Then the death had been described only as a suicide. I wondered what had changed. The face was familiar for another reason, but my thoughts were interrupted by Jess. "Any progress?" she wanted to know.

I rubbed the back of my hand into my eyes. "Ask me anything but that."

"Okay." She considered. "So how are things with Ethan?"

I thought about the attempted robbery, the conversation in the donut shop, the note he had left. "A few bumps. But better now, I think. I hope."

"You like him, don't you?"

"Yeah. I do."

"Long-term like?"

With slight surprise I found myself nodding. "Yes. Long-term like." Saying it made me realize how much I meant it. I found a couple of clean coffee mugs and poured us each a generous measure of scotch. We sat on the floor and Jess threw a little toy mouse across the store so Bartleby could charge crazily after it. "I swear he thinks he's a dog," she said as the cat trotted back to us, mouse in mouth, depositing it neatly on Jess's lap to be thrown again.

It felt good talking about something other than Care4 for a few minutes. "How's Linda?" Jess's fiancée was a pediatrician. We usually had dinner together at least a few times a month. I liked her a lot. There was a wedding planned for the following summer.

"She's good. Except we're going down to her family's place for Thanksgiving."

"That's a problem?"

"Orange County. I get to enjoy four days of beautiful weather and expensive restaurants, swim in a seriously big infinity pool, and listen to a lot of pointed questions about how much longer we'll continue our untraditional lifestyle."

"Don't tell me that's still a thing? In California?"

She took a swallow of scotch. "With Newport Beach Republicans? Very much so. Especially when they're convinced that the loving partner is only in it to inherit their millions. That's the thing about people with money. If you don't have it, they're convinced you must want it. And the more you protest, the more convinced they become."

I picked up the mouse and threw it. Watched the cat sprint across the floor, gray legs a blur. No doubt in his mind about what he was pursuing, I thought jealously. "You can't skip the visit?"

"Nope. Thanksgiving, every year. Part of the deal we made. Even though her father still won't have me at his damn golf course. One of those old-boys clubs that would rather choke to death than have to choke down some diversity."

"Well, let them choke." I finished my drink. The ZEBRAS were packing up their books and food. The store was empty. "You should get out of here. I can close up."

"In a few," Jess agreed. "Finishing some paperwork."

Upstairs, I looked up Brenda Johnson's number. If her husband had been at Care4 I wanted to learn why. But I dialed a different number first.

"Hey, stranger," I said.

"Nikki?"

"Vietnamese food," I answered. "How did you know it's a favorite?"

Ethan's voice brightened. "Some random girl once told me that everyone makes assumptions. Something about how the only question is if they're right or not."

"A random girl? From what I understand that's generally a very trustworthy type."

"So . . . I was right?"

I answered with a question. "You free tonight?"

"Sure," he said, surprised. "I mean, I'll have to ditch my friends for trivia, which means they'll probably lose, but they'll get over it. We usually lose anyway, to be honest. I tend to blame the questions. They're way too superficial."

"Tell me where," I said, "and I'll see you in an hour."

As I hung up I felt better. I wanted to see him again. I wanted to talk books or laugh or lean against his shoulder, feel an arm around me and not say a word. Not make decisions. I didn't even want to see a menu. I picked up the phone again, dialed Brenda Johnson's number. No answer. I'd try her later.

Meet me there at ten o'clock tonight.

I'll tell you everything I know.

But ten o'clock had been too late. Too late for Karen to tell me.

Too late for me to save her.

That afternoon. The look of fear on her delicate face. Her eyes showing frustration and helplessness all at once. Frustration, because there was so much I didn't understand. Helplessness, because there was so much that she did understand.

And I had sent her off to die.

I poured a new drink and started going through the photographs again. I'd stared at the faces so many times I felt like I knew each person. Who were they? Why did they want to do evil things to innocents? A handsome man with tousled hair walking out of a mosque. A woman with sad eyes and a haunted face, mid-step, black hair swinging in a frozen ponytail. A skinny man kicking a soccer ball in an asphalt lot. A woman with a round, determined face and high forehead, seated in a restaurant, fork halfway to her mouth. A tough-looking man in an overcoat, hurrying somewhere, a satchel clutched in one hand.

I stopped at one picture. A man with a missing tooth. The same man who had smiled out from the blurry newspaper photo. Someone who was now, according to the newspapers, a dead man. What did that mean? How did it connect? I stared at the photograph, feeling that there was something just out of reach. I pushed my frustration away, forcing myself to think logically through the possibilities.

One: he was an anticorruption blogger, just as it seemed, and he had committed suicide for whatever reason, just as they said. Which was completely possible. Families were notoriously unwilling to accept a loved one's suicide. Fairly or not, a suicide forced people to ask all kinds of unpleasant questions of themselves. Far easier to think of death as something involuntary, even unavoidable.

Two: he was indeed a journalist of some kind but his widow was right and he had been killed. Which could have happened for any number of reasons. Maybe he'd simply written the wrong piece that stirred up some unrelated trouble. Or just run afoul of some local gangsters, maybe had a bad debt, a gambling problem. Blogging about corruption didn't automatically confer sainthood.

Three: he wasn't a blogger at all, but something more sinister. If he'd been part of some kind of cell, it wasn't stretching the imagination to think that he could have gotten cold feet and been killed after trying to back out. Or government security forces had gotten to him. Egypt's security forces were notoriously violent, even for the Middle East. In recent years, they'd killed thousands, often for little or no reason. If they suspected a blogger or anyone else had even the most tenuous jihadist connections, his life would be worth nothing once they found him.

People will die.

Karen Li had told me that whatever I thought, it was worse. If there was a plot, and the people in these photos were involved, what was the target? The final week of October and I still didn't know who was being targeted, what milestone Care4 was approaching, or what these pictures had to do with it. And why did I have the unsettling feeling that I was missing something?

I flipped through the pictures, noting the foreign backgrounds and different languages. Arabic, Spanish, English, Cyrillic. What was being planned? What was I not seeing?

Feeling more than ever that I was missing something important.

The office had grown dark. The days were shorter, approaching daylight savings. I tried Brenda again, once again reached her voice mail. Mentally running through what I wanted to wear to the restaurant, I decided I'd just get in touch tomorrow. I wanted time to shower and put on a little makeup before dinner. I hadn't seen Ethan in a while. I wanted to look nice. Outside, Telegraph Avenue was busy with traffic and pedestrians. A black van with impenetrably tinted windows pulled up across the street and double-parked. One of the big Mercedes Sprinters used for airport pickups or to ferry around private school tennis teams.

Three men in suits got out of the van.

Not a tennis team.

The three of them approached the crosswalk.

One of them pressed the Walk button.

They waited.

I watched.

The flashing orange figurine froze white.

The three men crossed the street.

They paused in front of my motorcycle. I had parked it on the sidewalk near the bookstore. One of the men nodded toward it. As though expecting to see something, and then seeing it.

They continued toward the bookstore.

My ears vaguely registered a cracking sound. The mug I'd been holding had fallen to the floor. I hit the intercom button in a rush, my voice urgent. "Jess? Are you there?" Praying for no response. Silence would mean she had already gone home.

The men had almost reached the door.

I heard Jess's voice in the intercom. Casual, unconcerned. "Yeah, what's up?"

My heart was hammering. Danger. Not arbitrary. Not distant. Right on top of me. "When I hired you," I said. "You made me promise. No micromanaging. You remember?"

She was confused. "What are you talking about?"

"Have I ever told you to do anything?"

She was more confused. "Nikki, what is this—"

"I'm telling you now. You need to hide. Get out of sight. And no matter what you hear or see, *don't move*."

Even through the cheap intercom speaker I could hear the sudden fear in her voice. "Nikki, what are you talking about? Is this a joke? You're scaring me."

"Do it," I hissed. The three men were huddled around the entrance to the bookstore. One of them stepped forward. He tried the door. It was unlocked.

They walked inside.

I climbed onto my desk, holding the envelope full of photographs. A ceiling panel was loose. I slid the envelope underneath, got down from the desk, and unlocked my safe.

The monitors showed the three men dispersing into the store.

I pulled a customized pump-action Remington shotgun out of the safe. I'd removed the standard walnut stock and replaced it with a stainless-steel folding stock and pistol grip. More portable. Better for close range. I worked quickly, loading the shotgun from two different boxes of shells, back and forth. I glanced at the monitors. The biggest of the three men stood at the door to the downstairs office, which was now closed. The other two had fanned out in the store. The man by the door tried the handle. Locked.

He started to turn away.

I breathed out in relief.

He turned and delivered a savage kick. I watched. Trying not to think about the bedroom door of the Narwhal Cottages, forced open with that same strength. The man walked into the office. I couldn't see Jess but my eyes moved from a desk in the back of the small room, to a couch set against the wall opposite the door, to a Japanese-style hinged, three-panel screen accenting a corner. Jess would be under or behind one of the three.

She had to be. There was nowhere else to hide. The big man's eyes were on the Japanese screen. His feet took him a step closer to it. Couch, desk, or screen. A one-out-of-three chance she had chosen wrong. Like a card game, except the stakes were indescribably higher than in any casino.

Another step moved him within arm's range.

His hand shot out and ripped the screen away.

Blank wall.

Two places left.

The big guy's eyes turned to the couch. The couch, maroon upholstery on short cylindrical legs, was just high enough to fit a body under it, but low enough to the ground that someone standing would have to duck down to see all the way underneath.

The big guy stepped toward the couch, squatted down.

One gone, two possible places remaining. Down to a fifty-fifty chance.

With despair I saw movement from under the couch, like an arm shifting to pull back out of sight. She was there. The man saw the motion, too. He leaned forward on one hand for a better look, his big frame visibly tensing.

More movement.

Bartleby the cat emerged sleepily from under the couch, his gray tail unfurling.

Frustrated, the big guy reached a hand out and shoved Bartleby out of the way, hard.

Bartleby had been a shelter cat before Jess had adopted him. There was no telling what he'd been through early in his life. He was sociable by nature, but he valued his own space, too, especially fresh from a nap. And no one liked being shoved. He answered the intrusion by raking his claws hard across the extended hand with a motion so fast I could barely see it. Deep tracks of blood appeared instantly. The big guy leapt up, cursing silently on the monitor. He aimed a tremendous kick at Bartleby, who was already halfway to the door.

The man chased after him, holding his hand, and launched another kick that had even less of a chance of landing than the first. He reappeared back on the previous monitor, in between the shelves, shaking his head in pain or disgust and rubbing his bleeding hand. The cat had vanished. Bartleby probably knew the bookstore's space better than I did. If he didn't want to be found, he wouldn't be.

The big guy kicked a table over in frustration. Books scattered across the floor. The office search forgotten.

I pushed my relief aside as I saw the men regroup and eye the EMPLOYEES ONLY sign on the door leading upstairs. I had left it unlocked. On the next monitor the three men climbed the stairs. Their pace purposeful but unhurried.

Now each of the men held a gun.

My turn.

Shotgun braced against my shoulder, I knelt behind the open door of the safe, the steel blocking most of my body. I had a clear line of fire straight through to the door.

The first of the three men reached the top of the stairs.

When loading the shotgun, I had alternated between buckshot and metal slugs. Six in total. The buckshot would punch a circular, twelve-inch pattern through inch-and-a-half-thick plywood. The solid metal slugs could take fist-size chunks out of hardwood trees or stop a thousand-pound charging grizzly. The pump action would fire as fast as I could work the slide and pull the trigger. I could get off six rounds in less than three seconds if I wanted.

I breathed evenly. In and out. Trying to slow my pulse.

Time slowed, sharpened.

The first man who walked through the door would die.

That was a certainty. I'd put a two-and-a-half-inch steel slug traveling at 1,500 feet per second through him before he took a step. Didn't matter if he wore Kevlar under his jacket. Bulletproof was always relative. The metal slugs would go through a bulletproof vest like cheap denim.

The question was the next two men. It would be a firefight. Chaos. Bullets going everywhere. A lot would depend on their experience. How they'd react after their friend crashed backward toward them with a hole in his chest big enough to fit a softball. Whether they'd panic. A lot more would depend on dumb luck. The random geometry of which bullets happened to go where.

There were three of them. But I had a shotgun and a defensive position. I figured that gave me an even chance of surviving the next two minutes.

The lead man was at the door. I racked the shotgun. Took a breath in. Let it out.

It was time.

Then he did something strange.

He knelt like he was tying a shoe. He was putting his gun on the floor, I realized. He stood and reached into the inside pocket of his suit jacket. For an unsettling moment, I wondered if he had some kind of explosive he planned to use. Something I hadn't considered.

He looked up into the camera above the door. I saw a hardened face, a sharp jaw, and pale eyes. He raised whatever he held toward the camera. A piece of glossy paper. A Polaroid. He stretched his arm up. Slowly, the picture filled the monitor. And then I understood. The lighting wasn't great and the picture quality was only decent. But the face was one I would have recognized anywhere, regardless of bad lighting or fuzzy detail. A face as familiar as my own.

I was looking at my brother.

34

Shotgun at hip level, I walked across the room, opened the door, and stepped back. The three men stood in front of me without bothering to move out of the way of the shotgun barrel. Guns barely pointed at me. I wasn't going to shoot. Worse, they knew it.

"Nikki," the lead man said, stepping into the room. The other two moved in behind him. "We've been wanting to talk to you."

I held the shotgun barrel less than two feet from his chest. "Where is he?"

"May we come in?" His accent sounded Eastern European.

I backed up. "Where is he?" I repeated.

"All in due time. May we?"

"Don't play cute," I snapped. "Don't act like you waltzed in looking for a first edition. You have him. Where is he?"

"You seem anxious. I hope you will not accidentally shoot me."

"When I shoot you, I promise it will be on purpose. Where is he?"

"Your brother is somewhere safe."

One of the other two guys grinned. "He says hello to his big sister." The speaker was the one who had kicked in the door downstairs. With satisfaction I saw Bartleby's claw marks, lurid against his hand. He was the youngest and largest of the three, in his twenties, maybe six foot three or four, and the weight to match. He had the build and bearing of a hockey enforcer. The kind of guy who comes along for a fight and goes home disappointed if he doesn't find one. His face was pockmarked by old acne scars and his hair was long and greasy with some kind of product.

I ignored him and addressed the lead man. He was running the show. "What do you want?"

"We want to talk to you."

"Talk. Right."

He shrugged, his eyes pale and expressionless. "We have to ask some questions about what you know. Call it due diligence. Then, if the answers are okay, we all go home happy."

"I don't do a thing until I see my brother."

He smiled. "We would expect nothing less."

Expect. With a helpless feeling, I realized that everything I was doing and saying was playing into their hands. "Fine. Go get him."

"We go to him," the man corrected. "Put your gun down. You can ride with us."

"Not a chance."

His eyes were an unnaturally pale color and conveyed a reptilian disinterest. "You misunderstand. Maybe I've been too polite," he said. His smile was gone and his words, lightly coated by the accent, were clipped and careful. "Let me try again. Put that shotgun down and come with us, or our friend, who is babysitting your little brother, will use a hacksaw to remove his feet below the ankles."

I thought hard. Trying to see a way out.

There wasn't one. They knew it and I knew it. I could pretend I had choices, but I didn't.

I shrugged. There was no point in stalling. The sooner I could get to Brandon, the better. I placed the shotgun on the floor. "Let's go, then."

"First we check you," said the big one. Even as he spoke his hands were all over me. Unlike Mr. Ruby's, his search wasn't civil at all. I felt his hands rubbing against all the places where I didn't want to feel a strange man's hands. He took his time, finding the Derringer, the sap, the brass knuckles. Tossed the handful onto a chair and grinned up at me. "What's a sweet little bitch like you doing with the fun stuff? You like to play?" His breath was sour in my face. Between his manners and his looks, he couldn't have had an easy time getting dates growing up.

The third man, short and thickly built with a shaved head, was tearing through my office. There was a crash as he knocked over the file cabinet. He came back after a few minutes, holding my purse. "Nothing we want." The small measure of relief that he hadn't found the photographs was mitigated by wondering if it mattered; if I'd ever see the photographs again, ever learn what Karen Li had been trying to tell me.

They walked me downstairs and outside. The short man who had torn apart my office got behind the wheel. The lights from the dash glowed. The big guy sat behind me and the pale-eyed man next to me. The van eased into traffic and glided into the night.

We drove south on Telegraph in the direction of Oakland. The driver was cautious. He drove several miles under the speed limit, stopped at yellow lights, braked if a pedestrian was anywhere near a crosswalk. We weren't going to get pulled over. I figured they had Brandon in a warehouse or empty building. Probably one they had rented days or weeks before, to have ready for this kind of thing. I didn't bother to talk. There was no point. The glitter of downtown Oakland drew closer. People out on a Thursday night, happy hours and dinners and concerts. Then downtown faded behind us, the streets grittier, fewer cars. We passed rows of one-story houses, beat-up apartment buildings, and weeded vacant lots. The part of Oakland where tech employees didn't move and tech money didn't flow. The streets were familiar.

I realized where we were going. Not to some warehouse.

They had my brother at the most obvious place of all: his own apartment.

The van pulled up to the curb. The driver left the engine running and stayed where he was. The pale-eyed man opened the door and the big guy shifted behind me. They stayed close, watching me carefully. We walked inside as the van pulled away. In the lobby, there was a broken pipe or leak. Slow metronome water drops ticked against the floor. A fluorescent light flickered. A rat bolted across the lobby, long bald tail whipping from side to side.

We walked up the stairs. The big guy in front of me, the pale-eyed man behind.

No choices.

For a moment, it all looked the same. The mess, the smell of stale smoke, Brandon sitting on the couch as usual. Except now his hands and feet were duct-taped together. A man with dishwater-blond hair in a charcoal suit sat next to him, playing a game on his cell phone. He looked up at us and put the phone down, showing a salon-tan face and too-white teeth that looked like he gargled with bleach every morning. Everything else the same squalor—overflowing ashtrays and empty pizza boxes.

"Nik?"

"Brandon." I tried to run over to him and the big guy grabbed me by the shoulders. He was abnormally strong. He held me back easily, laughing. I forced myself to relax. I didn't want him to have the satisfaction of feeling me struggle. His fingers pressed painfully into my arms long after I'd stopped moving. The man with the pale eyes had brought my purse from the bookstore. He dumped it out on the coffee table and looked at the Beretta with mild interest.

"Are you okay? Did they hurt you?"

Brandon smiled and I saw the old, gentle humor in his eyes. "Hurt? Naw, Nik. I was bored. Sitting here all alone without anyone to talk to."

I turned to the man with the pale eyes. "What do I call you?"

His eyes slid off me. He shrugged. "Call me Joseph if you like."

"Let him go, Joseph. Then you can do whatever you want to me. He's not part of this."

"We do whatever we want to you now. No bargains. And he's your flesh and blood, which makes him part of this."

"What do you want?"

He gave me a long basilisk look. "Who have you talked to, Nikki?"

"What do you mean, talked to? About what?"

Joseph walked over to the coffee table. I noticed a large briefcase that had been placed on the floor. He set the briefcase on the table and opened it carefully. Wires. Red and black alligator clamps. And some kind of large metal cube the size of a shoebox.

A battery.

"I haven't talked to anyone," I said again. "Not about any of this."

He shook his head. "Forget it. Save your breath. We are going to use this on you regardless. And we will keep using it all night, back and forth between you and your brother. Until we are sure you are not withholding anything we want to know."

The big guy grinned. "We never really pay attention to anything the first hour. That's just getting-to-know-you chitchat."

I met his gaze. "I bet you enjoy that part."

His grin grew. Not denying it.

They sat me down in one of the armchairs. It took them about two minutes to tape my hands in front of me, then my feet. They were thorough. I didn't bother to struggle. Not even when Joseph placed alligator clamps onto each of my arms, just above the tape that bound my wrists. I watched as the stubby serrated jaws closed over my flesh.

He held something up. A rubber mouth guard.

I looked at it. "Why?"

"We need you to be able to talk. When it's time."

I shook my head. Trying to ignore the visible teeth marks embedded in the rubber. "No."

Joseph stared at me. His eyes were an almost colorless shade of blue. "Have you ever seen someone bite off their own tongue?"

I thought this over, then opened my mouth dutifully. Tasted the sour rubber, wondering how many other people had sat with this mouth guard against their teeth, feeling the metal clamps pinching into their skin, knowing what was coming. Brandon spoke up, the nonchalance stripped from his voice. "Please, guys. Don't hurt her. Do it to me, instead."

I tried to tell him to shut up but my voice was muffled around the mouth guard and I could only mumble. The big guy laughed. "Don't worry, junkie. Plenty for you, too. But first your arrogant bitch sister needs a drink of the juice."

"Before we start," Joseph was saying, "I'm going to do you a favor. I'm going to tell you something important. *Five seconds*. Do you understand what I mean?"

I looked at the wall in front of me. Said nothing.

"That's how long the first time will last. This is the only time I'll tell you how long. And this will be the shortest of the night. Remember that, when you're trying to count to five."

"Please," said Brandon again. Louder.

"Shut up." The man in the charcoal suit gave him a hard, open-handed smack against the face. My brother's head jerked back. I managed to get out of the chair but the big guy laughed again and pushed me down easily. I stopped struggling and focused on what was coming. Trying to put my thoughts far away. Away from this room and these men. Away from the rubber taste in my mouth and the cold clamps against my skin. The three of them were staring openly at me. Curious. Like I was a lab mouse. Wanting to see how I took it. The big guy watched me with special intensity. An almost sexual anticipation. Greedy, eager, like I was performing a striptease just for him.

"Ready?" Joseph asked. Wires ran to a control panel that he held in both hands, like he was operating a remote-control airplane.

I didn't answer.

He adjusted a dial.

He fastened his eyes on me and hit a switch.

Liquid fire filled me from arms to legs to face. My body was on fire from the inside out. My face was on fire deep within the skin. My eyes felt like they'd pop out of their sockets and I felt a horrible grip over my very organs, as if they were being squeezed into pulp. I was vaguely conscious of my teeth burrowing into the hard rubber in my mouth. I didn't know if one or one hundred seconds had gone by. Space and time had ceased to exist. Just pain. Nothing else.

The pain was gone as instantaneously as it had arrived.

I was conscious of the world again. I smelled burnt flesh and spat out the mouth guard. I became aware that I was screaming and managed to quiet. The screaming continued and I realized the sound was coming from my brother. The big guy was watching me with even more hunger. "Some people piss themselves, even the first time. Did you?"

Brandon was still screaming. The man in the charcoal suit slapped him twice more, hard. Brandon quieted, vivid marks on his thin cheeks. They were taking the clamps off of me, putting them on my brother's wrists. "Don't," I said. "He's got a weak heart. It will kill him."

The big guy looked at me. "Your junkie brother should pray to God he has a heart attack bad enough to finish him off. It would be the luckiest day of his worthless life."

I already knew I was going to try to stop them. They did, too. I could see it. I didn't care. The Beretta lay on the coffee table. Maybe, somehow, I could reach it.

"Ready, junkie?" Joseph asked. "Five seconds. Same as she got."

He fiddled with the dials again. His hand moved closer to the switch.

I took a breath. Blew it out. Tensing in the chair.

The front door opened.

All five of us turned our heads in surprise. It was Eric, with the green Mohawk. Standing in the doorway looking just as surprised as we were. The big guy moved quickly. Bounded over and pushed the door shut behind him. Joseph was on his feet. He glared at Eric. "How did you get in here?"

Eric swiveled his head toward Joseph and slowly lit a cigarette. He was high out of his mind. His pupils were shiny little points. He held an open Twix bar in one hand and a grease-stained McDonald's bag in the other. He took two slow steps into the apartment. "I have a key," he said. "That's how." He tucked his cigarette into the corner of his mouth and held up a brass key as if to offer proof.

"You gave *him* a key to your apartment?" I exclaimed. "Seriously?"

"He had nowhere to stay, Nik," protested my brother.

"What's going on?" Eric looked around suspiciously. He must have shot up very recently. An easy way to tell. Because he wasn't flat-out terrified. Any normal, sober person would have been frantically out the door after one look. But stoned as he was, Eric wasn't blind. A vague look of worry settled over his face as his eyes took in the three men. "Is this a bust?"

The big guy laughed. "He's junkie number two, that's all."

"Hey, man!" said Eric. "Screw you! I'm no junkie." He took a slow bite of his Twix. Chocolate crumbs flecked his shirt. "Who are these people, Brandon?" He took a closer look at my brother. Saw the duct tape and alligator clamps. He might have been high, but he wasn't dumb. Every instinct of self-preservation seemed to fire up at once. His eyes darted around. "I'll come back later," he said, and started backing toward the door.

"Wait!" said Joseph. "Take this, to be quiet about what you saw."

Eric looked over. Seeing the wad of hundred-dollar bills held in Joseph's outstretched left hand. Almost at the door, he stopped. Looking at the outstretched cash.

Hundred-dollar bills.

Irresistible.

"You should probably run, Eric," I advised. "Right now."

Instead he walked toward Joseph, hypnotized by the cash. "That's all for me?"

"All for you," Joseph agreed.

He picked up my Beretta from the coffee table and shot Eric in the head.

The Beretta was loaded with .40 caliber hollow-points. A very destructive round. The bullet blew out the back of Eric's head. He was dead instantly. Blood spattered the scuffed white paint behind him in a five-foot radius. The McDonald's bag dropped to the floor. Fries spilled out of greasy paper as blood pooled around the food. My brother was screaming again. "You didn't have to do that!"

I was trying to figure out how this changed things. The gunshot had been loud, but this neighborhood was no stranger to gunshots. Gang and drug shootings happened all the time, and many of the residents had a distinct aversion to police involvement no matter what the reason. There was always a chance that if someone had heard the noise they'd call it in, but I wasn't counting on this. These three men, though, had flown in from somewhere else. Hired guns. They probably went all over the world doing this kind of work. They didn't know the area. And they were in an apartment with a dead body and enough incriminating evidence to put them away for life on a dozen different charges. Joseph had to be in his midforties and looked like he'd already done plenty of terrible things in his career. Hitmen didn't tend to make it to their forties unless they had at least a modicum of caution.

The three of them, whispering urgently, seemed to reach a decision. Joseph looked over at me. "You two are lucky. You just avoided a very long night."

"You're letting us go?" Brandon asked. His voice was charged with relief.

The big guy laughed. "You can think of it like that, if you want."

"What are you going to do?"

"We're going to do what we came here to do," answered Joseph. "We're going to use you to tell a story. The only difference is we're just going to skip to the last chapter."

The big guy removed two other objects out of the briefcase. A small leather case the size of a hardcover and a narrow, two-foot tube wrapped in cloth. Joseph unzipped the case. A row of syringes gleamed against the black interior. "What are those?" asked Brandon.

The big guy snickered. "Should look familiar, junkie."

Joseph addressed my brother. "A synthetic opioid compound. Chemically almost indistinguishable from heroin. A toxicology report won't even show a difference."

"Why?" I asked, feeling sick.

Joseph looked to me. "You showed up tonight and found your little brother, overdosed." He jerked his head over at Eric's body. More blood pooled, the face an awful, unnatural shade of white. "You saw the scumbag who sold it to him and flew into a rage, pulled your gun, and shot him dead on the spot."

"Very likely. And then what?" I challenged.

"You realize what you've done. And you realize you only have one option left."

"Yeah? What's that?"

"That should be obvious." He smiled thinly. "Suicide."

"Right. People will believe that."

"Of course they will. After all, you showed up here already a murderess, already knowing they were closing in on you." He gave Eric's body another glance. "This one doesn't really change anything. Your brother was always going to OD tonight and you were always going to find him. And you were always going to have Karen Li's blood on your hands."

Now I was confused. "What?"

Joseph was unwrapping the cloth.

We all watched as the object was revealed.

A crowbar.

One end stained with what looked like spilled paint. I understood. He could tell. "Now you see, right? You'd been stalking her, out of control."

"That kind of cheap trick isn't something you'll get away with."

The big guy grinned. "We get away with way, way worse. You wouldn't believe what we get away with. This is nothing."

"I talked to the FBI. They know all about you. They know who you are."

Joseph shook his head. "No, they know who *you* are."

"They'll know it wasn't me."

"How hard will they bother to even look? Finding you in this slum, drugs everywhere, practically on top of a dead man who was killed with your gun. Finding the crowbar with the Li woman's blood all over it. That's what they call open and shut, I believe."

He was more right than I cared to admit, but it didn't matter. He thought he was, and was confident enough to move forward with the plan. If things didn't work out for them down the road, that wouldn't do Brandon or me much good.

"Which one of you actually killed her?" I wanted to know.

Joseph shrugged. "Questions like that—what's the point?"

I looked at the big guy. Thinking of the bookstore, his kick to the office door. "You?"

He grinned at me. Not denying. "What makes you say that?"

"Because you like it. I can tell."

His eyes flicked over me with that same hungry look. "You think I like it?"

"Yes."

He took a step closer. "I wish we had more time. I could have so much fun with you."

"Take it easy, Victor. We have work to do," said Joseph. He took one of the syringes and sat next to Brandon, searching for a vein in my brother's thin arm. I watched the needle probe fruitlessly.

Brandon smiled cheerfully. "Sorry. I used those up about ten years ago."

"Shut up." Joseph checked the other arm, to no avail.

Brandon giggled, hysteria under the levity. "I'm trying to cooperate. I really am."

"Goddamn junkie," Joseph exclaimed. He kicked the coffee table in frustration, knocking ashtrays and detritus and the open leather case onto the floor. I watched one of the syringes roll. It came to rest near my feet. I looked at it. A thin, translucent cylinder, the metallic needle jutting out. Almost invisible against the floor.

I stretched a leg out, grazing the syringe with my foot.

"Try his leg," suggested Victor. None of the three were looking my way as I inched the syringe closer. They were all staring down at Brandon like he was a puzzle of some kind. Joseph rolled up a pants leg and probed around the ankle, then slid the needle carefully into Brandon's leg. Brandon's eyes softened with involuntary pleasure. He sagged back on the couch as I used my outstretched foot to work the syringe closer. Everyone's eyes still on my brother as he breathed heavily, deep down in the stupefying pleasure of the drug. I leaned down quickly as they moved away from my brother.

I sat up. "Victor," I said. "That's your name, right?"

The big guy looked over at me. "Why?"

"It was you, wasn't it? You were the one who did that to Karen."

"Why do you care so much?"

"What does it matter?"

He shrugged. "Okay, why not, then? Sure."

"It was you?"

He nodded slowly. "She begged, you know. You should have heard her beg."

"And you liked that."

He wasn't bothering to pretend. Gave me that same hungry look. "I *loved* it."

Behind him, I saw Joseph retrieve the open case and remove another syringe. He didn't seem to notice one was missing. For the first time in my life I was grateful for Brandon's addiction. Addiction equaled tolerance. Right now, tolerance equaled life. The more he could take, the longer he could stay alive. The question was how much. He could handle a far greater dose than a normal person. Maybe a second syringe, or a third if he was very lucky. I doubted anyone could take more than that. And there had been six in the case. They'd keep shooting into his unconscious body until his breathing stopped.

If I was going to do anything, I had to hurry.

I didn't see any good options. But I had to do something. Even if that meant a great deal of extra pain for the slimmest of chances.

I made up my mind.

"You like hurting women?" I asked Victor.

He smiled, revealing a crooked overbite. I wondered how many women had turned down his advances over the years. "I like hurting *everyone.*"

"Think you could hurt me?"

He heard the challenge in my voice and his eyes sharpened, the pupils dilating slightly as if exposed to bright light. "I think I could do all kinds of things to you."

I shook my head contemptuously. "Bullshit. I know your type. Jackals, that's all. You prey on easy victims. That's all you're good for."

His face flushed. "No one ever taught you manners, did they, sweetheart?"

I took a guess and spoke deliberately. "Sweetheart? What a joke. Guys like you used to ask me out all the time. Bottom-feeders, buzzards. I used to laugh in their ugly faces while saying no." I looked straight into his eyes and laughed scornfully. "Just like I'm laughing in your ugly face right now."

Victor ran his tongue along his lower lip. His eyes flickered. "Just when it was going to be an easy night for you, you go and make it difficult."

"Think I give a damn about easy? You talk tough with a crowbar and a one-hundred-twenty-pound computer scientist begging for her life. Such a tough guy."

Victor's voice was dangerous. "That's what you think?"

"Deep down, you're a pathetic coward. I can see it all over your ugly face."

He was no longer smiling. "You're about to make your final hour hell on earth."

Behind him, Joseph held the second syringe, probing my brother's other leg. Like a vampire. I shuddered. I had to hurry. He was angry. Close to where I wanted him to be. But not quite there.

"I'm curious," I went on. "In high school, when all the other boys were dating, finding girlfriends, going to dances and parties, having fun—what did you do, Victor? Walk around setting cats on fire and pulling wings off bugs?"

I saw something click in his face. It was his eyes. For a second they grew fuzzy and unfocused. As though he had forgotten all about me. As though he was thinking about something completely different. Then the eyes sharpened again. In one quick motion he pulled a knife out of his back pocket, leaned down, and slashed the ugly triangle blade through the duct tape that bound my feet.

"What are you doing?" shouted Joseph.

Victor seemed to barely hear. "She's going to need her legs free for a while."

"She's supposed to be a goddamn suicide."

"Then we'll throw her off the damn roof," said Victor sullenly. "I don't care. But no one ever taught this bitch how to keep her mouth shut, so I will."

"We have to get out of here."

"You didn't let me play with the last one. This time I want to have my fun." Victor's tone was determined. His mouth pursed. Under different circumstances it would have been funny. Like a parent arguing with a petulant child over whether they had time to stop at a toy store before going home.

Only the child was a six-foot-four sociopath.

And I was the toy store.

That made it less funny.

"Fine," Joseph acquiesced. "But hurry." He gave a grunt of satisfaction as he found a second vein. Brandon's body stiffened and his eyelids fluttered. He was completely unconscious. I watched his chest as it moved almost imperceptibly up and down.

Victor put his knife back in his pocket and grabbed me. "Come on, bitch. This is as close as you'll ever get to your wedding night." He dragged me toward the bedroom door, my feet stumbling to keep up. As we got into the bedroom he shoved me. He was freakishly strong. Hands still taped in front of me, I lurched across the room and banged into the wall. From the light of the closet bulb I could see him pulling his jacket off, revealing a shoulder holster. The butt of a gun stuck temptingly out.

He headed my way. "Let's see what you have under those jeans."

I aimed a hard kick at his groin. I didn't think Victor was the father type, but I was doing my best to make sure of it. If the kick had landed, what was under my jeans would have been the last thing on his mind. But for a big man he was surprisingly fast. He shifted his weight and brought up a knee, turning so my boot glanced off his thigh.

He licked his lips and sneered. "Cheap shot."

He grabbed me again and I kicked him as hard as I could, this time connecting with the shin. With my hands taped together I couldn't do much more. He grunted in pain and hit me on the temple with a chopping downward blow. I rolled my head away but the force still knocked me backward and filled my eyes with slowly blinking sparks. I got in another kick and in response he slapped me hard across the face. The room spun crazily. I tasted blood. The sparks danced faster.

He got hold of me and then I was on the bed under him. A rough hand tore open the front of my blouse, the other fumbling at my jeans. I tried to kick but he shifted his weight onto my hips, sitting over me. My legs churned uselessly. His eyes were excited as one hand pulled the front of my jeans so hard I felt the button tear off. I was too full of adrenaline to feel sick at what was happening.

"Fight back," Victor said. "I want you to. It's more exciting that way."

He used his left hand to pin my bound wrists above my head. I struggled to free my arms, but with his strength and vantage he didn't even have to really try. His right hand went to his own pants. I heard the zipper of his fly. A zipper. Such a normal sound. Now, here, the worst sound. I wondered how many women before me had felt Victor's weight crushing down, heard that sound, thought those thoughts.

He smiled as he undid his belt one-handed. "Bet you wish you hadn't talked so much."

I said nothing. He was taunting me, trying to get me to struggle. There was no point in expending needless energy. Still easily pressing my arms down against the bed with his left hand, he leaned forward and stroked the fingers of his right hand tenderly against my cheek. I felt his fingers brush slowly down my face. Somehow that was a far worse feeling than any of his blows. I swallowed hard and forced myself to stay quiet as the fingers gently traced their way along the underside of my chin, my throat. I felt them on my lips and involuntarily tried to bite him. He jerked his hand away, laughed, slapped me hard with his right hand.

"That's not so nice on a first date." He seemed almost relaxed as he undid his pants, sitting forward slightly, his legs folded under him, eyes narrowed in excitement. His right hand went again to my unbuttoned jeans, first one hip, then the other, tugging them down. I bucked my hips hard but it was a losing battle. Victor had to weigh close to double what I did. With my arms pinned above me there was nothing I could do. We both knew it.

We were both startled by a loud jangle as my brother's old Mickey Mouse alarm clock on the night table went off, to my right and Victor's left. Victor's head turned sharply and I felt his weight shift as he instinctively prepared to face this possible new threat. Almost as quickly, he identified the noise for what it was. He cursed, hesitating as he realized the clock was out of reach of his right hand, and I felt the pressure against my arms free as he leaned over and seized the clock with his left hand, hurling it against the wall. It broke apart into plastic shards as he reached back to re-pin my arms. He had correctly reasoned that even if I was able to hit him once or twice, lying pinned on my back, wrists bound, he had little cause for concern. Even the hardest puncher in the world couldn't do much lying on his back, and Victor was too heavy for me to buck him off. The whole thing had taken him no more than a second.

A second was all that I needed.

In the moment that Victor's hand left mine I swung my arms up. The light from the closet bulb glinting off the syringe clenched between my hands. I didn't have the luxury of searching for the best spot. And I just had one chance. I played the odds and stuck the needle into the right side of Victor's neck. There were all kinds of important veins there. The external jugular, the superficial cervical artery. The needle punctured his flesh as his hand flashed up to grab my wrists.

I pressed the plunger in as his hand reached mine.

The effect was instantaneous. Victor's eyes rolled up in his head as his hand fell away. He tried to say something but failed. His weight shifted sideways and he slumped onto the bed like a crumbling statue. I didn't waste time watching. My hands were already in his back pants pocket where his knife had gone. I got the knife open and squeezed the handle between my knees. The position was unsteady but the blade was sharp.

The tape fell away and my hands were free.

I stood and breathed deeply, fighting to control the adrenaline pumping through me. Forcing myself to not think about what I had just barely avoided. There would be time for that later. I flexed my hands, getting the blood running through the fingers. The tape had been tight. I'd need steady hands for what was about to happen.

I looked from Victor to the closed door and back.

They'd had their chance.

Now it was my turn.

Joseph's voice called through the door. "Come on, Victor. Not all night. Finish up with her already. We have to go."

I had to move quickly. Victor's face was serene, blissful. The dose in the syringe had been powerful. Victor was far heavier than my brother, but he didn't have my brother's tolerance. He was gone. In another world. I leaned over his body and got his holster open. His gun was an HK45, Heckler & Koch. That would work fine. BMW, Siemens, H&K—trust the Germans to do cars or finely calibrated scientific equipment or guns better than anyone. Those Teutonic standards of perfection.

I paused by the closet light, pulled back the slide, and checked the chamber.

The brassy end of a .45 caliber cartridge peeked out.

I checked the clip. Full.

I flicked the safety off.

I stared at the closet bulb for a few seconds. Not letting myself blink. The living room would be bright. When I opened the door, I didn't want my eyes taking time to adjust.

I took a breath.

Blew it out.

My turn.

I opened the door.

In the first second, I had the advantage. Both due to surprise, and because the living room was brightly lit while the darkness of the bedroom left me obscured. Across the room, someone sat in one of the armchairs behind a raised newspaper. I could make out the ornate lettering centered at the top of the front page that faced me. The *San Francisco Chronicle*. I couldn't tell who was behind the paper. Just a hand holding each outside edge.

It didn't matter.

I fired a single time directly through the *O* in *Francisco*. Dead center between the hands. The inside of the newspaper flecked red and the hands released their grip. The pages fluttered down. The tanned guy in the charcoal suit leaned sideways, blank open mouth showing his white teeth as if in a wide yawn. A hole where the upper bridge of his nose used to be.

I stepped into the living room as I heard a curse and saw Joseph throw himself to the side. I sent two shots his way, cognizant of Brandon's supine form. Both missed. Joseph rolled behind an armchair. I fired twice more into the armchair, aiming about where his head would be. Figuring maybe the big .45 rounds could get through a bit of stuffing and cheap fabric.

I got my answer almost immediately. I lunged into the kitchen and down to the floor as a fusillade of bullets tore through the plaster wall above me. I was already crawling fast. Not wanting to stick around in the same place.

Two more shots ripped into the floor where I'd just been.

Lying prone, I saw a trace of arm sticking out from around the chair. I aimed carefully, letting the darkness of the arm blur into the background, the gun sight sharp in the foreground. I squeezed the trigger smoothly and was rewarded with a scream.

I rolled away as three more bullets tore through the wall. One angled up and went through the kitchen's overhead light. I threw my arms over my head as shattered glass rained down. I heard rushed footsteps. Gun up, I stood and peered into the living room. The front door was open. I checked behind the armchair, wary of a trick. No Joseph. There was blood on the floor. A spotted red trail led to the door. He was gone.

I used Victor's knife to cut the duct tape off Brandon. He was in bad shape. Three empty syringes next to him. His breaths came laboriously and his lips were blue. Spittle had dried across his mouth and his face was pale. I pulled up an eyelid. His eyes were glassy and unseeing. I pressed my fingers against his neck and felt a weak, uncertain pulse.

A textbook overdose.

With a prayer, I pulled open the drawer of the coffee table. The two white naloxone tubes I had brought were still there. I put one carefully up his right nostril. For the second time in five minutes I pressed a plunger.

Brandon lurched upward, cursing, arms flailing.

He wasn't happy, but my brother was alive. Very much alive.

It took me a few minutes to soothe him. When he finally quieted he looked around, taking in my blood-covered face, the bodies and the blood-stains, the bullet holes in the armchair and walls. He looked at me uncertainly. "Nik?"

"Yeah?"

"I think I might lose my security deposit."

I hugged him tightly. "You mean *my* security deposit, shithead."

35

I used Brandon's phone to dial a number from memory. "Jess."

Her voice was frightened. "Nikki, are you okay? Who were those people? What happened?"

"I'm going to give you an address. You'll see my brother outside. Take him to a hotel. My apartment isn't safe. He's going to be sick. You have to help him get through it."

She didn't hesitate. "Leaving now."

"When you arrive, Jess, don't come up. That's important."

I gave her the address, hung up, turned to my brother. "Wait outside for her."

His voice was unsteady but he could stand. "What are you going to do here?"

"You have to go, Brandon," I said. "Now."

He heard my tone. He went.

It took me a few minutes to tape up Victor. I was very thorough, cognizant of his abnormal strength. Even with bound hands and feet he would be a handful if awake. I wrapped him like a mummy, starting at his ankles, up to his trunk-like thighs, both arms cocooned down at his sides, and a nice wide strip across his mouth. I used just about the whole roll of tape. That was fine. I couldn't think of anything else I'd need it for besides Victor.

I burned plenty of calories dragging him from bedroom to bathroom. He was a big guy. There was a lot to drag and it was all dead weight. He didn't even mutter as his head banged hard along the wood floor and tiles. I hauled his legs over the bathtub rim, then shoved his torso over. He flopped into the tub, his legs following, and lay there on his back, eyes staring blankly upward.

I screwed the stopper into the drain and turned the faucet on.

Water began to puddle against the bottom of the tub.

I made another call. Another familiar number. Another familiar voice answered.

"It's Nikki. I need a favor. I'm going to give you an address. Come over, fast. And bring a car you really hate." Even if gunshots were commonplace I didn't want to draw things out any more than I had to. Not after what had happened. And not with what I was about to do. The sooner I was out of the apartment, the better.

There was a brief pause and then the voice said, "I'll be there in half an hour."

"One more thing," I added. "The car you bring. Make sure it has a big trunk."

I went into the bathroom and sat on the toilet seat, watching as the water line crept up. Thinking about Karen Li. The cabin. The water rose higher. Now it was above the back of Victor's head, submerging his ears. Nearing his mouth and nostrils. His eyes were still blank. He made no attempt to struggle. He looked like he was lying on silk pillows, being fanned by palm fronds. Blasted onto some other planet. Full of the weird, impenetrable bliss of heroin.

He'd drown literally without knowing that he was underwater.

I thought of Karen Li again. The cut on her hand. The broken pane of glass that was as close as she had gotten to escape. The bloodstained crowbar. Her shattered arm and broken face. Begging for mercy where there was none.

I took another look at Victor. His face was serene.

Somehow, it didn't seem fair.

I shut the water off.

Went into the living room, came back, and grabbed Victor by the back of his long hair. I held his head up and shoved the second tube of naloxone up his nostril. Again, the effect was instantaneous. He thrashed around in the bathtub like some huge, hooked fish. His bound legs made loud thuds as they kicked against the tub. I was glad I had used extra tape. His desire to get out of the tub was extreme. And he was very strong.

I made my way to the edge of the bathtub and looked down. He rolled his head around and glared up at me out of reddened, open eyes. Very much conscious. Full of the immediate sickness of withdrawal that the naloxone produced. He mumbled something around the tape. I couldn't understand what he was saying but I got the general message. I didn't suppose he was wishing me good things. As the exact nature of his location sunk in, the thrashing increased. His head jerked back and forth, banging hard against the sides of the bathtub. He didn't seem to care. Water splashed onto the floor.

"Victor," I said.

Somehow the mention of his name set him off again. More thrashing, more mumbling, more splashing.

"Victor. Pay attention. Please. I'll only talk for a moment. Then I'll leave you alone."

He scowled up at me.

"Who hired you guys, Victor?" I leaned down and ripped the tape off his mouth. Waited for him to temporarily run out of curse words.

"Who hired you?" I asked again.

It turned out he had a few words left. That was okay. I could wait.

"Who told you to kill Karen Li? Who told you to come after me?"

He glared up. "I don't know. Joseph handles all that."

"You must know something. Try to meet me halfway."

"Lots of people use us. We do lots of jobs. Joseph handles the bookings."

I held the H&K up so he could see it, and smiled brightly down at him. "I bet right now you wish you'd brought some dinky little .22 with you, right? Instead of this cannon?"

He stared furiously at me. I didn't feel he was getting my point.

"How'd you get my gun?" he demanded. "Where's Joseph? Where's Theo?"

"Joseph left," I answered. "He was in a hurry. Theo, I believe, is still here."

"I want to talk to them."

"Who hired you, Victor?"

"Go to hell, bitch," he said. "I'm not scared of you."

"Victor. Please. A little common sense. Are you sure you want to talk like that to someone pointing a .45 your way?"

"Go to hell," he repeated. He added a few words that made "bitch" sound mild.

I shot him in the left foot.

Right through what must have been a size twelve or thirteen black leather wingtip. Bits of leather and flesh flecked out against the sides of the white tub along with the blood. There wasn't all that much water in the tub. It turned red pretty quick.

Victor was tough. He got the initial screaming under control after a long minute, and with some effort stopped moaning entirely soon after. The cursing probably would have continued indefinitely except I held the gun up a second time, this time pointed at his right foot. What remained of the left foot bled red into the bathwater. The .45 was a big gun.

"You were saying."

"You goddamn *shot* me. You *shot* me."

"One foot left, Victor. If you care."

"Okay! Wait!" He took a breath and grimaced. "I'm telling you, Joseph handles the bookings. I don't know who he talked to except that it was someone at the same company that hired you. Care4. We knew you were following Karen Li up to Mendocino because we were, too. That's all I know."

"Why didn't you wait for me that night? At the cabin?"

The pain seemed to be increasing. He worked his jaw muscles and breathed with effort. "We didn't know you'd actually go into the cabin. We thought you were following at a distance. That's what we had been told. At that point, our instructions were to deal with her. No one had told us to go after you yet. That came later."

"Have you worked for Care4 before this?"

"No."

"Has Joseph?"

"I have no idea."

"Are you lying?"

"No!"

I turned the faucet back on and watched Victor's face as water began again rising up around his head. "You're sure you don't remember who actually hired you?"

"I told you! Joseph handles that. I just do the jobs."

"Okay, Victor. Good enough." Maybe he was telling the truth, maybe not. Either way he didn't have anything more to offer. A shame Joseph wasn't here as well. He'd know more. I stuck a new piece of duct tape over Victor's mouth. It was harder with all his flailing, but I managed. When I stood, I was soaking wet from splashed bathwater.

"These last few minutes are yours," I told him. "I can't tell you what to think about. But I hope you realize that Karen Li didn't deserve what you did to her."

Ignoring the increasingly frantic pleas issuing from under the tape, I walked out of the bathroom and shut the door. I heard plenty of thuds and splashing for the first few minutes. Victor was a strong and hardy man. He didn't have any wish to go along with what was happening to him. But sometimes there really wasn't any choice.

Eventually the noises lessened. Soon after, the bathroom became quiet.

I tasted blood. The inside of my mouth was cut from Victor's slaps, my lips already swelling up. I found some tissues and stuck them in the side of my mouth to absorb the blood. An old boxing trick that a cutman had taught me once. Then I sat still. Waiting.

Soon there was a knock.

I opened the door, gun in hand.

Buster wore black jeans and a black leather jacket. His black hair was tied into a ponytail. He looked like a giant, sinister cowboy. Most people, opening the front door to find Buster facing them, would have had nightmares for weeks. I felt so much relief I wanted to give him a hug. He walked in and looked around the room and whistled. "You don't get to make fun of the mess in my office anymore." He was staring at me, taking in my face, my ripped and soaked clothing. "You look like you got kicked by a damn horse."

"You should see the other guys."

He looked around. Taking in the two bodies on the floor. Eric, and the *Chronicle* guy, bloody newspaper still folded across his lap. "You mean these other guys?"

I found two cans of beer in the refrigerator, handed one to Buster, and cracked the other. "How big is your trunk?"

He smiled wolfishly. "Big enough for two."

"Three," I corrected. "Needs to be big enough for three."

He looked around again. "Never been one for math, but I always figured I could count all the way up to two."

I nodded toward the closed bathroom door.

Buster followed my glance. Drank off half his can of beer and shrugged. "It'll be a tight fit, but they won't complain."

Less than half an hour later, we were out of the apartment.

"Need a lift anywhere?" he offered.

"That would be nice. They sort of kidnapped me."

He patted my shoulder with a big hand. "And I'm sure they're very sorry they did."

WEEK FOUR

36

"Nikki, your face—were you in a car accident?"

"We can call it that."

"Do you need help? Have you gone to the police?"

"The police can't help me."

"I always thought that's exactly what the police were for."

"I'll be okay."

"May I bring something up, Nikki? Something that might upset you?"

"It's been an upsetting week. This will fit right in."

"I took the liberty of doing some research. Nothing fancy, just some basic internet searches with your name. Articles came up, archived stories from twenty years ago."

"Is that right?"

"Your parents—I'm very sorry. May I ask what happened to you in the aftermath?"

"I don't talk about that."

"You've made that very clear, but why not tell me a little? Stop if you like."

"Other people told me that, too. Afterward. 'Just talk, tell us just a little, we're here to help you.' It was too late for them to help, though. Too late for talking to fix things."

"I assume you mean other therapists? After it happened? Maybe this is different, now."

"Different? How? I didn't have a choice about seeing them. Same as I don't have a choice about seeing you."

"Five minutes, Nikki. Talk to me for five minutes, and then leave. That's all I'm asking."

"Five minutes? And then I can go?"

"Yes."

"Okay. Sure. Five minutes. Why not? I was twelve when it happened. My brother was three years younger. No relatives on my dad's side; my mom had an estranged sister somewhere up in Oregon. So at first we were wards of the state, until they found different families to adopt us. Like puppies, I guess. Easier to find room for one than for two."

"What happened then?"

"I was in Stockton for a few years with one family. Things started badly and ended worse. Then I landed in Davis, with new foster parents. They were different. I lived with them until college, and when I got into Berkeley, they helped me with tuition. I owe them a lot."

"And your brother?"

"Brandon ended up in Fresno, in a strict, religious household. Eat-your-peas or go to bed types. With what happened, it was the worst place for him to be."

"Is your brother better now?"

"He's had a hard life. Drugs. Addiction. We each got some money when we turned twenty-one. From the estate, which was mostly just the sale of the house. My parents didn't have a lot of savings. The house was sold before prices really shot up in Bolinas, but it was something. I bought a building, started a business. My brother didn't do those things."

"How about you, Nikki, right now? Are you safe?"

"I got dragged into something. Now I have to drag myself out. I have a week to do it."

"How do you do that?"

"I don't know."

"I hope you figure it out."

"Me, too. If I do, you'll see me next week."

"And if you don't?"

"Then, probably, you won't."

37

I ate a salad at a popular new place in downtown Berkeley and thought about faces. I had looked at the In Retentis photographs so many times I had started to memorize them. Like the photos of suspected terrorists that the U.S. military had printed onto playing cards and given to the troops after the Iraq invasion. I wondered if any of the faces I was looking at had been on those cards. Doubtful. That had been almost fifteen years ago, and terrorists weren't known for their long lifespans. Surely those men were gone, replaced by others equally willing to give up their lives to murder others. November 1. The days ticking by. Less than a week. What had Karen Li been trying to tell me? What was I missing?

I pushed my plate away. Faces. Who were they?

"Nikki?"

I looked up and saw Ethan. He had come in with a group of friends. I stood to greet him, and then with a rush of guilt remembered the Vietnamese place. With everything that had happened that night it had been the last thing on my mind. "I didn't mean to stand you up the other night. I'm sorry."

"Sure. No problem." His voice indicated the opposite. "Anyway, I'm with friends. I just saw you and wanted to say hi." He started to move off toward the counter. "See you around."

"I wasn't trying to be a Pamela Flitton, honest," I called after him. He was the first guy I'd ever dated who I thought might get an Anthony Powell reference.

He turned, half smiling in spite of himself. "Don't worry, she broke many men's hearts. You only crushed mine. You have a long way to go." He took a closer look at me and the smile was gone. "Nikki, what happened to your face? Are you okay?"

"I'm fine," I said. The last thing I wanted to talk about was my face, bruised and puffy after my recent encounter with Victor. "I mean it," I went on. "I'm sorry. I have a really good excuse." *The men with guns walking up the bookstore stairs. Victor on top of me, his weight suffocating. Fingers tracing nauseatingly against my skin.*

"Does your excuse have something to do with those bruises?"

"Let's not talk about that." *The noise of the zipper. The recoil of the gun in my hand. Victor's face glaring up from the red bathwater.*

Ethan motioned for his friends to go ahead. "Did someone else try to *mug* you?"

"Hey! Not fair." *Joseph standing over my brother with the needle. The exhausting thumps of heavy bodies being dragged down endless flights of stairs.*

He nodded. "Sorry. You're right. That wasn't fair." He wasn't done. "Look, I like you, Nikki, a lot. But if there's always going to be something that gets in the way, then maybe we should just admit that now, no hard feelings, before we get too far."

I hated the validity of his words. My voice was tight as I answered. "It's not like that. We'll spend so much normal time together you'll be bored sick. The closest we'll get to excitement is overtime in Boggle." *Bleaching blood off floors, picking bullets out of walls.*

He didn't laugh. "I don't think that exists. Are you in trouble?"

"I can handle a little trouble." *The smell in the tub. The big toe left stuck in the bath drain after the last of the red water had swirled away.*

The nonchalance of my reply, rather than defusing the tension, seemed to make things worse. He was trying to talk quietly but his words tumbled out in frustration. "I guess I just don't get it. I mean, you know so much about books, food, everything; you're beautiful and funny and charming; we have this great connection; but you have this other side—this darker side. A scary side. The violence, these situations you keep getting into that I don't even know about—I honestly don't feel like I know who you actually are. And if I feel like that, if I'm always going to wonder, how can this work? How can *we* work?"

I stepped closer to him and took his hand. "I want it to work. What do you want to know? I'll tell you."

He didn't move away, but his hand stayed limp in mine. "I want to know *you*, Nikki. I don't mean all at once, I don't mean everything, I'm not asking for your e-mail passwords or to share bank accounts, but for this to work I need to feel like I understand you. And right now, I don't feel like I do."

"Okay," I said. "If you want, I'll tell you about myself."

He glanced over at his friends again and I added, "But not here. Come with me."

We sat on the grass near the campus library, the sweeping pillared steps behind us, the four-sided clock tower of the white stone campanile lancing the sky. A group of students threw a Frisbee. Others clustered on the grass with books and blankets. His hand rested on my leg and he waited for me to talk.

"I guess it starts on a Saturday, when I was in sixth grade," I finally began. "This was in Bolinas, where we lived." I felt the giddy thrill of releasing a secret. Like standing on a high building preparing to leap. "I'd been down on the beach playing with friends, and eventually we all headed home for lunch, except on my way back I decided I wanted an ice cream so I stopped at a place in town. I remember I ordered chocolate, two scoops in a waffle cone, and I filled a bag of jelly beans for my brother because they were his favorite."

I went on after a moment. "That ice cream saved my life."

His hand was holding mine. "Saved your life?"

I didn't answer directly. Just kept telling the story. "My parents were having a bunch of friends over for dinner—my mom loved to cook, loved to entertain. When I got home I remember smelling seafood and saffron, hearing a pot boiling. But everything was so quiet." *A strange smell under the saffron. An alien, metallic smell.* "Then I looked down and saw the floor." *A red pool spread across the linoleum. A silver wedge, partly covered by the spreading pool.*

"What was on the floor?" Ethan asked quietly.

I didn't say anything and after a moment he asked again. "What was it?"

"A butcher knife."

Sight scored by clicking sounds. Jelly beans skittering on the floor. Colorful ovals rolling, slowing as they reached the red puddle's viscosity. I continued. Jaw muscles tight, eyes fastened on the clock tower. "My mother was in the kitchen. Behind the counter. My father was in the living room. I read the police report years later. He must have heard my mom's screams, come running downstairs. They stabbed him immediately but he was able to crawl into the living room." *Clips of memory stitched back together, unevenly. Hard to know what went* *where. The severed cord to the kitchen phone. Kneeling. Touching. Crying. Then that accidental glance over into the living room. More shock. Seeing the pair of eyes star-*ing out at me. "My brother was in the living room, too. Under the couch. He had been there the whole time, hiding." *Later, grown-ups would try to explain to me that he was silent not because he was angry at me but because what he'd seen had left him unable to speak.* "He started talking again after a month. And I'd been out eating chocolate ice cream while it happened. I've never been able to eat it since."

When my family had needed me most. I had failed them.

Abandoned them and left them to die.

Ethan hugged me as he asked, "Who did it?"

I moved away. I didn't feel like being held or touched. Not by anyone. Not just then. "Two men from a little East Bay city, Hercules. Jordan Stone and Carson Peters."

"Why?" he wondered. "What would make them do that?"

It was too much. "That's enough," I said. "We can talk more another time. Not now. But that's part of who I am. Like it or not."

"I had no idea, Nikki," he was saying. His words seemed to float in from a distance.

"How could you have? I don't talk about it. But, like you said, you had a right to know. And I wouldn't have told you if I didn't want this to work."

I was standing.

"Did I do something wrong?" Ethan said, getting up quickly.

I forced myself to smile. "No! Not at all. But right now, I think I should be alone."

I walked the two miles back home from the Berkeley campus, still wrapped up in my thoughts. That was the problem with memories. They could be disobedient. Once allowed out they didn't always retreat on command. At the time of the killings, Jordan Stone had been only seventeen, a high school senior. Peters was a few years older, a dropout with a string of arrests. Their plan had been a series of home robberies and then Mexico. As though they could go door to door robbing homes and end up with enough to retire. They'd broken into two homes before ours. The occupants had been lucky. They hadn't been home. Our house had been third. My mom had answered the door. They told her their car was broken down. She probably would have offered them fresh-baked cookies while they waited for the tow truck. According to Jordan Stone's testimony, it was Peters who insisted there be no witnesses. The cops got them two days later, down in Salinas, trying to hold up a gas station with a baseball bat and a meat cleaver. The entire spree had netted them a stolen car, some jewelry and cash, and a bag of Flamin' Hot Cheetos that Jordan Stone had taken from the gas station.

In return they had left an injured gas station clerk, some damaged property, and my dead parents.

The Surf Town Slaughter, the papers had called the crime. A high-powered San Francisco lawyer volunteered to defend Jordan Stone pro bono, the free media attention worth more than any fees. Almost overnight he worked out a plea bargain and a new narrative. A naive, susceptible kid who'd fallen under the Manson-like influence of the older man. They both looked the part. A cheap shirt and tie couldn't hide the ominous tattoos across the neck of Carson Peters, his menacing eyes and shaved head. He had been sentenced to death, which in California meant life. He currently occupied a comfortable single cell in San Quentin, at a cost to taxpayers of about $150,000 a year.

Jordan Stone looked like a scared teenager. Blond bangs falling over his forehead, blue eyes welling with tears. No prior arrests, a bright future, one mistake. He had been a star athlete on his school's track team. At the trial, his line of character witnesses stretched around the block, everyone from ex-girlfriends to his AP U.S. History teacher. His parents and siblings—who all still happened to be alive—told emotional stories about his generosity and kindness.

The trial taught me that people liked clear roles. Liked to see other people—strangers—and think they knew them. After the trial Peters went off to death row and settled into an endless round of appeals. Jordan Stone pled guilty to manslaughter, went off to juvenile detention, turned eighteen, and was transferred to state prison where he got his GED, attended chapel, tutored other inmates.

He did everything one would expect from a person seeking rehabilitation.

He had been a model prisoner, the parole board would unanimously agree.

After the trial, I was bounced around for a couple of years, from a tough state home to foster parents who I still tried hard not to think about. Eventually I wound up in Davis with a second set of foster parents, Elizabeth and Jeff Hammond. I arrived expecting the worst, but the Hammonds were different. She was a librarian, and every day that summer I walked to her library to read. The library was a modest, one-story building and soon it felt closer to home than anything I'd had in a long time. The smell of dry paper and bindings, the fresh ink and cedar of the newspaper rack, the sunlight that poured through the windows in the reading room and bounced dust motes around in a languid, silent dance. That feeling of wandering alone between high shelves, the outside world forgotten, neck craned sideways to better make out titles dim against dark hardcover spines, feeling with each step the pleasure of a solitarian mixed with a pioneer's fascination at a new discovery.

That summer, the last before high school, was spent almost entirely in the library. I reread all the classic children's books: the Little House on the Prairie series, *The Secret Garden, Little Women, Black Beauty.* I read *The Swiss Family Robinson,* wondering why there was no daughter, and pictured my own family, marooned on some island somewhere, out of my reach forever. Then *Island of the Blue Dolphins,* imagining myself on some similar island, again alone. I found *James and the Giant Peach,* poring over the beginning again and again—parents slaughtered by a rampaging rhinoceros, alive one moment, brutally dead the next, a small boy sent to live with the two horrible aunts, beaten and abused before being freed to explore the world. I spent hours paging through *From the Mixed-Up Files of Mrs. Basil E. Frankweiler,* raptly imagining myself as Claudia Kincaid, running off to New York with my brother and hiding out together.

I found my way to the adult section and read dozens and dozens more books, cutting eagerly across time zones and time periods. I never talked to anyone by choice. I disliked when library patrons commented on my concentration or the impressive thickness of the book I held, like I was a dog that had dug up an especially sizeable bone. Talking made me uncomfortable. Strangers made me uncomfortable. Grown-ups made me uncomfortable. I hated feeling looked at or noticed and so I made a habit of taking the books away from the comfortable armchairs of the reading room, preferring to sit on the thin carpeting in a corner, away from everyone.

At that point in my life I only trusted books. Nothing else, no one else. Not even myself.

One type of book drew me more than any other. I read *Wuthering Heights, The Hunchback of Notre Dame, The Count of Monte Cristo, Carrie.* Even then I was thinking about people who were wronged and people who did wrong. Even then I was wondering if wanting to do bad things to bad people made me the same as them, and if I cared. Even then I was thinking about Carson Peters and Jordan Stone. About the people in the books I read, and the many more people who must be out there in the world, planning evil. Hating the fact that I was a gangly teenager who had never saved anyone.

I had let my parents die. I hadn't been there for my brother.

I had failed everyone in my life who mattered.

The thing that separated me from all those characters in my books was that unlike them, I was helpless to help myself, let alone anyone else. At that time, I was filled with many different unpleasant emotions, but the helplessness was the worst. I hated it so much. I opened my eyes each morning thinking about Jordan Stone and Carson Peters opening their own eyes. I pictured them eating breakfast, walking around, talking, laughing. I didn't talk much to anyone. Mostly I read, and thought, and remembered. But as I read, as the summer days passed, I began to hate myself a little less. I had books to thank for that. Books saved me, that summer. If it had been up to me, I never would have left the library.

Instead, the summer ended and there was school.

From the first day, I had a hard time making friends. Talking about boys or complaining about biology homework seemed impossible. I pretended, wishing I could care, and my disinterest was noted. I joined the soccer team and hated it. Rumors about me swirled. Even though I was pretty and athletic I was branded a loner, a misfit. The problems started immediately, those first few weeks of ninth grade. A boy announced that the people I lived with weren't my real parents. That afternoon the Hammonds joined me to talk to the principal, who explained that while playground scrapes were to be expected, it wasn't normal for a boy to leave school with a broken tooth and needing stitches, even if he had instigated things.

The Hammonds took me home and talked about self-restraint. They were called in again a few weeks later. Different kid, different details, basically the same outcome. "Nikki has been through a horrific tragedy," the principal acknowledged. "And I gather that her last foster experience was . . . very difficult and ended quite badly. We all want to help, but she stuck a sharpened pencil about an inch into this boy's arm. He's lucky there wasn't nerve damage. And what if it had been an eye?"

The Hammonds lingered at the dinner table that night, talking in hushed voices. Before I went to bed that night I packed my clothes. Came down to breakfast the next morning with my suitcase. The two of them exchanged glances. "Where are you going, Nikki?" Elizabeth asked.

"You'll send me back," I said. "So I'm ready to go."

I hadn't meant to make her cry. She hugged me. "We never will," she said. "I promise."

That day after school, instead of me walking to the library, Jeff Hammond picked me up and we drove to a shabby building marked by a red pair of boxing gloves painted on plywood. Inside was a blue-floored square ring surrounded by a triptych of red padded ropes. Two older boys circled each other in the ring, gloved hands flashing out, bodies shifting subtly. I took in the cylindrical black heavy bags, patched with electrical tape. In front of a mirror a man faced his reflection, ducking and moving. Another guy jumped rope.

I didn't know it then, but Jeff Hammond had boxed in the navy as a young man. "Nikki," he said, "hundreds of years ago, boxing began as a sport of violence, where the bigger, stronger men always won. Gradually, other men began to study movement and technique. And then the stronger, more violent men started losing to the boxers who possessed control. A lot of violent people have come to places like this gym and learned control. I think it would be a good thing if you could, too."

I took another look around. "They're all guys in here."

Jeff Hammond followed my gaze. The trainers, the boxers—I was right. All men.

He looked back at me. "What's your point?"

I thought about it. "I'm not sure."

That day he didn't do anything but show me how to tape my hands up. He gave me a pair of cloth hook-and-loop wraps and wrapped my hands for me, starting at the wrist, working up around the back of the hand and over the knuckles. Then he unraveled the strips of black cloth. Did it again. Then had me try. Ten times, twenty. Until I could have wrapped my hands with my eyes closed. That night I slept with the hand wraps next to me in bed.

The next afternoon I was back in the gym. Jeff Hammond showed me how to place my feet, how to hold my hands, how to move. I was left-handed. That was the first time I heard the word "southpaw." He didn't let me throw a punch for a week. I didn't put on actual gloves for a month. By that winter

I was sparring, mostly against older, bigger boys. I was naturally good and got better. I started competing in amateur fights. At school, the problems stopped.

I wasn't able to become Brandon's legal guardian until I was eighteen. By then it was too late. Drinking and pot and disobedience had given way to harder stuff, worse misbehavior. I didn't buy the gateway argument. I figured whatever gateway Brandon had gone through, it had been a long time ago. Now there were just the symptoms. He ran away three times before he started high school. By the time I began my freshman year at Berkeley, Brandon had more or less stopped going to school. He was past the point where I had any idea of how to help.

By my senior year he had discovered heroin.

I did my best to get him out of trouble. He made it to my graduation. Sitting in the audience with the Hammonds as a stream of important speakers explained all the great things we'd go on to do. Everyone clapped. People liked a narrative, especially if it involved their own success. As for me, I had no idea what I wanted to do after college. No idea of what I might be good at or find value in. No idea about what I was supposed to do with my life.

It was a woman with haunted eyes and a rotted marriage who would teach me those things. A woman and, of course, her husband.

I pushed the memories away as I got home. I poured myself a glass of wine and sat on the couch, watching as the bright daylight filling the room was gently throttled by evening shadows. I got up for more wine, returned to the couch, sitting quietly in almost total darkness. The past didn't matter. Not right now. Now, I needed answers. Which meant I had another woman I had to see, another rotted marriage hiding more secrets.

And another husband.

38

The Johnsons lived in Pacific Heights, an exclusive San Francisco neighborhood full of commanding homes high above the Bay. Their street sloped upward in the kind of ferocious angle that would have been unthinkable in any American city except San Francisco. The Johnsons' house was a large Victorian set into the top of a hill. Curtained picture windows looked blankly out at the city. The weather was turning colder as October reached its final days. Halloween decorations were up, scarves and hats appearing with more frequency. I had stared at my face in the mirror that morning, seeing the same bags under my eyes, the same lines of stress, that I had seen on Karen's face in Mendocino. I wasn't sleeping well. Care4 was in my mind constantly. The company was getting to me. Too many shadows, too many unknowns. I needed time that I didn't have.

Brenda Johnson had been surprised to hear from me, but she suggested that we meet at her home willingly enough. I waited outside and saw her walking up the street toward me. She must have been coming from the gym, wearing white sneakers and plum-colored leggings and a stylish athletic jacket made out of some kind of stretchy composite fabric. The kind that was marketed to joggers and yoga studios with words like "sweat-wicking" and "air-flow" all over the labels. Athleisure. The word, summoned suddenly into existence by parties unknown, was everywhere.

"Hi, Nikki," she said. "It's good to see you."

I was glad that she looked good, flushed and healthy and confident. Very different from the anxious and uncertain woman I had last seen the month before. I held up a cardboard tray, two large cups stuck into it. "I brought coffee. It might be a little cold."

Before we sat in the spacious living room, she opened the blinds, revealing panoramic views stretching out to the Bay. The kind of room made for entertaining, clearly furnished by a professional decorator. The paintings fit the walls almost too well, as though they had been chosen chiefly for horizontal and vertical spacing. The house had an open floor plan, a large chef's kitchen separated from the living room only by a granite island. A bookcase ran against one wall. The books seemed a mix of leather-bound law texts and newer nonfiction titles. *Eat Pray Love, The Secret, A Return to Love, How to Sleep Alone in a King-Size Bed.* I made a mental note to send Brenda some fiction.

"How have you been?" I asked.

She sat comfortably, a glass coffee table between us. "Lots of changes, but I'm better. Definitely much better. I suppose there's been a lot to get used to."

"Is he staying here now?"

"Who, Silas?" That drew her first smile. "I had the locks changed that same week we met. You should have heard him squeal the first time he realized his key didn't work. I think he's in a hotel for the time being. One of those fancy places off Union Square that makes you feel like you're entombed on the *Titanic*. I hope they forgot to get rid of the asbestos."

I smiled but kept quiet. She wasn't done talking.

"As it turns out, the personal trainer was the tip of the iceberg. I found out more. A lot more. He'd been carrying on with different women for more or less our whole marriage." Her face wrinkled in distaste. "Not to mention the escort services and God knows what else."

"I'm sorry to hear that."

"It's okay—better that I know." She smiled again. "The divorce will take awhile to formalize, of course, but then I can make a clean start." She stirred her coffee even though she'd stirred it three times already. "Thanks again, Nikki, for your help. And for not . . . taking me up on that rash request I made. I know it wasn't a good idea. Maybe that's why it felt so good asking."

"You were angry," I said. "You had a right to be. I get it."

"Thank you for understanding."

"Can I ask you a question? How much did Silas talk about his work to you?"

She was surprised. "His work? His legal work, you mean?"

"Yes."

She considered. "A little, over the years, but never in great detail. Frankly, the corporate law he practiced sounded boring. He liked to name-drop, and he worked for a lot of high-profile people and companies, but he didn't tell me much about the work itself. Just boasted how we'd be invited to some movie premiere or sports event because of his work with so-and-so."

"Did he ever mention a company called Care4? In the last few months especially?"

"No, I don't think so. Why, did something happen?"

"Nothing you need to worry about."

She took that in. "Meaning something *someone* needs to worry about."

"Maybe."

Brenda took the spoon she'd been stirring her coffee with and put it down on a saucer with a clink. The coffee was untouched. The paper cup looked out of place on the glass coffee table, next to the china saucer and silver teaspoon. "May I be blunt with you, Nikki?"

I nodded. "I like blunt."

"Good. My husband is a piece of shit. He lied to me and deceived me for over two decades. He broke every marriage oath in the book and I wish him anything but well." Her eyes were hard and determined. "You don't strike me as the type to make random coffee drops. You came here to ask me something. Well, you did me a favor, once—a big favor. You helped me to see the truth about my marriage, and you didn't let me overreact after I found out." She leaned toward me. "I'd like to return that favor. I don't know what you want or what you're up to or how it fits in with my husband and, honestly, as long as it doesn't improve the quality of his life I don't care. Anything I can do— just ask."

The sun was coming in bright through the east-facing windows. I shifted a little so it wasn't in my eyes. "Last time we talked, you mentioned that you had copied the key to your husband's office. Do you still have it?"

She was surprised. "I can't believe you remember that. But yes, I think so. One second." She got up and went over to the kitchen island for her purse. She searched through it and came back over with a single brass key. One side was engraved with the words DO NOT COPY.

"Does he know you have this?"

"I did it secretly." She smiled. "It took me forever to find a locksmith who would do it in spite of the 'Do Not Copy.' I had to pay him an extra hundred dollars. Why do you ask?"

"You're right," I said. "I do need a favor from you. Can I borrow that key?"

39

People could be funny. They often seemed to like things to happen without caring much about how. For example, offices. People who worked in offices liked them to be clean, but they didn't like actually seeing the cleaning process. Partly a matter of convenience. No one wanted to be on an important phone call with a vacuum cleaner going in the background. There was something more, I'd always thought. People preferred not to think about someone scrubbing a toilet or mopping a floor. They just wanted the toilet to be pristine and the tiles on the floor to gleam like they'd never been stepped on. So it made sense that custodians tended to be nocturnal. The fewer people they encountered, the happier everyone was. They could work more efficiently, and employees could walk in each morning without having to think about coffee stains or dirty sinks. An arrangement that suited everyone.

At a law firm, plenty of people worked late. The junior partners tended to leave reasonably early and the senior partners earlier still, but the hungry young associates saddled with billable hour quotas were eager to have their late-night e-mails and punch-out times prove their worth as they chased promotion. Working until nine, ten, maybe eleven at night was no problem for associates in their twenties. Seventy, eighty hours or more a week was normal.

The custodial outfit that cleaned the offices of Gilbert, Frazier & Mann probably cleaned a dozen different sets of corporate offices each night. They were an efficient group. Six of them traveling in two minivans. They carried equipment with them and seemed to reach Gilbert, Frazier & Mann between eleven and eleven thirty nightly. The firm took up three floors of a skyscraper in San Francisco's Financial District. The kind of place that during business hours had security in the front lobby and a strict sign-in system for visitors. After hours the building relied on electronic readers and swipe cards. Law firms were busy places. They wanted their lawyers to be able to work late.

As the last of the six cleaners walked into the building, I stepped around the corner and waited until the glass door had swung closed. Then I kicked the door loudly with my foot. It hurt. I was used to kicking with motorcycle boots, not open-toe heels. The last of the six turned at the noise. I kicked the door a second time. Impatiently. As though annoyed at even a second of delay. He came back and opened the door, a small Hispanic guy in a Giants sweatshirt and baggy jeans. I walked in, barely nodding as I passed him. "Thanks."

He started to say something and then changed his mind. I was wearing a black skirt with a blouse and blazer. My hair was pinned up into a bun and my arms barely wrapped around a large cardboard shipping box, so full the top flaps couldn't close properly. I walked purposefully across the lobby until I was in the midst of the group waiting for the elevator. They watched me. One of them whispered something in Spanish to another. They seemed torn between wanting and not wanting to ask me something.

"Excuse me, do you work here, ma'am?" the second one finally asked.

I gave a curt nod without looking at him. The kind of short, impatient gesture that said my mind was on far more important things. There was a floor directory by the elevator. Gilbert, Frazier & Mann were floors ten, eleven, and twelve. I stood by the elevator and got one hand from under the box, juggling it on my knee as I tried to bring a lanyard and plastic card around to the card reader. It couldn't have looked easy. "Shit!" I exclaimed as the box I was holding started to fall. I tried to catch it, clumsily, and wasn't able to get my arms back around it in time. The box hit the floor and several manila folders fell out. Papers scattered over the floor. "Damnit," I said with more irritation, and knelt to grab up the papers. "Hold that, will you?" I called as the elevator opened.

It wasn't really a request. They held the door while I stuffed papers back into the box. It was a tight fit in the elevator. Pressing the box against the wall, I freed a hand and managed to hit the button for the twelfth floor. Silas

Johnson's Pacific Heights Victorian had been too expensive for him to be anything but a senior partner. He'd be on the top floor. The janitorial crew got out on ten, where the reception area and kitchenette would be. The most time-consuming floor to clean.

On the twelfth floor, the overhead lights were off and the hallway was almost pitch black. No one working late up here. I set my box down in a stairwell next to the elevator and pulled a bright LED flashlight from my purse. The offices all had little brass name plaques screwed into the hardwood doors. The doors were set apart at lengthy intervals. Spacious offices, up here on the partners' floor. I moved quickly. I didn't want to be in the building all night. I found Silas Johnson's office and used the key his wife had given me. Inside I kept the overhead light off and used my flashlight, turning it this way and that so that the room came into view. It was a large, comfortable office furnished principally with a black leather couch and a hulking mahogany desk. A bookshelf held the same sort of legal texts I'd seen at the Johnson house, all leather and gilt titles that gleamed like treasure as I shined the light along the spines. There was a steel file cabinet against the far wall. Five drawers, all locked. I didn't bother trying my key. I could tell by sight it was too big.

Busy lawyers needed quick access to documents. And in a locked office in a security-conscious building, people didn't think much about theft. I shined my light over toward the large desk. There was a vertical column of closed drawers on the left side and a narrow horizontal front drawer. I wasn't surprised to find the front drawer unlocked. The thin beam of the light illuminated standard office paraphernalia: paper clips, rubber bands, staples, pens. In a corner of the drawer there were two small silver keys. One fit the file cabinet.

I spent an hour going through the file cabinet drawers one by one. Judging by the dates, the cases seemed to be current. The firm would have archives of some kind where they stored the work of past years or decades. I worked as fast as I could, looking for any mention of Care4 or Gregg Gunn or In Retentis.

Nothing.

The desk was messy, covered in papers. Unlikely that any sensitive material would be left out in the open, but I went through everything anyway.

Nothing.

I checked the trash can, digging through a browned apple core and several empty Diet Coke cans, a copy of *The Wall Street Journal*.

The three vertical drawers of the desk were also locked. I tried the second key from the desk. It worked. I started at the bottommost drawer. It held a nearly empty bottle of Macallan eighteen-year single malt. Not a cheap bottle. Two unopened bottles of the same stuff lay behind it. Like a one-man supply chain. Two lowball crystal glasses were tucked neatly into the drawer next to several *Penthouse* and *Playboy* issues. The tanned, air-brushed girls on the cover looked about the same age as the scotch, and the same color.

The middle and top drawers held more files. I worked my way through them as fast as I could. Understanding anything about the nature of the cases would have been a far longer job, but it was easy enough to tell which people and companies were involved where.

I found the Care4 file in the top drawer. Three folders, rubber-banded together.

I had just opened the first folder when the office door opened.

I threw myself under the desk and clicked my light off as the overhead light turned on. I narrowed my eyes in the brightness and huddled under the desk. The front panel meant that I was invisible as long as no one came around to the back.

It also meant I didn't know who was in the office with me.

An unsettling feeling.

Footsteps moved closer and I caught a glimpse of an old white sneaker under a slice of loose jeans. I relaxed a little. Lawyers who drove Mercedes S-Class sedans didn't wear beat-up Nikes. If they wore sneakers, they'd be brand-new. I tried to figure out where these sneakers were likely to step next. The trash can. The cleaners would go office to office, emptying the trash cans. No one wanted to sit down in the morning and smell decomposing apple cores. I stayed very still. The cleaner's feet came closer. I heard a grunt as he bent down. The trash can lay less than a foot away from my head, separated only by the side of the desk. I held my breath and stayed absolutely still. I heard the trash can empty into a bag. Heard the rustle of papers and the more solid thump of an object. The apple core. I could hear plastic crinkling. A new bag, being shaken open.

Then silence. I couldn't see the sneakers anymore.

Five or six seconds stretched on forever. Finally, I heard footsteps again. Moving away from me. The custodian hit the light switch and the room was dark again. The office door closed. I let out my breath. Slowly getting to my feet, I switched the flashlight on again and sat at the leather desk chair, file in front of me.

It was time for some reading.

Gilbert, Frazier & Mann had been involved with Care4 for several years and appeared to have done a variety of legitimate work. As the partner who oversaw the Care4 account, Silas Johnson had been involved in much of this work. It was clear that the folders I was looking through were far from complete. There were probably thousands or tens of thousands of additional documents, filed somewhere on the firm's three floors. These folders offered only an overview. I learned that he had helped guide the company through equity financing in its early stages. I reached the second folder, which involved litigation and HR. One case, involving trade secrets with a rival company, had gone to court. Several contract disputes had been settled in arbitration. When it came to its employees, Care4 didn't hesitate to use its lawyers aggressively. The next folder was thinner and pertained mostly to financial and tax matters. Other lawyers were referenced. Silas Johnson didn't directly handle tax law. A different department.

After an hour I didn't feel like I knew anything more about what I was searching for. Silas Johnson's work seemed exactly what his wife had described it as: boring corporate law. The files could have been dealing with any corporation. Nothing stood out. No mention of In Retentis or strange photographs or murdered employees or criminal investigations. Nothing secretive or villainous. In fact, the most scandalous thing I'd found all night were the *Penthouse* magazines. I'd have to figure out a different angle. Silas Johnson was a terrible husband, but as a lawyer he seemed boring, capable, and nothing more.

Putting the rubber bands back around the three folders I stopped, interested. There was a fourth folder in the stack. I hadn't noticed it at first because it was completely empty. A plain olive-green filing folder containing absolutely nothing. The kind of folder that sold at Staples for about seventy cents. Just a basic organizational vessel to put papers in.

Or take papers out of.

Maybe this was nothing. Or maybe there had been other papers inside it. Papers that Silas Johnson didn't trust to a locked desk in a locked office in a locked building. Papers that weren't boring corporate law filed routinely for any company in the country. Papers that the lawyer would want to keep extremely close. I relocked the drawers and made sure everything was exactly how I had found it. When I was done, the only difference from when I walked in was the now-empty trash can, loaded with a new trash bag and ready for the next day.

The cleaners had long left. On to the next building, the next stop of their long night. I found the cardboard prop box where I had left it in the stairwell and headed down the stairs in the red glow of the emergency lights.

Thinking about the next step.

40

The Kingston Hotel was a block off Union Square, on Geary Street. It had a grandiose Art Deco feel. Not the sleek, minimalist luxury of newer hotels, but a more ornate style out of a Dreiser or Fitzgerald story. The lobby floor was white and black marble like a chessboard. Oil paintings in gold frames hung on the walls below crystal chandeliers. It was exactly the type of hotel that I would have imagined a wealthy, middle-aged lawyer would go to if kicked out of his apartment.

I didn't know much about Silas Johnson, but I knew that he liked women and he liked a drink. Those facts counted for something. So I wasn't surprised to find that he seemed to be a regular at the hotel bar. The hotel lobby offered a clear view of the bar. Basic architectural strategy: the more people that could see a place, the more likely they'd be to go in. The lobby was full of couches and armchairs. Easy enough to sit unobtrusively and watch.

The first night the lawyer unsuccessfully hit on a pretty Indian woman about my age who sat at the bar with a laptop and a glass of white wine. There was an unwritten rule that people on laptops weren't generally around to be picked up. They were there to work. To concentrate. Silas Johnson either didn't know about this rule, or didn't care. Maybe he took it as a challenge. I watched as he sent a glass of champagne her way, via the barman.

The woman drank the champagne but didn't seem much interested in the person behind it. The lawyer's face showed irritation. Silas Johnson clearly liked women who thanked him after he sent them unsolicited bubbles. A few minutes went by. I watched him lean over and say something to her. Her face froze up in the kind of polite smile that women all over the world are used to giving in those situations. I noticed the sparkle of a diamond on her left hand. Maybe the lawyer had noticed it, too. Maybe he hadn't. Even the best-intentioned men seemed to notice those details imperfectly. And Silas Johnson didn't seem like the world's best-intentioned man.

He also didn't seem like the kind of man to take a hint. He finished the Manhattan he was drinking, ordered another, said something else, and patted the empty bar chair next to him. Like he was calling a dog to sit. This time there was annoyance behind her smile as she shook her head. A moment later the Indian woman got up and carried her laptop and drink to the far end of the bar.

That night Silas Johnson went to his room alone.

The next night he was back in the same spot. The bar was a bit more crowded on the second night. The lawyer's gaze flicked around the room to different women but he didn't talk to anyone. He checked his watch several times. By the time he'd worked his way through his first Manhattan, a tall blond woman in a tight black dress walked in. She must have been thirty years younger than the lawyer. She had red nails and copious eye shadow and a pair of stiletto heels that looked high enough to let her wade right across the Pacific without getting her hair wet. The lawyer stood, smiling. The woman walked over and he kissed her on the cheek. She sat next to him.

He drank a second Manhattan while she put down three vodka sodas, one after the other. I couldn't blame her. In her position, I would have had six. He whispered something in the woman's ear and they got up with their drinks.

I watched him sign for the tab.

I watched the two of them leave the bar and head for the elevators.

That was the second night.

The third night he talked to me.

Nothing about the situation was ideal. I liked to spend at least a week following someone before any contact. A night or two wasn't nearly enough to learn someone's habits. I preferred to watch someone interacting with the people in his life, learn his routine. I didn't have the luxury of time, though. It was the twenty-ninth of October and I still had no real idea of what was going to happen on November 1. *People will die.* The words had been looping around in my mind until I felt like I was starting to go crazy. I knew increasingly how Karen Li must have felt in her last weeks. Too much uncertainty, too much stress. Care4 had taken over my mind. Whatever Silas Johnson had or knew, I couldn't wait any longer to find out. Even watching him for two nights had been pushing it. I had to act.

The first hint of his interest was a flute of champagne that descended in front of me, the small circle of glass clinking delicately against the zinc bar. I looked up inquiringly. Past the golden effervescence of the glass to the bartender who had set it down. "Did I order that?"

The bartender shook his head disinterestedly. His face was neither golden nor effervescent. He was a thin man with a wide forehead, a large reddened nose, and a mustache the color of calking putty. In keeping with the rest of the hotel, he was dressed formally in a white shirt, black tuxedo vest, and maroon bow tie. The bow tie was a clip-on and the vest was slightly too big. He looked like he'd done this routine a million times and expected to do it a million more. "From the gentleman down the bar," he explained.

He nodded in the direction of Silas Johnson.

I followed the bartender's look and met eyes with the lawyer for the first time. He was at his usual seat with his usual drink. He was a handsome enough man in a rumpled, affluent way. His brown eyes were set deep in his face and gave the impression of pugnacious shrewdness. He had a salt-and-pepper goatee and a square, heavy head. The knot on his tie was loosened and his checked blue sports coat was open, revealing a belly that the personal trainer had apparently been unable to do much about. He gave me a broad smile and raised his drink. I wasn't worried that he might recognize me from the Care4 parking lot, where I'd been wearing a full-face motorcycle helmet. I'd spent the last two evenings in the lobby, but the lawyer's attention had been focused elsewhere. He hadn't seen me.

I nodded without lifting my own glass and went back to my book. I turned a page and took a sip of my red wine. The champagne sat untouched on the bar. I turned a few more pages, not minding the passing minutes. *Portrait of a Lady* was a favorite. I drank more of my wine. My hair was down and I wore a simple black dress that showed my figure.

Finally, I heard his voice. "That champagne is thirty dollars a glass. You're not going to drink it?"

I looked up again. He was leaning toward me, voice raised slightly, smiling to show that he didn't really care about wasting thirty dollars on a drink. I looked from the lawyer to the champagne. "I'm not sure. But if I do, I know where to find it."

He gave me a look to see if I was being flirtatious or insulting. My tone had been neither. Just matter-of-fact. I was already back to my book. He called down the bar again. "Maybe champagne isn't your thing. Would you prefer something else?"

I gave him a polite smile and nodded at my wine. "I have something else."

I kept reading. Another slow night, the nightcap-after-dinner crowd long gone. The bar was almost empty. No other single women. No one else for the lawyer to order expensive champagne for.

Only me.

He tried again, changing tactics. "What are you reading?"

"This?" I looked up, as if trying hard to associate my book with the stranger in front of me. *"Portrait of a Lady.* Do you know it?"

He didn't look interested as he shook his head. "Afraid not. That's a big book. Looks worse than what they threw at me in constitutional law."

"Is that your way of telling me that you're a lawyer, or that I should be reading something easier?"

He grinned. "I always did like to kill two birds with one stone." He let the sentence hang there for a second and then went on. "I'm teasing. I'd never tell you what to read."

"Or what to drink." I went back to the book.

Reading a page of Henry James wasn't the quickest thing in the world, but this time I barely made it through a paragraph before I heard his voice again. "You're so far away. I feel like I have to shout just to talk to you."

"If you weren't talking to me you wouldn't have that problem."

He smiled. "But then I wouldn't be talking to you."

"All that logic," I observed. "Maybe you really are a lawyer."

"Not just *a* lawyer. I happen to be a really good lawyer."

"I'll be sure to call you next time I get pulled over for speeding."

He didn't love that. Humor often seemed to fall before ego. "I'm a partner in a firm that handles things a touch more important than speeding tickets. Come sit over here," he urged. "I promise you I'm more interesting than a book."

"You're setting a pretty high bar for yourself," I warned as I got up and sat next to him. He looked triumphant as he ordered another Manhattan. "And whatever she's drinking, another," he told the bartender.

The drinks were set down even though my first glass of wine was still more or less full.

"Now," Silas said, "I'm going to run to the little boys' room, and then you're going to tell me all about yourself."

For some reason, I'd always disliked men who called the bathroom the little boys' room. One day maybe I'd meet the exception to that rule, but it didn't seem likely to happen tonight. The lawyer got off his stool and headed toward the restroom off the main lobby. I sat there, the two drinks in front of me. Silas's Manhattan was a garnet color. A flat twist of orange peel curled on the rim. I looked over at the bartender. He was across the bar, busy taking glasses out of an under-the-counter dishwasher. I discreetly emptied a small capsule of white powder into the Manhattan. The powder immediately dissolved, leaving nothing more than a slight cloudiness in the drink. I glanced around again. No one looking anywhere near me. The whole thing had taken perhaps five seconds.

Silas was back. "Still here." He grinned. "I wasn't sure if you'd run away."

"I've never much liked running away from people."

The lawyer sat back down and raised his glass.

I watched the rim ascend.

The glass stopped just shy of his mouth. He was giving me a strange look. He put the glass back down on the counter.

"Everything okay?" My tone was casual but I was running the last several minutes, and several nights, back and forth in my mind, wondering. Had he seen something or recognized me? What could have given it away?

He shifted the glass around on the bar, still watching me. "Your face," he finally said.

"My face? What about it?"

His eyes were narrowed as if trying to place me. As if there was some kind of delayed-fuse recognition process occurring. Depending on what he said, I'd need to either bluff or leave the hotel. Quickly. And then figure out how to get what I wanted with the addition of a very suspicious lawyer who would be asking all kinds of questions on behalf of his clients. An outcome that would turn an extremely difficult problem into a hopeless one.

He pointed a finger toward my face. "Those bruises—what happened?"

I realized with relief he was just noticing the marks left by Victor in my brother's apartment. They had faded a little and I had used makeup to cover the worst, but bruising was still visible. "Slipped and fell," I said apologetically. "I guess maybe I'm just a bit of a klutz."

The lawyer smiled affectionately. "Now you don't have to worry. You have me here to catch you." He raised his glass again and gulped half the drink. His brow furrowed. He looked like he'd sucked on a lemon. He called over to the bartender. "You way overdid the bitters, Brian. Remake this, will you?"

The bartender came over and removed the offending glass. He emptied it into the sink and made another Manhattan and placed it back in front of the lawyer. "Apologies. Hope that's better, sir."

Silas took a judgmental sip. "Considerably." He turned his attention back to me. "Now, where were we?" He answered his own question. "Ah, yes. You were going to tell me all about yourself."

Like some men, he had the habit of meaning the opposite of what he said. I hadn't much felt like talking about myself, but I needn't have worried. What the lawyer really meant was that he wanted to talk about himself. And he did. I learned all about the important cases he handled and the giant settlements he negotiated and the huge fees he commanded. I learned about his unfortunate treatment at the hands of his ungrateful wife, and his upcoming divorce, and how unfair it was that he had to give her so much of his hard-earned money. "She had me followed!" he exclaimed, like he was still upset by the whole thing. "Photographed, even! Can you imagine?"

"I guess I can picture it."

The conversation shifted as he ordered another drink. I was still sipping my original glass of wine. He kept talking. I learned about his views on everything from why the Sundance parties were overrated to the mistakes we made on foreign policy. I learned about the beautiful, exclusive vacations he took and what great Warriors seats he had, thanks to having represented a friend of the owners in some long-gone case. "Play your cards right," he added, "and maybe you can come to a game with me. Bet you'd like that."

"I always try to play my cards right," I said, my voice soft and now a little flirtatious.

He finished his drink and turned to me. He seemed a little drunk. His face was flushed. "You know, you're very beautiful."

"Thanks."

"What's a beautiful woman like you doing all alone at a bar?"

"You really want to know?"

"Yes."

I looked directly into his eyes. "I've been watching you."

He liked that. "Really? You were watching me?"

I nodded. "I've been watching you like you wouldn't believe."

He seemed to like that even more. His eyes were all over me. "I have a beautiful suite upstairs," he said. "Best suite in the whole place. Come up for a drink."

"A drink," I repeated. "I suppose I could handle that."

His face lit up. He was happy. The night was going beyond well. "Perfect." He called over to the bartender again. "I'll take the check, Brian, and give me a bottle of champagne and an ice bucket, will you? Veuve, not Dom," he added more quietly. For all his ostentatiousness, the lawyer didn't seem opposed to cutting corners if he could get away with it.

While Silas signed the check, the bartender put a bottle of yellow-labeled champagne in a silver ice bucket. He loaded ice into the bucket and then folded a white napkin into a thin rectangle and draped it around the lip of the bucket. A nice touch. The lawyer seemed indifferent. He grabbed the bucket with one hand and my arm with the other. "Upstairs we go," he said.

He was right. He did have a beautiful suite. No way to tell if it was the nicest in the hotel, but it was a nice one. A big corner suite on the top floor. A large dining area and a living room substantially bigger than my own. A balcony revealing the lights of the city. There was a bedroom off to the side. Through lace-curtained French doors, a king bed lurked. With no forewarning, Silas embraced me and tried to sloppily kiss me. One hand felt its way to my behind. I pushed him away. "I thought you were offering a drink."

"Of course," he said. He didn't seem all that deterred. He shed his sports jacket and tie and busied himself with the champagne while I looked around. He had clearly been living in the hotel for a while. His presence was everywhere. There were clothes and bags strewn all over. I saw with interest that the desk was covered in papers. Next to the desk was a briefcase. Maybe more papers in the bedroom. Many people worked from bed. Especially in a hotel. Maybe Silas liked to get started first thing in the morning, comfortably horizontal, with a room-service tray and fresh coffee within arm's reach.

The lawyer was still occupied with the champagne bottle. He had unwrapped the gold foil and was twisting ineffectually at the cork.

"You look like that cork's giving you some trouble."

"Yeah," he said. "I'm okay . . ." His words were slurred and tired. He fumbled at the cork and almost dropped the bottle.

"Let me help you." I took the bottle from him. He didn't protest. He looked at me dully, shirt half unbuttoned. Thankfully, he hadn't gotten to his pants yet. His chest was covered by hair. I remembered it from my photographs. I twisted slightly, loosening the cork, and then got a thumb under the edge and applied pressure. I thought of his hand, squeezing my ass in the same possessive way that he had seized the ice bucket.

There was a loud pop. The cork shot out. It turned out that the bottle neck had been pointed Silas's way. The cork bounced off his nose.

He rubbed his nose and looked confused. "Oww," he stated. "That hurt."

"Sorry. My fault. Maybe you should sit down," I suggested.

"I'm fine," he said, but let me lead him into the bedroom all the same.

He sat on the edge of the bed and watched me as I found a water glass. I poured champagne into the glass until it was full. I handed the glass to him. "Cheers. Drink up."

The lawyer took the glass like a child and drank.

I watched him. He was sweating. His eyes were half-closed.

"More," I suggested. "You're almost there."

"More," he repeated as he drank. "More . . . more."

"Good boy." I patted him gently on the head. He had almost finished the glass when his hand loosened. The glass fell out of his hand and landed on his lap. Spilled champagne moistened his crotch. His eyes were fully closed. He slumped sideways onto the bed, breathing audibly. I picked up the glass and put it on the coffee table. Then I took a long, critical look at the lawyer. He had started snoring. I pulled his feet over onto the mattress so he wouldn't roll off. Silas Johnson looked like every marching band in the Big Ten could have been in the room playing at full volume and he wouldn't have even blinked. He'd wake up with a hellish hangover, but he'd be fine.

I went to work.

It took me under an hour to go through every single document in the suite, starting with the briefcase. The lawyer seemed to be simultaneously working on several cases. Some of the names were familiar from the search of his office, and some weren't. But I couldn't find anything about Care4. I was careful to put each paper back exactly in its original place. The last thing I wanted was Silas Johnson wondering if he'd had his room searched.

On the second pass through the room I pulled his pants off and checked his pockets. I went through his wallet, seeing platinum credit cards, a plastic room key, various insurance and membership cards, a driver's license, two condoms, a thick fold of cash, and several folded pieces of paper with phone numbers that I assumed to be the fruits of his bar-and-champagne routine.

I also found his car key. The Mercedes. It had been a silver late-model sedan, I remembered. An S550. I wasn't thrilled about having to check the car. It would be parked in the hotel garage. I didn't like parking garages. Cameras everywhere. It was one thing being in a hotel room. If anyone checked security footage, all it would show was me accompanying the more-than-willing occupant of the room and then later leaving alone. Hard to take issue with that. A parking garage was different. Tapes would show a woman unlocking and searching a car that wasn't hers. Not to mention the problems that could occur if there were monitors being checked in real time by security. All kinds of potential trouble. But I didn't really have a choice.

I took his room key from his pocket. No matter what I found, I would need to get back into the room to return the car key.

I was walking out when I saw the safe.

It was in the closet. A standard hotel safe, black-painted steel bolted into the wall, hidden behind a row of dark suits. A basic model with a keypad and small digital display. A small white square of paper was glued onto the front of the safe, offering simplistic directions for setting a code and unlocking it.

Hotel safes were designed with two considerations: security and convenience. The goal was to offer a basic level of protection while ensuring that the unlocking process wasn't so complicated that a stream of annoyed guests would flood the front desk with forgotten combinations. Hotel safes weren't even comparable to the really good home models. Just enough to satisfy a standard hotel insurance policy. This one was pretty average. Four digits, according to the instructions. Crucially, there was no cut-off feature. The safe wouldn't shut down after a certain number of incorrect guesses the way an iPhone would. Four digits was a lot easier for a guest to remember than six or eight digits. Four digits was also a lot easier to guess. Exponentially fewer combinations.

But even four digits meant ten thousand possible combinations.

That was a lot. Far too many to try one by one.

I spent the first few minutes running through all the basic combinations that people used when they were rushed or complacent. A handful of combinations covered a big chunk of the PINs and passcodes people chose. I began with the most obvious numbers. 0000 and 0101 and 1010 and 1111 and 9999 and 1234 and 4321.

None worked.

Next was more common stuff. 2222, 3333, all the way to 8888. I went through sequential, easy-to-remember combinations: 2345, 3456, 4567, 5678, 6789, 7890. Then back down: 0987, 9876. Trying any sequence that was easier to remember than a random group of four numbers.

Each time, just a blinking red light marking failure. If Silas Johnson had gone with a random combination, I was missing it.

The next stage was more personal. I pulled his driver's license from his wallet and tried his birthday, backward and forward. 6/2/1956 translated to 6256 or 6591. Nothing. His street address was 1004 and I tried that, backward and forward and mixed up. I tried digits off his credit card numbers and his medical record number from his health insurance and even combinations based on the phone numbers in his wallet. I didn't know his wedding date but that didn't matter. Soon-to-be divorced philanderers who had been kicked out of their apartments weren't thinking about their wedding day.

Nothing worked. I checked the time. Over two hours had passed.

I had to go.

The safe was probably empty, I told myself. Silas Johnson was a slob. His stuff was all over the room. He didn't seem like the type to take elaborate security precautions. If he had anything, it must be in the car.

The room door closed behind me. I headed down the hallway.

At the elevator bank I pushed the Down button and waited, picturing the car I was looking for. This hotel probably had a new Mercedes in every other parking spot. Silas's car had been silver, four doors. I remembered the curved, taut lines of the roof and distinctive five-spoke rims. There had been a vanity plate. I thought back, trying to remember it. Vanity plates were easy to recall. Too easy. I didn't understand why people paid to have them. I would have paid not to. LAW something. Numbers after the letters. LAW1981.

1981. According to his driver's license, Silas Johnson had been born in 1956. Assuming he graduated college at twenty-two, in 1978, and gone straight on to law school, he would have graduated and sat for the bar in 1981. Silas Johnson was many things, but he didn't seem like the type to fail the bar. In which case, by any measure—whether graduating law school, taking, or passing the bar—Silas Johnson had become a lawyer in 1981.

1981.

Four digits.

The elevator door opened.

I didn't move.

I turned around and headed back the way I'd come, hearing the elevator door close behind me. Back in the suite, I checked on Silas. He was sprawled on the bed, snoring with tremendous volume, mouth open. I went back to the safe and punched in the four digits.

1981.

This time the light flashed green.

I opened the safe. The first thing I saw was a stack of hundred-dollar bills. To pay the call girls, no doubt. Under the money was a white stack of eight-by-eleven papers. Papers that would fit perfectly into an olive-green document folder. The top paper bore two words.

IN RETENTIS.

I'd only read through the first couple of pages when I stopped and carried the pages to the kitchen counter. I turned up the overhead lights as bright as they'd go, took my camera, and started photographing close-up shots of the documents. There were over a hundred pages. So I took over a hundred pictures. Along the way, I started to understand why even a sloppy, drunken lawyer was so careful with security and concealment. Why the papers weren't sitting around his office or briefcase with everything else. I started to understand why Karen Li had been so frightened, and why she had gone through such elaborate pains to hide the photographs I had found.

I started to understand more about those photographs.

By the time I finished, I knew a lot more about Care4, and In Retentis, and what was going to happen on November 1. *People will die.* That's what Karen Li had said. She had been right. People would die.

But I had been completely wrong about who.

I had barely two days.

It was past two in the morning when I finished. I was even more careful to put everything back as I'd found it now. Because I knew more. I closed and locked the safe, resetting the code to the same four digits, 1981. Silas Johnson was still snoring in his king bed. I looked at him. The last few days hadn't endeared him to me, but I hadn't considered him much more than a mild form of dirtbag. My opinion had changed. With what I now knew, I would have liked to do all kinds of things to the man snoring in front of me.

I couldn't touch him, though. Silas Johnson needed to wake up without suspicion. Which meant that he'd avoid what he deserved. Things weren't always fair.

I pulled off the rest of his clothes and tossed them at various places on the floor. As though they'd been passionately stripped and strewn. The owner of the passionately stripped clothes lay on his back, naked and snoring. This was the second time I'd seen him naked. I could do without a third. I took one of the condoms from his wallet, opened it, and threw the empty wrapper conspicuously on the floor near the bed. The condom itself I flushed down the toilet. I was going to open the other as well for good measure but I held off. No need to further swell his ego. I put his wallet and car keys and room key back in his pants pockets and jotted a line onto the hotel stationery on the nightstand.

Last night was everything I wanted. You were perfect.

The pen was nice. I kept it. I poured myself a glass of champagne. The ice was mostly melted but the bottle was still cold. I went out to the balcony and stood watching the city and thinking about what I was going to do next. Wondering if I'd get through the next day.

I closed my eyes, seeing the cabin, the broken windowpane, the woman on the floor. I hadn't kept her safe. I hadn't protected her.

The odds were against me, but finally I understood what I was up against.

Now, maybe, I could redeem myself.

I opened my eyes.

All in.

41

I found an all-night diner on Van Ness where I drank coffee and ate scrambled eggs, thinking about that first diner, over a month ago, where I had met Ethan. I wondered if he'd called me since our conversation. I got up and used the diner's phone to check my voice mail. Nothing from Ethan, but there was a new message from Jess. It had been left an hour earlier and her voice was plainly stressed. "Nikki, it's your brother. Get over here when you can." I hung up with a stab of guilt. I shouldn't have left Jess with Brandon for that long without checking in. The Care4 case was affecting me.

It was late enough that the roads were empty. It took me barely fifteen minutes to get back into the East Bay. The wind was fierce and as I swept across the luminous Bay Bridge I could feel the gusts tugging and pushing at the motorcycle. The hotel was in Emeryville, a nondescript city wedged between Berkeley and Oakland. One of the ubiquitous chains found off every freeway in the country. Nothing compared to the five-star place I had left earlier that night. No ornate marble lobby or bartender pouring cocktails. A young night clerk in a wrinkled blue shirt slumped behind a glass window off the side of the empty lobby, his head resting on a paperback, eyes closed. The spine was turned toward him so I couldn't make out the title. Next to a stained table with an empty coffee urn, a rack of bright brochures offered discounts on local theme parks and haunted houses. I found the elevator and creaked up to the second floor at about half the speed of climbing a staircase. Jess was sitting in a chair by the bed.

"How is he?"

She nodded toward the bed. Brandon lay on top of the twisted sheets, naked except for a pair of boxer shorts. He was soaked with sweat and very much awake. Jess's voice was tired. "I've never seen someone go through withdrawal before. I keep wondering if I need to call nine-one-one. I've been taking his temperature every hour—he's running a high fever but it's not climbing anymore. Thank God for Linda being a doctor. She's come by twice today to check him, take his blood pressure and heart rate."

"I'll take over," I said. "I shouldn't have left you with him this long."

"You're sure?" She couldn't hide the relief in her voice.

"Of course. I'll stay with him tonight."

"Okay." She grabbed her jacket and bag, pausing. "Have you found anything more? The first of November—it's in two days, Nikki." She checked the clock, seeing it was well past midnight. "Technically, one day."

I tried not to sound irritated by the reminder. "I know, I know."

"Shouldn't you go to the police? If something does happen and you didn't warn people when you could have . . ." Her voice trailed off. She didn't have to finish the sentence. We both knew what that would mean for me. Morally, and quite possibly legally.

"I have it under control. Don't worry." The words were pushing hard at my aversion to mendacity. I knew I shouldn't even be in the hotel room. The moment I left Silas Johnson's hotel I should have been on my way to the FBI. I told myself I hadn't gone to them because my evidence hadn't exactly been obtained in a manner that would hold up in court. Regardless of whether we shared goals, I didn't particularly feel like confessing to Mr. Jade and Mr. Ruby that I had drugged a lawyer to steal confidential client documents. I had no interest in ending up as collateral damage in their quest to take down Care4. Besides, law enforcement was bound by rules. Search warrants, subpoenas— all kinds of judicial paperwork that took time we didn't have. Shutting down Care4 on November 2 wouldn't do much for the people who would die on the first.

There was something under that rationale, though. Something I was less comfortable admitting even to myself. Something darker. Something I knew was in me, even if I didn't like it.

They had killed Karen Li. Tried to kill my brother. Tried to kill me.

My battle with Care4 had become very personal.

I didn't want the FBI to come in and sweep things up.

I wanted to do it myself.

For almost my whole life I had been wrestling with this part of myself. Trying to control my reactions when sometimes it felt so much easier just to give in. I didn't know which way was right. I didn't know whether it was normal to be more frightened of myself, of what I might do, than anything out there. I didn't know . . .

". . . okay?" Jess was asking.

"Okay?" I had missed most of what she said, and assumed she was talking about my brother. When I looked up, though, her eyes were on me. Her face was worried and she was watching me closely. "Are you okay?" she asked again.

"Of course I'm okay. What do you mean?"

Her fingers brushed absently at a clump of gray cat hair on her jeans. "I know you pretty well, Nikki. We spend a lot of time together. Lately you've been walking around like a zombie, exhausted, like you're holding up the world. How can you be trying to handle everything yourself? You're up against an entire company, a huge conspiracy. People are being *murdered*. It's too much for any one person. Even *you*," she added pointedly.

"I have everything under control," I repeated. "Trust me."

The words sounded flat and forced even to me.

"This isn't what you do," Jess went on. "Going after some asshole tough guy who hits his girlfriend is one thing. This is completely different. I saw the man who came into the bookstore when I hid. I still have nightmares about him."

"I don't need help," I said tersely.

"Are you making the right decisions? Are you sure that you're not too deep in this to even know what the right decisions are?"

"Don't worry. I can handle it."

I knew I was just repeating the same forced words over and over. Jess stood, giving me a last look. She left. The door swung closed. I sat on the bed next to Brandon. Sweat filmed his skin and his eyes were filled with restless energy. I could see his ribs against his chest, and I put my hand on his forehead, startled by the intensity of the damp heat emanating from his skin.

"Brandon," I said softly. "Can you hear me?"

His eyes snapped onto mine. "Nikki? Nikki, you have to get me out of here. You have to get me something. *She* wouldn't—but you will. I know you will. You look out for me."

"We're going to stay here," I said softly. "I'm right here with you."

"*No!* I *need* something! You don't understand—I'll die!"

I tensed, startled by the surety in his voice. I went into the bathroom and found a clean towel. Soaked it in cool water and placed it gently against his forehead. "We're going to get through this, Brandi."

He thrashed on the bed and his fingers found my arm. "If you really loved me, you'd help me. If you cared that I was sick you'd help. You don't give a shit about me, do you?"

I said nothing. He shouted more things and I sat there quietly, dabbing the towel against his sweat-filmed skin, holding him. I looked around the room, seeing the untouched bowl of grease-filmed soup on a dresser, bottles of Gatorade and water, the plastic bucket next to the bed. His voice went on, raving, crying. I sat there with him, saying nothing, stroking his arm or dabbing his forehead with fresh towels.

Eventually he calmed. I thought he had fallen asleep but then he spoke again, his tone gentler, less tortured. "Nik?"

"Yeah?"

"Do you think Mom and Dad can see us now?"

I sat up. "What?"

"Mom and Dad. Can they see us now? Or are they just gone?"

"I don't know," I said. "I have no idea."

"Why don't we talk about them more?" His green eyes were fastened on mine with the most extreme lucidity.

I spoke slowly, unbalanced by the frankness of the questions. "It's hard to talk about. And I know what you went through—I'm scared, sometimes, of bringing them up. In case doing that makes it worse for you. Or maybe I just got used to not talking about them."

"Dad tried to save her. Did you know that? It didn't do any good, but he tried. I didn't try. I didn't try to save anyone. I just hid."

Tears had filled my eyes. I squeezed his hand. "If they had gotten you, I couldn't have made it. Honest. You being alive saved me. That's always been what's saved me."

Outside, the engine of a tractor trailer started up. The very dimmest light had started to filter through the curtained windows.

"I wanted to kill them," he said. "Both of them. That's all I thought about, for a long time. How badly I wanted them to die. I pictured it—every part, every detail—how it would happen. How I *wanted* it to happen. In my fantasies I killed them both a thousand times."

My fingers were over his, but that didn't feel close enough. I lay down next to him, held him, put my arms around him, willingly, gladly, feeling his sweat soaking into my clothing. "I did, too," I said. "That's all I thought about, too. It's okay to think like that."

"Carson Peters. They locked him up for good. San Quentin, right?"

"Right."

"Think he'll ever get out?"

"I hope so. Badly. But he won't."

"Jordan Stone."

"Yeah."

"The other one."

"The other one."

"I didn't see what they did to Mom. I was under the couch in the living room and they were in the kitchen. I couldn't see, but I heard it. I heard all of it."

"You never told me that."

"She asked why. That was the last word she said. Why. After she was after it had started. She screamed it while she could still talk. They never answered her. The last question of her life, and she never even got an answer."

"You never told me that," I said again. Holding him tighter. Choking on my own swollen throat, my own breath.

"We don't talk about it. But things we don't talk about still happen."

"I know they do."

"They released him, didn't they, Nik? He was paroled, right?"

I didn't answer at first. "Yeah. I guess they did."

"And then?"

A longer pause. "I guess he went back home."

"I tried to find him, you know. A few years ago, I finally got the nerve. He was from Hercules. Just up the road from here. I don't know what I would have done. I always told myself I'd try to kill him . . . but I don't know if I could have. Part of me hopes yes, part of me hopes no. Maybe I would have punched him, or tried to hit him with my car. Maybe just yelled at him. Maybe just cried or gotten beaten up. Who knows? But he's gone, so it doesn't matter."

"I guess it doesn't."

"It's funny, though," my brother continued in that same quiet, reflective voice. "That day that I went looking, I couldn't find out anything at all about Jordan Stone. No one seemed to know a thing. Like he went home and disappeared into thin air."

I held my brother. I felt his sweat, his body, his breathing, against me. I felt him so closely it was like I was inside his body, feeling in my own body the sluggish sickness of withdrawal, in his mind, the tremor and sensitivity of his thoughts my own. I'd never felt closer to him. We had come from the same place. Out of the world's billions, only us two, no one else.

"Nik?"

"Yeah, Brandi?"

"Can you tell me a bedtime story? Like you used to when we were kids?"

"A story."

"Yeah, a story. Tell me a story."

I breathed very slowly. My eyes were closed and my voice was quiet. "What should the story be about?"

"Tell me a story about what happened to Jordan Stone after he went back home."

I didn't say anything for a long time. Just lay there with my arms around him, watching the cracks of lightness seep out from behind to frame the curtain. "You mean it?"

"It's just us, Nik. Just me and you. No one else. So tell me a story. Tell me that story."

Some of the thoughts hurling through my mind found purchase, steadied.

"Okay. If you want me to, I will."

When they paroled Jordan Stone in the spring of 2005, he moved back to his parents' house in Hercules. A small city of about twenty-five thousand on San Pablo Bay, just north of Berkeley. He had just turned twenty-eight and was dead broke. Heading home was logical. Not that Jordan Stone had a choice. Living at home was a condition of his parole. There weren't many conditions, but that was one of them. Federal and state laws were remarkably tough if you were, say, a sex offender. If Jordan Stone had been convicted of even a crime such as having sex with a seventeen-year-old girlfriend when he was eighteen, he would have faced all kinds of harsh restrictions. Register as a sex offender for life, check in with the local police station anywhere he moved, no living near schools or parks, name and address permanently in a publicly accessible database. But a convicted murderer? Society was more trusting.

Sure, he wasn't going to be voting or buying guns, but beyond that, his only real responsibility was to meet with a parole officer once a week and avoid trouble.

Back at home in Hercules, Jordan Stone seemed to live quietly. His whole release had been quiet. No media attention. No stories in the papers about the reformed killer returning home. No op-eds thundering for or against his release. Nothing.

His family was middle class. His father owned a small contracting business. He had two siblings, an older brother and a younger sister, now both married, with kids of their own. The sister in San Diego and the brother in Richmond. They didn't seem close with their middle brother.

Not many businesses made a habit of hiring felons, especially those fresh out of prison for murder, but Jordan Stone was in luck. His father knew a painting crew that either wasn't too particular or was willing to do a favor. He got a steady job almost right away. Spent Monday through Friday on job sites and enrolled at Contra Costa, a local community college. Courtesy of the State of California, which had already paid about $50,000 a year to lock him up, Jordan Stone now began working toward a college degree.

His days were simple. Work, check in with his parole officer, sleep at home. As part of his parole he couldn't drink. He didn't hang out at bars or clubs. He didn't have many friends. Occasionally he met up with a few guys he'd probably gone to high school with, played pool or went bowling. He usually went to the arcade once or twice a week at least. Spent hours and hours in the NASCAR simulator or battling zombies. Beyond that, his life didn't seem to have much else.

With one exception. Jordan Stone loved comic books.

There was a comic book store in town. He went in at least three or four times a week. Most of the customers were regulars. They hung out. Knew each other. Almost all of them boys, men, ranging from preteens to middle-aged. A community. There was a back room where Magic: The Gathering tournaments took place on Friday nights, and there was a section with Dungeons & Dragons games and another for Japanese anime and manga. But mostly comic books. And Jordan Stone loved them. He hung out in the store for hours, flipping through old issues. The few times he smiled seemed to be when he was staring deep into the vivid pages of a comic book or graphic novel.

I knew all this because I followed him to Hercules.

The parole board had decided that he was rehabilitated.

They felt he deserved a second chance at life.

I wasn't so sure.

I rented a room in a shared house in Berkeley. Living with five or six undergrads who were barely younger than me. They partied and studied and cooked and forgot to wash their dishes. Bought plenty of cheap vodka and boxed wine but always seemed to forget toilet paper and dish soap. All the usual undergrad stuff. Fine with me, as long as they left me alone. Berkeley was convenient. Only ten miles south of Hercules. Close, but not too close.

After a few weeks I knew his schedule probably as well as he did. The painting, the arcade, the comic book shop. I'd never followed anyone before. I had to teach myself as I went along. But I had an advantage. Not only did Jordan Stone not know what I looked like, he didn't expect to be followed. So I watched. And learned.

Soon I knew what I had to do.

I set out to give myself a crash course in comic books.

I'd thought it would be easy. Brush up on some Spider-Man and Superman and be ready to go. I'd never much liked comic books. Growing up they were probably the only books I didn't read. Superheroes, superpowers, supervillains. Everything super-something. People were enough for me. I didn't need super.

To my surprise, it turned out that the world of comic books was overwhelmingly vast and intricate. Thousands of characters, hundreds of beloved writers and illustrators, intersecting plots, rival companies like DC and Marvel with different ecosystems, some characters and worlds mixing, merging, a whole interlocking universe. I was shocked to learn that some of these little paper books sold for insane amounts of money. The big conventions each year drew tens of thousands of people. A huge amount to learn.

Fortunately, I'd always been a good student.

I spent a month studying comic books every day. By the time I was through, I didn't know everything. Not an expert degree of knowledge by any means.

But enough to begin.

The first time I walked into the comic book shop I didn't say a word to anyone. Just browsed for two hours. I was the only girl. I got plenty of looks. Some curious, some checking me out, most a combination of the two.

I ignored it all. Just read. And watched.

I went into the comic book shop a week later. The second time. This time I went in a half hour before Jordan Stone was due to get off work. Gambling that he'd show up. Based on his habits, it was even money that he would.

Sure enough, he came in about an hour after I did.

There was a stereotype of the convicted felon. Covered in crude ink, bulky with jailhouse muscles. Jordan Stone was living disproof of that. He wore wire glasses and his wheat-colored hair was shoulder length. His build was lean to the point of skinny. He had the kind of boyish handsomeness that would fade by the time he hit middle age, but for the time being it was there.

After he walked in I continued to read my comics for a while, ignoring the looks as usual. Then I walked over to the counter and asked if they had a *Marvel Feature* #1, from 1971, with a first appearance by the Defenders. The guy behind the counter was impressed. He wore glasses and smelled of pot and Old Spice. "You know your shit," he said. "But sorry, we don't. That's a rare one."

"I know. That's why I wanted it." Again, I was the only girl in the store. I'd dyed my hair black, with purple highlights. I had black glasses and wore dark plum lipstick and heavy eye shadow. A tight-fitting black Batman T-shirt and black jeans and black Vans sneakers gave me a look that was not quite Goth but somewhere in the vicinity. I could feel Jordan Stone glance over at me. Furtive. My skin prickled.

I felt his eyes like an iron pressed into my cheek.

A few days later I was back. They knew me a little, now. Just enough. Old Spice nodded hello. Someone else said hi, too. An older man. I gave him an uncomfortable look and crossed my arms protectively over my chest as I walked past him. I took a few comics from different shelves. Went over to a corner and sat cross-legged on the floor. I could feel glances now and again but I said nothing. Never looked up. Just turned pages with a frown of concentration.

Finally, I got up to leave. Happening to walk across the store at the same time Jordan Stone was standing there. I paused. Nodded toward the comic he held. New *X-Men*.

"That's by Grant Morrison, right?"

He looked at me. Nodded. "Yeah."

The first words we'd ever spoken to each other. I felt so dizzy I wanted to sit. Blood pounding against my temples. All I said was, "He's good."

Jordan Stone nodded. "Yeah. Really good."

That was enough. I left.

All those hours in the store taught me plenty about comic books. They taught me something else, too. Something more fundamental. I began to understand that people wanted fantasies. That they wanted things so badly, often they didn't stop to think too much about the whys. Jordan Stone, the clerk, the men browsing—they wanted an introverted, not-trying-to-be-sexy girl in a tight Batman T-shirt to be sitting in the store with them. A girl who knew and loved comic books. A fantasy.

The same way other people thought about and wanted other things. The way lonely men drinking alone at bars fantasized about the woman who would walk in alone, sit next to them, talk to them. Choose them. Understand them. Maybe go home with them. The way some of the military guys wanted the tanned chick in cutoff jean shorts who could tell you the difference between rimfire and center-fire and liked to hit the range before splitting a six-pack. Or the recovering alcoholics or health nuts, searching for the woman who did triathlons and Ironman competitions and spent her Friday nights at CrossFit. Others looking for someone who had a strong preference between Swift or C++ or Python. The men who dreamed about falling in love with a woman who could tell a Rembrandt from a Rubens.

Eventually I'd meet them all. All types. Looking for themselves in others. Everyone wanting something. Fantasies. Usually pretty easy to see. To identify. To embody. I'd been all of them at some point. Back then, I didn't realize fully that deception wasn't really about lying. More about just showing people what they already wanted to see. Telling them what they already wanted to hear. And letting them form their own assumptions.

The next week when I walked into the store, Jordan Stone said hi to me at once. Asked me what I was reading. I showed him. *Spawn* #1. Then I went and sat cross-legged in my usual spot in the corner. Read quietly. When he came over to me an hour later, he was clearly nervous. "Hey," he said.

I looked up at him. "Hey."

"I'm Jordan."

"I'm Ashlee," I said after a second.

He shuffled a foot nervously and scratched his jaw. "Look—I was wondering. If . . . like, if you wanted to maybe get a burger or something. If you have time, I mean."

"Like, together?"

He shifted his weight. "Yeah. If you want."

I thought for a few seconds. "When?"

The question seemed to catch him off guard. He stammered a reply. "Um, I mean, like, tonight, if you're around. Or some other time."

I bit my lip and fiddled with a strand of unfamiliar black hair. "Uh, yeah. I could do that, I guess. But I gotta be home early. I have class tomorrow."

Jordan Stone smiled. A genuinely happy smile. He nodded. "Yeah. Same."

He was shy. We went on three dates before he tried to kiss me. I'd been bracing myself for it. We had hung out at the arcade, played Skee-Ball and video games, won long chains of red paper tickets that we'd used to buy little trinkets that China probably pumped out by the trillions. We walked to the parking lot together. Paused by the old Ford truck that I happened to know was registered to his father. I saw the tense mix of desire and fear in his face and he said, "Well, anyway, see you around." I nodded, and as I did he leaned over and put his hand gently on my hip and his lips found mine.

It took everything I had. The blood pounding in my head with a sick dizzy feeling. But I let him do it. Let him kiss me. Even reciprocated, slightly. He stepped closer. I could feel his thin frame against me. His pulse against mine. He was hard. I felt it against me. Thinking about that possibility, I thought it would make me sick. Instead I just felt a strange dispassion. Noticing it without feeling it. Feeling it without feeling it.

After an infinite moment I pulled away. "I should go."

"Okay," he said.

"'Night."

"'Night, Ashlee."

I had to be careful. There was a balance. He had to like me. Had to want me. Had to trust me. But not to the point that he'd start telling people about this new, black-haired comic book girl in his life. Not to the point where he'd ask me to come over for Sunday supper so he could introduce me to his parents. Not to the point where he'd ask me to hang out with his friends. Not to the point where we ended up in a bedroom together.

So I chose the third week. Starting from when he'd kissed me in the parking lot. The third week of going to the arcade or the movies, once driving into San Francisco and getting pizza in North Beach, making out in his truck and letting him feel me up with increasing excitement. He liked me a lot, by then. I could tell. It was obvious.

Why wouldn't he?

I was perfect for him.

"We should go somewhere," I suggested one night. Sitting next to him in his truck. We had parked by a quiet overpass up in the hills. It was a clear, cold fall night. Below us I could just hear the traffic on the freeway. The windows had fogged up and for a while we had been making out without saying much.

"Where?" he asked.

"My family has a house a few hours from here. Between Tahoe and Reno. A ski place. They come up in the winter but it's empty now. We could go hang out there," I said meaningfully.

I could see his eyes. Thinking. Wanting. Desiring. "When?"

"Why not tomorrow? I have off from work and I don't have class." As far as he knew, I waitressed part time and was enrolled at Cal State East Bay down in Hayward.

The thought seemed to scare him. "I gotta work."

"So ditch. Call in sick."

He shifted his weight, looked away, uncomfortable. "Look, Ashlee—I'm not really supposed to go out of the state."

It was the first time he'd mentioned that. I asked the logical question. "What are you talking about? Why not?"

He shook his head. Still looking away from me. Out the window. "I got in some trouble a long time ago. I'm supposed to stay local."

"Oh," I said. "Never mind, then. Just an idea. Anyway, I should get home."

He started the engine. We pulled back onto the road. But the hook was there.

The next day, when I saw him, he was in a good mood. He smiled. Kissed me. "You know what? Let's do it."

"You're sure? You won't get in trouble?"

"Let's go. It'll be fun. If we leave now, I'll just miss work tomorrow. Not a big deal."

I held his hand in mine. "I guess if you're missing work I can skip class. I'll drive."

We drove east on the 80 for a few hours, through Sacramento, the traffic growing sparse. If we'd stayed on it for another three thousand miles we would have ended up somewhere in New Jersey. We neared the Sierra Nevada range and the road snaked into the mountains as we approached the infamous Donner Pass. It peaked, then dropped sharply through the forested mountains that led to Lake Tahoe. We stayed on the 80 as the ground flattened again and then hit the Nevada desert, just scrub and brush in the darkness.

"You're quiet," he said. "Everything okay?"

"I guess."

"You nervous?"

I gave him a look. "I'm not sure."

"It's not me, is it?"

"Can I ask you a question?"

"Sure."

"Comic books. Why do you like them so much? What made you like them?"

He considered. "I guess when I was a kid they were so exciting. More exciting than real life. Real life seemed boring." He thought more. "Now it's different. Now they're about possibility. Anything can happen. Like, anything is possible. Characters can always get to the next page, the next issue. No matter how bad things get."

I nodded.

"How about you, Ash?"

I shrugged. "I don't know what I like about them."

When I finally turned off the highway it was almost nine o'clock. The unpolluted desert sky crammed full of bright stars. A scimitar of moon. The barren landscape enveloped us.

"They live pretty far out," he said. His voice casual but clearly nervous. "You're not lost, are you?"

"I'm not lost."

"Are we almost there?"

I nodded. "We're almost there."

I turned onto another road. This one just a narrow unpaved strip, narrow enough that I would have had to slow and pull over for an oncoming vehicle. The car bounced up and down against the rough road, pebbles kicking up into the undercarriage with sharp pings. "This is a ski house?" he asked uncertainly. "Where are the mountains?"

"They couldn't afford Tahoe. So they picked something a little farther out."

"Oh."

We kept driving. I flicked through radio stations, looking for any music. Some country song came on, a baritone voice furred with static.

"Where are we, Ashlee?" he asked again. There were no houses in sight. No vehicles. Nothing. Outside the windshield the world was pitch black except for the headlights and stars and yellow light that melted off the moon like tallow.

I slowed as we came up on a narrow turnoff, took it.

We left the road entirely, bumping across dirt tracks.

He didn't bother to hide his nervousness anymore. "Ashlee? Where are we? There aren't even any houses here."

"We're almost there," I said again.

We bumped along another fifty yards.

I stopped.

In front of us the headlights cast twin pools over scrubland.

"Ashlee. Is this a prank? Let's just go back home. C'mon. This was a bad idea."

I looked at Jordan Stone. "It's too late, now. It's too late to go back. Come on. I'll show you where we are."

He started to say something, but I was already getting out of the car. I left the lights on. After hesitating, he got out and joined me. We stood in front of the headlights, looking out at the blank landscape. Shrubs and low cacti threw strange shadows over the earth.

"Ashlee. What is this?"

I looked at Jordan Stone directly. "The trouble you mentioned. Why you couldn't leave the state. You never told me what happened."

His face paled in the glare of the headlights. "What are you talking about?"

"What did you do? That you aren't supposed to cross state lines?"

He flinched like I'd hit him. "Nothing. Just something stupid. A long time ago," he muttered.

"You don't want to tell me?"

"I don't want to talk about it. I just want to go home, Ashlee. I'm cold. I'm hungry. I don't know where we are. I need to get home."

"Maybe my name isn't Ashlee."

He stared at me. "What are you talking about?"

Now that it was finally happening I didn't know exactly how I felt. Something was missing, though. The feeling of triumph that I'd always imagined. That wasn't there. Everything just felt flat. Empty. Like the scrubbed and shadowed ground around us. "You don't recognize me, do you?" I said. "You have no idea."

His face was paler. He took a step back. "Recognize you? What are you talking about?"

"But why would you, I guess? Although people always told me I had my mother's eyes."

He was utterly confused. "Your mother? What does she have to do with this?"

"Everything," I said. "See, Jordan, she has everything to do with this."

And then, slowly, Jordan Stone understood.

His face seemed to gain in years and he started backing away from me. Slowly. As if his feet dragged weights. Inching his way backward toward the car.

He stopped when he saw the gun.

"Ashlee," he said. "Please. Whatever you think I did."

"I don't think. I know." Still none of the thrill or satisfaction I had imagined. Instead just a dull anger and a chilly, spreading tiredness. I didn't want to be there either. Part of me wanted to just get back in the car, drop Jordan Stone off in Hercules, take a hot shower, and never see or think of him again.

But that was impossible. I was too far in. Besides, I knew better. I'd spent the last ten years trying not to think of Jordan Stone. It didn't work. He was always there. He always would be.

"What are you going to do to me?" He inched farther away.

"Stop," I said. "We're not through. Not yet."

His feet stilled. His face drawn in thought. "So this whole time. The last month. The dates and the arcade and the making out and the comic books. Just a bunch of lies."

"I didn't lie."

He gave a bitter laugh. "Of course you did! You lied about everything— even your name." He gestured around with a furious, futile energy. "The ski house in the goddamn desert. Everything. You never stopped lying. Just to bring me here."

"Yes," I acknowledged. "To bring me here."

"Why?" he asked helplessly.

"Why did you do it?" The question that had burned me up for the last decade.

"Carson," he said. "He planned it. I was a kid. I was stupid. I just went along with it."

"Save that for the courts," I said, suddenly furious. "All his fault, sure. Corrupting you. Bullshit. The papers lapped it up. The jury lapped it up. The parole board, too. But not me. Not me. You helped to slash my mother's throat with a butcher knife. You didn't have to. But you did."

Jordan Stone looked queasy. He huddled into himself, shrinking down. His shadow looked monstrous, stretching away over the dark earth. "He said he'd kill me if I didn't help. He meant it. He would have. He said if I didn't do it, too, then he couldn't trust me."

"You could have said no. You could have stopped him. You could have let them run. You could have called the cops. You could have done anything. But you didn't."

He bit his lip and he was suddenly crying. "I pray to God every day to forgive me."

"*I* don't forgive you. That's what matters here."

"I suffered. You have no idea. In the juvenile home, in prison. You know what the gangs did to me? A skinny little white kid?"

"I don't care."

For the first time in my life I pointed a gun at someone. It was a little black Ruger .22 semiautomatic. I'd bought it on my twenty-first birthday. A present to myself.

Already knowing what I planned to do with it.

I drew the slide back, racking a cartridge into the chamber.

His face lost still more color. His voice shook. "You have no idea. You think you do, but you don't. You might think it ends when you pull that trigger. Trust me. It only begins. Killing haunts you forever. You think I've slept through a single night in the last ten years? You think a single night's gone by when I didn't wake up screaming?"

My hand was shaking, too. I didn't want to talk to Jordan Stone anymore. Didn't want to know any more about him. "I'll take that chance."

"They'll catch you," he said. "I told people I was with you. Told them about tonight."

"I don't think you did, but I'll take that chance, too."

"Do you really want me dead?"

"I don't know," I said honestly. "But you being alive doesn't seem to work."

His voice was loud and uncontrolled with fear. "Why don't you kill Carson? Why does he get to live? And not me?"

My finger tightened on the trigger. "I think about Carson Peters every day."

"You lied to me," Jordan Stone said again with great bitterness. "Just like everyone else. Just like the whole shitty world. You tricked me."

"I guess I did."

"Why won't you just let me go? I tried to turn my life around."

"Why should that matter? After what you did? Why should you ever get that chance?"

"Don't you believe in mercy? Redemption? Don't you?"

"Not when it comes to you, I don't."

He started crying and got down on his knees. Face upturned, less than a foot from the end of the barrel. "I'm begging you, Ashlee. Please. I *liked* you. I thought I was falling in love with you."

The thought disgusted me more than anything he'd said. "Shut up. You don't know me. You never knew me. I was a fantasy to get you here. Everything about me was a fantasy. You don't know anything about me."

"Please."

It was too much talking. The more I heard his voice, the harder it was. I wished I had shot him the second we got out of the car, before he ever opened his mouth. "Shut up," I said again. "Stand up and take it like a man, at least."

"No!" There was unexpected vehemence in his voice. "You can kill me but you don't get to tell me to be a man about it. The guards told me that in prison, too. Just be a man. Like that somehow makes it better." He was weeping, and mucus ran from his nose down to his lips. He curled into a ball and put his arms over his eyes, the side of his face pressed into the dirt.

I aimed the barrel just above the top of his ear. The small caliber didn't matter. The first shot would kill him. The .22 was popular with hit men and assassination squads all over the world. Quiet, lethal. It would be a quick, instantaneous death. The opposite of my parents'. But the point wasn't some precise balancing of the scales, some karmic repositioning of the universe. The point was that Jordan Stone would be gone from the world.

That was all I wanted.

Right?

Hit men. Assassins.

I realized I was still holding the gun, the front sight lined up perfectly with the tip of his ear. No chance I'd miss. .22 ammo was cheap. I'd fired over five thousand times from this gun, aiming at targets at a much greater distance than Jordan Stone was right now. The sight formed a perfect triangular point just above his ear. Nothing would go wrong. He would be dead, just like I wanted.

Hit men. Assassins.

Murder.

That was them, though. *Them.* Not me.

I looked at the curled, convulsing body on the ground. Even without the gun I would have felt completely safe. By the time I'd finished high school I'd had over fifty amateur fights, sparred over two thousand rounds in the gym. The gun in my hand barely mattered. I would have felt fine taking on Jordan Stone without it.

He deserved to die. Which left only one question. Who did I want to be?

I made a decision. Pushed all the doubt away.

I pulled the trigger.

There was no recoil. Just a brittle snap that echoed into the night.

Jordan Stone screamed and his body stiffened.

The echo spread through the air and faded.

I spoke. "Get up."

An eye peeked up fearfully from under an arm. "You shot me."

"Get up," I said again, more impatiently. There was an almost undiscernible mark about a foot away from his head, where my bullet had pocketed into the dry earth. "You're fine."

His voice was quiet and frightened. "What are you going to do to me?"

"If I had meant to shoot you, I would have."

He slowly got up and looked at me, arms crossed in front of his chest, hands almost on his shoulders. He looked very small. "You're not going to kill me?"

I ignored his question. "You're going to head in any direction you want except west. Stay out of California and never come back. That's the deal."

"But my parole officer. They'll put out an arrest warrant for me if I don't check in."

"That's your problem."

"My friends, my family—everyone I know is in Hercules."

"You took my family from me," I said. "Forever. You think I feel guilty?"

I didn't want to be there with this sniveling, begging demon who had chased me through so many dreams. I felt sick. All the subterfuge of the last months hit me all at once. The revenge stories I had loved as a girl hadn't prepared me. They made revenge sound thrilling, exhilarating. I didn't feel anything of the kind. Without another word I got back in the car.

"You can't just leave me out here!" he shouted after me. "It's the middle of nowhere!"

But I did.

I left him and drove away, and that was the last anyone heard of Jordan Stone, as far as I knew. I never saw any mention of his name in the papers. He had vanished. There was one thing he'd said, though. His accusation about my lies. I didn't like that he'd been right. I had lied. "So I decided I wouldn't lie anymore, to anyone. I never saw Jordan Stone again."

I lay in bed next to my brother. Seeing the light scrabbling at the curtains. It was fully dawn. My brother's forehead was no longer feverish; now his sweat felt cold against me. I found more towels, ran warm water from the tap, mopped hot compresses across his face and chest. My clothing, my skin, soaked in his sweat. It didn't feel unpleasant. It was him. My brother. It just made me love him more.

"Nik?"

"Yeah?"

"I think I'm feeling better."

I hugged him. "Good."

"Who were those men who came for you, Nik? What did they want?"

"They wanted bad things."

"They're after you?"

"Yeah. I guess they are."

"So what happens now? We hide again? Run somewhere else?"

"No." I watched the light pulse against the curtain. Knowing the day that stood in front of me. "We don't hide from them."

"If you don't hide, then they catch you. That's how it works."

"That's okay," I said. "They can find me. They can catch me."

He looked at me, frightened. "I don't understand."

I answered with my eyes still on the window. Thinking of another window, in the cabin, that cracked and useless exit that had come to represent a final, slender plank between life and death. Karen Li, trying to escape the unescapable, fist beating glass with the futility of a moth's wing. *They* had come into my life. I hadn't sought them out. They had found me, taken her, tried to take my brother. Tried to take everything that mattered.

That had happened once to me. People taking everything away.

I wouldn't let it happen again.

I wanted Brandon to understand. "It's not just that they're after me."

"What is it, then?"

"I'm after *them*."

42

I went home, showered, slept for a couple of hours, and got to the bookstore by mid-morning after placing a brief call to Charles Miller. We agreed we'd meet for a coffee that afternoon. There was something I wanted to give him. I was trying to ignore the fact that I was utterly exhausted for what would likely be the most challenging day of my life. The week before, with Halloween around the corner, Jess had stacked a row of pumpkins, hung witches and devils from the walls, and created a special Horror section with titles by Stephen King, Mary Shelley, Robert Bloch, Anne Rice.

Halloween—October 31.

November 1 was a single day away.

I knew what I had to do. Pulling it off was another question entirely.

I had arrived intending only to have a quick word with Jess, but it was busy enough that we didn't have a chance to do more than nod hello. A beefy guy in camouflage shorts and a floppy safari hat had come in with a dolly stacked with boxes, over three hundred books he wanted to sell in one go. I found myself trying to explain Old English to an international student while a grad student pestered me for books we didn't have.

The dolly guy checked his watch. "How much longer will this take?"

"Will I have to read other books in Oldest English?" He was a tall, black-haired Korean boy wearing bright green glasses and gold sneakers.

"What's your course?"

He unfolded a syllabus. "Survey of English Literature, Beginning to 1500."

"It's a definite possibility," I informed him, pulling a copy of *Beowulf* from the shelf.

He looked like he was going to cry. "Can you tutor me?"

"I'd come back, but I rented this dolly by the hour," the beefy guy was saying. He wore a tank top that showed off an astonishing amount of chest and back hair.

I felt my forehead start to throb. "Be patient, please." Too many voices, too many people asking for things, wanting things from me. Too much to do.

"My dissertation is on Gibbon," the grad student was complaining. "What am I supposed to do without volume five of *The Decline and Fall*?"

"I don't know what to tell you." I was getting a sharp headache.

"I think it's only fair that you should split the dolly rental with me."

I felt a small piece of something within me snap. "Take your damn dolly and stick it—" I headed for the door as he sputtered. I had to push my tiredness aside and start readying myself for the coming night. I'd catch up with Jess later.

I was halfway out the door when I was bumped by someone coming in.

Zoe.

The day changed again.

It took me a moment to recognize her under the blackened eye, the bruised arm, the tear-stained mascara that looked like it hadn't been washed off from the night before. The last time I had seen her, when we had sat comfortably on the beanbags, seemed a world away. Now she was shaking, her voice raw.

I helped her sit. "What happened?" One of those pointless questions. Like wondering why an earthquake hit. Reasons didn't always matter. Sometimes just damage.

Short phrases came in between sobs. "I was out at a club and some guys were there, dancing with us, nothing bad. Luis came in with his friends and got jealous. There was a fight, he got arrested. This morning when he got home he blamed me for starting it."

Jess was next to us. "I'll get her to the hospital."

"I'm going to talk to Luis," I said to Zoe. "I need your address."

She grabbed my arm. "No! You don't understand what he'll do to you."

I barely heard her. There was something singing in my ears that drowned out the words people were saying to me. The singing noise seemed to be pushing me along so I didn't have to think at all about what I was doing. I didn't even feel tired anymore. All the doubt that had filled my mind recently now seemed wonderfully distant. Even Care4 didn't seem to matter as much.

"I need your address," I said again.

Zoe glanced from me to Jess, then back to me. Still not saying anything. Unsure.

"Last time he hurt you," I said. "This time, he hurt you worse. Next time—and there will be one, because there always is—there's no telling what he'll do to you. Or whether you'll be able to get away. So please, Zoe, give me your address."

Her eyes were large and frightened. She looked down and was quiet for a few moments.

She looked up and, hesitantly, she told me the address.

I started toward the door without another word.

"Nikki, not when you're angry," Jess said. "You always say the planning is what matters."

"You're right. I should wait," I acknowledged.

Jess relaxed a little. "Good."

I walked out of the bookstore anyway.

The singing noise pushing me mindlessly along. Not just that, though. There was pragmatism mixed with my anger. I didn't know what would happen to me in the coming night. No matter what, while I could act, I wanted to do this last thing. I wanted Zoe to be safe.

Zoe lived in Pittsburg, northeast of Berkeley by about twenty-five miles. A rough city, too far from removed to have soaked up the tech money that spread like a vast stain from the epicenter of Silicon Valley and San Francisco. The money. Endless amounts of the money. Soaking through what had once been flat green farmland and orchards and russet hills. Now infinite acres of luxury townhomes were set into those hills, development after identical development, postered by garish billboards advertising the newest in materials and finest in amenities. The money. Everywhere. In San Francisco, five coffee shops on every block and each one cuter and more perfect than the last, the whole city choking on construction cranes that wound around it like wisteria. People like Gregg Gunn, creating the money faster than the Treasury presses in D.C.

For whatever good that did.

I pulled up to a one-story house with an attached garage. In the driveway there was a black Escalade with shiny custom rims, windows tinted far past the point of legal. The small front yard covered equally by children's toys and beer cans. I got off the motorcycle. Knowing that I was breaking all my rules. Not caring. The singing noise in my ears still pushing me along. I didn't bother with my gloves. Left my purse on the seat and the keys in the ignition. I wouldn't be long.

I'd been thinking so much. Trying to fit together pieces that refused to fit. Now I didn't need to think. I didn't need anything to fit.

I only needed Luis.

The garage door was open but it might as well have been closed. It was too bright outside to make out anything within. Like looking at a black curtain and wondering what lay on the stage beyond.

I walked right into the darkness.

I stood on a pitted cement floor. An old red Mustang with no tires rested on stacks of cinder blocks to my left. Bared, the axles looked obscene. Across, on the far right, the adjoining door to the house was closed. Besides the sun streaming in from the open bay door, the only light came from a single bare lightbulb that hung off a thick orange cord from the ceiling above me. Hard rap music pounded from a subwoofer. I smelled sweat and motor oil and marijuana. There was a weight bench in front of me. A shirtless man in sneakers and mesh basketball shorts was doing bench presses. He was powerfully built, grunting with effort as he heaved up a bar loaded with discs of iron.

The man was Luis.

Without breaking my stride, I walked up and jammed my foot down against the bar he was pressing up. With the loud music he hadn't even heard me walk in. There was a rattling sound and a fleshy thud as about two hundred pounds of iron-loaded bar fell onto his chest. He let out a gasp and rolled sideways off the narrow bench onto the cement floor. Weights spilled down and the bar clanged loudly.

"Hi, Luis," I said. I took another step forward and kicked him in the mouth with the reinforced toe of my right boot. His lip split like it had been peeled apart, but the teeth held. I felt vague disappointment.

"Who the fuck are you?" he managed, raising his head.

"We've met. You'll remember." I brought up the heavy heel of my boot and drove it down into his left ear. Another thud as his head bounced off cement. Blood from his ear trickled down his cheek and joined blood from his lip.

"Shit!" He clutched the side of his head. "What do you want?" His words were fuzzy. Harder to talk with a split lip.

"Everything."

Even through his pain, his face was bewildered. "What?"

"I want you to feel everything. Because everything you did to that girl in the last five years I'm going to do to you in the next five minutes."

He managed to get up on one knee. He looked up at me. "I'll find both of you. You and that whore. I should have kicked her onto the street years ago. I'll find you both."

"Find me. Feels like everyone's trying to find me. We'll talk about you finding us. Right now, though, I found *you*." The music was too loud. I jerked the subwoofer's cord from the wall and the garage was quiet. Luis was poised to rise, eyes fixed on me, bulky pectoral muscles heaving as he breathed. He wiped blood from his face with the back of a hand.

"Go on," I said. "Get up. I'll let you."

His body tensed but he remained frozen on one knee, suspecting a trick. There was no trick, though. I wanted him to stand up. So that we could continue. In my mind was a kind of grocery list of things that I intended to happen to Luis in the immediate future. He probably had his own list for me. We'd see who got to do what. "Get up," I repeated.

We watched each other. Preparing. Then three things happened.

The interior adjoining door between house and garage opened.

Two men walked into the garage.

And Luis stood up.

"What the hell?" asked the guy on the left. He looked as surprised as I was. He had a broad frame with about twenty extra pounds spread around his gut. In his doughy face his eyes were small and malicious. He looked from me to Luis as if suspecting a joke. He was wearing a black muscle shirt and colorful board shorts and held a six-pack of Corona Extra bottles in his right hand.

I backed toward the bay door, my anger gone. Things had changed.

The guy on the right seemed to have read my mind. He was shorter than his friend, with a scruffy black beard and heavy boots. His hand shot out and hit a button on the wall as I backed up. The garage door began to close behind me. I backed up faster. I didn't want to be in the garage anymore. Not with three of them. That's what I got for going in angry.

I stopped backing up when Board Shorts let go of the beer and pulled a gun out of the back of his baggy shorts. A cheap black semiautomatic. He got the gun pointed at me about the same time as the beer smashed into the floor.

"Don't move!" he said. The hand holding the gun quivered with adrenaline. No way to tell about bullets or safeties. A gun was pointed at me from maybe fifteen feet away. That was all I knew. Not very far. Fifty feet and I'd run from a handgun every time. Twenty-five and I'd be tempted. Any closer drastically lowered the odds of escaping unscathed. Even a stoned, shaky shooter could hit something from fifteen feet away.

I stopped only a couple of feet shy of the door, wondering if I should try to roll under as it closed. That seemed a decent way to get out of the garage. Also a decent way to get shot. I stayed where I was. The bright daylight faded to a thin crack and then was gone. The only light in the garage coming from the overhead bulb. Shadows appeared in sharp relief. With the door closed I had fewer options. None of them seemed good.

Luis spat blood, rubbing his ear. Board Shorts and Boots moved closer so that we formed a rough scalene triangle. Myself, Luis, and his two friends, farther away. "You're from that bookstore," said Luis. He laughed, as though realizing how ridiculous it sounded. "She sent you?" he added. "To do this to me?"

He took a step toward me. He was angry enough I thought that he might rush me on the spot. That would lead to chaos. Chaos wasn't necessarily bad, but I hadn't made up my mind. I didn't want chaos at this exact second. I wanted to think.

"I sent myself." I leaned down and grabbed the steel weight bar. Standard dimensions, about forty-five pounds, maybe seven feet long, each end pebbled for grip.

Enraged as he was, Luis didn't relish the thought of catching that bar in the face. He edged back out of range, stopping six or seven feet directly in front of me. I stole a look at the other two. They had fanned out but were still side by side, about ten feet behind Luis at a forty-five-degree diagonal. Behind them the adjoining door to the house. The only viable exit. I thought of the scalene triangle again, and then for some reason of ninth-grade geometry. The angles of a triangle add up to 180 degrees. The shortest distance between two points is a straight line. Solid, logical foundations for the world to operate upon.

I addressed Luis's friends directly. "This isn't between us. Walk away and we have no problem."

Board Shorts laughed and cocked the gun. "We're not the ones with the problem." I saw him struggle as he pulled the slide back. Rust, maybe. I could see more rust on the barrel. The gun was a Cobra. Not a company synonymous with quality. Cobra made cheap guns that were purchased by people who didn't want to spend money on better guns. They were all over the streets. Take a cheap semiautomatic pistol and throw in an owner who didn't know or care about cleaning it. Maybe a few owners. Guns like this one were passed around a lot. Used guns were like used cars. They could be immaculate, or junk, or anywhere in between. With this gun, possibly a long chain of indifference to care and quality. Meaning a definite chance it could misfire. I filed that thought away.

"Why'd you hit her?" I asked Luis. I wasn't talking for answers. I wanted a little more time to think.

"She's crazy. I never touched her."

The lies were always so easily told, but I was barely listening. I was thinking, adding things up. Possibilities. Three men. The only accessible door blocked by two of the men. A gun. The bare lightbulb dangling almost directly above me. The third man in front of me. No way out unless I ran through the two men between me and the door. In which case Board Shorts would likely empty his gun straight toward me.

"Toss the bar," Boots advised. "Maybe we'll be nice." He sounded cheerful, unconcerned. The way most people would be in his situation. His chin came to a sharp V and he had sideburns that jutted down his face like a frame around a painting. He had picked up an aluminum baseball bat from a corner of the garage and held it casually, like he was popping pitches at Sunday softball.

I made up my mind.

I bent down but didn't drop the weight bar.

Instead I unbuckled my boots. I pulled them off and placed them next to me. Noticing with some small part of my mind that the left tip was smudged with Luis's blood. From when I'd kicked him. That seemed a long time ago. I stood there in my socks.

The three of them were looking at me curiously. Like I had cracked up.

Luis grinned through his bloody mouth, rubbing his left ear as though it itched. "You can take the rest off, too," he said. "Or maybe I'll help with that."

I took one more look around the garage. Thinking again of that geometry class, almost twenty years behind me. A name came to me. Ms. Irvine. My teacher. She'd be glad I was still thinking about the course, all these years later. She'd always claimed that geometry was the most applicable branch of mathematics.

"What's it gonna be?" asked Board Shorts. His voice was impatient. "Lie down or lights out?" With his colorful shorts and pistol he looked like an aging, murderous frat boy. Spilled beer foam and broken bottle glass littered the floor around where he stood. That only added to the image of partygoer gone wrong.

I flexed my toes against the cement. Took a long, even breath. "Let's go with lights out."

I took a half step forward and swung the bar up in a sweeping vertical arc.

The three of them watched, surprised. Not bothering to step back. Knowing they were comfortably out of range. Not having time to wonder why instead of swinging the bar toward them I was swinging it upward. Toward the ceiling. As the bar connected with the lightbulb above me, the last thing I saw was the same surprise threaded across three different faces.

I felt glass shower down, heard startled exclamations, as we were plunged into total darkness.

There were plenty of species that had no problem with night. Thrived in it, even. Lions, wolves, raccoons. Certain monkeys and birds, domestic cats. But not humans. As a species, we'd never grown comfortable in darkness. We were biologically wired to move in day and not night. Not seeing meant you could run into a tree. Or walk off a cliff. People grew cautious. Froze up until their brains could get some information flowing and figure out what to do. So I wasn't surprised that I didn't hear any immediate motion of any kind.

I was already moving.

I took two careful steps forward. Two feet a stride, counting in my head. I couldn't see Luis, but I hadn't heard him move. Meaning he would now be between three and four feet directly in front of me. I held the weight bar tight with both hands, crouched, and swung it at ankle level, sweeping around through the shoulders and pivoting my whole body into the swing.

There was a crack like I had hit a fastball. I felt the impact through my arms.

Luis screamed. The scream was useful. It provided me with more information. I shifted my stance and swept the bar back toward the origin of the noise, fast, before the scream even stopped. I felt a second impact jolt through the bar. The scream stopped as suddenly as it had started. I heard the sound of a body collapsing.

Someone who sounded like Boots called out, "Luis? You okay? What happened?"

"Shut the fuck up!" another voice hissed. Board Shorts. A smarter voice.

I was already moving again. The voices made it easier but I didn't need them. Trying to see was pointless. I was listening. Listening, and counting in my head. *One-two. One-two.* The same careful two feet per stride. Stepping along the imaginary diagonal line that led to the two remaining men. I placed my feet softly, with great care. I felt like I could almost see the line I had memorized, blazing like a tightrope.

The shortest distance between two points. Basic Euclidian geometry.

My socks made no sound against the cement floor.

No way they could hear me coming for them.

I heard a crunching sound in front of me. The sound of a boot stepping on broken glass. The crunching sound helped. In the darkness it was like hanging a bull's-eye on a target. I brought the bar back with both hands and then lunged forward, ramming the bar ahead like a spear. Mentally aiming for a point about three feet above the crunching sound. I felt the bar encounter something soft and yielding. Stomach or lungs, maybe, or genitalia.

There was a terrible groan and a clatter that sounded exactly like a dropped aluminum bat hitting cement.

Most people, taking a blow to that area of the body, tended to double over. Involuntary, reflexive. I raised the bar about two feet and rammed it forward a second time. This time there was a kind of gurgle. I had brought the bar back a third time when the quiet was broken by a series of explosions. Bright flashes of fire tore out as the semiautomatic fired. In the enclosed space the noise was deafening. I leapt backward. Away from the gurgle. Away from the most recent source of noise. In case Board Shorts was doing the same thing I'd been doing and following sound. I closed my eyes to preserve what was left of my night vision and dropped down. The cheap Cobra hadn't jammed after all.

I counted three shots, each one deafening in the enclosed space. I could hear the actual bullets cracking and bouncing. I stayed down. Could see the muzzle flashes through my closed eyelids. He was firing wildly, as fast as he could pull the trigger. Nowhere near me. I was counting the reports carefully. It was doubtful the full clip had contained more than ten rounds, and definitely not more than twelve. He had pulled the slide back to chamber a round, meaning there hadn't been an extra in the chamber. People didn't tend to carry extra clips of ammunition when they were sitting around a garage drinking beer with their friends.

Twelve shots, maximum. Then I could move again.

We never got there.

After the fourth shot there was a scream of pain and then a crash that sounded like someone falling into some kind of metallic objects.

The shooting stopped.

A stream of anguished profanity issued from the direction of the crash.

I stood up and stayed perfectly still for a moment. Mentally adding up how much I had moved from my original position. Adjusting my steps, I walked toward what I hoped was the adjoining door, wincing as I felt a piece of sharp glass dig into my heel. The glass was okay. It told me I was more or less in the right spot. My foot brushed a raised line. The doorjamb. I felt around against the wall until my finger found the garage door button.

I pressed it and the garage door opened. The most normal sight in the world. Familiar to millions of suburbanites all over the country. The bright sunlight unscrolled as the door rose. A sign for most families to pull the car out or go look around to grab the golf clubs or rakes. Any of the normal things that people kept in normal garages.

I looked carefully around. This garage looked different. Decidedly not normal.

Luis lay crumpled on the floor. Except for the blood running from a cut on his head he could have been asleep. Boots was curled into an awkward seahorse shape. His breaths were raspy and uneven and both hands were clasped around his throat. If I'd had to guess, I would have figured something to do with the trachea. More likely bruised than crushed, based on the fact that he was breathing. No long-term damage, but he wouldn't be moving much for the next few minutes. My gaze continued to Board Shorts, who lay on the floor in the other direction, both hands clutching his leg. He'd fallen into a row of empty paint cans, which had caused the clatter. Wildly firing a semiautomatic pistol in an enclosed area didn't always pay off. No telling which way a ricochet might go. One of his bullets must have bounced back at him, hot sharp metal sizzling with kinetic energy. There was blood coming from his leg.

I walked over, kicking the gun away out of his reach even though he didn't look like he wanted to be anywhere near it. I knelt down and took a closer look at his leg. "Your lucky day," I said. The bullet had gashed the leg but it hadn't lodged. Not enough blood to mean anything life-threatening. I straightened. "I wouldn't mention the gun when you're getting that stitched up. There's no bullet in you. You can get away with that."

He nodded, understanding.

"Use your shirt, tie it off." I nodded at Boots. "If you call an ambulance you'll have some explaining after they arrive. If I were you, I'd have your buddy bring you in. Luis isn't going to feel like driving."

He looked around the garage toward his friends. "Why not?"

I didn't answer. I was already pulling my boots back on. "And for God's sake don't pull a gun next time you're in a fight. That's not who you are." Luis was stirring. I watched his fingers slowly clench and unclench as he groaned. His right ankle was the size of a Valencia onion. I watched his fingers move. His hands flattened and braced, crablike, against the concrete, and he started pushing himself up. He was muttering something that I couldn't make out. He looked pretty out of it.

I picked up one of the circular forty-five-pound weights that had fallen off the bench press. I had to strain to carry it. I walked over to Luis and lifted the weight with both hands, still needing to squat a little so I could push up with my legs. Not for the first time, I thought with mild astonishment about gender difference when it came to physical strength. How men like Luis could lift six or eight of these weights with no problem. And yet be knocked out cold same as anyone. Somehow that felt fair.

With an effort I raised the weight to shoulder height.

The metal disc was poised directly over the spread fingers of his right hand.

I released my grip.

The weight fell.

There was an awful crunching sound and he let out the worst cry yet. Not a nice way to wake up. His left hand clutched its damaged partner to his body and I saw tears of pain in his eyes. I bent down over him. "Luis," I said. "Pay attention." His face was drenched in sweat and patched with blood. Quite possibly concussed and an ankle he wouldn't walk on for a long time. And the hand. His fingers. I caught a glimpse of them as he cradled them protectively. They didn't really look like fingers anymore. The hand was a flattened, crooked mess.

I had his attention. "We need to talk about Zoe," I told him.

He looked at me, face drawn tight with pain. "What about her?"

I spoke slowly and clearly so he'd be sure to understand. "She'll come by for her things. You'll receive advance notice. It's very important that you not be home when that happens. In fact, I'd spend the day in a different city entirely. Take a trip somewhere. You understand?"

He nodded. He understood.

"Then it's over. For good. You leave her alone."

He nodded again. Sick with pain. But he seemed to understand.

The epinephrine that had flooded my body began to recede and I was filled with the strange chemical depression that always hit after violence. I didn't want to talk anymore. I didn't want to be in the garage anymore. I didn't want to be around people. I wanted to go find a quiet room and lie down and go to sleep. I walked outside without lingering. Gunshots might mean police whether Luis wanted them or not.

Five minutes later I was back on the freeway. Riding in the rightmost lane, letting the faster traffic flow by on my left. Part of me wondering why people like Luis did the things they did. The way I always wondered. The other part, with what I knew of people, didn't bother wondering at all. I'd been learning that for most of my life.

After college, it was something I kept learning.

After graduating, I moved around the Bay a few times, restless, feeling unfulfilled. I ended up back in Berkeley without any idea about what I wanted to do. One afternoon I stopped while walking past a women's shelter in Oakland, remembering two long years spent with my first foster family. A week later I was in a certification course, and within the month I started working as a first responder. Like the name suggested, meeting women immediately after an incident, wherever they were. Offering comfort, support, creating a safety plan with them. The training emphasized how to help them heal, gain the self-confidence needed to start afresh, but my job meant different things. Maybe helping them find employment, or sign a lease for the first time.

Maybe helping them stay alive.

There was a problem. Many of the women who walked out of the shelter healed tended to return. When they returned, they were not healed anymore. And there was a formulaic truth: the more often they came in, the worse shape they were in. I began to feel that as fast as we could help them find their feet, there were unseen forces out there knocking them back down. Unseen people, actually. Only these people weren't unseen. They were right there in the open.

It was Clara that did it. A fun-loving Haitian woman with a happy smile and scared eyes. The first time I saw her she had a bruise under her eye. The second time, a chipped tooth. The third time, a broken wrist. It turned out that her husband was ex-military. When he got drunk he seemed to think he was still in combat. And that the hostile forces were principally his wife. After the third time, I convinced her to leave him. Using all of the persuasive arguments and rhetorical techniques I'd learned in training. Making every salient argument about reclaiming her life and finding her inner strength.

She agreed. I was happy. She was happy.

She left him. It took courage. I was proud.

I hadn't considered something significant. Just because one person made up her mind to leave, the other person could still go and find her. I'd imagined that leaving was the final step. Actually, it was only the first. And the most dangerous. I began to see that the women who dared to leave often fared the worst. As though exercising free will was the greatest possible insult. Maybe it was humiliation, maybe rage. Maybe, with some of the men, just an impersonal tendency to apply violence to any part of their life that didn't seem to be working. Some would kick a dog, woman, kid, TV set, all with the same matter-of-fact brutality. Others just seemed unfathomably depressed. They could be the most dangerous. I wasn't a psychologist. I didn't know why. Maybe a murder didn't seem so bad if there was a suicide planned five seconds behind it. Maybe just a general nihilism or indifference to life.

I did what I could to learn. As usual I turned to books, reading everything from *The Gift of Fear* to *The Woman Who Walked Into Doors*. I read articles and sociological journals and legal cases and nonprofit reports. I learned about Battered Women's Syndrome and the cycle of violence, an endless looping pattern of anger, violence, apology, calm.

The violence kept happening. All around me.

The fourth time I saw Clara was in the hospital. She wasn't in good shape. On the other hand, she hadn't broken her neck. Being pushed down a staircase could do all kinds of things. It was hard to stand in a hospital with a bruised and terrified woman and think about words like "lucky." But maybe she had been. I decided then and there that I didn't want there to be a fifth time. The cycle had to be broken.

Once that decision was made, one step seemed to lead naturally to the next. Like shooting pool. Each shot lining up the next. Finding Clara's husband was simple. Most people had to live somewhere and work somewhere. Most paid bills and received mail and frequented bars and gyms and grocery stores, had social circles and habits.

First a name. Then an address. Then watching, studying. Just like I had with Jordan Stone. I learned when Clara's husband went out and when he went to bed. I learned who his friends were and what he did for fun. I began to understand that a lot of little facts could become important. Whether someone was a vegetarian or loved fried chicken. Whether someone walked a dog every evening or bothered to raise the shades after getting up in the morning. Whether someone's idea of a good time was getting drunk or going on a hike.

Everything mattered. The less important a detail seemed, the more it might matter.

Sink a shot. Line up the cue. Aim again.

The next step.

I hadn't known exactly what I wanted to say to Clara's husband when I stopped by for a talk. Before I knew it, I had lapsed back into my training. Applying reason, logic, debate. I was a decent talker and I was trying hard. I gave Clara's husband every good reason why he should allow his wife to move on.

He made my next choice an easy one. He reacted aggressively.

And then everything seemed to click.

Staircases were unpredictable. Someone could go down a dozen different times and end up a dozen different ways. Clara's husband happened to go down pretty hard. He had been drinking, which hadn't helped. Later I found out that he ended up with a broken hip, a separated shoulder, and a few less teeth from where his face bounced off the banister.

Nothing said I needed to break his right wrist after he landed. But it felt fair, so I did.

He was ex-military. He had guns. He liked to shoot. And he was a drunk. A dangerous combination. After he got better, I visited him again. In the morning, when he was still in bed and most likely to be sober. I reminded him that other people had guns, too. I showed him one of mine. I explained that his wife was going to be single, and that only he could decide whether she should be a divorcée or a widow.

Breaking the cycle.

And he understood.

That week I quit my job at the shelter. I had started to feel that talking was inefficient. Clara's husband helped me understand that certain people were wired in an unusual way. Like they had a switch that had been mistakenly preprogrammed in the Off position. So that their default mode was not wanting to listen. Talking to them first was pointless. They'd never hear a word. It was important, with those people, to reset the switch to On, so that they were in a position to take in important information.

Then they could hear just fine.

Everything became much easier. First reset the switch, then talk. Two steps.

The danger wasn't alleviated just because of my talks. Over time I'd gotten good at reminding the men I spoke to that they could meet new people, act differently. Hopeful things. I didn't want them descending into such pits of depression or rage that even the worst consequences seemed unimportant. Several times, throughout the years, my talks hadn't worked. Those were terrible moments. But usually I accomplished what I wanted.

Word of mouth was a powerful thing. Pretty soon I got a call from a different woman at a different shelter. One followed the next. Later, other people started coming to me for other work. Finding information, finding people. Not especially exciting. Mostly following, watching, staying in the same place for hours. I liked the work, though. I was solitary by nature. Irregular hours, time alone, it all suited me well. I was okay at what I did.

I kept at it and got better.

43

Woodside was supposedly one of the most expensive zip codes in the country. A quiet area in between Palo Alto and San Francisco, full of hidden mansions and estates. I bought a coffee and a sandwich in the small town, then rode a few miles out until I reached a winding driveway blocked by a black gate. The gate was about ten feet high, made up of vertical iron rods set two inches apart, topped by a row of little ornamental spikes. Designed to open outward in two halves, each half folding out from the middle. I passed the gate and pulled over on a side street, turning around so I could see the main road. I opened my sandwich and made myself comfortable.

An hour later the sun had set. I returned to the driveway. The security was straightforward. One camera on either side of the gate, mounted high up so as to take in the surrounding area. Next to each camera was a motion-activated floodlight. The system was clear. Any nocturnal motion would trip the lights, which would then illuminate the area for the cameras. The cameras probably fed into a security system off-site. Simple and effective.

Except that without lights, at night, the cameras wouldn't be much use.

I used a BB gun from across the road. Far enough that I wouldn't trip the sensors. Aiming not at the bulbs but at the motion sensors underneath, each marked by a tiny red light that I assumed meant they were on and working. Like a pair of eyes in the darkness. A harder shot, a much smaller target, but doable because of the twin red dots. And worth the effort. The sensors would be less obvious when cracked. The floodlights were there to facilitate the cameras, not the other way around. Meaning the lights didn't have any camera pointed at them. Two shots did it. The two red dots disappeared. The vertical rods on the gate were easy to grab. I climbed up, swung one leg and then the other over the spikes, and let myself down on the other side.

Gregg Gunn's house was perched high up on a hill. The house glowed like a spaceship. Low-slung, modernist architecture, all long, clean lines and sweeping expanses of glass. A glowing blue pool and emerald hot tub sat upon terraced hills in front of the house. If this was what the gated parts of Woodside looked like, no wonder it was up there in the per capita charts or whatever the economists used to measure that kind of thing.

Gunn's Tesla was parked outside. The only car in the circular driveway. I moved quickly. There were surely more cameras. I tried the front door. It was locked. I walked down the side of the house and saw another, smaller door. The kind of informal entrance that a homeowner would use day to day when coming in with bags of groceries.

This door opened.

I found myself in a vast, icy kitchen, impersonal as a laboratory. Cold recessed LED lights pinpricked down. The eight-burner stainless steel Wolf range looked like it had never been used. The floor was moody gray tile, travertine, maybe. Someone had gone and dug up a granite quarry and spread it liberally for the countertops. The counters seemed untouched, as if a crumb would be a traumatic new experience. I walked through the kitchen into a living room that was furnished with Japanese touches, soft earthy tones and bamboo floors, several silk screens taking up corner space. Floor-to-ceiling glass windows and a glass sliding door looked onto a wide stone patio. I could see the blue from the pool and, far below, points of light from other homes.

I found him in his study, although there wasn't a single book anywhere in the room. A gleaming samurai sword hung against one wall. Another silk screen embossed with Japanese characters. Gunn sat behind a walnut desk, dressed casually in a black T-shirt and yoga pants, one of those cold-pressed juice bottles next to him. His expression was contemplative, as though he was pondering the world's weightiest problems and making considerable progress.

The only thing wrong with the image was the hole in his forehead.

I looked around carefully. I was alone. I walked over to take a closer look. A single gunshot had killed him. A vertical line of blood had traveled from the wound, down over the right eye, along the cheek and chin, and finally onto his shirt. The back of his head was in worse shape. Stickiness over the brown curls of his hair. There was a stainless-steel Colt revolver on the desk, close enough to his right hand that it was impossible to tell by looking if it had fallen out of his hand or been placed there. It might have been loaded, or not. I wasn't going to find out. There was no way I'd put my hand on that gun.

I noticed a spattering of marks on the upper half of his face, like freckles. Gunpowder burns. A close-range shot, suggesting suicide. Equally, someone could have just walked up and stuck a barrel in his face. Impossible to tell whether he had shot himself or someone else had.

I had shown up with a long list of questions. I had been looking forward to a long talk. We wouldn't be talking after all.

The house was quiet.

It was time to go.

I found a pay phone in town. When Mr. Jade answered he sounded dispirited, but his tone changed when he recognized my voice. "Nikki? Is that you?" His words were eager. "We've been wondering when we'd hear from you. Have you found anything?"

"Doesn't sound like you have." Usually I didn't like rubbing it in. But it was the FBI, and I couldn't resist. I might never have the chance again.

"We're desperate," he admitted. "We have no idea what's going to happen tomorrow, much less how to stop it. We tried everything. Whatever Karen Li had for us, it's gone."

"That's because you've been looking for the wrong thing this whole time."

Mr. Jade sounded almost plaintive. "What do you mean?"

"I mailed you something. It will reach you soon, in the next couple of days. Just in case we don't get a chance to finish this conversation."

Now he was more confused. "Why wouldn't we?"

"Because there's still something I have to do tonight. If I can."

He started to say something, but I wasn't done. "In the meantime, I'm going to start by giving you an address belonging to a certain CEO. Probably not a bad idea for you to pay him a visit."

Now he was frustrated. "That's easy for you to say. Whatever corners *you* might have cut, there are rules. For us, anyway. You know that we can't just show up and walk in without a warrant."

"You can if someone tells you a crime has been committed."

"But no one—"

I had grown impatient. "*I'm* telling you, okay? As a concerned citizen, or whatever you want to call it in your report. And I'll tell you the rest soon. I don't have time now. Make sure I can reach you tonight. And if for some reason you don't hear from me by morning, don't forget to check the mail."

"Wait—where are you going, Nikki? And what did you mean, something you have to do?"

I ignored the questions. "Like I said, pay him a visit. I wouldn't wait."

I hung up. Picked up the receiver again. Put in more quarters. Dialed again. This time I didn't have much to say. "Charles," I said. "What we talked about—it's time."

I hung up again but kept the phone to my ear. A third call. The last one for now. More quarters clinking into the coin slot. More ringing. The voice that answered this time was suspicious. "Who is this?"

"Oliver," I said. "We need to talk."

"What are you talking about? Why are you calling me?"

"In person. Tonight."

"Meet? Are you crazy? I told you not to even call me anymore. I don't know who this is," he said loudly as though the NSA and Pentagon were both tucked into bed with him and the microphones were poking him under the quilt. "Good-bye! I'm hanging up now!"

"It's important," I insisted.

His voice was reluctant. "Then tomorrow."

"I found out what In Retentis is. I think you'll want to see what I have. Besides, tomorrow might be too late."

His voice changed. "You did? What is it? And what are you talking about, too late?"

"Too late for you, Oliver."

"What?" Now he was bewildered.

"They just visited Gregg Gunn. Which means they probably intend to visit you next."

44

The Port of Oakland was a massive sprawl along the eastern side of the Bay, big enough to handle the thousand-foot container ships that plodded back and forth across the Pacific, decks piled high with rectangular shipping containers. Stacks and stacks of multicolored corrugated boxes carrying the world's trade across the globe. Above, hundreds of cargo cranes poised like silhouettes of giant herons with metronomic eyes of blinking red, frozen on the verge of dipping into the black water.

I reached the maze of streets that belonged to the Port itself, my motorcycle bouncing along asphalt that had been chipped and potholed from endless lines of heavy trucks. I turned several times until I reached a one-lane road marked only by the yellow diamond of a dead-end sign. Steel and asphalt were the only markers of human presence. I could have been five hundred years in the future, staring at the deserted ruins of some anachronistic metropolis.

The night was quiet except for an electric hum and the faint noise of cars dripping off the freeway. In front of me was a reinforced four-foot metal gate. A sign said EAST BAY E-Z-STORE CUSTOMERS ONLY. I pressed a button on a plastic fob that hung off my keychain and the gate slid open. Inside, the ground was packed dirt. Stretching around me were stacks of the ubiquitous shipping containers, each twenty feet long and ten feet high, each stack a half-dozen containers high. There must have been hundreds of them, lining the yard like an industrial hedge maze. The storage facility was a squared pancake of a building, thick walls painted a depressing beige.

I waited.

Twenty minutes later I saw headlights. A small white car came into view and I pressed the key fob as the car slowed. The gate opened and the car drove slowly into the yard. Oliver rolled down the window two inches and peered up at me suspiciously, his thick eyebrows furrowed. "This really couldn't wait?"

"Come on. We don't have all night."

He turned the engine off and warily got out of the car. He was dressed as though I had told him we'd be jumping out of a helicopter behind enemy lines, a black hooded sweatshirt under a black windbreaker and a black ski hat. The ski hat had a tasseled pompom. Looking at him, I thought that Oliver must be the first special ops soldier in history to have a windbreaker emblazoned with the Sierra Club logo. He rubbed his eyes. "What did you mean about them visiting Greggory?"

"Gunn's dead."

He stopped rubbing his eyes and blinked. "Greggory? Dead? What are you talking about? He can't be. I just saw him today."

"I saw him tonight."

Oliver looked at me as if I had told him a joke in poor taste. "You can't be serious! What happened?"

"Either he shot himself or someone gave him a hand."

Oliver groped for his orange plastic bottle of antianxiety pills and dry-swallowed several. "Karen Li talked to you and she's dead. Greggory talked to you and now he is, too."

"I didn't hurt Gunn, or Karen, and I don't intend to hurt you."

"Why should I believe you?"

"Come on. We'll talk more inside."

Plenty of people used storage facilities for normal things. A couple downsizing, or someone stuck in a four-hundred-square-foot studio who needed more space. But storage facilities attracted some definite weirdos, too. Loners, often nocturnally inclined. Plenty of middle-aged men storing survival gear or hoarders filling space with crumbling newspapers. So storage facilities like this one usually offered 24-7 access. If a guy in combat boots and camouflage wanted to go digging around for his hunting rifles, maybe better that he not do so while a family was picking up a couch. The unrestricted access suited me fine. I'd always liked to be able to come and go.

I used a key on my key ring to open the padlock on the front door and we walked into a bleak grid of hallways, rolling garage-style doors set at intervals. The fluorescent lighting was spotty. Some of the light panels flickered and other patches seemed aggressive, as though they were cannibalistically leaching wattage from the sick ones. The walls were an ugly institutional green that had probably gotten a fresh coat of paint back around the first Gulf War. Oliver looked around suspiciously. "What are you showing me, anyway? You found something new?"

I stopped at one of the doors, unlocked it, and we stepped into a room that was twenty-five feet by ten feet. The room was filled floor to ceiling with books stacked in triple rows along cheap wood shelves, more books rising in vertical stacks set upon the topmost shelf. The books far exceeded the shelf space and the overburdened bookcases craned forward with excess weight. The walls of the storage unit were cement and so, rather than bolting the shelves to the wall, I had run restraining lengths of yellow nylon rope across the front of the shelves to stop them from tipping over. With the weight of the books pressed against them, the ropes were taut as guitar strings. More books were piled on the floor, rising in places to waist height and creating an overgrown jungle effect.

"What is this place?" Oliver wondered.

I sat on a mint-colored file cabinet against one wall, moving an open paperback copy of *The Iliad* to make room. "I run a bookstore, remember?" It felt strange having someone else in the room with me. I was used to being alone here. I liked it better that way, I was deciding.

Oliver shook his head impatiently. "The last thing we should be talking about is books. What did you learn? What's being planned? Is it an attack like we thought? Who's the target?"

"Right. An attack. What we talked about on the ferry—that the people in the photographs were some kind of terrorist cell, that there was some kind of attack being planned overseas. An attack that would happen tomorrow, November first. No one seemed to really know anything for sure, but everyone was guessing at the same thing. That was the part I didn't like, actually."

He was confused. "What do you mean, didn't like?"

"I tend not to trust anything that seems too certain."

"I don't understand."

"Someone recently reminded me of something I'd said once. That everyone makes assumptions, and the only question is if they're right or not. Take this, for instance. Everyone seemed to assume that the people in the photographs were up to no good. Criminals, extremists, whatever. Even the FBI was convinced there was some kind of plot, and they hadn't even seen the In Retentis photos. They were just guessing off the bits and pieces Karen Li had shared, assuming some kind of terrorism connection. Guesswork based on where Gunn was traveling and the fact that she'd told them something bad would take place on the first of November."

"FBI?" He was startled. "What? Since when have you been talking to the FBI?"

"Come on, Oliver, don't get coy at the eleventh hour. You have to know the FBI are actively investigating your company."

"Fine," he allowed. "I've heard rumors. But weren't we right?"

I thought of the Egyptian blogger with the missing tooth. Jumping off a roof, leaving his wife and children behind. "Maybe. Maybe not."

"What are you talking about?"

"The governments that Care4 has been dealing with—the places Gunn's been visiting, the places in the photographs. Saudi Arabia, Chechnya, Egypt, Iraq . . . sure, they're hotspots for extremism, terrorist activity. They also have something else in common."

"Which is?"

"They all happen to be some of the worst violators of human rights in the world."

Oliver took off his hat, sat down on a pile of books, and wriggled around, trying to get comfortable. "What does that have to do with anything?"

"I started wondering. What if we were coming at it from the exact opposite angle that we should be? What if none of the people in those pictures were bad guys after all? Flip the assumption. What if the bad guys were after *them*?"

He looked more confused than ever. "Why would they be?"

"Human rights and LGBT activists, anticorruption bloggers, journalists. In the States, maybe you get some nasty tweets aimed your way. In these countries?" I thought again of the man with the missing tooth. "You get pushed off a rooftop."

"But if it's not a pending attack, what is it?"

"Care4's real business isn't the cameras or the baby monitor stuff that your PR people hype. That's common knowledge within the company. Practically everyone must know the surveillance game is your bread and butter."

Oliver's face showed no disagreement. "Like you said, common knowledge. But what does surveillance have to do with November first?"

"I'll get there. For years the company has been pouring money into deep neural network research. Care4 wanted to become the first company in the world to create a surveillance system that wouldn't just operate without needing any human control but one that could *actively teach itself to get better at finding people.*"

"I think I might know a bit more about that field than you do," Oliver said mildly. His phone beeped from a pocket. He took it out, jabbed a quick reply, put it away.

"Absolutely," I agreed. "What do I know? I don't even have a smartphone. Anyway, Care4 has been selling more basic versions of the system for years, all over the world, which must have demonstrated the high demand for its products. So somewhere along the line, they decided to go all in on AI-driven surveillance software. Your company has been working practically around the clock to get this revamped version up and running by the internal launch date: November 1. In Retentis was always at heart a software project."

Oliver didn't look sold. "We have multiple internal launch dates every year. Every company does. What does that matter to anyone outside Care4? And what does that have to do with terrorism?"

"That's not the point. Terrorism was never the point. Teach a computer to recognize a face, to pick a person out of a crowd, and it doesn't care whether it's looking at bin Laden or Mother Teresa. You can use it for anything, good or bad."

"So?"

"Karen warned us that people would die. And that got the FBI on the wrong track immediately. Because that's how they're trained. That's what they're trained to look for. An airplane going down, a truck being driven into a crowd. After nine-eleven the Bureau's whole focus changed to terrorism. They're so preoccupied with stopping plots that this threat seemed to fit neatly into their worldview and they never really questioned it. Assumptions, again. They saw what they wanted to see. They thought Care4 was concealing crucial information about some plot out of greed, not wanting to alienate any of its international clients. That was never what Karen meant."

"What *did* she mean, then?"

"These people—in the pictures—*they're* the victims. Or they're about to be."

"Why?"

"Care4 hadn't accidentally collected info on some terrorist plot. It was selling a state-of-the-art AI system that would allow totalitarian governments and dictatorships all over the world to locate and round up the people they most hate and fear: men and women who risk their lives to expose injustice and corruption. The physical cameras are already up and running—God knows those places have no shortage of cameras all over. Everyone was just waiting for the network to go live so that computers could begin flagging faces and pointing to them in real time. And then security forces and secret police squads could just pluck these people right off the streets. There would have been huge sweeps in all these countries, beginning the day the system went live. No one would have known why journalists and activists were suddenly disappearing across the globe. And over time, the Care4 system would snow-ball, steadily teach itself to become increasingly accurate, to scan metadata and social networks to find friends, families, supporters, sources. All over the world, political opposition, the press, everyone standing up to these governments would be tracked, located, and whittled away."

Oliver's voice was slow and puzzled. "Why would Care4 do that? What's in it for them? Why risk breaking the law?"

"What law? They're selling a product, not telling people how to use it. Morally, it's a different question, but the rationale is the same reason that just about any company does anything—profit. Don't get me wrong, Oliver, I don't think that Care4 *wanted* people to die, but they also weren't willing to give up lucrative security contracts all over the world to stop that from happening."

"That's a lot of guessing." He sounded doubtful.

"Maybe so." I fell quiet, thinking. "The way I see it, Care4's attitude was basically similar to that of the U.S. gun lobby. Selling as many guns as possible is what matters, and they're not responsible for what buyers do with them. Stop a bank robbery or rob a bank—it's all up to the individual." I reflected. "I'm sure some countries would have used the system to stop terrorism or crime. For all I know ours is one of them."

"So how do you know that *all* of the countries aren't using this for good? Who says anything bad will even happen to these people you're talking about?"

I didn't hesitate. "One of the men in the photographs Karen got her hands on was an Egyptian blogger who had supposedly jumped off a roof. Police said suicide, his family said murder. Guess who was right? These countries weren't just waiting around for Care4, naturally, they were going after anyone they could find in the meantime. They just happened to get to this poor guy without needing the In Retentis network. If it's not a 'suicide' these countries always label anyone they kill a terrorist or security threat. You would think they'd never killed an innocent, none of them, ever."

Oliver stood and looked at me skeptically. "So explain Karen Li's death. That still doesn't make sense. If my company isn't actively trying to hurt anyone, how could they have been involved with whatever happened to her?"

I nodded somberly. "I couldn't figure that out at first. Even if they were morally bankrupt and had no general problem with someone being killed, why would they risk the heightened exposure that comes with a dead body? Especially an American citizen killed on U.S. soil?"

"And? Why?"

"Again, a common enough reason for human motivation. They felt they didn't have a choice."

"What do you mean, no choice?"

"What do you know about Karen Li?" I asked.

The question clearly surprised him. "I don't know—I mean, I worked with her, I saw her résumé, she was very good at her job . . ."

"Do you know anything about her parents? How she ended up here?"

Oliver shook his head impatiently. "Of course not. Why would I? I wasn't dating the woman, I was her coworker. I care about her programming skills, not her family tree."

I thought of the timeline. The photograph from the cabin. The little girl held in her mother's arms. The GPS records showing the nonprofit where Karen must have volunteered, Tiananmen Lives. "She came to the U.S. in 1990 from China. She only gained U.S. citizenship later on. Something had happened to both her parents at the same time, probably the year before that. 1989 Beijing. Want to take a guess where?"

He saw where I was going almost immediately. "Tiananmen Square?"

"They were almost definitely student protesters. They probably died side by side. Afterward she came to the States to live with relatives. The woman had a lifelong hatred for any government willing to kill its own civilians for protesting abuse of power. To her, that was far more important than money or a career. More important than anything. Once she found out what In Retentis was about, she was never going to just walk away and let people die."

"So Care4 didn't have a choice? That's what you're saying?"

"I'm sure they would have far preferred any other option than murder. They probably ran through everything. But fire her? She could sue, or turn whistleblower, or go to the press—any number of things. Buy her out, bribe her? Well, she valued some things more than money. Intimidate or scare her? God knows they tried. Everything from threatening her with lawyers to hiring me to follow her. The pressure took a toll without a doubt. If Care4 could have stressed her to the point of a breakdown I'm sure they would have been delighted. But she was tough, and the woman was driven by something more important to her than even her own physical safety. She wasn't going to walk away. And if they just ignored her? Then—"

"She gets the FBI information that shuts down In Retentis," Oliver finished.

"Exactly."

"When you put it that way, they really didn't have a choice," Oliver said thoughtfully.

"Wrong," I corrected sharply. "Of course they had a choice. They could have chosen to place innocent lives above profit. They could have said no to blood money. They could have refused to sell their technology without stipulating how it was used, even if that cost them financially. And, most of all, they could have decided to face up to consequences, or chosen to take on their employee in court if they felt she was wrong—anything except choosing to murder her in cold blood." I gave Oliver a hard look. "They had a choice, all right. They just chose the wrong way."

He looked away from my eyes. "The guesswork is impressive, but how do you know for sure? Do you have proof?"

I got up and opened the top drawer of the file cabinet I had been using as a stool. I took out a sealed manila folder and opened it with a penknife that I left on the file cabinet next to the open paperback. I pulled out a sheaf of photographs. Each a page of Silas Johnson's file from the hotel. "Take a look," I said, extending the documents. "Attorney-client privilege goes pretty far, but I've never felt it should cover complicity in murder. The lawyers Care4 hired were helping to handle the In Retentis contract negotiations with foreign powers. I'm sure they were getting paid very well for their efforts."

Oliver glanced through the first few photographs carefully, then looked up nervously. "You know they could sue you into the poorhouse just for having this stuff?"

"I'll take my chances."

He took a candy bar from his pocket, tore off the gold wrapper, and chewed with small, rapid bites. "So what do you need me to do?"

"Help me log into the Care4 systems. Tonight, before it's too late. We stop the system from going live, we shut down In Retentis, and that saves these people and hundreds or thousands of others, too."

Oliver blanched. "That's impossible."

"You helped build their security system. If anyone can pull it off, you can."

"What if I get caught?"

"Right side, wrong side, Oliver. You said it yourself. Where do you want to land?"

"Isn't there some other way?"

I shook my head. "Not this time."

He thought some more. "You're not exactly asking me to hack into a lemonade stand."

I was growing impatient. Impatient, and edgy. Only a handful of hours remained. "I'm not going to argue with you all night. Either you help me, or say no, so that I can go find someone who can. We have to hurry."

He looked around uncertainly, stalling. "This is too risky. I need to think it over."

"We don't have time. Yes or no? Make up your mind."

I started toward him, then stopped abruptly.

Joseph stood in the doorway.

He was dressed similarly to when I'd last seen him, at my brother's apartment. A dark suit, dark shirt, black polished shoes. One difference was his right arm, which was now in a sling. A .45 would do that. Impossible to tell exactly where he had taken the bullet, but his upper arm bulged slightly under the shoulder of the well-tailored suit. The kind of bulk that a layer of thick bandages might add. He held his gun in his right hand and a pair of heavy bolt cutters in his left.

I backed away fast. Last time Joseph had walked into a room with me, his pale eyes had been flat and empty. Eyes that said he was utterly indifferent to my fate. No longer. Now, his eyes surged with hatred. "You," he said. "I've been thinking about everything I want to do to you." He gestured significantly with the bolt cutters, raising the black stainless steel jaws toward me. "I'm going to make sure that it's a very long night, and I'm going to keep you alive to the very end."

45

"How'd you get in, Joseph?"

His voice was thick with animosity. "You think I can't cut a lock with one arm?"

"I hope that's on your résumé."

He called me a couple of names that no newspaper in the country would have printed. He was holding the gun in his right hand, even with the sling. I wondered what Joseph would do if he decided to use it. Whether he'd switch hands so he could bring it up and sight, or if he'd stick to the right hand and shoot from the hip. He might still be a good shot. He might not be. "I can kill you and be out of the country long before they find your body," he finished.

"Sure," I said. I nodded toward Oliver. "But can *he*?"

Maybe the antianxiety pills were kicking in, but Oliver didn't seem so nervous anymore. He didn't seem so surprised to see Joseph here either. In fact, he hadn't even seemed to wonder who Joseph was. "I thought you were helping me, Oliver," I said. "Disappointing."

"What are you talking about?" he said.

"It's okay. You can drop the guardian angel bit. We're past that."

"I am helping you, Nikki," he insisted. "Of course I am."

I nodded at Joseph. "And I'm supposed to believe that he just took a wrong turn and ended up here? Come on, why keep lying? What's the point?"

Eyes on the ground, Oliver considered this in silence. "I was helping you at first," he finally said, looking up. "But you were too good. You started finding out too much."

"Why help me at all?"

He didn't hesitate. "An insurance policy."

"Insurance?"

"Greggory had a fairly low opinion of your abilities. He didn't think you'd get anywhere—except where we wanted you to get. Out of the two of us, I've always tended toward caution. I wasn't sure where you'd end up after Greggory first approached you. I thought it would be better to know your thought process. I didn't give you any information or idea you weren't going to reach eventually on your own. We didn't know if you'd ever get to In Retentis, but if you did, we wanted to know about it—and the more convinced you were that terrorism was the answer, the less you'd be thinking about it being anything else."

I sat again on the file cabinet, next to the open book folded spine-up. "Why me?" There was a gun in the top drawer. A .357 stainless-steel revolver with a big four-inch barrel. I had left it loaded and cocked. "Why come to me in the first place? Why risk getting an outsider involved?"

He shrugged. "We needed someone like you. You were perfect."

"Perfect how?"

"We needed someone who actually did this kind of work for it to be plausible, but the true ideal was a loner with proven antisocial tendencies. Someone without close friends or family. Without a big network of people who would come asking questions if anything happened to her. As far as your established record of violence, the anger management therapy, the arrest for assault—well, we couldn't have asked for anything better. For any*one* better. We spent a long time searching carefully for potential candidates, and you, Nikki, were the very best."

I didn't much like hearing that. "The plan was to frame me for Karen's murder?"

"We needed to establish causality. We'd hired you to follow her, but you became fixated, got out of control. When she learned you were following her and demanded you keep away, you grew angry, issued threats. You had become paranoid, obsessed with the idea of protecting her from unknown enemies. And then, finally, when she refused to accept your help, you became frustrated and lost your temper."

I nodded, remembering the bloodstained crowbar Joseph had brought to my brother's apartment. "So with the police right on my heels, I would have been found as a suicide, right next to the murder weapon, everything tied up nice and neat. And killing Karen, rather than . . ."

I didn't need to finish my sentence. "You were right," he agreed readily. "We agonized over the decision. It was a radical new step for us, and it was the last thing we wanted. Well, *almost* the last thing," he modified. "If there had been any other way to get her to be quiet or just go away, we would have gladly taken it. We were shocked by the woman's stubbornness, her refusal to listen to reason. We couldn't understand that—but of course, we didn't know about her parents. That obviously left her less willing to compromise. Karen Li needed to be out of the picture, but we couldn't just have the police pursuing an open-ended murder, especially with the FBI already suspicious. We needed a why, and most of all we needed a who."

I took that in. "That was why Gunn had me start following her on that particular day. You knew she was meeting the FBI. You didn't need me to follow her. You needed *them* to see me following her. To set me up for later."

He nodded. "Surveillance, Nikki, was the last thing we needed you for."

"So why expose your company to this kind of risk? Why not just make money by selling your system to countries who would actually have used it to make their populations safer? Why deal with the worst of the worst?" Pulling the .357 from the file cabinet and killing Joseph would take less than a single second. If he tied his shoe. If he blew his nose. If he got an eyelash in his eye. None of those things happened. Joseph's eyes never left me.

Oliver drummed his hand against his thigh impatiently. "Don't you get it? You practically answered your own question. Do you not understand that my company has made an extraordinary and unprecedented technological advance? Our system will fundamentally change the way we *live*. How can you not see that?" His normally forgettable voice had taken on a new quality and his eyes shone. "To know where people are, to be able to locate them anywhere—can you not see how limitless that power is? A child strays away from his mother—feed a photograph of his face into the system and he's found, probably within seconds. A criminal goes on a rampage—police find him instantly. A child molester wanders near a playground, a convicted bank robber shows up near a bank, and real-time alerts are triggered. And the system keeps getting smarter, learns to recognize new things, *teaches* itself at an exponential rate. Eventually far faster than a human could ever learn.

Crime can be virtually eradicated—but not just crime. Think of public health! Someone walking around with influenza, exhibiting symptoms of some highly contagious disease—they can be taken away for treatment or quarantine before they infect others. A drunk driver could be recognized and stopped before he ever gets in his car. All the chaos and unpleasantness of the world can be addressed and fixed." He took a breath. "Are you starting to see what I mean, Nikki?"

"What does that have to do with a dictatorship murdering a journalist?"

Oliver's voice smoothed out, became patient, as though he was explaining things to a child. "We're addressing problems on a *global* scale. For this to work we can't pick and choose. You can see that. We need our network to spread everywhere, all over the world. It's useless if we can only see here and there. The more it sees, the more it learns, the faster it teaches itself. We don't have the luxury of cherry-picking who we work with. You think we want clients to abuse our system? Of course not. But what we created has to be allowed to take root, and if you want to call a tiny handful of people growing pains, so be it."

"Innocent people," I pointed out.

"You know how many lives we've already saved?" Oliver retorted heatedly. "Far more than the number being threatened, I promise. And there are some very high-up officials in our own government and military who have shown themselves to be extremely receptive and supportive of what we are doing."

"Assholes in government, there's a shocker," I observed drily.

"Come on, Nikki! We turn a blind eye to far worse every day! You know how many dictatorships, how many human rights abuses, our country looks away from, ignores, every day, in the interests of national security?"

I leaned back comfortably and used the penknife to trim at a hangnail. "It feels so good being right."

He wasn't done. "Like I said, you were too good. We never thought you'd find out so much so fast. That was the only thing that surprised us—well, that, and how personally you took the Li woman's death. We didn't understand that. You barely knew her. She didn't matter—certainly not to you, of all people."

"She did, though. That's the thing. She mattered a lot to me."

Oliver's face lost its animation and grew disinterested. "No point in splitting hairs. We need to wrap things up. Actually, the biggest surprise to me was that you were foolish enough to get trapped here tonight. Such a basic mistake, and at such a crucial moment. I had grown fond of seeing your resourcefulness in action, truth be told. I expected more from you. I still can't figure out why you allowed yourself to be so careless when it mattered most."

"Maybe you should have asked yourself that an hour ago."

"Huh?" He peered at me, bewildered. "It's doesn't matter. We're here."

"Exactly. We're here." I slowly reached for the open book on the file cabinet. "Don't worry, it's a book," I called to Joseph as his gun inched up. "It can't hurt you."

I moved the book aside, revealing a little white object that looked like a golf ball.

"Look familiar?"

Oliver's face changed. "That's not—"

"When Gunn gave it to me, the day he hired me, I didn't know what to do with it. So I just left it sitting in my office. Then, later, I could never figure out one thing. When Joseph and his friends grabbed me at the bookstore, they didn't walk in randomly. They waited until after I had gone upstairs and settled in. The timing seemed too perfect. But they didn't know someone else was hiding in the store, downstairs. Like they could only see into my office on the second floor. And on the ferry, you seemed surprised that I had Karen's photographs, but not *that* surprised. Not as much as I would have thought. Because I had looked at the photos in my office. I realized that this little sucker had been streaming live audio and video the whole time. Gunn gifted me a Trojan horse. The oldest trick in the book, and I fell for it."

His face was very pale. "Nikki, that hasn't been—"

"On? Recording? Now?" I shrugged carelessly. "You know me, Oliver, I don't do tech. I doubt I would even know how to turn it off." I held up the little camera and turned it idly in my hands. "I did have a friend take a look at it. Turns out it's easy enough to point the live stream in a different direction. To somewhere safe, say, where people have access to everything we talked about no matter what happens to me tonight."

I pictured Charles Miller, probably a cup of coffee in one hand, hunched over his laptop, watching and listening intently. Given the many unhealthy things that might happen to the people in this room tonight, I wasn't about to let Mr. Jade and Mr. Ruby watch me in real time. Not with my intentions. We were helping each other, but they were still sworn to uphold *all* laws. I wanted a bit more flexibility. Yet I had given Charles the contact information for the two agents just the same. If worse came to worst, he'd know where to send his recording of the night's events. "If you two hadn't been so busy today planning your boss's murder," I finished, "you might have noticed that you weren't watching my office anymore."

Oliver looked around the room warily. "You brought me here to trick me?"

I didn't bother to answer.

He flushed, thinking, then made up his mind. "I didn't know I was being recorded. None of that's admissible in court. Give me the camera. Now."

"No."

"Give it to me," he demanded.

"Come and get it."

"Get the camera from her, Joseph," he said.

Joseph looked like he'd been hoping for exactly those words. Without hesitation he walked eagerly toward me, his pale eyes murderous. "I'm looking for an excuse," he said, his gun pointed directly at me and the steel bolt cutters held loosely in his left hand like a hatchet.

I picked up my penknife again. "What are you going to do with that besides cutting your pretty little nails?" he sneered.

I didn't bother to answer. Just reached across fast and slashed the yellow ropes nearest to me. The sharp little blade went through the taut nylon and the ropes slid away, limp with released tension. I was already on my feet, backing a safe distance away from the wall.

Joseph shook his head. "Come on. No more games."

There was a single thud as a hardcover dropped off the top of a bookcase, bounced off Joseph's shoulder, and landed at his feet.

He looked down at the book curiously.

Then he looked up to see where it had come from as the entire length of the bookcase lurched forward, hundreds of books toppling down all at once. He tried to get out of the way, tripped over a pile on the floor, fell, and then the lower half of his body disappeared as the long wooden shelf came down on top of him.

By then I had the .357 in my hand. No more banter. I was all business.

Oliver was watching me with the look of someone who'd just watched a tiger jump its fence at the zoo and was now wishing he hadn't been poking it through the bars. He shrunk away from me, timid once again. I could see Joseph moving under the pile of books and kept my eyes focused on him. As

I walked past Oliver, I threw a hard elbow into the bridge of his nose. Hitting him felt very satisfying. He'd had it coming for a long time.

He clutched his nose and gasped in pain, then again as I kicked him hard in the side of the knee. I saw him fall in my peripheral vision, saw Joseph's good arm bracing itself as he tried to push himself up. "Joseph," I called. "Keep your hands empty or I'll shoot them off your damn wrists. Stand up."

I watched Joseph struggle to his feet, disheveled. "Your stupid tricks," he said furiously.

Hitting Joseph across the face with the barrel of the .357 felt even more satisfying than hitting Oliver. He went down on one knee, a gash spilling blood down his forehead. The .357 barrel made a nice straight line between my hands and Joseph's head. "Get up."

"Stop, Nikki, right there."

I turned my head for a quick glance, not wanting to take my eyes off Joseph. My elbow hadn't done Oliver any favors in the beauty department. Blood had spread all over his lower face and chin and he was panting loudly through his mouth. But his hands, holding a semiautomatic pistol, were reasonably steady.

"I wasn't going to shoot you, Oliver," I said, eyes still on Joseph. "I was going to make sure you were held accountable, but not shoot you."

"That's easy to promise when I'm pointing a gun at you."

"You're missing my point. You just changed things. I wasn't. But now I might."

He picked up the little white camera and threw it on the ground as hard as he could, then ground his heel into the pieces for good measure. "Put your gun down, now."

I had to make a decision quickly. If I pivoted and shot him he probably wouldn't have time to react. He hadn't done this kind of thing before. There would be that fragment of shock, delaying his reaction, as he realized he had to pull a trigger with an actual person in front of him. But multiple guns in a small room meant almost anything could happen. And as soon as my gun shifted, Joseph would throw himself at me. He was already inching closer, reading my mind. He wouldn't care if I shot Oliver. Not if that let him reach me. He hated me that much. I thought of Board Shorts, catching a ricochet in the garage. I pictured the three of us here, bullets bouncing randomly off concrete in a small enclosed space.

I didn't love the odds.

"Put it down," Oliver said again. There was more tension in his voice. The gun was shaking now, his hands clenched tightly around the grip. He looked like he was starting to panic. I imagined the pain from his nose mixing with stress and adrenaline. An unreliable combination.

He might shoot me without even realizing he had pulled the trigger.

I made up my mind.

"Okay."

I put the .357 down on the ground.

By the time I'd stood back up Joseph had his gun pointed back at me, just like before.

Except this time, I didn't have a plan.

46

We walked single file. I led, Joseph and Oliver behind me. Joseph was a professional. He stayed back far enough that I couldn't reach him, but not far enough for me to duck around a corner and run. Oliver carried the envelope with the Care4 documents under one arm. Outside, the night was warm. A slice of moon in the sky, garnished with orange vapor thrown off by the Port lights.

"Why'd Gunn have to die?" I asked.

Oliver's voice came from behind me. "Why do you care?"

"I don't. I'm curious. You two worked together for years. Why kill him?"

"If you must know, the pressure of the FBI investigation was getting to Greggory. He lost his nerve at the worst possible time."

There was a beep as he unlocked his car. Headlights flared as if in greeting. On the other side of the gate I saw a nondescript dark sedan. It was parked with the bumper almost touching the gate, so that a person could step easily from the hood and scale the bars.

"Where are we going?"

"Shut up," Joseph said. "Just get in the goddamn car. Up front, passenger side."

"Okay." I opened the front door of Oliver's car, then paused. "Almost forgot." My keychain was extended in my hand. "To open the gate."

"Give it to me," Joseph said.

"Here you go."

I threw the keychain over his head as hard as I could.

It sailed into the darkness of the empty lot and was gone.

What I had done took a second to sink in. Neither one of them was happy. Joseph was all for shooting me on the spot. Partly out of personal animus, but another reason, too. Several times, now, I had done things he didn't expect that resulted in outcomes he didn't like. Joseph didn't say it outright, but he was starting to feel that me being alive was a risk to his safety.

Naturally, I felt the same about him.

Oliver wouldn't allow it. The last thing Oliver wanted was to end up with his car trapped on the wrong side of a gate, with a dead body right there for anyone to find. Finally, they reached the obvious conclusion: the only option was to go find my keys.

"Where'd they fall?" Oliver asked.

Joseph made a vague gesture that took up about two acres. "I was watching her."

"I think I saw," I volunteered helpfully.

They had me walk in front of them. A logical decision. They couldn't leave me alone, they wouldn't trust me anywhere behind them, and they weren't willing to walk next to me. Joseph was adamant about that. He'd seen Victor walk into a room with me. I'd been the one to walk out. Joseph wouldn't let me get within arm's length if he could help it. We started walking, the high rows of shipping containers dwarfing us. "It's not much good without a light," I said, holding up the same LED flashlight I'd used in Silas Johnson's office. "We'll be out here all night."

"I hope you try to run," Joseph said. "I really do."

"When have I ever done anything you wanted, Joseph?"

Joseph cursed. I laughed. We walked.

Oliver and Joseph had been watching me when I threw the keys. But I had been watching the keys. I had a pretty good idea where they'd landed. I had started off by heading intentionally too far to one side of the dark lot. No need to rush. Now I was easing us toward where I thought the keys actually were.

Oliver wanted to know something. "When did you start to suspect me?"

"I suspected you from the moment we first met. When you came up to me in the parking lot of the gym. Of course I did."

He sounded annoyed. "Such a Sherlock. Always a million steps ahead of everyone else." His voice was sarcastic. "I'm sure you noticed a single hair out of place, or some miniscule paint fleck on my car, and then suddenly all the answers just instantly came together in your mind."

"Not what I meant. I didn't just suspect *you*. From the moment Gunn hired me, any new person I met was suspect. That's how these things work. Obviously, though, I wanted to find out for sure. So on the ferry I told you I might go to the police with Karen's photographs."

"And?"

"I couldn't help noticing that no one tried to kill me until I told you that. Then the next day I had Joseph and company at my doorstep. If they were out there watching me, I wanted to flush them out, although I hadn't figured they'd be mean enough to go for my brother. That was a mistake." I was actively scanning the ground but continued talking. The more people talked and listened, the harder it was for them to think. "But I still didn't *really* know until tonight."

"What happened tonight?"

I threw a look over my shoulder. They were a few steps behind me, still carefully out of arm's reach. "You showed up here."

"What does that have to do with anything? You told me to show up."

"Exactly. An innocent man wouldn't have listened. Especially not after he's told his life's in danger. He might call the police, he might hide or lock himself up in his home. The one thing he doesn't do? Show up to a strange warehouse in the middle of the night, all on the word of someone he barely knows." I worked the beam of light back and forth over the ground. "You showed up because you needed to see what I had."

"Why not just have the FBI here waiting? Why take the risk of meeting us alone?"

Glancing back at them, I nodded toward Joseph. "You can thank him for that."

"What do you mean?"

"Joseph is cautious," I said. "In his line of work, if you're not, you generally don't hit thirty. I couldn't take the chance that he'd sense a trap or see the FBI guys and get spooked. I needed you to show up tonight, but I also needed *him* to be here. That part was important."

"Why?" This time it was Joseph asking. He sounded genuinely puzzled. "You must know what I'm going to do to you."

"You tried to kill my brother," I answered frankly. "And you're just as responsible for Karen Li's death as Gunn or Oliver or Victor. You think you get to just walk away?"

"But I will walk away," said Joseph. "Right after I'm done with you. And before I get on a plane I'm going to do two things. I'm going to grab your junkie brother a second time, and then I'm going to tie him up in that god-damn bookstore of yours, soak him in gasoline, and burn it into ashes."

I ignored him. If he was thinking about the future that was his problem. I was focused on what was right in front of me. Specifically, a glint of metal on the ground.

"Found them."

I picked up the keychain and held it up obediently. The flashlight in my hand had momentarily angled toward them. The direction of the light made it difficult for Joseph and Oliver to see me, while making it correspondingly easier for me to see them. I took a step toward them, hands held wide and unthreatening, and sprayed Joseph full in the face with the pepper spray clipped to my keychain. Then I flung myself down and to my left, to the out-side of his right shoulder. His sling pinned his right arm to his body. He'd have to twist his whole body around to aim.

Joseph yelled in pain and flung a hand across his face even as two bullets cracked out toward where I'd been standing a moment before. Then I was exactly where he hadn't wanted me: within arm's range.

He was trying to rub his eyes, turn, and shoot all at the same time. I came up with my left hand in a twisting uppercut and hit him as hard as I could. Not in the face or body or groin or any of the places I usually would have aimed for. I hit Joseph just under the right shoulder in the thickness of his bandages. The gunshot wound was only a few days old. He cried out in agony and the fingers of his right hand loosened. His gun fell to the ground.

We both dove for it. I felt a big hand against my face and bit hard into the fleshy part of the palm. Joseph yelped and kneed me in the stomach while relocating his bitten hand to my hair. I got my own hand into his crotch and twisted, hard. He made an unappetizing sound and then drove his good elbow into my forehead. I felt skin split, got two fingers around his earlobe, and did my best to annex that piece of territory. He got another knee into my stomach and a finger hooked into my nostril. My teeth found their way back into his hand for the second time. It was that kind of brawl. Not pretty. No rules. Not any kind of event that Kentucky ladies would have donned flowered hats to see.

I got one hand on the gun and felt Joseph's hand close over my own. He was much stronger than I was, even one-handed. He got the gun angled up and then toward me. I head-butted him, but in my prone position I couldn't get my weight behind it. I felt the barrel of the gun nudge into my body and tried frantically to push it away, but he was too strong. He had me. We both knew it. The barrel of the gun poked into my stomach and I jerked my body around and under his in a desperate attempt to get the barrel off me.

There was a sharp report and the pungent smell of gunpowder filled my nostrils.

Something was wrong.

There was no pain.

It took me a moment to realize the gunshot had come from above. Joseph's hand fell from the gun. His body went limp and eased away from mine. Oliver stood over us. That last movement of mine had put Joseph between me and the bullet Oliver had fired down at us. Oliver's hands were shaking and his face was covered in drying blood, but he kept his gun pointed down at me.

"Roll away from the gun," he said. "Slowly."

I rolled. Once, then again, blinking my eyes to try to clear the blood running down my forehead from Joseph's elbow. "You just shot Joseph. I'll assume it was an accident."

Oliver was breathing raggedly, his eyes fierce and determined. "He was expendable."

"You say that about a lot of people."

"A lot of people are."

I was still curled into a protective ball. My hand brushed at my boot as his eyes wandered to Joseph's body, then retreated as he looked back to me. "How are you going to explain this mess?" I wanted to know. "Are you forgetting the camera? I wasn't kidding about that. A copy will go to the FBI. They'll know you were here tonight."

Oliver didn't seem overly worried. "You made things awkward, yes, but it's nothing we can't handle. Anyway, *this* isn't recording, now, and"—he nodded at Joseph's body—"I'm starting to learn that dead people make excellent scapegoats. As far as the fallout, I have friends who understand how crucial it is that we be allowed to go live unimpeded. Starting tomorrow, our network will provide U.S. intelligence services an invaluable window into the world. You think that will go unappreciated? Even the FBI backs off with national security at stake." He ran a hand across his nose, which was still trickling blood. "This is as vulnerable as we'll ever be. After tomorrow we'll never be threatened like this again."

"There was one part that really had me stuck," I said.

He sounded only mildly curious. "Oh yeah? What was that?"

"You."

"Me? What about me?"

"Who you are, Oliver—or Martin Gilman, I should say."

He was startled. "How do you know my name?"

"Missing a Clipper card?"

His eyes narrowed, remembering the ferry ride. "That was you? You resorted to that kind of cheap pickpocketing? I'd think that was beneath you."

"I wanted your name. Even in Silicon Valley, low-tech solutions still work." Each Clipper card was marked with an individual number so it could be reloaded electronically from a personal account. Finding Oliver's personal information had taken Charles Miller less time than it took me to finish a cup of coffee.

He shrugged. "Fine. So you have my name. So what?"

"I couldn't figure out why you were mixed up in everything if you were just a salaried employee at Care4. It didn't make sense to take the kind of chances you took. Look at you. You're more committed than Gunn ever was, and he was the damn CEO. I guessed at all kinds of things: blackmail, maybe you two were jockeying for power and working at cross-purposes, but none of it quite added up."

"And what did you conclude?"

"I kept coming back to the only answer that worked. Care4 wasn't actually Gunn's company at all, was it?"

Oliver looked at me without answering for a long moment. "What do you mean?" he finally asked.

"On paper, Gregg Gunn seemed like the classic Valley success story—Stanford dropout, gets a taste of finance on Wall Street, gets into trouble, fresh beginning in the start-up world. But there was something wrong with that narrative that I kept coming back to. He didn't seem to be very *good* at any of it. He didn't drop out; he flunked out for bad grades. In New York he almost ended up in jail for insider trading. I'm sure the fines eclipsed any profit he made. And every company he started out here lost money and folded. Three of them, I think it was."

Oliver's face stayed neutral. "Interesting assessment."

"Interesting? Sure. What *I* found interesting was that I'm not the only one who made it."

"What do you mean?"

"*You* did." I said. "Years ago. I arrived at a conclusion recently that you'd reached long before we ever met. Gunn was broke. He'd lost money for investors every time at bat. No one was about to trust him with more money. Care4 was *your* idea, not his. But you were already thinking ahead. Maybe you just didn't like the spotlight or found it distracting. Maybe you wanted someone who could be the face of the company, and, if necessary, a lightning rod, while you quietly ran things from behind. Even someone you could send all over the globe on your behalf—or, for that matter, someone you could send to hire a private detective while you played both sides, buddying up in case she found out too much. Assigning yourself to a boring division like the security department was clever. You could plausibly know what was going on without attracting interest. And Gunn was perfect for you. A charismatic, extroverted stooge. Someone greedy enough to skirt the law, smart enough to act the part, and dumb or shortsighted enough to go along with everything you wanted without asking too many questions."

"And how exactly am I supposed to have met this perfect person, at a bus stop?"

"No." I thought of the transcript Charles Miller had given me on the Berkeley fishing pier. "Gregg Gunn was your freshman-year roommate at Stanford. Then he flunked out. Maybe you stayed in touch, maybe not. But later on—long after you graduated and decided to found Care4—you had the perfect person for your purposes. You tracked down your old down-on-his-luck college roommate and made him an irresistible offer. To do what he'd always wanted: lead a successful company."

Martin Gilman stared at me, then nodded slowly. "In retrospect, we could have made our lives much easier by finding someone less good at her job," he said. "Live and learn, I suppose. A shame I have to kill you. If I didn't, I'd hire you for real." There was a beeping sound from his pocket. His eyes flicked down as he used one hand to reach into his pocket and silence his cell phone.

This time my hand found its way all the way down to my boot.

"Anyhow," he said, "we don't want to be out here all night." He held his pistol again with both hands. "Care4 is a company with limitless potential, Nikki. We've been cultivating many important relationships, not just around the world but also in D.C. Next time something like this happens, we'll be untouchable."

The tiny .32 Derringer wasn't good for more than a few feet of accuracy, but the man in front of me wasn't more than a few feet away. I brought my hands up fast and fired upward. There was a small crack, barely more than a cap gun would make. The bullet hit him in the throat and within that fractional space of time his life expectancy changed from about another forty years to another forty seconds. He dropped his gun and sat down on the ground, holding his throat with both hands as it leaked blood. The Derringer was a two-shot gun. I could have shot him again but I didn't. It wasn't that I wanted to prolong things. I was just tired of shooting people. I could have been fine never seeing another gun. I was overcome by one of those sluggish, unhappy sensations where the entire universe seems pointless.

The man who had called himself Oliver was trying to say something, but he couldn't talk because of his throat. He made unpleasant sounds as he shifted from a seated position to supine, slowly, as though in a reclining dentist chair.

It took him a little while to figure out the whole dying thing, but he figured it out eventually.

I wasn't entirely surprised to hear sirens. Like many parts of Oakland, the Port was blanketed with a network of ShotSpotter microphones, designed to pick up gunshots and relay the location to nearby police. If gunshots occurred anywhere outdoors, there was always a decent chance police would soon be headed for the noise.

I was standing in between two bodies, one shot dead with a gun registered to me.

No matter what might happen later on, there was no way that I'd be allowed to just walk away.

I reached into Martin Gilman's pocket and took out the iPhone that had distracted him so fatally. I used his limp right thumb against the fingerprint sensor to unlock the screen and dialed from memory. "It's me," I said.

Mr. Jade's voice was tight with adrenaline. "Nikki? We're at Gunn's house, we found his body. Where are you?"

"I'm at the next stop."

"Where?"

"I have the documents Karen Li was trying to get you, but I need your help. The Care4 servers need to be shut down from their offices tonight. Tomorrow will be too late."

He didn't sound particularly fazed. "It won't be the first time I woke up a judge. If you have the evidence to prove why we have to get in there, we'll handle that part."

"One other thing. Some people tried to stop me tonight."

"Tried?" He heard my voice and understood. "I see. Tried. Are you okay?" Worry laced his tone. Unsentimentally, I wondered if it was for me, or because he risked losing the same evidence twice. I gave him the benefit of the doubt and figured it was a bit of both.

"Oakland's finest are about to show up. I need you to be here to explain the situation. Make sure they understand that I was working with you. I have a very comfortable queen-size mattress at home. Memory foam, coil-free, all that good stuff. I'm used to it. I like sleeping on it. In fact, I don't much feel like spending the night anywhere else."

He got my point. "Give me the address. We'll leave now."

I gave him the address.

"Oh, and Nikki?"

About to hang up, I kept the phone to my ear. "Yeah?"

"If we were wrong about everything, like you said, then what was actually happening? Were people in danger?"

I nodded, even though he couldn't see me. "Just not the people we thought. When you get here I'll explain everything, but hurry. Until you reach the Care4 offices, they're still not safe."

I put the phone down, walked over to a row of shipping containers, and sat. I slumped against the ridged metal, hearing the sirens getting louder. I was tired enough that I could have fallen asleep leaning against broken glass. My face hurt. My body hurt. Every part of me hurt. I could see blue lights beyond the gate. I watched the lights get closer.

WEEK FIVE

47

"My goodness, Nikki. The last time I saw you, you looked bad. Now you look . . . worse."

"Thanks, I guess."

"Your reticence can make you really extraordinarily difficult to work with. I mean that with equal measures of frustration and affection."

"Everyone likes a challenge."

"Challenge, yes—I suppose that's one way to put it. You're through with these sessions, you know. This is our last one. I submit my papers to the court and you're all set. But you're free to keep coming back, voluntarily."

"Choices."

"Choices, exactly."

"Can I ask you something before I go?"

"Of course."

"Do you think we're defined by what we do?"

"Defined?"

"Like, do you think doing bad things makes a person bad?"

"I'm not sure how to answer that. I think it must depend on what is done, and why. Maybe a question that a spiritual or religious adviser might answer better. For what it's worth, Nikki, you strike me as many things, but bad isn't one of them."

"But you don't know me."

"I don't know what you've done, and I doubt I ever will. That's true, but maybe if I did I still couldn't answer your question."

"I've always been scared of being, you know, like a Becky Sharp out of *Vanity Fair*. Someone who can think, take care of herself, tough, resourceful, but inside . . . nothing. Just her own well-being. Sometimes I think that would be worse than—worse than a lot of things."

"Nikki, you've never come out and said as much directly, but I get the distinct impression that you have no problem putting yourself in danger to save others. Out of all the things for you to worry about, I wouldn't worry about a lack of empathy."

"Maybe. But I still do."

"The ones who don't worry are the ones who should worry, I'd say. I'll tell you what. I'll keep next week's slot open for you. Same day, same time. Just in case."

"Sure. Just in case."

"All right, then. I'll see you next week. Maybe."

"Maybe it is."

48

The cemetery was in Monterey. I parked my motorcycle by the gated entrance, near a small office. Inside, I found a groundskeeper in jeans and work boots reading a newspaper with the day's date, November 2. As he put it down on his desk and got up, I saw bold headlines on the front page: a tech CEO dead, a middle-of-the-night FBI raid, chaos. A second, smaller headline announced that a San Francisco law firm had also been implicated. There was an inset picture of Silas Johnson. He didn't look so cocky as the last time I'd seen him, at the hotel bar. Handcuffs had that effect on people.

Outside, the groundskeeper pointed me in the right direction and then returned to his newspaper. I strolled slowly along a paved path, feeling that odd juxtaposition of tranquility and despair that hung in the air at any cemetery. It was a cool, pleasant morning. The ground slanted down toward a dark-green lily pond and groups of large white geese marched with self-satisfied purpose among polished granite and marble. There was a playground across the street, the top of a yellow slide just visible, and happy children's voices filtered lightly through the air.

I found her grave after a few minutes of searching. It was new enough that a headstone had not yet been put in and the rectangle of ground was still raw. There were numerous bunches of flowers, though, and someone had set a photograph of her on the ground, propped against a small pile of ocean-smoothed stones. I had my own bouquet that I placed carefully on the grass. I stood quietly in the sunshine for a few minutes and finally sat cross-legged facing the picture, not minding the dewy grass against my jeans. "We saved them, Karen," I said out loud. "I'm sorry you can't be here, I'm sorry I didn't get the chance to know you better, and most of all I'm sorry for letting them get to you—but we saved them."

There was a simple stone bench nearby, within sight of the grave.

I sat there for a long time before I left.

49

The restaurant was a tiny place on San Pablo Avenue. Just a few tables, all bunched a little too close together so that a person had to squeeze a bit sitting down. An open galley kitchen ran along one side, a battered and ancient gas stove topped with huge pots. The restaurant was run by a Vietnamese couple. The husband cooked and the wife, a tiny woman with black hair and wrinkled cheeks, greeted me warmly and seated me at once.

She looked at the second place setting inquiringly.

"I'm meeting someone. Also, would you mind if I used your phone?" I added, before she walked away.

"No cell phone?" She looked surprised.

"Afraid not," I said. "No cell phone."

For some reason, she found this very funny. She broke into peals of laughter. "I thought everyone had cell phones. My mother is ninety-two. Her village only got electricity last fifteen years, but even she has a cell phone." Still chuckling, she led me over to the front of the little restaurant, where a cord phone was fastened to the wall.

Jess picked up on the second ring. "Who is this?"

"It's me."

I heard the relief fill her voice. "You're okay? I've been reading the papers."

"I'm okay, yeah. How's he doing?"

"He's better, now. Much better."

"Can I have a word with him?"

"Of course."

There was a pause and then Brandon's voice came on. His voice sounded clearer, more alert than it had been in a long time. "Nik? Are you okay?"

"I'm okay. How are you?"

"I've been thinking about what you said," my brother answered. "Maybe it's time I moved on from that place where I've been. Maybe I could move closer to you. If that's still okay?"

I swallowed. "It's still okay. Yeah."

"Thanks, Nik. For everything."

Back at the table, I took an envelope out of my jacket. I opened it and looked through the pictures inside. Faces. One, then another. A young woman with brown eyes and a resolute expression, a spray of freckles across her skin. A Middle Eastern man in his forties, smiling easily as he pointed to something out of the frame. A black woman about my age, wearing a colorful silk shawl, an infant held in her arms. People. People who were alive. People who weren't being thrown in prison cells or being beaten or lined up and shot. I wished Karen could have been sitting with me. They were her pictures. She had gotten them. I wished that the people in the pictures could know about Karen Li.

"What are you looking at?" Ethan's voice.

I put the photographs back in the envelope. "I'll tell you some other time."

I stood to kiss him and he looked at me, shocked. Between Victor and Joseph, I wasn't going to be turning heads for a while. Not in a good way, at least.

"What happened?" he asked hesitantly, as though even asking would somehow jar me and cause new pain. "Are you okay?"

"Everyone keeps asking me that."

"I wonder why. You look like you picked a fight with Mike Tyson."

"Mike Tyson's retired."

"Maybe he's onto something."

I shook my head. "I don't play golf and I don't fish."

"You could take up knitting, maybe. Something safe."

The talk went on like that for a bit. Keeping it light. As though we were getting to know each other again. We ordered, and the food came out quickly. With food things felt more comfortable. Soon we were slurping rice noodles from big bowls of beef pho. I used chopsticks to dip the beef into a side plate of hot sauce and spooned up more of the hot liquid. The food felt good. Sitting there with Ethan felt good.

He finally pushed his bowl away. "Can I ask you a question?"

"Sure."

"It's going to make me sound like an eighth-grade girl."

I pushed my own bowl away. "Exactly what I've always wanted in a relationship."

He smiled at me, a noodle trailing from the corner of his mouth, and I had to laugh. He blushed and wiped his mouth. "Seriously, Nikki. The last couple of weeks, being worried, telling myself that I was overreacting. Except seeing you now . . . I can't help thinking that instead of worrying too much, maybe I wasn't worrying enough."

"That wasn't a question."

"I guess my question is—is this normal?"

I took a gulp of water, my mouth burning from the hot sauce. "This has been one of the least normal months of my life."

"Oh." He thought that over. "That's good. Because if it was, like, an every-week thing . . ."

I laughed. "If this kind of thing happened every week, I really would retire."

He insisted on paying. We walked outside and stood together, his arm in mine. The air was cool, the fall coming to an end. It had briefly rained that afternoon and a neighboring bar's neon signs threw blue glimmers onto a sidewalk puddle. Cars drifted past, traffic sparse. "Do you have to be somewhere?" he asked.

"I don't have anywhere to be."

"Me neither."

I hesitated, then spoke. "We can go for a ride. If you want."

"A ride?"

I nodded toward the red motorcycle parked across the median on the other side of the street. "I have a second helmet. We wouldn't be breaking any laws."

"Where?"

"There's a place I sometimes go. A little town up the coast. There's a house I sometimes visit there."

He understood immediately. "Bolinas? Where you grew up?"

"I never thought I'd bring anyone else there. But I've told you a little about it, and we can talk more when we're there. Maybe sit by the ocean, watch the sun come up. If you want."

His hand was in mine. "I'd like that."

We crossed San Pablo and climbed onto the motorcycle. I felt his weight behind me. Felt his arms around me. I hadn't had anyone ride with me for a long time. Two people felt different. It felt okay, though. The balance was still there, even with two. With motorcycles, balance was the important thing.

I started the engine. Nudged my left foot down, clicked the bike into gear.

We glided into the quiet street.

Soon we were on the freeway, heading north. Toward the bridge, toward the shadow of San Quentin, but beyond those forbidding walls the road continued, climbing and twisting up over Mount Tamalpais before finding, eventually, the open water. The moon above, the water of the Bay, the sprinkled lights of the homes built into the East Bay hills. I was aware of all those things. The darkness ahead of us retreated, pushed back by the headlight, as we continued on.

ACKNOWLEDGEMENTS

I have tremendous gratitude to my agent, Victoria Skurnick, who decided to take a chance on a writer she'd never met and a character she barely knew. Many thanks for sharing her enthusiasm, editorial skills, vast knowledge of the publishing world, and a first-class lasagna recipe. Thanks also to James Levine and everyone at LGR Literary Agency. I'm indebted to my incredible editors Amy Einhorn and Christine Kopprasch at Flatiron Books, for believing in Nikki from day one and for challenging me with edits that left this book far stronger than when it first reached them. I'm also grateful to Bob Miller and everyone at Flatiron who worked so hard to help bring this to publication.

Many people gently advise would-be writers to consider a different career, and I'd like to thank a few in my life who didn't. Bill Pritchard, David Sofield, and Lisa Raskin of Amherst College have all been readers, teachers, and friends long after my college years, and I am deeply grateful to Don Pease at Dartmouth College for his unflagging support. Thanks also to Dick Todd, Tom Powers, and Dan Weaver for valuable advice and feedback on my writing and to the Dartmouth MALS program for setting me on the right track. Tim Colla proved uncomplainingly willing to read everything I threw at him over the years, and thanks to Catherine Plato for offering a fresh eye whenever one was needed as I revised this book.

My brother, Daniel, has been extraordinarily supportive of my writing throughout my life. From literally the day I began this book he was, as always, on hand to offer support, ask questions, and deliver the occasional stern pep talk whenever my progress risked flagging. More than anything, I am grateful to my parents and always my first readers, Alan and Barbara. As making any effort to tally up all they have done for me would require far more pages than I have at my disposal, suffice it to say that their belief in me has shaped me as a writer.